HEARTSTRINGS

Second Chance
AT L♥VE

CATHRYN LYONS

Cover art by Steamy Designs

Cover image by Wander Aguiar photography

Model: Valerio

Edited by Michelle Fewer

ISBN 9781969897009

HEARTSTRINGS

Second Chance
AT L♥VE

CONTENT WARNING

Cathryn Lyons and team respect our readers and want you to be well-informed. If you would like to know if this book contains elements that may be of concern for you or triggering in a way that would prevent your enjoyment, please visit the Content Warnings section of www.CathrynLyonsAuthor.com.

*"In three words, I can sum up everything I've learned about life:
it goes on."*
Robert Frost

PROLOGUE

TIERCY

There is a hazy moment in the thin veil between asleep and awake. That is where I find you, my love. Surrounded by the misty dark, accompanied only by the sound of my quiet breaths, you are with me. It's like it never happened. My mind simply, benevolently, reverts to "Before." And in that magical moment, everything is as it should be. I'm at peace. I'm happy.

Then, inevitably, the veil dissipates.

And you are gone again.

Chapter One

"What's past is prologue."
The Tempest, William Shakespeare

TIERCY

Tiercy Somerville could sort her life neatly into one of five categories: Way Before. Before. That Day. Right After. After.

It was how she thought of everything.

She knew better than to go to Right After too often. The penetrating pain would overpower her, robbing her of any hard-won ability to cope.

As for That Day—she refused to let her mind, and her heart, go there.

Then why had she agreed to attend this event? First, it was a Thing. (Tiercy hated Things.) Second, it was about *him*. Third, and most damningly, it was right after the fifth anniversary of That Day. It was a trifecta of bad ideas.

"Ground control to Major Tierce. Come in, Major Tierce."

Her best friend's voice cut through Tiercy's ruminations. Perched on the end of the double sink in the en suite bathroom of the apartment she rented, red toenails shining against the dull white of the builder's grade vanity, Ross downed her Kir Royale, eyeing Tiercy with obvious concern. One sculpted eyebrow arched in question as she motioned to Tiercy's empty flute with her own. "More Dutch Courage?"

"This is a bad idea," Tiercy admonished herself—and Ross, in the mirror—as she gulped a restorative swallow, her second refill. "In my defense, it's not nearly as big as a red wine glass," she muttered.

"What's a bad idea? Another glass or tonight?"

Tiercy knew Ross had been examining her for fissures in her outwardly calm reserve. No one knew her better than her lifelong best friend. Tiercy had managed to scrape herself through the deepest of agonies, one grieving atom at a time, to a place of peace in her life—and harbored a powerful reluctance to disrupt that peaceful stasis. She'd vacillated about this event before finally agreeing to it. And, according to Ross's bathroom mirror, the doubt on her face was as clear as the blue eyes she'd inherited from her father.

"I think both are bad ideas."

"Well, you know my motto, as stolen from the late, great Bette Davis: 'There comes a time in life when the only thing that helps is a glass of champagne.'"

"That's your motto? Since when?"

"Since now," winked Ross.

Tiercy laughed, the touch of best-friend-induced relief soothing her torment as she handed Ross her empty flute. "Cheers!"

They were drinking champagne with Chambord, the Kir Royale cocktail being Ross's latest drink preference. It was a thinly veiled attempt by her bestie to help Tiercy gird herself for the evening ahead. Except it wasn't working.

"Dead soldier." Ross waved the empty bottle. "Getting more. BRB."

Tiercy leaned into the bathroom sink and let out a long sigh, almost as deep as her recent gulp of fizzy drink. Despite her best efforts to compartmentalize, she was succumbing to fleeting flashbacks of That Day.

The police officer.

Shake it away, Tiercy commanded herself, refocusing on shaving her legs so as not to slice herself.

The harsh fluorescent lights of the ER.

Tiercy resolutely pushed the unwelcome memories away. Eyeliner under one bloodshot eye, administered with a trembling hand...

She couldn't let her carefully built walls crumble. That she was even in this situation was regrettable. At first, she had determinedly ignored the invitation. But then Brinder had interceded. Dear, wonderful Brinder, with his soft brown eyes and tender heart. Tiercy had caved, and now was stuck in that wretched place between regret and aching need.

Tiercy caught movement in her periphery, eyes flicking to catch Ross standing silently in the doorway, sadness etched on her bestie's face. "How long have you been standing there?"

Ross handed her one of the refreshed glasses. "Long enough to see my bestie valiantly trying to compose herself and prepare for this evening. Also long enough to see you've made exactly zero progress getting ready and then zoned into your la la land." She smiled at Tiercy with a knowing gaze. "You seem to be doing a remarkable job procrastinating."

"I just wish I hadn't agreed to this. We should have stayed at the beach."

For the last four years, Tiercy's unwavering M.O. had been to ignore the painful memories embedded in the anniversary of That Day. The first year, Jemma had been a newborn, and it was a blur organically—a topsy-turvy blend of new baby, mind-numbing sleep deprivation, misery, joy, despair, and the hope that comes with a precious new life. That year, her parents and Ross came over, but no one else. Tiercy wouldn't allow it. At that point, she was refusing in any way to acknowledge or discuss That Day.

The next three years, Ross and Tiercy took a couple days off, loaded little Jemma into the car, and drove to Ross's Great-Aunt Francesca's beach house on the Delaware shore. It was quiet at the beach during the week in early May. They'd hang out, build sandcastles, and then go back to the beach house, where they'd rinse off, hang their sandy clothes on the line to dry, then eat crab cakes and partake in Ross's drink du jour. One thing they would most definitely *not* do was talk in any way about That Day.

But this year was different. It started with an email she'd received six weeks ago from Dr. Ben Lopez—Luke's former boss and the vice president of medical affairs at Fellowship-Unity Medical Center:

Subject: Fundraiser for new building

Tiercy, I hope this note finds you enjoying the beautiful spring weather. Coralee and I think of you often and hope you and Jemma are doing well. Attached is an invitation to a fundraising event at the Manchester Inn, near the hospital.

I'm not sure if you've heard, but we are building a new medical pavilion on campus. It will feature a conference center and a simulation lab for training our clinical staff. There has been some recent discussion about naming the residency training center for Luke. It's hard to believe it's been five years. There has been a groundswell of support from the medical staff and the Emergency Department team, and it looks like it's going to happen. We will have some high-profile potential donors at the event, former residents just like Luke, along with some other stakeholders, and we thought your presence might be helpful to cultivate support.

I want to be upfront about the date. Brinder Desai reminded me that it is right after the anniversary of the day you lost Luke. By the time we realized the timing situation, it was too late to reschedule. I recognize this may be difficult for you, but we'd love to have you there, even for a short bit. If you cannot attend, of course we'd completely understand. If you do, you are most welcome to bring a guest.

Dr. Desai wanted to invite you himself, but I insisted on reaching out to you. Luke was very special to Coralee and me, and to the entire hospital. We all miss him. I hope you can make it. The details are on the attached invitation. (Actual invite is in the mail to you.) And you can always call me.

Ben

She'd opened the .jpg invitation and her eyes immediately fixed on the date, blurring with tears and coming into focus again as she dashed them away with the back of her hand. The day after That Day. The day she woke, knowing in her gut something was wrong, but unable to place it...until she remembered. And felt a dagger of pain slash her heart. *He was gone.*

Tiercy hated the day after That Day almost as much as she hated That Day. So, go to a Thing about Luke just after the anniversary of That Day? Not a chance in hell.

She'd started to hit delete, but her hand hovered over her keyboard, shaking. Tiercy had reread the note, remembering how much Luke loved his residency at Fellowship-Unity and how committed he was to physician education. She'd read it a third time and felt deep pride on Luke's behalf that this was even being considered. And, yet, she couldn't fathom attending.

For nearly a week, she did a bad job pretending it didn't exist. Until her regular Thursday pizza dinner with Jemma and Brinder. It was Brinder, who had been Luke's best friend, and had become one of her closest friends, who'd gently nudged her that night.

Five weeks prior

Tiercy and Brinder sat quietly at the kitchen table. He motioned to the box, eyeing the single slice of deep dish remaining. "You want this last piece, love?" he asked, the British accent of his upbringing only slightly diminished after fifteen years in the U.S.

Tiercy leaned back in her chair and groaned. "Have at it. As Ross's grandmother would say with her lovely manners, 'I've had a sufficient amount.' That said, I do believe I have room for a bit more vino." She smiled at him across the table, a gesture he returned with deep warmth in his handsome face.

He topped off her glass and polished off the last piece in the remarkable two-bite way he and Luke seemed to have perfected in med school. He started to say something, and then stopped.

Tiercy watched him with affection, but also a twinge of dread. They'd become close in the past few years, and she knew very well when he was tiptoeing around something. In this case, the event invitation, to which she'd yet to respond.

"Spit it out, Brin. I know what you're going to say. You've been dancing around it in your head all night. In addition to our yummy pizza and wine, we have an uninvited elephant in the room, so let's acknowledge it."

Brinder looked up and smiled sheepishly. "Busted." He let out a deep sigh, brow furrowed. "Are you planning to go to the fundraiser? I know it's right after," he paused and swallowed, "you know...the anniversary."

Even five years later, Brinder still had trouble saying it, too. He reached for her hand across the table, and gently stroked his thumb over the back.

Tiercy's eyes were fixed on the rhythmic, soothing motion as she battled against the lump in her throat. "I can't, Brinder," she finally whispered, head bowed. "I can't be around people—at least, not so close to his..." Like Brinder, it was agony to finish that sentence. She shook her head. "I need to go to the beach with Jemma and Ross, to be away from here. The last thing I can do is be in a room of his friends and colleagues and try to talk about Luke, and schmooze—which I'm terrible at anyway—as everyone looks at me with sympathy. It feels impossible. It's a bad idea all around."

Brinder gave her hand a gentle squeeze. "I understand, love."

They sat in silence, each grappling with their emotions, as Tiercy fiddled with the edge of the empty pizza box. Across the hush, they heard Jemma's sweet voice in the other room, singing a song from *The Little Mermaid*. Tiercy looked up at Brinder, who had turned his head in the direction of the living room, a wistful smile on his face.

Good gravy he was gorgeous. Tall, dark, and handsome...and incredibly kind and smart. Not that it could ever go anywhere with him. He was like a brother to her. She shook her head, knocking any romantic thoughts of him out of the way. It felt incestuous to even consider.

"She's been asking about him a lot lately. Her dad. As she gets older, she sees her friends' fathers, and then I get an incessant barrage of questions about Luke."

Brinder nodded. "I think that's pretty normal."

"Whatever 'normal' is in a horribly abnormal situation," Tiercy responded wryly, hooking her fingers into air quotes. "I do the best I can to answer. But it's hard. In so many ways, he's a fantasy character to her, like Prince Eric. I struggle with making him real to her, to convey all those small, wonderful things about him." She closed her eyes. "I know I can never do him justice."

Brinder's voice was low and tender. "I know it likely won't resonate with her now. But...perhaps having something lasting named after her father would mean a lot to Jemma later in life. It would be a way to honor Luke and show Jemma just how incredible her father was."

Tiercy's shoulders slumped fractionally. "I don't know, Brin. They can raise money without me there."

"Possibly. But I think your presence will convey a lot—will make a difference. And, who knows, it could even be healing for you to do something like this for him."

"Possibly," she retorted, using a fake British accent as she tried to lighten the mood, causing Brinder to break into a wide grin that she knew had weakened the knees of many females. Luke had told her the nurses on staff called his best friend 'Dr. De-siiiigh." She chuckled at the memory, and Brinder cocked his head at the sound.

"Anything you want to share with the class, Teacher?" He smiled. Brinder was always so proud and supportive of her work at the high school where she taught English.

"Oh, nothing. Was just thinking the one entertaining thing might be to watch the females fall all over themselves to get to Dr. De-siiiigh," she singsonged with a grin, relieved to shift the topic at hand.

Brin rubbed his hand over his face and groaned. "Not you, too. Bad enough I have to hear about it at work."

They smiled at each other and, in practiced unison, stood to clean up dinner, easy banter filling the evening—a tacit understanding to cease the sad and uncomfortable conversation about the event.

And yet, as they said goodnight a bit later, Brinder offered to accompany Tiercy to make it easier, and suggested she also bring Ross for a second steadying crutch of moral support. Tiercy balked, but promised to think about it. How could she not? Brinder's line of reasoning made sense. But in the land of grief, reason and sense were awkward strangers.

Later that evening, she and Jemma followed her daughter's bedtime ritual. After saying her prayers, Jemma kissed the photo of Luke that was in a frame on her nightstand. "Goodnight, Daddy. I miss you."

Her precious daughter, blonde hair damp from her bath, was wearing Spider-Man pajamas, which had softened and faded with frequent washing—the byproduct of her desire to wear them on a regular basis. She was the spitting image of Luke.

Tiercy's heart squeezed. No matter what she did, she could never bring Luke back to Jemma...and to her. But she could do the right thing and help create something lasting to honor Luke.

Back in her own room, Tiercy forwarded the email to Ross. "Hey... got this from Ben Lopez (Luke's former boss). Look at the date on the invite...I think I actually might go. I'll leave the beach a day early. Want to be my plus one?"

Then she texted Ross.

TIERCY

Just forwarded you an email from Fel-U. Fundraiser for a new hospital bldg. They want to name something after Luke. Check out the date.

How twenty-first century, she thought wryly, to text someone that you've just sent an email.

The gray dots flashed in impending reply.

ROSS

Just opened the email. Wow. Impressive. But...the date? You sure?

TIERCY

Can you talk?

ROSS

Not really. At a restaurant with a guy I met on Hinge. He's in the loo right now. I don't want to be one of those obnoxious people talking on their phone in a restaurant. But I can text.

TIERCY

Gotcha. You can tell me about your date later.

ROSS

Won't be much to tell. I can already see that he's the clingy type. Looking for a wife. He'll be a one-and-done date. Distract me while I wait for Mr. Clingy to return. Tell me about this event.

TIERCY

I don't plan to stay long. A little schmoozing. For Luke. I feel like I need to do this for him, and for Jemma. We'll do the cocktail party chitchat for a bit, and then maybe you and I can grab some drinks in the bar of the Manchester Inn. I've been wanting to go there. And Brinder will be there.

More dots from Ross.

ROSS

Three thoughts. 1: How random that it's right after the anniversary. 2: Despite that, my gut says you should go. And 3: Yay…I get to be a third wheel with you and Dr. Hottie McHot Pants. (I'm texting that last part in a snarky voice, BTW.)

TIERCY

Let's clarify: Brinder and I are not 'two-wheeling.' (Back at you with the snarky voice, BTW.) You know this. He's like a brother.

ROSS

Nice euphemism, T. You sure about that?

TIERCY

Can we not discuss this now? I've told you a million times that's a no-go situation. Focus, Beaufort. I need to know about the event. Can you come with? I need you there…

ROSS

Like you even have to ask. You know I'll be there for you.

TIERCY

Thank you.

ROSS

That's what friends are for. (Crap…did I just quote Dionne Warwick?)

TIERCY

Ha! Love you. Thank you.

ROSS

Gotta run. Mr. Clingy is coming back. Gah… he even walks in a clingy way.

TIERCY

Is that even a thing?

ROSS

It is now. Ugh. Bye, Hooker Hips.

TIERCY

Sorry you got Hinge Singed. Bye!

Smiling at her bestie's hijinks, Tiercy took a deep breath and sent her response to Ben. She would attend.

CHAPTER TWO

TIERCY

Five weeks later, Tiercy was preparing—with the greatest dread —to make an appearance at what she'd coined "Luke's Thing." It was the opposite of what she'd wanted. And, yet, something hummed inside her. Maybe it was the milestone—five years. Maybe it was just adrenaline. Maybe it was even another piece of her ravaged heart knitting back together—different, irrevocably changed, but healing. But Tiercy found that a tiny, secret part of herself was somewhat looking forward to the evening. It would be a chance to hear Luke's name spoken aloud. And to speak it aloud herself.

Even now, she didn't say it a lot. It was as if she rationed the use of it. It was too special a name to just *say*. She had to honor it. Say it with meaning. Feel the shape of it formed in her mouth. Perhaps she feared overuse would dilute the power of his name over her...*within* her.

From the very beginning, his name evoked emotions that were

astonishing in their strength. Way Before, it was the thrill of the new. Of a handsome, funny man who, for some crazy reason, really dug her. And then Before, it was the name of her person. Her boyfriend. Her fiancé. Then her husband. *I, Tiercy, take thee, Luke.*

And That Day, it was the screaming of his name. The sobbing of his name. The begging and pleading of his name. Right After, it was the toneless, numb shock. The disbelief. The anger. And deepest sorrow. Whispering his name, as if the trueness of her grief, expressed in the breath of his name, could erase time and make it all go away. Could bring him back to her.

And After, she wouldn't use it indiscriminately. His name was a treasure, a legacy to be savored.

One word. One name. With so much connected to it.

Luke.

There was an illicit thrill in saying his name, and hearing it said. Tiercy felt like a junkie. Just a little taste, that was all she needed. Just a little taste of Luke. One night to revel in Luke. One night to get lost in memories. One night to hear stories from those who knew him well. To allow the treasured gift of sharing Luke out loud. The verboten would now be sanctioned by his widow—*God, she hated that term*—the only one who could grant that freeing permission. The only one who could allow friends and co-workers to loosen their respectful restraint and share Luke with abandon.

Just one night wouldn't hurt.

The afternoon of the fundraiser, Ross took Tiercy out for body scrubs and mani-pedis, where Tiercy tried not to remember the similar spa treatments they'd gotten for Tiercy's wedding day. Instead, they indulged in their ongoing joke about Ross's "sausage toes," which were rather short and ugly compared to the willowy body they helmed. They read trashy celebrity magazines, mocked freakishly puffy Kardashian lips, swooned over Chris Hemsworth, and debated the merits of which *Marvel* character was the hottest. They were both MCU addicts, with Tiercy first watching the movies with Luke while dating, and then Ross jumping on the bandwagon when she realized what she called the "Hottie Quotient." Tiercy was all in for Thor, while Ross had it bad for Captain America.

Later, slapping along in their salon-issued throwaway flipflops, they'd gone back to Ross's apartment to get ready for the party. Tiercy couldn't face her house that day. *Their* house.

"I wonder how Jemma is doing?" Tiercy exited the bathroom, walking away from the frustrating exercise of getting glammed up. She flopped down on a chair in Ross's bedroom, giving in to inertia, and possibly one too many Kir Royales. She'd stopped drinking when she felt herself getting both silly and more maudlin than even her dread for the upcoming evening had induced.

She, Ross, and Jemma had returned from the beach house late the evening before, opting to spend the night at Ross's. She especially couldn't stand to be in her home on the anniversary of That Day. This morning, Tiercy and Jemma went to the tire park, a playground made of recycled tires that was their favorite place. Jemma's preferred section, and Tiercy's, was a set of side-by-side tire swings, reminiscent of her childhood home. It was tender, sweet, and fun, with her daughter's gleeful giggles soaring across the blue May sky.

But, like so many things since Right After, there was a surreal quality—almost as if she were watching herself playing a role in her life in which she was terribly miscast.

"I'm sure she's fine. She's with your folks, so you know she'll get spoiled. She'll get to watch *Frozen* ten times, eat grilled cheese, and stay up past her bedtime." Ross waggled her eyebrows at Tiercy as she adjusted the belt of her silk robe, stretching out onto the bed. Tiercy suspected she, too, was feeling the cocktails. "Ma and Pa Flynn are the best."

Ross had a smile on her face, but Tiercy was as attuned to her best friend as Ross was to her, and she could see the sadness creep into her best friend's eyes. Close to twenty years prior, Ross's parents had died in a car accident. Tiercy's parents had essentially raised Ross after that.

Some people would cringe to be so close to their parents, but not

Tiercy. Cate and Neal Flynn were funny and cool—the kind of parents her high school friends had wished they'd had. Tiercy's house had always been the gathering place among her friends for as long as she could remember, and her mom had served as a non-judgmental, kind, witty confidante for countless schoolmates. Teenage Tiercy had tried to be annoyed with her folks, because it seemed like the thing everyone else was doing. But try as she might, Tiercy had never experienced much of the seemingly requisite I-hate-my-parents angst.

Her mom and dad had a fun, loving marriage. They would "get their Irish up" and fight, and then make up just as colorfully...and romantically. It was somewhat embarrassing as a teenager and only child, but as an adult, and now a single mom, Tiercy took wistful solace in their affection, and she very much relied on them as a source of support for her and Jemma. They represented a nutty, Irish calm in the sea of upheaval that had been the last five years.

Tiercy nodded wistfully, smoothing her thumb over the pale pink manicure on her ring finger. "*Romanza*. That's what the nail lady told me this color was called. Romance. Nothing romantic about going to a party to raise money to honor the memory of your dead husband."

Her head dropped back as she closed her eyes, breathing deeply through her nose and fighting for control. There. She'd said it. Out loud.

"Oh, honey." Ross rolled across the bed and swept over, fragrant and lovely in her robe. She drew Tiercy up and into a hug.

It was hard not to feel like a troll sometimes next to Ross, especially on a night like tonight when she could barely summon the energy to do her makeup properly. She sniffled back her incipient tears.

"I'm going to fucking lose it." Tiercy's voice was muffled against her friend's head. "I swear, I fucking hate this."

"The f-bomb. Good," Ross cooed gently, stroking Tiercy's thick auburn hair. "When your Irish gets going and you cuss, I know you're going to be OK."

"Am I?" Tiercy pulled back and eyed her friend warily.

"Indubitably. You will."

"Nice SAT word, Bestie." This was an ongoing competition with them since high school—throwing SAT words into casual conversation, calling each other on it, and one-upping the other at the next opportunity. It was a touch of normalcy in a day that had sunk in her gut like lead. "Your certainty is quite absolute," Tiercy responded drily. "Do you know something I don't know?"

"I know that you are the strongest, bravest chick I've ever met. You're tough stuff. You've got this, Tierce. And I've got your six. So…"

"I can see you've been reading Brittney Sahin's military romance novels again." Tiercy winked at Ross, again grateful for the infusion of normalcy.

She inhaled deeply, restorative oxygen flooding her system. "So, I guess I'm doing this. And I'm irked at Brinder for bailing on me at the last minute." She glared balefully at her phone, on which sat an apologetic message from her friend.

"Not really Dr. McHot Pants's fault. He *is* the chief of radiology. You can't blame him for two docs on his team calling out with a stomach bug. He said he'd do everything he could to get coverage and swing by."

"Ross, I appreciate you trying to defend him. But I spent a long time as the wife of a doctor. I know what happens in these situations. He's not coming."

Tiercy wasn't sure if that was a good or a bad thing. Ever since Right After, Brinder had been there for her. As Luke's best friend, he'd immediately stepped forward, offering her friendship and a comforting shoulder to cry on. They had both loved Luke so much. Sometimes it seemed Brinder was the only one who really grasped the depth of her loss.

Yet, lately, something had shifted with him. A subtle movement in the subterrain of their friendship. Barely palpable, and yet there.

"Well, anyway, *I'll* be there— Crap, now that earworm is going to be in my head." Ross's response startled Tiercy from her reverie, her bestie singing like the Jackson 5.

Ross always could sense when Tiercy was teetering on the edge of losing it. So far, she was doing an A-plus job getting Tiercy through this evening.

"Now come on, Tiercella." Ross smiled gently, using an old nickname for Tiercy. "I'm your fairy-best-friend-mother—"

"What the hell, Ross?" Tiercy giggled, mouthing the phrase before repeating it aloud. "Fairy-best-friend—"

"Just go with it. I've had a lot of champagne. Now, chop chop, spit spot—"

"Now she's quoting Mary Poppins," Tiercy muttered under her breath with a helpless laugh at her gorgeous, goofy, steadfast bestie.

"—it's time for your dress. I feel like Flora and Fauna, or was it Merriwether...I can never remember, even with as many times as I've watched *Sleeping Beauty* with Jemma," Ross muttered, dragging Tiercy back to the bedroom. "I want to wave a wand and yell, 'Pink. No, blue!'"

"You are a mess." Tiercy laughed as Ross disappeared into the walk-in closet. "I'm just going to raid your closet for something long enough that it won't air out Miss Kitty."

Tiercy had struggled to find the right outfit. It was a fundraising event, during the evening...but also on a Thursday night. She figured many hospital and business attendees would be coming from work, thus wearing their suits and corporate boringwear. Of course, the casual capris and shirts she normally wore to work would not be appropriate. *See, this is why I hate Things.* Disgusted with her choices, she'd tried on and discarded the outfits she'd thrown in a garment bag earlier in the week. Nothing looked right.

She wrapped her robe tighter and decided she'd just wear that. Ha! That would be memorable.

"I knew you were going to be cranky about what to wear, so I decided to further cement my status as the most prodigious friend in the world by getting you something new." Ross swept into the bedroom, wearing a triumphant grin and brandishing a garment bag. Ross herself had changed from her robe into an emerald-color sheath, which set off her neatly coiled dark hair and green eyes.

"Way to take advantage of my weakened, pathetic state with yet another SAT word, Ross." Tiercy narrowed her eyes in fake anger.

"I'm nothing if not competitive, dearest," Ross rejoined, tossing her long dark hair over her shoulders. "Now take a look at what your fairy-best-god-whatever-the-fuck-I-said-earlier got for you, Tiercella."

"I'm wearing your muumuu from Hawaii and a baseball cap.

Nothing looks good and my hair is going to end up a frizzy mess anyway," Tiercy whined.

"Just try this on," Ross cooed, speaking in a tone Tiercy had heard her use with Jemma when she was being a mule. Ross unzipped the bag and handed the contents to Tiercy.

Tiercy stepped into the form fitting, sleeveless, navy dress. It had a modest slit in the front right—just enough to tantalize with a bit of thigh—and Tiercy was glad she ran five miles early that morning. The wide boat neck grazed just below her collarbones, then dipped to the middle of her shoulder blades, leaving the tops of her shoulders bare. It was simple and elegant.

"You're the best. You know that, right?"

"I *do* know that," Ross called from her closet where she was rummaging around. "I figured tonight would be hard for you, so I thought I'd try to remove at least some of the stress." She came out with a pair of nude strappy heels, which she tossed to Tiercy. "It always pisses me off that you are so much taller, but we wear the same size shoes. Ah, well. C'est la vie." She shrugged her shoulders and navigated Tiercy back to the bathroom. "Now for your hair. No baseball caps tonight." She guided Tiercy to face the bathroom mirror. "So, what should we do with your lovely locks tonight?"

Tiercy fussed with her hair in the mirror over Ross's sink. Unseasonal May humidity, partnered with the need for a haircut, triggered more volume than usual. "If I try to flat-iron it, the second I walk outside, my hair will poof up anyway. I think I'm just going to let the Irish wave win out."

"Yes, good thinking. I love your hair long and wavy, but let's throw some loose curls in, just to tame it a bit."

Luke had always loved it when she wore her hair down. Her hair was shorter now, grazing just below her shoulders, with more layers. She'd contemplated cutting it much shorter After, but couldn't seem to let go of that link with Luke. In the way of amputees still feeling lost limbs, she could still feel her husband gently wrapping her hair around his hand, stroking the tresses. The practical side of her also recognized the benefit of being able to throw her hair in a ponytail on school days when

Jemma was giving her trouble and she was in a hurry to get to work before the high school bell rang.

Without waiting for Tiercy's assent, Ross prodded Tiercy onto the vanity chair in front of the mirror. Under Ross's patient fingers and the ministrations of a curling iron, Tiercy soon had long auburn waves framing her face.

With a sigh of relief, she worked on her makeup, as Ross kept up a steady stream of chatter from the kitchen, where she was cleaning up her cocktail prep.

Luke always told Tiercy she was a natural beauty with no need for cosmetics. Yet whenever she did dramatic eye makeup with pale lips, Luke would give her The Look. Which would always end up with her having to reapply her makeup after their passionate lovemaking. Luke would watch her touching up her face, a lascivious smile playing on his lips. "You know I'm just going to mess it up later." And Tiercy would laugh and pretend to push him away, when really all she ever wanted to do was pull him closer.

Tiercy examined herself, nodding a thank you to her mom, and possibly a long line of ancestresses with nice racks, as she studied her silhouette in the flattering dress. Childbirth and several months of nursing hadn't taken a visible toll. Maybe her boobs weren't as perky as they used to be, but, heck, she was also thirty-three (almost thirty-four, she sighed at the inexorable passage of time) and now fighting the pull of gravity and age.

Tiercy remembered another dress Ross had played a role in—a splurge purchase on a trip Tiercy had taken to Manhattan to visit Ross at her new office many years ago. The little black dress had been Luke's favorite. It was clingy and landed three inches above her knees. Held up with the thinnest of straps, there was a low cowl neck draped in the front and a deep vee in the back. The first time she wore it, Luke had looked up and given a low growl. He'd moved toward her, eyes intent. It's a wonder they'd gotten out of the house. Later that night, when he was peeling it off her one delightful inch at a time, Tiercy had mused that the fabric was infused with elements of sorcery. From that moment, the dress was coined Sex Magic.

"Stop it, Tiercy," she whispered to herself in the mirror as she attempted one last touch up, accepting that she'd likely cry it off later anyway. "You'll never get through this if you wallow in Before."

Fueled by determination and Kir Royale, Tiercy strode out of Ross's bedroom, intent on finding her best friend and getting on with the evening's torture. It was a quick trip, as the floor plan of Ross's apartment was compact. Ross was perfectly able to buy a larger, more permanent place. But to an avowed commitment-phobe, owning a home felt too permanent, so her bestie just rented places over the years. It could have been a corporate apartment, such was the generic nature of the furnishings.

Her kitchen was the exception. It featured neatly organized cabinets of high-end bakeware and always smelled of Ross's culinary treats. When she wasn't editing, she was baking. Tiercy regularly teased Ross that she only used her for her blueberry muffins. And her cakes. And the pies. "How you stay so thin, I'll never know," Tiercy often complained, usually with her mouth full of a decadent treat.

Rounding the corner into the kitchen, she found Ross sitting on a counter barstool with her feet up on another, scrolling through her phone.

Ross looked up at Tiercy and let out a low wolf whistle. "Damn. As my grandfather would say, 'Hubba Hubba!'"

"You are such a flirt," Tiercy tossed back. "But we all know I'm not your type. You like a smoldering romance novel hero. Oh...and Captain America."

"Mmmm...true. El Capitan can rest his shield on my bed any day," Ross replied in a sultry tone as she looked at her watch. "All that said, you do look smoking. I am a freaking awesome fairy bestie-mother. The Mouse has nothing on me, I tell you. Now, Tiercella, off to the pumpkin. Or our Uber, as the case may be." Ross moved toward the door and then halted.

Amidst the joking, the mood had shifted infinitesimally. Only a best friend could pick up the subtle vibration of sorrow emanating from Tiercy. And there was no doubt her best friend was attuned to it.

"You OK, Tierce?" Ross placed a gentle hand on Tiercy's shoulder, compassion shining in her eyes. "We can back out. If it's too much to do this, we could just...not go. I know you hate Things. And this will definitely be a Thing. I have more hooch. We can stay here, drink ourselves silly, and watch *Steel Magnolias* and *Beaches* so you can have an epic cryfest and blame it on the movies."

It would have been so easy to bail. To just not show up. People would understand.

As Tiercy weighed her options, she caught a glimpse of herself in the hall mirror. It was Luke's wife reflected. She watched herself as she made her decision. She needed to go and honor her husband. This was about him, not her.

She reached for her best friend's hand. "Let's go."

Chapter Three

Cole

Cole leaned against the bar, scotch in hand, enjoying the bustle of activity around him. Normally at fundraising events, he had two purposes: make the necessary connections that led him to the event in the first place, and avoid the ring-starved single society women who seemed to frequent these things.

But tonight was going to be fairly low key for him. As the lead contractor for Fellowship-Unity's expansion, he was expected to attend. But he didn't really have a role other than to support his client and shake a few hands. And then he could head home. Thank Christ. It had been a long day and even longer week. He was spent. More than ready to climb into bed and hope for a decent night's sleep before rising and returning to the grind.

He sighed deeply, recognizing once again that what used to be fulfilling now depleted him. His days had become one tedious cycle of work, working out, rinse, repeat. Something was missing in his life. He was out of balance, and he knew it.

He dragged his hand through his hair, not caring if the action ruffled the thick dark locks he'd inherited from his father, along with ice-blue eyes people often referred to as gray. He'd started his day at the office at six a.m., navigating an issue with permits. While he ultimately handled it to achieve his desired outcome, it had drained him. He'd been tempted to blow off the reception, but the hospital was part of a larger system, and there was a huge contract coming up. He wanted his company to win it. So, he'd donned his trusty slate gray custom Tom Ford suit, along with a deep blue tie, and summoned the energy to schmooze.

The room was filling rapidly, the hum of chatter rising to the din so common with these events. He took a sip of his liquor and tuned into the string quartet in the corner. The cellist was absorbed in a haunting solo, and Cole relaxed, letting the music sweep over him. He was a music lover, finding pleasure in a variety of genres. If memory served, this was "Elegy" by Adam Hurst. Earlier she'd played "Cello Suite No. 1 in G Major." Years ago, Cole had the transcendent experience of listening to the great Yo-Yo Ma play that piece live. It led to a deep fascination with cello pieces.

Watching the attractive cellist, his eyes slid across her, noting her dark skin, almond eyes closed in focus, and heavy black tresses. She was lovely. And, yet, nothing stirred in him.

He rubbed his hand down his face in frustration. It wasn't just work that had him feeling...unsatisfied. Lately, no one seemed to rev his engine. The dating scene carved out his spirit, leaving him hollow. It was just...utterly bankrupt of authenticity. He'd tried dating sites. Everyone and their mothers offered to set him up, and occasionally he let them. But regardless of how they came about, the dates always began and ended the same. Zero connection. Zero chemistry.

As a result, he was also in his longest dry spell since losing his virginity after his junior year homecoming football game. The starting tight end, he'd scored two touchdowns on the field—including the winning one—and then scored again later that night in the back seat of his first car. With the head coach's daughter.

That was the start of a string of physically satisfying yet emotionally meaningless encounters with the opposite sex. Until lately, it never bothered him. In fact, it had suited his lifestyle perfectly.

What had shifted? Perhaps it was just normal maturation for a man tipping over the other side of his mid-thirties. Maybe it was seeing his siblings happily married with children. Or, could it be...that he was lonely? In his busy life, surrounded by family and friends, when he returned to his house, the emptiness was ironically *suffocating*.

He was thirty-five, and truly had never been in love. Oh, he'd been in lust many times. He'd been in deep "like." Once, he even thought he could fall for someone, only for her to relocate for a promotion, and him to realize after a short period that he didn't even miss her. So, definitely not love in that case.

Perhaps it was because he wanted what his father and late mother had. Theirs had been a marriage of passion, of friendship, of partnership. It wasn't perfect, and they'd argued plenty of times, with his mom delivering epic doses of the cold shoulder when she was peeved. But they always made up, and seemed stronger for it.

Seeing firsthand the kind of marriage he wanted, he just couldn't summon any enthusiasm for the dating scene. It left him with a sense of longing for what he feared he'd never find. And, yet, there was a dancing ray of hope that stayed with him. Deep inside, he knew she was out there. He just had to find her.

What would she be like? Dark-haired or blonde? Short? Tall? Curvy and full-figured, or perhaps slim with small breasts he could nuzzle to both of their hearts' (and bodies') content.

Cole recognized he didn't have a type. Over the years, he'd met and bedded all shapes, sizes, and colors of women. He loved the suppleness of their skin. The slide into their snug, wet channels. The tightening and the explosion. He was a connoisseur of lovemaking as much as music. And yet, the former left him empty these days, only the latter doing some small part to fill his playboy soul.

In the end, he didn't want to be a player. He wanted a partner to cherish, to ravage in bed, to build a family with, to love—a deep, unconditional, and forever kind of love that would be new to both of them and would sate them individually and together in a way they could never have imagined.

Cole scanned the room, so deep in thought he barely registered the path of his eyes. His mind wandered to his best friend, Xander—an architect who dabbled in a myriad of projects. Since Xan's ex-wife left him and their newborn son years ago, he'd been adrift. One of his projects had been this very venue, which he'd purchased and successfully rehabbed before heading off to Europe with Petey, his young son. Cole swirled his liquor in the catering-grade rocks glass. Xander thought he'd found that kind of love, only to have his heart shattered.

Cole knew he'd only ever embrace a truly powerful love, the kind that knocked you off your feet. Anything else was a pale imitation. He wanted the real deal. And though he'd never experienced even a glimmer of that shining city on the hill of love, he held out hope that one day he would.

Okay. So he was a romantic playboy—one who apparently was turning into a stereotypical teenage girl eager for love. And that type of musing wouldn't help him get through the tiresome night ahead.

His perusal of the room earlier showed exactly what he'd expected— more of the tedious same. Cole wished Xan were there to keep him entertained. He missed his best friend, and made a mental note to call him in the morning. It was already past midnight in Italy, which was the last place Xan had checked in from.

He closed his eyes again and allowed himself to get lost in the music, just for a moment, and then he'd work the room until it was time to leave.

"Are we putting you to sleep, Mr. Colburn?"

The sweet, deeply southern voice shook him from his musings. He shifted, looked way down, and offered a genuine smile to Coralee Lopez, the diminutive wife of Dr. Ben Lopez, the hospital's vice president of medical affairs and one of his primary points of contact for the construction project. They had been introduced upon his arrival earlier in the evening. Coralee was one of the lead planners of the reception, and carried a lot of influence with her husband. They, too, were an obvious love match. It was evident as Ben was introducing them, and perhaps that example of the kind of bond he wanted had triggered this evening's melancholy.

Regardless, it was in his best interest to put his most charming foot forward. At six-foot-four, he was tall by any standards (except maybe most NBA teams). But Coralee was pintsized. Almost a foot and a half shorter than him, he had to bend low to press a kiss on her dimpled cheek.

He summoned a mostly authentic laugh. "No, not sleeping Coralee. And, please, call me Cole. I'm just engrossed in the music. You did a wonderful job selecting this string quartet. The cellist is quite talented."

Coralee's dimple popped again and she lightly tapped his arm. "Well, I could be persuaded to make an introduction. I'd be as happy as clams at high tide to do a little matchmaking." Now Cole laughed for real, and Coralee's grin grew wider. "I bet that pretty thing would love a tall glass of sweet tea like you."

He shook his head and held his hands up, enjoying her evident pleasure at the idea of serving as a human Hinge. "While I appreciate the offer, I think my plate is full right now with this construction project. It wouldn't be fair to start dating anyone while I'm in the thick of it. I'm just dating my desk these days."

"Sure, sure," Coralee winked, examining him in a non-flirtatious, almost businesslike manner, and then turning her scrutiny to the cellist. "No, as I ponder this, I think that dog won't hunt."

"What does that even mean?" Cole was enjoying her burst of southern charm. Honestly, she'd knocked him right out of his lovelorn musings. No wonder Ben was nuts for her. She was the epitome of the phrase 'ray of sunshine.'

"It means I can see you two would never suit. You need a woman who will compel you away from your desk by the sheer force of her presence. And if it were to be our dear cellist, you would have already been over there working your charm instead of holding up this bar listening to her music."

"Touché, Coralee. Touché." He downed the last of his scotch, leaving the empty on a waiting tray. "Now, who should I meet tonight —for work purposes, not for matchmaking?"

"Leave it to me, Cole." She patted his bicep again and winked. "You just leave it to me."

Chapter Four

"The power of a glance has been so much abused in love stories that it has come to be disbelieved in. Few people dare now to say that two beings have fallen in love because they have looked at each other. Yet it is in this way that love begins, and in this way only."
Les Misérables, Victor Hugo

Tiercy

When she and Ross pulled up to the Manchester Inn, it was aglow with gas lighting in period-style fixtures. Buoyed by the impressive ambiance and the comforting presence of Ross, Tiercy resolutely climbed the steps to the restored Victorian mansion that was the latest rage for parties in the main house and for dinner at its smokehouse restaurant on another part of the property. In the main house, they'd taken the dining room and parlor and blended it into a bar area, with high tables, deep chairs, and a series of liquor carts that formed the "bar" itself. It was like stepping back into the nineteenth century, and Tiercy was captivated by the romanticism of the environment.

Ross was at her side, equally enthralled. "What a picturesque location for a fundraiser. It feels like Mr. Darcy is going to come around the corner and knock us off our feet!"

The deep resonant notes of a cello greeted them as they turned the corner into the main room. Ben Lopez immediately spied Tiercy and headed straight for her, gracefully exiting a conversation with a tall man whose back was toward them. The man and Ben's wife, Coralee, were talking and gesturing animatedly. Tiercy adored Coralee and Ben. They had galvanized tremendous support for Tiercy, Right After.

"Tiercy, hello! You look lovely!" Ben kissed her on both cheeks. Born and raised in Puerto Rico, he still retained his wonderful accent even though he'd lived in the mid-Atlantic U.S. since completing medical school some thirty years earlier. "I'm so glad you could make it." Holding her hand, he smiled warmly. "I worried maybe this would be too much for you. Five years is both a blink and an eternity when it comes to grief. How are you?"

'How are you' number one of the evening.

She murmured a noncommittal, "Fine, thank you," in response even as she stifled a sigh amidst her mental tally.

How many times had she heard that question in the last five years? No one ever knew what to say to her, especially Right After. But if she had a dollar for every "how *are* you?" she'd been asked, she'd be able to finance a trip around the world, where she and Jemma could live incognito and never have to hear that sympathy-tinged question again. In this case, as in most when that question was asked, Ben meant well, so she offered him more grace than she did for the casually concerned, digging deep into the energy stores she knew she'd have to tap this evening.

He squeezed her hand. "Thank you for helping us honor his memory."

"Luke would be thrilled. He loved Fellowship-Unity."

There. My first 'Luke' utterance of the evening. It felt good. The trick was not to gorge on saying it. Just roll it around in her mouth, like a decadent morsel to be savored.

Ben nodded, eyes damp, and turned his attention to Ross. "And you are Ross, correct? I remember meeting you at a party years ago. Thank you for coming."

"Dr. Lopez. It's a pleasure to see you again," Ross replied, offering her most flirtatious smile.

Tiercy giggled inside at Ross's reaction to the handsome Ben, with his more-salt-than-pepper hair and his lovely Latin manners. When he stepped aside to quickly respond to a staffer's question, Ross took the opportunity to whisper sotto voice to her friend, "Please tell me he has a single younger brother."

"Sorry, kid," Tiercy whispered out of the side of her mouth.

Ross fake pouted and then announced, "I'm hitting the bar. Shall I bring you something?"

"A glass of champagne. Thank you." Her Kir Royale buzz had worn off, but Tiercy would have to track her consumption or her bestie would have her three sheets to the wind by the end of the evening.

As Ross slipped away to the bar, Ben resumed their conversation. "Sorry about that. The philanthropy director wanted to know if we are almost ready to begin. The hospital president and I, and a few other folks, are making some brief remarks shortly." Spying his wife heading toward him, Ben called out, "And here is the loveliest of brides. I swear, querida, you still take my breath away."

Tiercy opened her mouth to greet Coralee, but her breath momentarily escaped her. The tall man who had been talking with Coralee had turned around and was walking toward them. Walking? Too tame. This man commanded the space around him.

Tiercy registered Coralee welcoming her with her charming, syrupy southern accent as she was enveloped in a fragrant embrace. She automatically returned the hug, offering mindless platitudes in response. Coralee was very petite, and, mid-hug with the much shorter woman, Tiercy's gaze was drawn to the man standing just behind Coralee. She was incapable of taking her eyes off him.

He was tall. At least six-foot-four, because she herself was over six feet in heels, and he still had several inches on her. Broad shoulders were encased in a dark gray suit that looked tailored to fit his obviously muscled body, and a crisp white shirt met tan skin. Dark brown wavy hair set off the most interesting shade of light blue, almost pale gray eyes.

Coralee ended the hug and pulled her in for another quick one. "I am just so glad to see you." Coralee had her blonde hair twisted into an updo and was wearing the highest heels Tiercy had ever seen. Even with them, Coralee was barely five-foot-five.

She began chatting away and then turned to the man who'd followed her over. "Oh, do forgive me. How rude. I've been busier than a moth in a mitten tonight and I forgot my manners. Tiercy Somerville, please meet John Colburn."

This John Colburn specimen also hadn't disconnected eye contact with her. His extraordinary irises fixed on her in a way that sent a shiver cascading down her spine. Goosebumps chased across her skin. For a moment, neither of them moved.

Then he broke the moment, extending his hand toward her. Tearing her eyes away, Tiercy watched her own hand rise to meet his. Warm, solid fingers wrapped around her hand. "A pleasure to meet you, Tiercy. My friends call me Cole."

"Nice to meet you...Cole," Tiercy offered, her voice sounding far away.

She was horrified to find herself rendered largely mute in the presence of this attractive man. Her mouth was dry and she prayed for Ross to appear with her drink, if only to motivate her saliva glands into working again.

He smiled at her and she reflexively returned a genuine smile of her own. In that moment, she had the strangest feeling of being alone with him, even though they were surrounded by people. Suddenly, she realized that he was still holding her hand...and she was holding his.

As if reading her mind, Cole let his gaze wander onto their joined hands. He offered a soft squeeze—the gentlest of pressure—and slowly let go. Tiercy had to resist the temptation to bring her hand to her lips.

What in the hell is going on with me?

Seemingly oblivious to this strange moment, Coralee chattered away. "Tiercy, Cole is the building contractor for the new pavilion. He is overseeing the entire project. He's quite amazing. Maybe later he can show you the renderings."

Ben interjected, "And Cole, Tiercy is our special guest tonight. Her late husband, Dr. Luke Somerville, will be honored with an in-memoriam naming of the residency training center in the new building."

Cole's face registered shock at the words 'late husband,' and then just as quickly he composed his features. "I've heard about Dr. Somerville. I am very sorry for your loss. I hope we can honor him with a wonderful learning space."

Tiercy nodded, blinking away a quick surge of wetness in her eyes. At the same time, she was frustrated at her absolute inability to make basic conversation. What was it about this man that made her speechless and—if she admitted it—a bit shaky.

She was saved from any further ponderings, and her own lack of coherence, by Ross. "I come bearing the gifts of Bacchus," Ross announced, stopping with admiration at the sight of the handsome stranger.

Good. John Colburn will get a gander at Ross and I'll be off the hook. An unexpected frisson of jealousy sliced through her at the thought.

Tiercy gratefully accepted the champagne and quickly took a sip, using the activity to finally tear her eyes away from the man who had inexplicably transfixed her. Coralee might have been oblivious to the electricity that hummed between Cole and Tiercy, but it was clear Ross most definitely was not. She darted a glance between Tiercy, her face now hidden in a champagne glass, and this gorgeous man who was looking as poleaxed as she felt.

Ben offered his apologies and headed into the other room, where they were setting up a microphone and speaker. Coralee offered air kisses and flitted away, promising to be back "in two shakes of a wooly lamb's tail." She had clearly already enjoyed a cocktail or two, and Tiercy wished she could pound a few more glasses of champagne to try to calm the emotions roiling inside her.

"I'm Ross Beaufort, Tiercy's best friend." The sound of Ross's voice startled Tiercy back into focus. She watched, still transfixed, as Ross held out her hand in a businesslike fashion. An amused smile crossed her bestie's face, but her signature flirtatious manner was unusually absent.

"John Colburn. Cole for short. Tiercy's *newest* friend."

Ross laughed, and Cole joined in. Deep, sexy bass. *Good lord.* Tiercy was captivated and mute all at once. A long dormant stirring between her legs horrified her. Was the *mere presence* of this man making her wet...and at an event designed to raise money for her late husband? As Coralee would say, Jesus wept!

Horrified, Tiercy downed the rest of her champagne, reached blindly for a passing tray of the bubbly elixir, trading her now-empty flute for a full one, and drank that too.

"So, John-Colburn-Cole-For-Short, it is *very* nice to meet you." Ross put emphasis on the word 'very' and Tiercy shot her a quelling look. "I'm sure our paths will cross again this evening, but I need to grab your *newest friend* for a moment. She is needed in the other room. Would you please excuse us?"

Having offered a pathetic total of six words in the conversation, Tiercy allowed Ross to maneuver her in the direction Ben and Coralee had gone, somehow both relieved and disappointed at the same time. At the entrance to the other room, a little voice in her head told her to turn around.

She glanced over her shoulder to find Cole was just standing there, watching her, a smile playing on his mouth. He lifted his champagne glass in a silent toast.

Tiercy turned back slowly, a matching smile on her own face.

CHAPTER FIVE

"Hear my soul speak: The very instant I saw you, did my heart fly to your service."
The Tempest, William Shakespeare

TIERCY

"WHAT the everloving fuck was *that*?" Ross's voice was a cymbal crash through her reverie.

"What was what?" Tiercy responded with a calmness that didn't reflect the churning inside her.

"Don't play dumb with me, Tiercy Flynn Somerville. I leave you for ten minutes to get us some libations, and I come back to find you having clearly impure thoughts with *People* magazine's sexiest man for eternity. And it was reciprocal. The guy was gobsmacked."

Tiercy started to vociferously object and realized there was no way she could deny it. Instead, she offered a helpless shrug of her shoulders.

"Stranger danger! Jeez, Tierce. I could practically cut the sexual tension with a knife." Ross had cornered Tiercy. "Well...?"

Tiercy opened her mouth. Nothing came out. She closed it, opened it, and tried again. "I...he...he was nice," she all but squeaked.

"*Nice?? Nice????*" Ross whisper-hollered. "He's a freaking walking orgasm. In fact, I was pretty sure you were having one while he held your hand...for a very long time, I might add," Ross noted primly. "Who is this hottest of Hottie McHot Pants?"

Tiercy flushed. "He's the lead contractor for the new building. Coralee introduced us. I'm sure he's married. Or gay. Guys that hot have to be gay. Or douches. Anyway, it doesn't matter. I'm not interested in... anything." *There. That was like, fifteen words, or more. I am recovering my powers of speech.*

"Oh, I can assure you that Mr. 'Cole' most certainly is not gay. And as for being a douche, I honestly didn't catch that vibe off him. And my douche-dar is pretty accurate."

Tiercy's eyes wandered to the doorway, where Cole had just entered the room.

Ross fixed a knowing stare at her, eyebrows raised sky-high, following Tiercy's gaze to Cole. Her bestie's eyes practically popped out of her head as Cole's gaze traveled an immediate path to Tiercy, locking on her and warming up places that had no business being warm tonight of all nights. And yet...yes...her lady parts were definitely singing while her nipples danced along inside her lacy bra. Good God, what if she had headlights while schmoozing? Tiercy's face heated up.

"Holy Get a Room, Batman," Ross muttered, rolling her eyes. "Not interested in anything, my sausage toes," she added under her breath.

The sound of microphone feedback jarred all three to attention.

Tiercy turned to Ross, grabbing her wrist and hissing urgently, "I need to get out of here. I can't do this."

Ross lay a gentling hand on top of hers. "Yes, you can. Are you freaking out because this is a Thing, or because a hot guy is interested in you and your body is all-in?" She cocked an eyebrow as Tiercy self-consciously covered her chest. "Because as your best friend in the universe, and all the multiverses, I have to tell you, Tiercy, you are allowed to be interested in men. It's normal."

"Not *tonight*. Tonight is about Luke." Tiercy closed her eyes. "I knew this was a bad idea."

Ross responded in a low, firm voice. "Tiercy Niamh Flynn Somerville, tonight is about raising money. You honored Luke yesterday at the beach and earlier today with Jemma. For now, just enjoy the evening. And if a Hottie McHot Pants wants to flirt a bit with you, no harm-no foul. I promise."

"My bestie is the bestest," Tiercy whispered, grateful for the billionth time since That Day—and the gazillionth in her life—for the support of her best friend.

Ross squeezed Tiercy's hand, and Tiercy tried to ignore the trembling of her own hand as she squeezed back.

Ben's voice filled the room, followed by the hospital president's, and then some other talking heads. Ross fidgeted impatiently, and after twenty torturous minutes, her stomach started growling. Tiercy and Ross giggled. "I'm going to go find some hors d'oeuvres," Ross nodded toward the other room. "I'm tired of all this 'blah blah blah.' I need food. Want anything?"

"No thanks. They should be wrapping up, and then I'm sure Ben will want me to meet some possible donors."

"Have fun," sang Ross as she headed toward the main entry.

Tiercy observed Cole offer Ross a warm, but not flirtatious smile on her way out.

Definitely not gay, mouthed Ross behind his back, with a huge grin.

Tiercy closed her eyes and took a deep, calming breath, just as her therapist had taught her. She sensed him moving toward her, as if drawn by an invisible magnetic field that gripped her on the other end. She knew he was going to come over—discerned it deep in her bones.

Please, please, let me be coherent this time. Witty would be fantastic, but I'll settle for coherent.

"Hello again." Cole had reached her side, and he smiled.

Who knew gray eyes could be so soft and warm. "Hello again, yourself." *Oh yeah, very witty.*

Cole turned to face the speaker, now one of the top hospital donors. They were facing the same direction, and he was close enough that she could feel the brush of his sleeve on her bare arm. He leaned in and whispered, "I always find these things painfully boring."

"Me too. It's a 'Thing.' I hate Things," Tiercy whispered back. "Part of me wants to sneak out and the other part of me wants to make an embarrassing scene—start yodeling or something—so I never get invited back. But they want me to meet some donors, so I'll be a good girl and behave."

The corner of Cole's eyes crinkled with his grin. "And do you know how to do that? Yodel?"

Ignoring her panties melting away at his sexy smile—with straight, white teeth, and just a hint of five o'clock shadow—Tiercy laughed quietly. "No. Only what I learned from singing 'The Lonely Goatherd' from *The Sound of Music*."

"Lay ee odl lay ee odl-oo," he softly sang, and they burst into laughter.

Several guests turned at the disruption, staring at them. Tiercy worked to swallow her mirth, and saw Cole doing the same.

"How did you—" she began.

"My older sister, Margot," he responded, not needing to hear the rest of the question. "She made me watch it with her over and over again and she'd have us siblings all act out scenes. I had to be Kurt."

They laughed again, this time quietly, taking care not to disrupt the proceedings.

He turned to her with suddenly serious eyes. "I am very sorry about your husband. I've been working on the plans for the training space, and in the process, I've heard his name mentioned many times. He was very well-respected." Cole paused, and Tiercy wondered if his thoughts were as scattered in the moment as hers. "I knew he was young when he— when he passed. And I knew his...widow would be here tonight. But I wasn't expecting...you. You know, so...young... and lovely." Cole looked away, a blush creeping up his tanned neck.

Tiercy had a sudden reckless desire to put her lips there. Somewhere inside, she knew she should be deeply saddened by the conversation. Not to mention horrified by the timing. And she loathed being referred to as a widow, the baldness of it always jarring her. But somehow, coming from him, she wasn't offended at all. He was clearly struggling to make conversation, and the thought occurred that maybe he indeed was as affected by her as she was by him.

She looked again at his handsome profile, with its elegant nose and strong jaw. *You wish, Somerville.*

Cole shifted to face her again. "So, having just completely put my foot in my mouth talking about your late husband and then trying to cover my own frustratingly absent social graces..." He shook his head. "Listen, before Ben and Coralee sweep you away to charm some donors, would you like another drink? Dutch courage?"

Tiercy bit her lip and smiled. "You sound like Ross. She uses that saying. And, yes, I could use something."

Cole held out a blazered arm to her, and Tiercy could see the muscle definition of his biceps. *Sweet Jesus.* Tentatively placing her arm through his, and pressing against the hard muscle of his upper arm—*Oh sweet Jesus*—Tiercy followed him wordlessly to the bar.

CHAPTER SIX

*"He knew she was there by the joy and terror that took possession
of his heart...Everything was lit up by her. She was the smile that
brightened everything around."*
Anna Karenina, Leo Tolstoy

COLE

Care of his four siblings, Cole had several nieces and nephews. They were always throwing around Gen Z lingo like "skibidi" (no clue on that one) and "rizz." The latter he understood, and up until this point in this life, he'd considered himself pretty adept on the rizz front. Yet, within the last ten minutes, any ability to summon the charm and style that had earned him the "player" nickname in college seemed to have deserted him.

From the moment he saw Tiercy Somerville standing with Ben Lopez, he'd been riveted by her. Thick, auburn hair, falling in waves just past her shoulders, which she'd push behind her ear as she talked. Those eyes—the color of a blue topaz ring his mother once had—that, despite a sadness about them, were arresting as they'd locked gazes earlier. High cheekbones. A cascading laugh that made him smile just to hear it.

Slender build, but not too skinny, with sexy curves set off by a slim-fitting navy dress that was modest, and yet incredibly alluring. Elegant collarbones rose from the neckline, and a peek of toned thigh teased through the slit of the dress. She was tall, more than six feet in those amazing heels.

He was transfixed. He'd been with many sensational women, but Tiercy Somerville seemed different. Behind the sadness that emanated from her, and with good reason, there was an energy he found captivating. One thing was certain, he wasn't letting her leave tonight without getting her number.

Steering her toward a more private corner where a small bar had been placed, he allowed himself another quick (and he hoped discreet) glance at her. *Christ.* She was stunning. It was evident from her dress that she had a glorious rack. He wondered what those breasts would feel like in his palms. The color of her nipples. Were they responsive? Was she the type he could bring to orgasm just with nipple play, or did she fly when that decadent vee between her legs received the attention it deserved? Cole swallowed, imagining those long legs draped over his shoulders as he tasted her and brought her to completion.

His cock stirred in his pants. Jesus. Time to take that train off the tracks before he popped a boner at a fundraiser for this woman's deceased husband. *Tacky, you assbasket.*

With her still tucked next to his side, fitting perfectly with his own height, he focused instead on the warmth of her body. The delicate curve of her hand on his bicep.

Shit. They had arrived at the bar and he was still lost in cataloguing her beauty. Cole cleared his throat, running his free hand through his hair.

"Would you like—"

"This place is—"

They both began, and then laughed.

"Please, go on," Tiercy motioned, a slight blush creeping up to her cut-glass cheekbones.

Cole allowed himself a momentary fantasy of brushing his lips along them, toward the delicate shell of her ears.

"I just wondered if you'd like champagne, which I noticed you drinking earlier"—*when I couldn't take my eyes off you*—"or if you'd prefer something else?"

"Champagne would be lovely, thank you." She offered him a shy smile as she pushed her hair behind her ear and then bit her lower lip, quickly looking away toward the string quartet.

God...now he was fantasizing about licking and nibbling her lips. *Cut it out, horndog.* And, yet, he knew it was going to be next to impossible to stop. She was intoxicating, and he found himself drinking up as much of her as he could.

"Okay. Now your turn." He returned her smile, his gaze dropping briefly to her lips.

She faced him, and her gaze also dropped for a moment to his own lips, which curved into a broader smile. When was the last time he broke into a genuine grin of delight with a woman? Ages.

"This place is amazing," Tiercy marveled, looking around. "The attention to detail is incredible. I feel as if I've been transported to the late eighteen hundreds."

Cole handed her a glass of champagne and they lightly tapped the flutes together. "It is pretty incredible," Cole agreed as their eyes collided and locked again.

He wasn't sure if he meant the Manchester Inn or the immediate connection they were feeling—or at least he was feeling. Whatever it was, as sudden-onset nerves gripped his belly, a gremlin took over his tongue and he proceeded with a mortifying rush of word vomit.

"A good buddy of mine from college actually owns this place. Not sure if you know the story. You probably don't. But it's printed on the brochures by the entrance so maybe you read it already." He motioned toward the location, and then battled not to smack himself in the head. Hard. *Yes, you babbling derp, I'm sure she immediately grabbed a damn piece of paper and read it. And she definitely wants to hear you ramble about the inn.*

Tiercy tilted her head, only curiosity shining in her topaz blue eyes, and blessedly no sign of recognition of his random awkwardness. "I didn't notice the brochures. I think I was feeling a bit... overwhelmed...when we arrived." He watched sadness flicker across the fine bones of her face. "But I'd love to know the history. If you don't mind..." She placed her hand gently on his arm, as if sensing his discomfort.

The warmth from her hand calmed his now-racing heart, and it took all his control not to lift it to his lips and press a kiss there.

Tiercy's eyes caught on her hand and she quickly pulled it away, clearing her throat and taking a sip of champagne. A bloom crested on her cheekbones.

He took his own fortifying swallow. "It was private property," he rasped past the fucking throat gremlin, and then mirrored her own throat-clearing.

Tiercy tipped her chin down, a small smile playing on her lips. He shrugged his shoulders and cocked his head in acknowledgement, a smile playing at his own lips as he continued.

"It, uh, it was owned by the same family for two hundred years. The property had fallen into complete disrepair, and no one in the family wanted to deal with it anymore. They put it up for auction, with the expectation that it'd be bought for the land and the buildings would be torn down. Instead, Xander—that's my friend—bought it all and immediately started rehabbing the entire property."

"Wow, that's impressive. Is your friend here tonight?" she asked, looking around.

He tried (and failed) not to be distracted by the graceful curve of her neck as she surveyed the room. What would it be like to kiss his way down from her ear to those tantalizing collarbones. He bet he could drink a bit of champagne from the delicate hollows, then trace his tongue back up the line of her throat.

Suddenly sensing an awkward conversational lull, he realized she was waiting on his response. Yep, no rizz whatsoever tonight. But instead of looking annoyed, she looked...flushed. Almost aroused? He thought he could see the faint beat of her pulse in her neck. He'd been so absorbed in his perusal—and fantasy—he'd forgotten to actually answer her question.

He forced himself to focus. "No, he's in Europe right now. He donated the rental of the Inn this evening and thought he might make it back in time, but his plans are pretty variable these days."

Hopefully, there'd be time in his future to examine every inch of her...with his lips. Hopefully.

"Mmm...General contractor called in a favor to look good in front of the hospital execs?" Tiercy teased.

He loved the intoxicating glint of laughter in her blue eyes. "Something like that." Cole grinned back. "Never hurts to look good in front of the client."

"Well, it's a phenomenal location. Your friend should be proud."

Cole nodded, ignoring the tendril of sadness for his friend that coiled in his gut. He owed this magnificent woman his full attention. "He's had a tough time. The development of this place was important for him."

"I get the sense there's more to the story." Tiercy's smile was soft and knowing.

It was almost as if she could read him, which would be unusual, as he had developed an excellent poker face out of work and social necessity over the years.

"There is. But that's a story for perhaps another time." He hoped fervently there would be many more times to be with her. "I'll tell Xan you love the place. Now," he made his voice lighter, "tell me about yourself before I lose you to your duties."

"Only if you do the same."

"Deal."

He tapped his glass with hers again.

They shared the briefest biographical information. She told him she taught high school English. He gave her a summary of his construction company, which was a family business based in the Maryland suburbs of Washington, D.C. She showed him a picture of her daughter Jemma on her phone, wearing a ballet tutu and a camo army vest. Cole smiled, charmed by the little girl. He let it drop that he was the middle child of five siblings.

"Holy gravy! Five siblings?" Tiercy's eyes popped, her laughter finally erasing the sadness in her eyes. "I'm an only child. I cannot fathom that many brothers and sisters. The closest to a sibling I have is Ross." She motioned across the room to where Ross was deep in clearly flirtatious conversation with one of the donors he'd briefly met earlier.

"She and I grew up together and she even lived with my parents and me for several years." Tiercy's eyes shadowed again.

Unable to stop himself, he tipped her chin up to look into her eyes. "I sense there's more to the story," he said, intentionally echoing her earlier statement. It drew the intended, albeit small, smile from her in response.

"Touché. There is. Perhaps another time."

He took the opportunity to drift his fingers down the side of her neck, and was rewarded with a little shiver from her. *Good. She's feeling this too.*

Clearing his throat, Cole shifted the conversation back to lighter topics. "Let's proceed with Tiercy and Cole 101, Teacher." Yep. He was hot for teacher alright. "What was it like not to have to compete for parental attention? Snacks? The shotgun seat in the car?"

Tiercy's musical laugh filtered around them and Cole's insides tingled at the sound.

"I assure you there was plenty of chaos at my home growing up... usually caused by Ross, her Irish twin Gaby, and their hyper black lab, Shirley."

Cole was charmed at the image of a young Tiercy with her friends and the dog.

They talked about movies they enjoyed. Cole started telling her about one and blanked on the name. He smiled sheepishly and promised to send it to her once he remembered. For a moment, he had the impetuous thought of inviting her to watch it with him....

Too soon, Colburn. Too soon.

Instead, he contented himself with her presence. She smelled faintly of oranges and spice, a scent that traveled straight from his nose to his libido. The semi he'd been struggling to contain since he'd seen her across the room, as Coralee guided him to meet Dr. Somerville's widow, made a resurgence.

Tiercy Somerville was not what he'd been expecting.

She was a billion, mind-blowing times better.

As she chatted about her daughter and her work, breaking into laughter, Cole was spellbound. Her eyes lit up whenever she mentioned Jemma. And it was clear she loved teaching and her students. He smiled along, basking in the sheer beauty of her personality. Tiercy was lit from within. There was an accessible charisma about her that drew him in... and knitted him to her.

How was this possible? He discreetly checked his late grandfather's Rolex, which he treasured as a keepsake of his favorite family member and life mentor. They'd only met a half hour ago.

And yet...he was overtaken with the sensation of...recognition. As if he'd known Tiercy all along in his soul, and now life was finally catching up.

He'd just opened his mouth to ask if she was feeling the same, when Ben Lopez swept in to pull her away from him and to her duties for the evening.

"Are you ready to make the rounds, Tiercy?" Ben, bless him, seemed reluctant to interrupt.

"As ready as I'll get," she replied.

Was it his imagination, or did her face fall at the untimely interruption?

He shook Ben's hand and then reached for Tiercy's. Her long, tapered fingers draped around his hand, and he swore they trembled a bit.

"It was a pleasure meeting and talking with you, Tiercy."

Tiercy. What an unusual name, for an unusually beautiful woman. He took a chance and lightly rubbed his thumb along the back of her hand.

A small frown line appeared between her brows, and then she smiled, although this time it didn't fully reach her eyes. He thought he'd blown it, been too forward—especially in this scenario. But then she squeezed his hand, the corners of her eyes crinkling in a genuine smile. "My pleasure entirely, Cole."

When he reluctantly released his hold, he saw her square her shoulders and take a deep breath before turning toward the other side of the room, where Coralee was holding court with what appeared to be a gaggle of donors.

Holy fuck. Suddenly the evening was far from tedious.

Chapter Seven

"There are years that ask questions and years that answer."
Their Eyes were Watching God, Zora Neale Hurston

TIERCY

As anticipated, Ben swept in to collect her.

Tiercy tried, and failed, to suppress her disappointment at leaving Cole. The past half hour had been unexpectedly freeing. Instead of the pervasive doom and sadness that had taken residence in her gut since she'd received the invitation, there was a lightness in her heart. Conversation with the handsome (*fuck it*...and beyond sexy) contractor was effortless. He made her laugh when that expression of joy was the last thing she expected. And when he swallowed his champagne, and her eyes tracked the movement of his Adam's apple, Tiercy acquiesced to a long-dormant feeling—the aching hum of desire.

While chatting about movies, she had gotten the distinct impression he was going to invite her to watch one with him that he'd really liked. And then she watched as he almost physically checked himself.

So, that was a no. But maybe just a no-for-now?

"Are you ready to make the rounds, Tiercy?" Ben's eyes were kind... and curious?...as he eased next to her.

"As ready as I'll get." Tiercy hoped her smile looked genuine.

Cole shook Ben's hand and then reached for hers. "It's been a pleasure meeting and talking with you, Tiercy."

Almost out of body, she watched as she placed her hand in his. Cole's much larger hand, warm and comforting, enveloped hers. His thumb softly swirled against the back of her hand. Her throat was suddenly arid and she could barely swallow. "My pleasure entirely, Cole," she croaked and then smiled, squeezing his hand before reluctantly releasing it along with her fantasy to run away with him.

"Cole, you are most welcome to join us."

Was this connection with Cole that obvious? Tiercy wiped damp palms on her dress, pretending to smooth a nonexistent wrinkle. It was time to sing for her supper. Or Luke's training center, as it were. As much as she was reveling in her time with Cole, there was a knot of discomfort at the notion of Cole accompanying her while she inevitably discussed Luke.

Cole's gaze snagged on her. His eyes were soft and kind. Knowing. "I feel terrible for monopolizing your guest of honor for so long. I will do my own rounds and leave you both to your fundraising." Then he shifted, just infinitesimally, closer to her, his eyes still locked on hers.

Tiercy fought the insane urge to burrow against him and beg him to take her away. Instead, she managed a heartfelt smile, praying he couldn't see her lips shaking. "Best of luck with the construction, Cole."

"Thank you, Tiercy. Building new things is always special to me." He nodded with a sexy half smile and eased toward the Board chair.

Holy double entendre.

T iercy stabilized her shaking legs and turned to Ben. "May we please stop for a water? I'm a bit parched."

"Absolutely, my dear. We'll get one on the way to Mrs. Jenkins. She's ready to make a large donation and is so eager to hear about Luke from his wife."

Tiercy stifled a sigh and plastered a smile on her face. "Wonderful."

After inelegantly chugging a much-needed glass of water, Tiercy allowed Ben to guide her around the room, introducing her to donor after donor. After a while, Tiercy's face began to hurt from smiling. Surprisingly, the myriad mentions of Luke didn't hurt as much as she'd worried. The ache was there, but not the stabbing agony of loss that plagued her on the anniversary, and countless days in between.

As she tried to focus on each new person, she could feel Cole watching her. Each time she entered a new section of the party, she found herself scanning the room for him. And when she saw him, would catch him already looking at her with those arresting gray eyes. As a result, she was only partially present in every subsequent conversation. Her mind—and let's face it, her lady parts—were distracted by the sexy presence of John Colburn across the room.

There was a part of Tiercy that thrilled at the realization that Cole managed to always be in the vicinity of the "donor arc" through which Ben and Coralee led her over the next hour. Whatever room she was in, he would be there as well. A few times, he just happened to be speaking to a donor whom Ben wanted to connect her with, and Tiercy was able to enjoy being part of a group conversation with Cole. This no-pressure context allowed her to observe him subtly. At least she hoped it was subtle.

He would angle his head toward the women, an engaged but never-flirtatious bearing about him. With the men, he would assume the role of a man's man, always participating in their jokes and asking about hobbies. In every case, he asked good questions and seemed to make everyone feel they were at the center of his focus.

As he was the center of hers, even when talking with others. He was like a tuning fork, causing the air molecules around her to compress and expand, rendering her incapable of ignoring the vibrations his presence produced.

Another thing was certain. Her bestie hadn't missed her reaction to the sexy contractor. With her back to most of the room (including, thankfully, Cole), Ross gave an exaggerated wink, eyes flaring in his direction. Her friend experienced firsthand the hole Luke left in her life, and her heart. She'd been after Tiercy for ages to start dating—in particular, shipping her and Brinder with single-minded focus. But that would never happen, even if Tiercy suspected Brinder would absolutely be open to it.

Tiercy ran her thumb across the back of her left ring finger. Last summer she finally took off her wedding rings during a besties' trip to Barbados for what would have been her and Luke's eighth wedding anniversary, and tenth as a couple. Even then, despite her ever-present grief, Tiercy knew she was slowly turning an emotional corner.

Grief and sadness about Luke would always be a part of her, like a gray streak in hair that you could cover up but never actually remove. However, she recognized her own healing. Sometimes she fought it, the pulse of her grief her last emotional connection to Luke. Other times, she could almost hear Luke chiding her that it was time to come out from the haze of her grief and start living fully again.

It was after one of those silent conversations with Luke that Tiercy had eventually slept with someone—a disastrous encounter that had left Tiercy an emotional, guilt-ridden wreck. After, she decided she preferred celibacy to the bastardization of the lovemaking she and Luke had enjoyed.

And now, something seismic had happened. The timing was horrifying to her. She should be focused on Luke. Instead, her mind and her gaze sought and found Cole, again and again. Tiercy looked around the room and wondered if anyone else noticed. But the rest of the guests mingled, unaware of the connection being forged in the room that evening.

As if reading her friend's mind, Ross looked from across the room. Tiercy had been drawn into Cole's orbit yet again. He had conveniently been talking to a blue-haired woman dripping in diamonds when Ben, Coralee, and Tiercy came by, initiating a group conversation. Ross's eyes were questioning. She mouthed, "Everything OK?" and tilted her head in Cole's direction.

Tiercy dipped her head and couldn't contain a smile. Suddenly, she had to talk with her best friend. She quickly extricated herself from the conversation, making an excuse to use the ladies room. Gah. That was embarrassing TMI, but her addled brain couldn't think of anything else in the moment. Her *Cole-addled* brain, that was. And even more? She didn't seem to mind a bit.

CHAPTER EIGHT

TIERCY

She scurried toward the alcove that housed the entrances to the bathroom. Within moments, Ross was by Tiercy's side.

"Managed to tear yourself from the charms of Cole-Thor?" teased Ross, gripping her arm and playfully tugging her into the lavish "ladies' parlor."

"Cole-Thor—?" Tiercy burst into laughter. "I guess he does resemble our hunky Chris Hemsworth, albeit with dark hair. And mesmerizing eyes. Now don't make me laugh when I have to pee."

Tiercy and Ross disappeared into adjoining stalls.

She truly did have to use the loo. Her bladder, never the same after nine-pound baby Jemma barreled through in her hurry to join the world, was screaming at her. And yet, if Ross hadn't dragged her in there, she probably would have kept standing with Cole—content to enjoy his intoxicating proximity, urinary tract health be damned.

Other than an epic orgasm, which she hadn't experienced in more than a half a decade, nothing was more satisfying than emptying an excruciatingly full bladder.

She sighed, finished her act of nature, righted her dress, and stepped out at the same time as Ross.

"Pee jinx," Ross laughed. "We are bladder simpatico besties."

"Ha, nice SAT word." Tiercy chuckled, heading to the sink next to Ross and washing her hands.

Tiercy cast a quick glance at herself in the mirror. Gadzooks. She was flushed bright red. The jig was up. No way would Ross let this one go.

"Now can we talk about John Colburn? You two seem to have hit it off," Ross continued in a leading voice.

Tiercy attempted a noncommittal tone...and failed. You can't hide from your best friend. "He's pretty great. I—I think he likes me..."

"Oh, you think so? Thanks for the sports report, Stan. Now let's throw it to Tiercy Somerville at the anchor desk, to report the obvious." Ross threw her head back, snorting with laughter at her own joke. "Girl, he's been following you around like a lost puppy. A hot thirst trap of lost puppy, albeit, whose muscles seem to have muscles and who I bet has a huge di—"

"Stop it. Ssshhh," Tiercy shushed, fighting embarrassment while also secretly pleased that Ross concurred with her.

Ross wasted no time tucking her arm through Tiercy's, leading her back toward the main reception space.

Tiercy's heart picked up cadence, her senses telling her Cole was nearby. She glanced at her watch. Ten o'clock. When had it gotten so late? She'd told her parents she'd be back by nine-thirty at the latest. It was a school night for her, and she needed to be up early to get a workout in before taking Jemma to her preschool/daycare.

Ross examined her and Tiercy squirmed at the attention. She knew from experience Ross could read her like the memoirs she edited for a living.

Her bestie grinned. "You wanna leave but you don't wanna leave."

Tiercy shook her head. "It's time to go. I need to text my parents and tell them I'm running late."

"I'm sure they figured it out. They're smart like that."

"Ha ha, Ross. I just don't want them to worry." She dashed off a quick text, and her mom quickly replied that Jemma had fallen asleep soon after they brought her back from their house, and they were happy to stay as late as she needed.

Tiercy didn't let Ross see the text, sure her friend would try to finagle a one-night stand for her and Cole if she did.

Her stomach skipped. Did she want that? A night with Cole? Or maybe even more than one night? Holy gravy. She hadn't experienced this kind of immediate attraction since the day she met Luke. Guilt punched her in the stomach.

"Did you and Thirst Trap trade numbers?" Ross probed, a bestie dog with a juicy bone.

Bone made her think of Cole with a—nope, not going to think about Cole with a boner. Agh. She pictured it. And now it was in her head. Head. Her mouth watered at the thought of her mouth on him—

"Hello? Princess Space Cadet? Did you hear me?"

Tiercy forced her focus back to Ross, ignoring both the ache in her heart along with the inconvenient ache that had started pulsing between her legs. "Not yet. There hasn't been an opportunity. And, well, it needs to happen...you know, organically."

If she even should offer her number. The thought of it, though thrilling, made her sad too. Like she was cheating on Luke, or at least his memory.

Ross snorted. "Organic-shmorganic." She pivoted them to the left —bringing them practically face to face with Cole. "Aaaand...no time like the present." Ross gently elbowed her in the ribs to alert her to Cole's presence. As if that were necessary.

Tiercy pushed her hair behind her ears, beyond mortified that he might have overhead them.

"Ladies." He smiled at both of them, but a thrill danced through Tiercy when his eyes landed and stayed on her.

"John-Colburn-Cole-For-Short, fancy meeting you here. Crazy how you two kids keep running into each other."

Tiercy hid her eyeroll. Ross was as subtle as a train whistle.

"As much as I hate to leave the glorious goings-on at the Manchester

Inn," Ross continued, never one to be deterred by what she perceived as a challenge, "I have an early meeting, and my friend has to be at school by seven forty-five a.m. to educate the bright young minds of the future. Thus, she and I both need to hit the hay..." She held out her hand, which Cole shook in return, his eyes finding and catching Tiercy's once again before returning to Ross. "It's been a most interesting evening. And it was...fascinating...to meet you. Would you like my friend's number?" Ross added with wide-eyed faux innocence.

Tiercy's jaw dropped. She wasn't sure whether to strangle Ross or hug her. Both. She'd do both. Not clear on what order, though.

Cole reached in his pocket for his phone—Tiercy tried but failed not to notice the tug of fabric across his arm porn—and Ross recited Tiercy's number. "Now, call her so she has your number."

Cole complied obediently. Then he turned to Tiercy, gray eyes searching her face and resting on her lips. She imagined him kissing them over and over. And then she imagined those lips doing other things.

Focus.

She cast around for something charming, coming up with, "It was very nice to meet you, Cole." Hopeless. She was hopeless. She held out her hand. He reached for it and she startled at the jolt as they connected.

"Thank you, Tiercy. It was—incredible to meet you. I...enjoyed myself. Here's, uh, here's my card, too. In case, you...um...you need my work number." An adorable flush crept up his neck.

She took the card, proud that her hand didn't shake.

He leaned in, pressing the barest, gentlest of kisses against her cheek, his hand hovering above her arm. She shifted closer, breathing him in, just for a moment.

A burst of laughter from across the room startled them apart. And for the second time that evening, they found themselves locking eyes, neither one breaking the contact.

To her right, Ross cleared her throat. "Well, night-night, kids. Come on, Tiercella. I'm about to turn into a mouse or a pumpkin or whatever."

Cole blinked a few times and grinned. Tiercy's own smile mirrored his.

"Good night, Tiercy Somerville. Safe travels home."

"Good night, John Colburn. You too."

It was simple, inane, end-of-the evening conversation, but the words were loaded with promise and possibility.

She reluctantly turned away and let Ross lead her to the door. As they waited for their Uber, Ross grabbed her phone and added Cole as a contact.

Tiercy took her phone back, noticing Ross put "Cole-Thor" in the name field, along with two fire emojis.

"Well, that was *funexpected*, hmm?" Ross nudged her. "Have you somewhat revised your opinion of 'Things'?"

But Tiercy didn't respond. She was lost in thought, somewhere far, far away. Images of Luke and Cole tumbled through her mind. And her traitorous thoughts kept returning to the wrong man.

CHAPTER NINE

TIERCY

By ten thirty p.m., Tiercy had hugged her parents, assured them she was fine and had made it through the event sans breakdown, and gotten an update on Jemma, who'd been good and had quickly sacked out after roughhousing with Gramps.

Tiercy tiptoed in to kiss sweet Jemma goodnight. Her little girl, golden locks splayed on the bed, didn't even stir, soft snores emanating from her slack lips. One arm was wrapped around her favorite stuffed animal, a purple elephant she named Lola, which came out as Yoya when she was younger. Tiercy chuckled at the sight of a Han Solo figurine loosely wrapped in her daughter's hand, which still retained some of its baby fat. She'd found Han—Jemma's newest obsession—in a box of Luke's old stuff his mom had shipped.

Tiercy watched her daughter for several long moments. Even in sleep, her resemblance to Luke was so strong. It was like getting a small piece of him back. Sometimes it hurt to see it—to be reminded of what, and who, she'd never have again. But most of the time it felt like little gifts from Luke from beyond. He left her with a glorious piece of him and she was forever grateful.

She went to her room and tried to settle in for bed. She was in the weird place between wired and tired—twired, Luke had coined it somewhere during year two of his residency. She shifted her pillow so it would touch "his." It was bizarre, but it always made her feel better. She ran her hand over his pillow, remembering the times they'd lain in bed, reading and talking, and of course making love.

But tonight, she had something new on her mind. Or, more precisely, some*one*. A pulse of guilt beat through her, but didn't stop her from reaching over to the nightstand for the small piece of cardstock she'd placed there earlier.

I'm sorry, Luke.

She studied the business card. John Sims Colburn. General Manager. Colburn Construction. Feeling somewhat ridiculous, but compelled to do it nevertheless, she brought the card up to her nose and inhaled. Maybe it was her imagination, but his business card seemed to carry traces of his spicy, woodsy scent.

Holy gravy, she was on the Hot Mess Express, as Ross liked to say. She had been so discombobulated by Cole that she'd neglected to say her goodbyes to Ben and Coralee. Oh, well. She'd send him an email apologizing when she woke up.

Tiercy sighed. She was beyond twired. Giving up on sleep, at least for a little while, she opened the nightstand drawer. Her "Rose" vibrator and a Moleskine notebook rested side-by-side.

She contemplated the toy. In truth, her body was aching for release. She reached for it, and then her hand stalled. It was always Luke's face she pictured when she used her trusty toy. Tiercy had a trove of sexy memories stored that never failed her. But what if another face crept in? A tall, muscular body. Dark hair. Arresting pale slate eyes.

No. She couldn't do that to herself. Wouldn't do that to Luke. It was tantamount to cheating. Wasn't it?

Sighing, she reached for the notebook, willfully ignoring the protest between her legs.

Right After, and for a couple years beyond that, Tiercy had journaled regularly. It had been a coping mechanism recommended by a support group to help her through the dark days. As a rule, she never reread her earlier entries. That would be dangerous, the potential to be sucked under by Right After too powerful.

Although she journaled only sporadically these days, tonight the urge to process through writing was strong. As she picked up her pen, the words flowed from her, as if relieved to finally make their escape from her head, where they'd been bottled up since she and Ross left the fundraiser.

> For 12 years, I've been a teacher. In that time, I've read the Great Gatsby just as many times, in addition to when I read it in college. Tonight, an excerpt kept coming into my head.
>
> "There was something gorgeous about him, some heightened sensitivity to the promises of life...an extraordinary gift for hope, a romantic readiness such as I have never found in any other person and which it is not likely I shall ever find again."
>
> John Sims Colburn. There. I wrote his name. There really is something gorgeous about him, and it's not just his looks (although those were quite spectacular, if I'm being honest). I feel a little melodramatic writing this, and looking back over the evening, I wonder if my reaction isn't a tad over the top. Maybe I just imagined it. Maybe I just wanted to feel something again. Maybe I'm just tired of being sad, and a handsome man paid

attention to me, and maybe I've let my very active imagination fill in the rest. I don't know.

Am I exaggerating? Such a lost cause that I created some fantasy chemistry? I don't think so. I <u>felt</u> something when we shook hands. I <u>know</u> he was watching me—I caught him watching me several times as I worked the room with Ben and Coralee. He was always conveniently in the same area in what was a very crowded event, spread out over several rooms. I am pretty sure he was interested. So...what's the next step? Ross was obnoxious about the phone numbers...but I'm glad she did it. Now I'm sitting here wondering if he'll text me. It's been so long. I don't know the rules of the game.

I'm not even sure I want to play the game.

Yesterday was the five-year anniversary of That Day. Our love feels as real and present to me as ever, Luke.

I know you only get one love of your life. And I had mine. Ross thinks I can fall in love again. Even if I could, I don't want to. Because it wouldn't be fair to you, to me, or to the other person. You will always be my Number 1. That means anyone else would have to be content with being second to you in my heart—and that is a horrible thing to do to a person. They would resent you. Resent me.

But then tonight happened.

I have to ask myself...what *was* that when we touched hands?? It was so intense. Or is it just the *yearnings of a lonely woman? I'm 34, not 14. This is stupid. Whatever. I need to go to sleep. Besides, I guarantee he hasn't given me another thought.*

Even as she wrote it, Tiercy sensed maybe that wasn't quite true. She turned out her bedside lamp, slid under the soft cotton sheets, and proceeded to toss and turn until she fell into a fitful sleep.

CHAPTER TEN

*"They slipped briskly into an intimacy from which they never
recovered."*
This Side of Paradise, F. Scott Fitzgerald

COLE

Within moments of Tiercy Somerville's departure, Cole had said his goodbyes and headed home. He slid into the seat of his 1967 Jaguar XKE, a present to himself when he took over from his father as general manager.

Tiercy.

It suited her, lovely and unique...just like her. He could imagine whispering it as he kissed a trail down her spine on his way to feast between her succulent thighs.

Christ almighty. He adjusted himself. He'd need to take himself in hand tonight for sure. Cole had been half-mast most of the night and he knew this wouldn't go away until he took care of it.

His sister, Margot, had a term she used during her wedding speech about when she met her husband for the first time: gobsmacked. He always teased her (and his brother-in-law) about it. It had seemed silly, even if a part of him longed for that sensation.

Now he understood.

Never in his life had he experienced such a connection with one person, or the riot of emotions that accompanied it—Fascination. Shock. Lust. Affection. Even tenderness every time her eyes would go a bit soft and hazy and he knew she was thinking about her husband.

Jealousy.

That was another emotion that made itself known. He barely knew this woman, and yet each time he heard Luke's name through the evening, a bolt of jealousy zagged through him. That Tiercy had obviously been devoted to him—clearly still was. That she'd been his—to love, to laugh with, to bring to and share heights of sweaty passion. He didn't even know the guy, and a part of Cole hated him just on principle. Luke got to have what Cole wanted.

And there was another emotion. Guilt. What kind of assbasket was he, resenting a dead man who passed so tragically? Craving his wife. Fantasizing about all sorts of filthy things he could do to her slender, sexy body. Dreaming of taking her to ecstasy she'd never experienced before. And he would. Yes, he could own her body, if she'd let him.

But, as tempting as that was, what he really wanted to own was so much...more. Was it bonkers to say it so soon—after one short but memorable evening?

He wanted to own her soul.

Cole looked around and blinked. Somehow he'd arrived in his own driveway, and he had no memory of getting there. Fuck.

Tiercy Somerville was in his head, under his skin...and circling his heart.

Impossible, right? He'd always scoffed at love at first sight. Attraction, of course. Lust, definitely. Even infatuation. But love? Didn't that take time to germinate and grow?

Then what was this? The glimmer of love? The bud of possibility?

He shook his head and pulled into the garage. Pulling his phone from the console, he hovered his thumb over her name in the contacts.

Tiercy.

Five hours ago, he'd never even heard of her name. Hadn't even met her.

And now...he had the distinct sense of his life calving into two sections. Before and After.

He strode abstractedly into his colonial revival home in Highland, Maryland, lost in thought. Its location right between Baltimore and DC, allowed him easy access to both cities, plus relatively short commuting into Philly, New York, and south to Richmond. It was definitely too big for one bachelor, he acknowledged, tossing his keys and wallet into their place in the warped ceramic bowl his niece Lizzie had made in art class and given to him last Christmas. But when his last apartment lease was up a year ago, coinciding with his father's retirement, Cole decided to invest in a house and property. It seemed wasteful to pay the high rents of the region when that could go to a mortgage. He'd taken one look at the brick colonial, with its massive side sunroom surrounded by windows (perfect for working, reading, and relaxing), and the five acres of property (unusual for this area), and knew he had to have it. Within a couple months, he'd moved in and never looked back.

He often had company, making the home feel less empty, less vast. His father, his siblings, and their families invaded frequently. The Colburns were close-knit—sometimes obnoxiously so. They all had access to the house's entry code, and didn't hesitate to use it. Thankfully, he never brought women home. Given the number of times his family had just "popped over," it could make for an embarrassing situation. He wasn't opposed to bringing someone back, he'd just never met anyone he wanted to share this space with—even for a night.

What would it be like to have Tiercy there? And her daughter. Jemma. He'd only seen one photo, but it was clear the little girl took after her dad.

Was that what he really wanted? To court a widow...and her daughter? To take a chance that she'd even want a relationship, much less the all-in he knew was his end game?

Yes. It was absolutely what he wanted. And the look on her face at the end of the night, when he'd chanced a kiss on her beautiful, soft cheek, told him she felt the same.

Tomorrow, he'd begin making that happen.

Tiercy was his.

Chapter Eleven

"Then in the spring something happened to me. Yes, I remember.
I fell in love."
Long Day's Journey into Night, Eugene O'Neill

Tiercy

The following morning, Tiercy was ridiculously distracted. The blame for her preoccupation could be placed solidly upon John Sims Colburn. Cole. His name, his handsome face, his intriguing eyes, and his voice—all vying for her attention—popped into her mind again and again as she attempted to go about her normal routines. It was preposterous.

She put the milk in the pantry and the cereal in the refrigerator. She walked around for five minutes looking for her key fob, which was in her hand the entire time.

Jemma raised her eyebrows at her mother, her hand on her hip, and assumed a tone of adult consternation that sounded a lot like Tiercy. "'Dis is what happens when you don't get a good night's sleep, young lady," she'd admonished.

Tiercy had cracked up, swinging Jemma into her arms, their laughter filling the air.

Later that morning, when she dropped Jemma at daycare, the teacher alerted her that she had on one brown sandal and one black one. Worse, they weren't even remotely similar. This mix-up involved a drive back to the house to switch out one sandal, putting her fifteen minutes behind schedule, and then she had to rush to get to her first period class on time.

Once there, she couldn't maintain a train of thought. Her disloyal mind kept wandering, and she'd see pale blue-gray eyes and the sexy smile. Her best student, Nora, interrupted her ruminations. The students had been reading passages aloud, and apparently had been finished for quite some time.

"Ms. Somerville? Did you want us to continue?"

Tiercy startled, suddenly aware of an awkward silence in the classroom while her students darted curious glances in her direction. Her obvious discombobulation caused an undercurrent of laughter among the teens. It wasn't malicious or mocking, just little titters that confirmed her dreaminess had been duly noted by her students. The grins on their faces had her wondering if she'd had a dopey smile on her face, too. She dropped her head momentarily in her hand and started laughing, grateful for her rapport with these amazing young adults.

Tiercy knew she was a popular teacher, and tried to make herself approachable. This was a vulnerable age, and she was determined to be a strong, caring presence for her students. And, yes, the student (and fellow teacher) grapevine ensured everyone knew of her widow status. Among her students, there was always much teasing and speculation about her dating habits.

One student raised his hand. "What's up, Ms. S? Hot date last night?"

Tiercy flushed, momentarily speechless. She was acting silly.

"Ms. Somerville?" Nora again, this time to the rescue. "Would it be OK if we worked on our essays for a while since we're finished reading aloud? A lot of us would appreciate the extra class time to work on them."

Tiercy, grateful for the Distraction Life Preserver, flashed Nora a smile and quickly provided her endorsement of the suggestion. In the subsequent quiet of the classroom, she abandoned all pretense of teacherly focus and allowed her mind to wander unencumbered to thoughts of a certain sexy construction firm CEO.

That first moment, turning around and being frozen in a forcefield of...something unnameable. Laughing with him. The smile-lines at the corners of those striking gray-blue eyes. His broad shoulders. The faint scent of spicy cologne. Tiercy heaved a sigh worthy of any high schooler in the throes of a crush, and sunk into reminiscence.

After ten minutes of reliving every Cole-dominated moment of the previous evening—in painstaking detail—Tiercy shook herself. She truly was acting like a besotted teenager whose heartthrob had just paid her a bit of attention. There was no way she wasn't overplaying this in her mind. Clearly thousands of days without the tender touch of romance had warped her ability to casually flirt.

Get yourself together, Somerville. Here you are lost in fantasy land and he probably hasn't given you a second thought.

But apparently he had. As her second period class filed in, a text notification flashed on her phone. From him. Her mouth was dry as she unlocked her phone. Then she giggled as she saw the name Ross had assigned him.

COLE-THOR

> Tiercy, this is Cole, from last night. I really enjoyed meeting you. I remembered the name of that movie. It's "In Bruges." You'll love it. -C

Tiercy hadn't thought so hard about written words since her master's degree thesis. She tried a few responses, deleting everything because they all sounded wrong, and settled for simplicity.

TIERCY

> Thanks for thinking of me. I will look for it on one of my streaming services. It was great meeting you, too.

Tiercy waited a bit. No other response from him. A small but undeniable twinge of disappointment manifested itself every time she glanced—okay, somewhat obsessively—at her dormant phone. *Girl, you barely know him. He was probably just trying to be nice to the widow.*

Tiercy sighed, and then focused with renewed determination on her students.

Another text came in while Tiercy was eating lunch and scrolling social media, the silent home screen notification startling her far beyond what was normal. She practically threw her sandwich in the air. The two other teachers in the breakroom looked up, alarmed by her sudden movement.

"Sorry about that." Tiercy's blush was hot on her cheeks. "Instagram reel took a surprising turn." Tiercy offered an apologetic (and embarrassed) smile and quickly opened the text, turning her phone so no one else could see it. Good gravy. She was acting just like her students.

For as much as she loved her bestie, she swallowed her disappointment at the text's sender

ROSS

Hey there…can you meet up for drinks tonight? I'm knee-deep in an editing project and I need a Kir Royale break.

TIERCY

I don't know. Will text Mom. She's watching J after school because I have a faculty meeting after classes. Shouldn't be a problem, other than my mother guilt at two nights in a row away from her.

ROSS

You are an amazing mother. And I'll make sure you're home long before Jemma's bedtime. Plus, we need to talk about Cole-Thor. Has he asked you out yet? I pretty much came just looking at him. So did most of the women in the room and about a third of the men.

TIERCY

Lovely image. You need to take a shower or get laid.

ROSS

Srsly. Clingy Guy was hot but gave off major needy vibes. No headboard hockey with him. I'd never shake him after.

TIERCY

Incorrigible friend.

ROSS

Nice SAT word. Now Cole-Thor on the other hand...

TIERCY

If you are hot for him, go for it.

Why would she write that? Even as her thumbs typed the last message on the keyboard, a tug of jealousy pulled in her gut at the thought of Cole with someone else. *Stupid. You barely know the guy.*

ROSS

As if I had a chance. I was chopped liver to him. He's hot for teacher. Which one of us got his card and which didn't? You know you dig him. More, you want to quench your "thirst" with that hot trap. I think your self-imposed dry spell is about to be broken. 😏

TIERCY

Niiice. Let me text my mom. Unless I text otherwise, I'll see you at The Wine Bar at 5:30.

ROSS

<happy dance gif> <smooch emoji>

The bell announcing the next period rang, and Tiercy fired off a quick text to her mom.

TIERCY

> Hey, Mama. Ross wants to meet for a drink after work. Text me if it's a problem to stay with Jemma a bit longer. If you can't, no worries. But if you can…thank you for the gift of two nights out in a row. Love you. Also, meant to tell you that your new haircut looks AWESOME!

As her tenth-grade American Lit students filed in, Tiercy saw a response come through.

COLE-THOR

> Hey, yourself. But I think you meant this text for your mom and not me. Have fun with Ross tonight. I can just imagine the hijinks, and I barely know you both. Thanks for the compliment on my hair. I wasn't sure about the new cut, but I'm feeling better about it now. 😊 And, BTW, your hair looks awesome too.

Color flooded Tiercy's face as she read the text. And reread the text. *He's funny. And he likes my hair.* Her embarrassment giving way to amusement, Tiercy had a Cole-induced smile on her face as class began.

At five p.m., as Tiercy was wrapping up her faculty meeting, a text alert came through. Tiercy never got texts at work, and now she'd had more than a dozen in one day. *Please don't be mom backing out. I could use some time with Ross to talk through this confusing mess of feelings.*

But it wasn't her mother. It was Cole again.

COLE-THOR

> This is your social secretary reminding you that in 30 minutes you are scheduled to drink cocktails with Ross.

Tiercy burst into laughter—a girlish sound not unlike that heard near the lockers as the high schoolers flirted. Her team lead looked over questioningly. "Sorry," Tiercy apologized. "Just a funny note from a friend." She tapped a quick response.

TIERCY

> Ha! You made me laugh out loud…in a meeting. But it's a boring one, so thank you for the distraction. And thank you for the reminder of my BFF date night.

COLE-THOR

> . . .

(She really had to change his contact card.)

COLE-THOR

> Your new social secretary lives to serve.

Tiercy smiled again. The dots kept coming.

COLE-THOR

> Perhaps I could interest you in a date night with someone other than Ross? I checked with your social secretary, who thought it was a great idea.

Tiercy felt just like the girls in her class when the cute boys asked them out. She pushed her hair behind her ear and typed a response.

TIERCY

> Far be it from me to argue with my new social secretary. I hear he's very sensitive. What's good for you?

COLE-THOR

Only when it comes to you. Otherwise, he's pretty normal(ish)—unless you ask his older sister. Next Saturday OK? I wish I could meet up sooner, but I am knee-deep in this project.

TIERCY

Next Saturday sounds great.

COLE-THOR

Where do you live? (I swear, I'm not going to stalk you. I just want to pick a convenient location.)

TIERCY

I live in Columbia, about 30 minutes south of Baltimore.

COLE-THOR

That's close to me. I'm about 10 miles south of you, in Highland. Drinks and dinner at the new bistro on Charles St? 7 pm?

Highland was a nice area. There were some beautiful homes. She and Luke had looked at a couple places there, but decided they wanted to be closer to I-95 for ease of access to his hospital.

TIERCY

7 is good. Meet me there or...?

COLE-THOR

May I pick you up?

Tiercy's heart skittered. Was she going to do this? No men other than her father, Brinder, and the occasional contractor, had been in her house since Luke passed.

TIERCY

Yes.

Yes, apparently she was doing this.

COLE-THOR

Just send me your address. Your secretary
will duly note it for future use.

Tiercy fixated on the last sentence. *He said 'future use,' implying more than one date.* And for the second time in a day, Tiercy broke into a private smile caused by Cole.

CHAPTER TWELVE

"Friendship is certainly the finest balm for the pangs of
disappointed love."
Northanger Abbey, Jane Austen

TIERCY

One week later

Tiercy's eyes flew open. 10:27 a.m. Five hours past her normal time to get up, but not unprecedented. There were times—especially Right After—when her body, in its miasma of grief, seemed to abandon its normal circadian rhythm. Her mind wandered to that dangerous territory, only to shut itself off out of habitual self-preservation.

She sat up, rubbing the sleep from her eyes.

Tiercy still slept on "her" side of the California king poster bed that had been their first big purchase as a couple. Five years later, and that hadn't changed. Her side of the bed, rumpled and twisted. His, still smooth. Untouched. A waiting canvas of lovemaking, intimacy, and sleep they'd never fill together again.

Tiercy's eyes went reflexively to his side of the bed…and froze. It was rumpled. The pillow had a head-sized depression in it. Her heart raced in her chest, and her hands began sweating. "Oh crap!" she breathed sharply.

Tiercy grabbed for her iPhone, sending up a quick prayer that Ross was around, and fired off a quick text.

TIERCY

U around? I need to talk.

She was rewarded immediately with the little gray dots flashing an impending response. Thank God. She needed Ross.

ROSS

What's up?

Screw this. She hit Ross's name on the screen. Tiercy needed to talk faster than either of them could text. Ross answered quickly and they both started talking at the same time.

"Ross, I need to talk to you—"

"Tierce, holy hell. You sound terrible! What happened?—"

"Stop! I go first," Tiercy hollered into the phone. She had learned the hard way from Jemma how to demand attention. "Where are you? Something happened last night. I need to talk to you. How fast can you get here?"

"I already have my keys and I'm walking to the car. I just finished working out. I'll be there in fifteen minutes max."

Tears welled in her eyes. Despite her adrenaline burst, she was hungover, she was hungry, and she was weepy.

"You sound hungover, I can hear you're about to cry, and I *know* you're hungry because you always are after a bender," Ross announced into the phone, doing her BFF thing and reading Tiercy's thoughts before she even had a chance to fully form them.

"Yes," Tiercy managed to croak. "Yes, to all."

"Aunt Ross is on the way, with her famous blueberry muffins. Very medicinal and helpful for sore hearts, hungover bodies, and sorting out the messes we create. All of which sound applicable here."

Tiercy laugh-sobbed. "Hurry. And bring extra muffins. This one is a doozy."

"Shower," Tiercy muttered to herself. "Must shower. And coffee." Tiercy darted another look across the bed, regret flooding through her, as a hangover bullet whizzed behind her eyeballs. Her mouth was dry as cotton and tasted awful. She inhaled deeply and let it out, smelling stale breath. Her head hurt too much to think straight and her thimble-sized bladder demanded attention. Slowly she girded herself to face the exactly nine Tiercy-sized steps into her bathroom. Rising gingerly, swaying with the irregular beat of not-yet-metabolized alcohol in her system, Tiercy crossed the room, her feet sinking into the thick cream rug that crept out under the bed over the original hardwood floors.

Having taken care of nature's call, she stared at herself in the mirror, marveling at how if you look at yourself in the mirror for too long, even normal features start to look odd. Like a Picasso portrait, with certain features being emphasized and others fading. Being leftover-drunk probably added to the optical trickery.

Her self-assessment reminded her of another one just like it, five years ago.

Tiercy blinked hard, fought the urge to fall into the memory, and refocused. Auburn hair, more red than brown, looked like it was combed by an eggbeater, as her dad would say. Mascara smeared under her left eye, and totally gone on the right side. Puffy blue eyes.

Tiercy was one hundred percent Irish, with a mom who her dad pridefully called his "fiery ginger," and a dad whose now mostly gray, leonine hair had been deep brown with glints of auburn in his youth. Tiercy's hair was a blend of her mom's and dad's. Her eyes, both the sky-blue color and the almond shape, were straight from her mom. Tiercy had read once that a blue-eyed redhead is the rarest combination. Her mom was a rare creature for sure—and one of those people who always seemed to have it totally together. She had been Tiercy's rock in so many ways. Especially Right After. She could picture her mom's blue eyes, filled with worry and unshed tears.

Despite the bloodshot redness from drinking, the blue of her own eyes was magnified with tears just aching to be wept. Since she was a little girl, she'd often been told they were her best feature, which always made her wonder what was the worst? Once, she'd wondered it aloud when she and Luke were having pillow talk. He began to catalogue her features, making her laugh, and at the same time feel as if she were the most beautiful woman in the world. Such was their special magic.

"God, Luke. I just want you back." She squeezed her eyes closed, remembering.

"Your worst feature, Kal?" He squinted thoughtfully in his nearsighted way, using his special nickname for her. "Well, let's inventory them, and then I'll let you know. First," he said, running his hands through what was then almost waist-length wavy hair, "there's this hair. Too long. Too shiny." He captured a handful of it and wrapped it around his tapered hand, a hand that touched and healed so many. "It's very... distracting. Like when you walk by, and I picture it falling like a curtain around us as you lie on top of me and make love to me." With that, he grabbed her from the pillow where she'd been resting and pulled her across him, her legs straddling his boxer brief-clad hips (they were black with red, Tiercy remembered) as he lay back. She laughed, as her pulse quickened in anticipation.

"Then you have these legs. So long. With your delicious calves from all that running. Just too sexy. That's a problem." He ran his hand along her calf, the tips of his fingers leaving a trail of goosebumps behind them.

"We should also talk about these. They could be a problem feature." He cupped a hand reverently around one breast and then the other. "These two are beautiful, but they are so competitive with their friends here," and then he oh so gently flicked each nipple. Tiercy gasped, moving her hips in reflexive desire, and felt him shift under her. "The only way to deal with that kind of competition is to give equal attention to all." Which he proceeded to do...gloriously.

Tiercy was breathing fast and aching for more when he flipped her over, wedging himself between her legs and tipping her chin up, holding her face tenderly. Consumed with yearning to be physically connected to him, she pushed up against him...and caught the look in his eyes. So serious.

"Tierce, you want to know your worst feature? It's that you can never know how much I love you. But that's not your fault. It's mine. I will never be able to put into words or into action just how my heart feels with you in my life. I have this amazing woman, and a love for her that is bigger than I can explain or show. So, you'll just need to trust me and know that your worst feature is that you have a man who loves you bigger than eternity."

Overwhelmed by the intensity, Tiercy choked out a laugh. "So...not my nose?" She almost always defaulted to self-deprecating humor when she was uncomfortable.

He laughed softly but his eyes were solemn. Tiercy would never forget how beautiful his hazel eyes looked at that moment. As if he knew somehow what was coming. "No, Kal. Not your precious button nose. I know you hate it, but I love it." He dropped a kiss on the tip. "I love you, babe. You are the love of my life."

"I love you too, Luke. You are the love of my life."

Tiercy lifted herself onto her elbows and kissed him, softly. First on his lips. Then his sweet hazel eyes that were most often the color of honey, but in the soft light of the bedroom had taken on more of a green hue. Then his lips again. Top lip. Then bottom. She pulled away for a moment, and then Luke crushed her to him, kissing her in a way he never had before.

Luke flipped her again, her hair falling like a curtain around them. "Distracting...dangerous..." he murmured with a sexy smile, and proceeded to love her first with raw passion, and then excruciating tenderness, followed by an exquisite, sated sleep wrapped in each other's arms in the bed they had just purchased.

Ross told her that this kind of daydreaming was like astral travel meditation...where you slip into a parallel place and get lost. Tiercy didn't often allow herself to go to Before. And definitely not to That Day. Sometimes, though, Way Before was OK. She could do that. It didn't hurt as much as it used to.

But when the eviscerating pain inevitably emerged, it felt as if her back was turned to the calm ocean as she enjoyed a view of the beach. Then, out of the blue, a massive wave—formed out of nowhere—would hit her, tumbling her over and over. She couldn't breathe. Fought to upright herself. So disoriented. Which way was up? She felt like this time she wouldn't surface.

Then, mercifully, it would recede. And she would be left, shaking and drained, chastising herself for going in the water. She knew better. It was just flirting with danger.

Tiercy headed to the kitchen, began brewing much-needed coffee, and downed a cold glass of water on her way back to the bathroom. Slightly restored, she peeled her bra and panties off and hopped into a steaming shower, trying to organize her thoughts about last night.

Shower thoughts. That's what Luke called them. It was his favorite time to think. He'd be in there for ages, thinking about work and a solution to a challenge there. About a diagnosis for a patient, about how to fix the faulty wiring in the 1950s bungalow they were restoring. It was so bad that about two weeks after they moved in together, and fourteen cold showers later, Tiercy decreed that from then on, she'd take the first shower.

For their second anniversary, she surprised him with a fifty-gallon water heater, which she'd had installed while he was working a shift at the hospital. He'd roared in laughter when he saw the big red bow on the enormous tank in their basement. Then he dragged her upstairs to the en suite bathroom where they did something even better than thinking in the shower.

"Damn, Somerville. That's twice this morning you've gone to Before. Enough!" Tiercy chastised herself aloud. This was a slippery slope—and at a dangerous time for memories like these. If she wasn't careful, she'd go under. And there was Jemma to think about, who was with her parents this weekend, helping to create last night's unfortunate scenario that she'd unpack with Ross. Widowed mothers didn't have the luxury of going under, despite the temptation of even a temporary oblivion to outmaneuver the pain.

Her daughter's sweet face popped into her mind. Soft blonde curls with her dad's hazel eyes, and the ever-mutinous set of her jaw...always so *determined* about everything. Her four-year old legs still retained that last delicious toddler chub, but were on their way, Tiercy could already see, to having her own length. She'd be a tall woman, like Tiercy, but Jemma was every inch Luke's daughter, in both looks and temperament. Precocious. Opinionated. Tender. Curious. Assertive. Smart.

She was a natural leader. In her preschool class, Jemma was often the ringleader among the kids—boys and girls. If there was a project, she was in the middle of it. If there was trouble...she was also in the middle of it. Jemma, like Luke, was going to push boundaries. Her funny, inquisitive mind would not let her just follow along. She had to question *everything*.

Ross once sent her a hilariously accurate meme that said *My daughter will either be a CEO or run her own prison gang. Jury is still out.* Tiercy shook her head. Her baby girl was, as Brinder would fondly say, "a piece of work."

The thought of Brinder affected her like a physical shake, knocking Tiercy out of her shower musings—hard. She felt her hangover haze drop away, forcing her to fully confront what had transpired last evening. And with that, surfaced sorrow and regret...and horrifying guilt.

Tiercy jumped out of the shower and dried off quickly, stepping into a pair of faded, well-loved jeans, a T-shirt bra, and a clean, white shirt she'd found neatly folded on her dresser. Her mom must have done a load of laundry yesterday while Tiercy was at work.

Tiercy had one thought and she clung to it: *Hurry up, Ross. Talk me off the ledge.*

Chapter Thirteen

*"The companions of our childhood always possess a certain power
over our minds which hardly any later friend can obtain."*
Frankenstein, Mary Wollstonecraft Shelley

TIERCY

Ross and Tiercy had been best friends since they were little girls. Tiercy couldn't remember a time without Ross in her life. In fact, her first memory was the day Ross, her older sister, and their parents moved in next door.

The way her mom told it—Tiercy didn't remember this part, but she'd heard the story so much, it was like her own memory now—Tiercy was hanging around the front yard, fixated on the goings-on of the new neighbors. She'd seen two girls, clearly close to her age, going in and out of the house. Her mom had urged her to go over and meet them, but Tiercy, a shy child, stubbornly wouldn't do it. (*OK...maybe Jemma got some of it from her...*)

Now this next part she did remember. She was sitting on her tire swing, holding a big red ball—the kind found in a large wire container in the middle of store aisles, which drives parents crazy because you can't wheel a shopping cart past it without the brightly colored balls crying out desperately to be purchased. Which was exactly what had happened the day before. Tiercy was on the tire swing (she *loved* that swing), holding the rope with one hand, her new red bouncing ball nested against her chest with the other. Suddenly, a huge black blur came flying toward her, knocked the ball out of her arm, and set the tire swing spinning.

There was loud barking. Someone crying hysterically (that had been her). The sound of a screen door slapping and shoes running on flagstone. Adults talking. And a wetness on her cheeks that wasn't her tears. It turned out to be dog slobber from loving Labrador kisses, courtesy of the new neighbors' one-year-old black lab, Shirley.

And then the feel of a hand sliding into hers. Tiercy remembered that most of all.

It was the hand of lifelong friendship.

A lispy voice said, "I'm sorry. That's my dog. I'm Ross." Which sounded like "Roth." And then the red ball was being handed back to her...graced with slobber and static-adhesed black fur.

The visage attached to the hand became Tiercy's "go to face" from that moment on. Dark brown hair. The greenest of eyes. A missing bottom front tooth. And a way about her that said, *Trust me. I got this.*

CHAPTER FOURTEEN

"What is a friend? A single soul
dwelling in two bodies."
Aristotle

TIERCY

True to form, the ever-punctual Ross was pulling into Tiercy's driveway within fifteen minutes. Tiercy stood at the door, like a kid waiting for her mom.

Wordlessly, Ross pulled Tiercy into her arms and hugged her tight. "You OK, T? I mean, really?"

"Yes. I just really need to talk through last night."

"You say you're OK, but you look like shit. Here," she waved a container of muffins, "I'll put these in the microwave for a few seconds to warm, and I'll get us coffee. I can smell it from here." Tiercy listened to the comforting clatter of Ross in the kitchen, and the beep of the microwave. "Where's Jemma?"

"With my mom all weekend. Mom is convinced I have some PTSD from going to the anniversary event last week instead of staying at the beach, so she insisted on doing a weekend with Jemma. To, you know, *give me time.* She picked her up after preschool was over yesterday and will bring her back Sunday afternoon. So, it's just me and the house," sighed Tiercy, sinking into the family room couch as Ross came back with a tray of coffee and warmed muffins. "And I hate it."

Ross handed her a plate with a muffin. "Here—eat this. It'll help. Better for a hangover than any hair o' the dog." Ross turned and settled into the chair across, getting goosed by an action figure leg in the process. "Ah...I love my Goddaughter! When other mothers and aunties are suffering through the obnoxious cost of American Girl dolls, my little Jemma is playing with a retro He-Man doll."

"She loves it. Anything that was Luke's." Suddenly ravenous, Tiercy devoured the muffin. "Gawd...these are sinful."

She polished it off, pondering the He-Man Ross had tossed at her. "In some ways, I'm worried that his mom saved it all and gave it to Jemma. I feel like Jemma won't develop her own taste because she knows it makes Grammy happy to see her playing with Luke's stuff. She just wants to be close to her dad, you know?"

Tiercy swiped her eyes and motioned to the plate of baked goods. "I think I need another muffin. I am getting maudlin. Maybe if I stuff my face, I'll shut up."

"Ha...good SAT word, and extra points for use in a hungover state! When the book editor and the high school English teacher get together...good times!" The friends laughed. "OK, girlie. Enough. What in the hell happened last night?"

Tiercy cringed. Flashes of the previous evening played across her mind. She held out her hand. "Muffin."

"Talk to me, Goose."

"I had to let him go, Mav."

"Nice adaptation of an OG *Top Gun* line," Ross teased, cajoling a small smile out of Tiercy. "Let who go? Cole?"

Tiercy inhaled a steadying breath and began.

Chapter Fifteen

TIERCY

Last night

Thursday Pizza Dinner Night was their tradition, dating back from a particularly bad day when Jemma was about two years old. Tiercy had called Brinder that afternoon in tears. She'd had a horrible day at work, her car was making a strange rattling sound, and she'd come home from getting Jemma from her preschool/daycare to find the powder room toilet had overflowed. Her parents were away, and she'd begged for his help.

Of course, he came right over. Within forty-five minutes, he was at her door, hot pizza and Cabernet in hand, plus a plumbing snake in the trunk of his car. He snaked the line, cleaned up the mess, and then had dinner with her and Jemma. Later, he rubbed the knots out of her shoulders as she shared her bad day. Thus the tradition had started. Only his work shifts and emergencies impacted the routine.

And, much like that first pizza night, Tiercy was frazzled...and something else. Distracted. And guilty about her upcoming date with Cole.

Brinder had missed last Thursday's Pizza Dinner for work, plus it was the fundraiser. Tiercy had drinks with Ross the following night, and then another round of his insane working hours had forced the postponement of this Thursday night's dinner. As a result, Tiercy hadn't seen Brinder in almost two weeks. It was the longest stretch she'd gone without seeing him in years.

"I'm so glad you could make it tonight. I missed you. Two weeks is too long. And I missed the pizza." She walked over and embraced him in a warm hug. He kissed her on both cheeks, lingering perhaps a second too long.

And it paled in comparison to Cole's kiss the week before.

What the fuck? Holy gravy (her substitute for cursing since Jemma was a myna bird), that man was under her skin. She pulled away and scurried into the living room.

Brinder strolled in after her, as comfortable in her home as Ross. "I'm sorry I missed the fundraiser. Here I talked you into it and then I had to bail. I felt like I abandoned you, and on the worst night." Brinder raised his hands and then dropped them. "I feel terrible."

"Oh, Brinder, come here. Let's sit." She tugged him onto the couch next to her and passed him a glass of wine. "Don't feel terrible. Luke would have loved it." Her voice softened. "It was the right thing to do. I'm glad you made such a sound argument to go."

Brinder smiled at her in obvious relief. "I wanted to go and honor him. Instead I was at work. I feel like I let him down too. He was my best friend, and I spent that day utterly consumed with work when I should have been focused on him." His eyes filled with tears.

He turned his head away, but Tiercy gently turned his face back to her. She smiled softly at him, tears in her own blue eyes. Brinder was such a good man. Not for the first time, Tiercy wished she could have developed feelings beyond friendship for him.

"It's OK to cry, Brin. He was your best friend. He loved you like a brother. He would have loved that you lobbied for me to go. And he above all would have respected that you put your patients first."

With that, Brinder gave in and wept silently. Knowing his pride and his British reserve so well, and what it cost him to display any kind of emotion like this, Tiercy sat quietly, holding his hand.

When he regained his composure, he gathered Tiercy in his arms. It was a moment of shared friendship and grief. "Tiercy, he loved you so much. He would have wanted you to be happy. And he'd be so proud of you, and how you're raising Jemma—"

"Stop," Tiercy half-laughed, half-sobbed, leaning away from him and resting her hand on his chest to create some space. "I told myself I wouldn't wallow at the event, and I didn't. And I refuse to do it now." She took a shaky breath. "Now, I have a plan. It's Friday night. I don't have school tomorrow. You don't have work. Jemma is with mom. Let's grab that bottle of tequila in the kitchen and do Luke Somerville proud."

She waved in the direction of the other room, to chivvy him toward the liquor. Instead, Brinder took her hand and gently kissed the back of it. "You are an amazing woman, Tiercy."

There was something unspoken in Brinder's eyes.

Oh fuck, oh shit. Nope. No. This could not happen. Not now. Not ever. Her Spidey-senses tingled that he was about to make a proclamation. And that could not happen.

Brinder inhaled, but before he could say anything she called out. "Tequila! Code Shot—stat!"

It was a long-standing joke. Years ago, on one of the guys' rare nights off during their first year of residency, Tiercy, Luke, Ross, and Brinder had coined the term, cracking themselves up at what they thought of as a witty play on hospital codes.

A fleeting look of disappointment crossed Brinder's face, which he quickly replaced with a smart salute and a bright smile.

"Yes, ma'am. I'll be right back."

She heard him in the kitchen getting glasses and the tequila from the very high cabinet where she'd hidden it so even a climbing Jemma couldn't reach it. Tiercy knew she was just delaying the inevitable. All these years, she'd been careful never to lead him on. But she could see the want in his eyes. There had been a few other times she was sure he was about to declare his feelings, and she would silently will him not to say anything.

Please, she would implore in her head, *please don't ruin it. You deserve so much more than I can give you.*

He never did say anything. But he didn't need to. It was always there, written on his face.

And yet, sometimes she wondered, why not go with it? A love with Brinder would be a gentle love. He would always be good to her and to Jemma. He was handsome and funny. He would be a tender lover.

At the thought of the word 'lover,' Cole's face flashed in her mind.

Brinder walked back into the living room, his long legs quickly closing the distance. He held the tequila bottle triumphantly and beamed at her. She found herself smiling back, her face flushed. He was lovely. Sexy. Kind. Perhaps this is what Luke would want.

Tiercy reached out her hand to him. "Let's do this."

Brinder and Tiercy were laughing so hard the tears were falling. As he finished a story she'd never heard, Tiercy hiccupped and threw her head back, wiping her eyes.

"Oh holy gravy, Brinder. I cannot believe you and Luke brought your dates into the cadaver lab in med school. Were you trying to impress them or freak them out?"

He laughed, a gorgeous, posh sound that had melted so many hearts over the years. "Well, we thought it was a good idea at the time. We weren't counting on the formaldehyde smell, which hadn't seemed so terrible that day in class. Or the weak stomach of Luke's date. She barfed, and then her friend—*my* date—turned out to be a sympathy puker." Tiercy gasped with laughter. "Luke had to hustle them both out of the lab, leaving me to clean up the puke. And we'd had pizza for dinner. It was utterly revolting. I'm very impressed with my resilience that I can still even eat pizza." He grinned at her.

Tiercy giggled again. "I can just picture you both. Why didn't I hear about this years ago? I thought I'd heard all your crazy bromance stories." She leaned back against his legs, while he rubbed her shoulders.

"Well, it was just a couple weeks later in that first semester of med school when Luke met you. I guess the story got lost in the shuffle of true love. It was, you know? It hit Luke like a ton of bricks. He saw you, and that was it."

And with that, the room shifted under Tiercy, the power of memory and tequila working against her. She sat very still, knowing she was about to get sucked under, waiting for it to pass. *Breathe, Tierce. Breathe*, she reminded herself. It was so easy to get tumbled by the waves. But then she looked back at Brinder's devastated face. Here he'd been trying to make her laugh, and instead she was about to lose it.

"Nope. Not gonna do it!" she slurred resolutely. "I've had a very, very lot to drink and I refuse to wallow and waste this wonderful moment of being fabulously 'pissed,' as you Brits say."

She turned to face him, her arms propped on his knees, and held out her empty glass.

"You're the boss," chimed Brinder.

He poured the final shots for him and Tiercy, and they downed them.

As she dramatically clanked the glass onto the end table, her eyes collided with Brinder's.

Chapter Sixteen

TIERCY

"And that's when he kissed me." Tiercy heaved a sigh. Their coffee had grown cold and the muffins were long gone.

Ross had moved onto the couch and was holding her friend's hand. "I knew he had a major thing for you," she murmured.

"You did?" Tiercy squeaked, pushing her damp hair behind her ears and twisting it into a ponytail. "Why didn't you say anything?"

"Why didn't you?" Ross challenged back. "You knew he had a thing for you too, didn't you?"

Tiercy opened her mouth, closed it again, and then exhaled. "Yes," she admitted. "I've felt it for a while. I just didn't want to say anything because I didn't want to gossip about Brinder. He's just too *good*, you know? I didn't want to hurt him, even by simply acknowledging what I was thinking to my best friend."

"Same here," agreed Ross. "Dr. McHot Pants rocks. I wish, I totally wish, I could have crushed on him. When Luke was alive, I thought about jumping Brinder's bones. We'd have made a fun foursome. We could have gone on vacations, played bridge together—"

"You don't play bridge, Ross. Neither do I, for that matter. And you don't 'do relationships,' remember?"

"Hey...it was my Holly Homemaker fantasy. Don't ruin it. Besides, after Luke died and Jemma was born, it was clear that Brinder was falling for you. I thought maybe you might have started to feel the same way..." Ross finished quietly, trailing off.

Tiercy just sighed deeply in response.

"So, don't keep me in suspense. What happened next? I'm waiting for the raunchy part."

She ignored the comment. "It was like he dumped cold water on me. Or like an electric shock, but not in the good, romantic way." She flashed to the moment she met Cole and the zing of electricity between them. "And then I ran to the powder room and barfed," Tiercy finished miserably.

"Nasty." Ross interjected. "Nothing worse than a tequila hurl." She shook her head in commiseration.

"It gets worse," Tiercy moaned. "He came into the bathroom, washed my face off, and made me rinse my mouth. Then, he carried me upstairs and put me into bed."

"Ohhhkaaay," led Ross. "Did he undress you?"

"No, you horndog. He didn't. But he did tuck me in. Remember how I cried at the beach on the second anniversary? Well, I engaged in a dramatic reenactment. I just let it out. I cried and cried. And then I cried some more. I didn't think I could cry like that anymore. All I could think of was that I've cheated on Luke's memory three times—that guy in the bar a couple years ago, the kiss with Brin, even if I didn't kiss him back, and," she hiccupped, wiping a tear that had fallen, "and with Cole. I was crushed with guilt. And the worst was I kept thinking I'd just cheated on *Cole* with Brinder!"

"Oh lordy. Tequila and guilt do not mix."

"There's more, Ross!" Tiercy wailed.

"Hit me with it, girl. I'm here for you."

"Brin climbed in the other side—Luke's spot, Ross—and just held me until I calmed down. I think he thought I'd fallen asleep. He got up, left me a glass of water and some ibuprofen, and as he was closing the door, I heard him whisper it."

"Whisper what, babe?"

"He said 'I love you.' I mean, obviously he didn't expect me to hear it. But I did, Ross. And now I don't know what to do. I can't lose him. He's so dear to me."

"Nooooooo." Ross flopped dramatically back on the couch. "I knew he liked you. But a love declaration? That's huge."

Tiercy nodded, resting her head in her hands. "I think my head weighs fifty pounds," she moaned.

Ross shook her head, processing Tiercy's revelation. "Oh, Tierce. I am so sorry...and also slightly riveted, I have to admit." She shrugged guiltily at Tiercy and winked.

"I waited, frozen in place, until I heard him leave and the front door close. Then, I walked downstairs, locked the door, finished the tequila, and apparently passed out in my bed in my underwear."

Ross let out a low whistle of admiration. "Damn, girl. You win this week's award for Big Drama. Even more than my sister. You've set a high bar."

Tiercy shot a quelling glance at Ross. The topic of the icy divide between Ross and Gaby was more than she could handle this morning. Clearly recognizing that, Ross rolled her eyes in capitulation and raised her hands in front of her.

"Sorry. Sorry. Won't go there. Not the day. Not the time. Bad Ross Bestie. Do better." Ross sat quietly for a moment, pondering all of it. "I'm sorry. I saw this coming and I didn't say anything."

"You don't need to apologize, Ross. That whole scene probably needed to happen. Maybe not quite in this fashion. But it needed to happen."

"So, what's next?"

Tiercy gave a resigned laugh. "I wish I knew. I thought you were supposed to have the answers."

"Ha! When did I become the relationship expert?"

"You aren't. But you are good at dumping people. You've had a lot of practice."

Ross's jaw dropped in fake horror. "Low blow. But totally accurate."

Despite it all, Tiercy chuckled.

"OK, Tiercy. Here is my prescription for next steps. First, we need to clean this place up. It smells like tequila and unrequited love. And then, we need to get you laid—preferably by Cole-Thor. And then we need to get Brinder laid. I bet any number of women at the hospital will step up to the Dr. McHot Pants plate," mused Ross.

"Stop!" laughed Tiercy again.

"Speaking of getting you laid...isn't tonight your date with Cole-Thor?"

"With *Cole*, yes." Tiercy shot a warning look at her friend. "There will be no getting laid with him. I think one close call is enough this weekend." *Bullshit*, her lady parts contradicted her.

Tiercy tried to ignore the wave of desire that surged through her at the mention of Cole. Then there was the guilt she experienced for kissing Brinder when Cole was the person occupying her thoughts nonstop. It truly was almost like she had cheated on Cole. Which was ridiculous. Any guilt should be directed toward her husband, not a man she'd only met once and texted with a few times.

"I should just cancel. I'm hungover and I'm sure I look like shit."

Ross dramatically eyed Tiercy up and down. "Well, I have seen you look better..."

"Thanks." Tiercy put her head back in her hands.

Laughing, Ross put her arm around Tiercy. "Come on, I was just teasing. Besides, this is why God made ibuprofen and under eye concealer. And maybe some glimmer powder, which is truly proof that God is a woman, and she loves us and wants us to be happy. Well, that and our ability to orgasm multiple times in a short period."

Tiercy smiled fondly at her friend. "Thank you for being here for me. It's not the first time you've come running to scrape me off the floor."

"And feed you muffins."

"And feed me muffins." Tiercy was quiet a minute. "Ross? What if I'm wrong. What if I should give Brinder a chance? What if I'm being foolish throwing away something good and kind with a lovely man?"

"Tierce?"

"Hmm?"

"I know in my bones you're not the person for Brinder, and gorgeous and charming and sweet as he is, he *isn't* the person for you. Besides, the way you talk about him is the way his mother would talk about afternoon tea. *Good, lovely.*" Ross put air quotes around each word, using a bad *Bridgerton* British accent.

The friends laughed and then Ross took her friend's hand, her face serious. "But you're also wrong about something, and I've waited a long time to tell you—until you were ready to hear it. And I think now is that time." Ross took a deep breath. "Here goes. This is me being deep, OK? I believe in life after death. I know there is more for us after we 'shuffle off this mortal coil.' I've always believed that Luke is going to send someone for you, Tiercy—someone you can love really big. It will scare you. But Luke is looking out for you. He wouldn't want you to be alone. He will send someone. I know it."

"Ross, you are turning into a sap on me," Tiercy hugged her friend fiercely, grateful for the kismet or Divine Hand or dumb luck that brought Ross into her life. "I wish you were right. But you're not. I'm like a swan. I mate for life. And my mate is dead. There is an unfillable hole in my life...in my heart. And to be with someone else, but not be able to love them fully, seems cruel to them. But I'm OK. I've had an amazing love. It's more than many people get in a lifetime.

"It's going to be me and Jemma, going it together. And one day, she'll find her own love of her life. And I'll get old and watch her have the things that were cut short for Luke and me. I'm good with that. I have to be good with that."

With a shaky sigh of resignation and a rueful glance toward the empty bottle of tequila, Tiercy engaged in the hard-won skill of getting herself moving, despite the pain. "Now, let's clean up. I'm going to get Jemma from Mom and Dad's. I feel the need to have those sweet arms wrapped around my neck."

As Tiercy headed back into the kitchen to clean up, she heard Ross whisper. "Luke is going to send someone, Tierce. In fact, I think he already has."

CHAPTER SEVENTEEN

*"I can't go back to yesterday because I was a different person
then."*
Alice's Adventures in Wonderland, Lewis Carroll

TIERCY

Jemma was singing at the top of her lungs, "Let it go, let it goooo!"
while Tiercy cooked Jemma's favorites for lunch on the grill—Old
Bay turkey burgers and corn on the cob.

Tiercy tried to concentrate on flipping the burgers, her
stomach skittering every time her mind wandered to the evening's
dinner plans. *Focus.* Being with Jemma was a partially effective
distraction from thoughts of her upcoming date with Cole, which
managed to tease the corners of her mind (and her lady parts) as she
battled to contain them.

She cast an amused glance at said distraction, sitting at the patio table,
playing with her Han Solo figurine and singing the *Frozen* hit to a
Skeletor figurine that had been Luke's. Tiercy laughed at her preschooler's
juxtaposition of the Disney classic with *Star Wars* and a 1980s cartoon
character. It was incongruous...and perfect. Han and Skeletor were

dancing, rather closely, Tiercy observed. Suddenly Jemma looked up, nose scrunched up the way that generally signaled she wanted to ask a question.

"Mommy?" she asked.

"Yes, lovebug?"

"I know dat Daddy is in heaven, playing basketball wif the angels and fixing their broken wings and stuff." Tiercy smiled. She had worked with a pediatric counselor at the school system to help formulate a way to begin acclimating Jemma gently to the realities that her father had died. "Can you have a boyfriend?"

Tiercy dropped a burger, barely saving it from becoming porch fodder. She looked at Jemma, at a total loss for words. But that didn't matter, because now Jemma was on a roll.

"Marie said you are still married to Daddy, so you don't get to have a boyfriend. But den her mommy said you can. So, can you?"

Tiercy engaged in the age-old parental skill of evasion by answering a question with a question. "Jemma, what makes you ask this?"

"Marie's sister, Anapaula, is fourteen and has boobies. Her mom said she can have a boyfriend, but she can't kiss him. Mr. Dom said he wants to lock Ana in her room 'til she's thirty, but I think dat's just being a meanie."

Tiercy shook her head, trying to follow the four-year-old train of thought. "And...?" she prompted.

"Mr. Dom and Ms. Giorgia are married. So dey can kiss. But you and Daddy can't kiss 'cause he's in heaven. And Ms. Giorgia has a new baby in her belly. She got dat from hugging Mr. Dom. Dat's what Marie said. So what if you wanna kiss a boy? Ana says dat's what boys and girls do. But I think Han and Skeletor wanna kiss." And she promptly pushed their plastic faces together.

The warmth of the grill and unseasonal May heat had Tiercy sweating. Or maybe it was a conversation about kissing, and more, that she hadn't been prepared to have for a long time. She wiped sweat from her brow as a droplet rolled between her breasts, removed the burgers and corn from the grill, turned off the gas, and moved toward the table. Han and Skeletor had finished their plasti-kiss, but Jemma wasn't finished.

"Do you wanna kiss boys, Mommy? Do you wanna baby in your belly? You need to find a man to hug so I can have a baby brother."

An image of Cole flashed in her mind along with one of her belly full with his child. *Holy gravy.* "Well, I miss Daddy very much. And I would love to kiss and...*hug*...him again, but I can't," she added sadly.

"Dat's when you kiss the screen during your wedding show."

Jemma loved to watch Mommy and Daddy's "wedding show"—which is what Jemma called their wedding video. Tiercy didn't realize she'd been observed by her daughter doing that secret ritual. She had to ask, "When did you see that?"

"One night when I was 'apposed to be sleeping but I wasn't 'cause I needed to poop. I saw you kiss Daddy on the TV downdairs."

"I guess I have done that. I miss him. He was even better than a boyfriend. So, Mrs. DiNatali is expecting a baby? How nice! Marie will be a big sister!"

Jemma smiled at her mom. Her first baby tooth had fallen out recently, and the one next to it on the bottom was loose. She wiggled it intently. Given the vagaries of the four-year-old mind, Tiercy wondered if it would be enough of a distraction for Jemma, because she really hoped the conversation was over.

"Come on. Let's eat."

They dug in, chewing companionably. A short while later, four deer wandered into the backyard looking for their own food. Tiercy motioned for Jemma to be still, but that was impossible.

Jemma squealed, "Bambi!" and the deer leapt through the yard. "Dat's nice! Dey like our yard. So, do you?"

"I like our yard too. It's fun."

"No, Mommy. Do you wanna kiss a boy? Ms. Giorgia told Marie that mommies who don't have daddies in deir house because the daddies are in heaven could have a boyfriend. And if you are older than Anapaula it's OK if you kiss your boyfriend. And den you could hug him and get a baby in your tummy."

The entire conversation was mind-blowing to Tiercy. She wasn't even sure where to begin. One thing was certain, there had clearly been some discussion between Jemma and her friend about how babies ended up in a mommy's tummy. Tiercy also made a mental note to get a congratulations card and present for Giorgia and Dom.

It was a touch of kismet, Tiercy had to admit, that Jemma was broaching the topic just hours before Tiercy was going on her first date in a long time. The thought of Cole kissing her caused a flutter in her belly. The thought of him *hugging* her caused an entirely different feeling, lower.

She puffed out a deep breath. At times like this she wished she could cuss out loud, but she'd quit the habit cold turkey one day when Jemma, then three, parroted a particularly lush curse she'd uttered. These days, the strongest expletive she allowed herself was "holy gravy."

"You know what, Jemma Cathleen? I'm not sure about a boyfriend. But grownups do need time with other grownups—"

"Han and Skeletor like to kiss." Jemma interrupted to inform her, very seriously.

"Well, ah, yes, that's nice for them. They make a lovely couple."

"Princess Leia isn't happy."

"I can imagine that she'd be jealous." Tiercy realized that no parenting book could ever prepare you for a conversation with a precocious four-year-old who spent a lot of time with adults.

She tried again. "Jemma? Would you be OK if mommy went on a date?" She hadn't been planning to say anything about her upcoming date with Cole. Jemma often spent the night at her parents to 'give Tiercy a break,' but Tiercy knew Lovie and Gramps were just so enamored of their only grandchild that their altruistic excuse was more accurately a convenient cover story.

Jemma put her hands on each side of her mother's face and kissed the tip of her nose, echoing a gesture that Tiercy often did with her. Tiercy thought her heart might burst with love for her gentle, funny daughter. "Mommy, I love you a bushel and a peck..."

"...and a hug around the neck."

They hugged in the summer sunlight.

"I think you can go on a date with a boy," Jemma pronounced seriously, and then added with a waggle of her small finger, "but ask Lovie if you can kiss him."

Tiercy wiped the tears of laughter from her eyes.

"I am so glad I'm not sitting in the quiet car," Ross hooted. "I have been snort-laughing nonstop."

After they'd cleaned up that morning, Ross had hustled to the train station, catching the Acela so she could be in Manhattan early that evening. And as soon as Jemma went down for a nap, Tiercy had called her to tell her about the conversation with her daughter.

"Oh my gosh, I love that girl. You birthed a Luke Somerville clone, you know?"

"I know!" Tiercy exclaimed, filled with love for her little girl.

Jemma was the light of her life. She thought about when she was pregnant and convinced that Jemma was a boy. She would have loved a boy, but she couldn't imagine life without Jemma. It was hard enough living life without Luke.

A wave of sadness washed over her. "Ross, remember how everyone would say Jemma was a miracle baby? I think the miracle is that our lives have somehow managed to be relatively normal. Even with that, I just want her to have what I had growing up. Two parents who doted on me and who loved each other—still love each other—beyond words. This isn't how it's supposed to be. My four-year-old isn't supposed to be talking to me about my kissing and dating. It's just not right. It's not fair. This *isn't* how it's supposed to be. This isn't the life I was supposed to have."

Tiercy began crying silently. Ross was quiet on the other end. Of her many friend gifts, among the best was Ross's ability to remain comfortable with silence and not fill in the gaps.

After a time, the hush broken by sniffles and the sound of Tiercy blowing her nose, Tiercy gathered her thoughts and continued. "I also want Jemma to have what I didn't have—meaning siblings. I know Gaby drives you crazy and you almost never see her. But it wasn't always that way."

Tiercy knew she was treading in dangerous territory. She could hear the shift in Ross's breathing. Tiercy quickly changed the subject back to her own dangerous territory.

"I've been thinking a lot about our conversation after the Brinder debacle—and, no, to answer your next question, I haven't talked to him yet. I wonder if I'm meant to be alone, or if maybe I will have a second chance at love. Not a really big love, like I had with Luke. That is once in a lifetime. And not Brinder, because he deserves his own really big love. But maybe a good love. A trusting one. A kind one. A father for Jemma. And a person who'd have to be OK knowing they can't be the love of my life. It's a tall order." Tiercy sighed.

Ross was quiet. Her own parents had died almost twenty years earlier in a horrific accident. The locusts chirped their summer symphony in the background as Tiercy remembered a terrible July many years ago, and a life of Ross's that might have been and could never be.

"Tierce," Ross began, softly, carefully. "I think we get the life we get. It's not always what we expect. But it's the only one we have, so we'd be fools not to make the most of it. Along the way, we get moments of grace to cherish. You had one of those today with Jemma. You know I struggle with the whole benevolent God thing, but I guess I've been around long enough to recognize a God moment when I see one. You've been through hell, and you're raising a daughter by yourself. Stop overthinking it and just...*be*. You don't have to have it all figured out. Just take care of the step that's in front of you and cling to your moments of grace. It will all work out."

The friends were quiet for a long time. Tiercy could hear the sound of the conductor making his way through the train car and warm tears slid down her cheeks.

"Hey, Tierce?"

"Yeah?" Tiercy's voice was clogged from crying.

"About Cole? You should totally tap that..."

Tiercy laughed through her tears. "You are so bad!"

"I think 'incorrigible' is the word your mom uses for me," Ross teased.

"Good SAT word," Tiercy noted.

"Have *fun* tonight, Tierce. Love you," Ross chimed, snickering.

"Ha," Tiercy chuckled, rolling her eyes. "Love you, too."

CHAPTER EIGHTEEN

COLE

Why did time rudely creep by when you were looking forward to something? Cole had risen before the sun, eyes popping open in anticipation of the day. That wasn't the only thing that had risen. His cock, clearly thinking about Tiercy as much as he had over the last nine excruciatingly long days, had throbbed for attention from the moment he awoke.

Taking it in hand, he turned to his favorite fantasy of late—one that involved Tiercy, a bottle of champagne, that sexy hollow in her clavicles, and him burying himself inside her. As was par for the course over the last week, it didn't take him long before he was spurting his release. *Better not be that fast when you are with Tiercy. If* you are, he amended. No, *when* you are, he corrected again. Because he would be with her.

Tiercy.

Even her name echoing through his head was enough to make him stir again, despite the force of his explosion moments ago. He'd taken himself in hand at least twice a day since meeting her. Cole was surprised he didn't wear a callus on his cock. He looked down his body and sighed. Taking care of himself was nowhere close to the sublime pleasure of sinking into a woman. Into Tiercy. He had been beyond preoccupied with thoughts of her all week—not all of them impure. Thankfully work was so busy, it had managed to form a decent distraction.

Now the day loomed long before him. He wished Xander were around. It was time for him to stop traipsing around Europe with Petey and come home. He missed having his friend to bounce things off of live and in person. Phone calls and video chats were not enough.

He envied Tiercy having Ross at her side the other night. He imagined Xan at his shoulder, an epic wingman since their first false ID-driven forays into the college bars. Although Cole thought he did well enough on his own with Tiercy, Xander's easygoing ways always managed to grease the skids of any social interaction. He chuckled, this time imagining Xander flirting with the ball of fire that was Tiercy's best friend. Ross would wrap him around her finger in a hot second.

Images of Tiercy playing through his mind, Cole stretched an arm behind his head, enjoying the pull of muscle from his workout the night before. Work. Workout. Rinse. Repeat. His cycle.

Except tonight the cycle was breaking. For her.

Rolling out of bed, he stretched and looked at his phone. And groaned. 5:15 a.m. No way was he going to be able to fall back asleep. Sighing, he tugged on the fresh workout clothes he always left on his dresser. No excuses for missing a workout. That always managed to clear his brain anyway.

After working out (cardio and leg day)—and not at all preening at Tiercy's reaction to his muscles, nope, not at all—he spent a couple hours in his home office cleaning up emails he hadn't been able to get to during the week. A trip to the grocery store, which he hated, killed another forty-five minutes. He needed yogurt, coffee, and something else to fill the interminable hours between now and his date.

That done, he drove to a sports park and messed around at the batting cages and then hit a bucket of balls. What was it with guys and their sticks and balls, his mother had often wondered aloud. Sliding into his car, Cole grinned at the memory. Poor woman dealt with five children and a husband with a huge personality. Christ, he missed her.

He wondered if she would like Tiercy?

His musings were interrupted by his phone ringing through the Jag's Bluetooth system—a modification to the classic car that pained him but was necessary given the amount of time he spent in it. Smiling, he answered.

"Brother, what's up?"

Xander's voice echoed through the vehicle. "Hey, brother. I'm just sitting on my hotel room balcony and drinking sambuca. Thought I'd call and check in."

Cole checked his watch. "What time is it in Italy? Gotta be ten, right?"

"Yes, if I were still in Italy. But I'm in Athens now, and it's eleven here. Petey's long asleep. I just finished reading the latest issue of Architectural Digest on my iPad and realized I hadn't called you since the fundraiser at the Inn. How'd it go?"

"Dude...now Greece? Isn't that your," Cole counted in his head, "fourth city in six months? Aren't you exhausted from all that?"

"Fifth," countered Xan. "And yes. Getting that way. I have some updates on that front, but first tell me how my Inn looked."

Cole laughed, driving along the two-lane road that was the best, albeit often traffic-congested, way to his neighborhood. "Yes, Xan, I'm great. Thank you for asking," Cole teased. "How are you?"

"Oops. Sorry. Sambuca brain. How's my Inn and how are you?"

Cole paused, picturing Tiercy standing in the foyer of the Inn as they said goodbye. The gaslighting playing gently with her features, her pert nose so incongruous with the elegant planes of her face. Her shining auburn hair. Those clavicles.

"Brother...did I lose you?"

"Sorry, Xan," Cole shook himself back to the present and thought about both questions. How was the Inn? How was *he*?

"Spectacular." Yep, that was the word. He was feeling spec-fucking-tacular. And in two-and-a-half hours, he could leave to pick up Tiercy for their date.

"You or the Inn?"

As he motioned for a mom with a little girl to pass safely in front of him at the pedestrian crosswalk, his thoughts turned to Tiercy and Jemma, and his heart gave a thump of anticipation.

Cole smiled. "Both."

"Reeeally." Xan drew out the word.

"Yes, your Inn was perfect for the event, and I overheard a lot of the guests raving about it. The event planning team outdid themselves."

"Glad to hear it." Cole could hear the pride in Xan's voice. "And you are spectacular too, brother, becaaaause..." Again Xander drew out the word.

Cole hadn't told anyone about Tiercy yet—hadn't wanted to—and now the words were bubbling out of him. "I met someone. A woman. At the event. She was—Christ, Xan—she's incredible. Funny. Sexy. Sweet. Tall. A loving mother—"

"A mother?" Xan interrupted. "Dog, we don't swim in other men's pools."

"I know that, assbasket. She's a widow. She was married to the doctor they're naming part of the new building after."

"How old is she? You digging a cougar?"

"Young, dickhead. I heard the story from their lead doc, Ben. Her husband died unexpectedly and tragically about five years ago."

"Fuck. That sucks. And they have a kid?"

"Yeah, a daughter. I learned that part too from Ben. She found out she was pregnant after Luke Somerville," he swallowed past the jealousy as he said her husband's name, "died."

"Shit." The sound of a glass being placed on a table filtered over the phone. "That's terrible. So the kid never met her dad? Jesus, I can't imagine the heartbreak of Petey not knowing me."

Unspoken by either of them was the fact that Petey's mother wasn't in his life—by her own choice. Something that had broken Xander's heart and eventually sent him on this vagabond tour of Europe to escape the painful memories.

"Her name's Jemma. Cute little girl."

"You've met her?"

"No. Just saw a picture on Tiercy's phone—"

"Tiercy. That's the widow?"

"Yeah, and...brother...I gotta tell you," Cole let out a huge exhale, "I've got it bad for her."

"How many times have you seen her since the event?" The surprise in Xan's voice carried clear over the line.

"None."

"None?"

"Nope. But I texted her the next day—"

"You're supposed to wait two days, King Rizz. You know this."

"Shut up and let me finish," Cole chided, shaking his head at his friend, who was clearly starting to feel his sambuca. "Fuck, I almost texted her that night after I got home, but it was close to eleven and I didn't want to be a douche. She had to be up early. She's a teacher. And she had to get Jemma to daycare."

"Keep going."

"So I texted her the next day. I was busy that weekend—Margot's birthday and then various games for the nieces and nephews where I'd promised to go and cheer. And then work is intense. She has Jemma, so I didn't think a weeknight would be good. So I suggested today. Tonight. And I've been practically crawling out of my skin because this fucking day couldn't go any slower."

"Fuuuuuck." Xander let out a low whistle. "So let me get this straight. You met this woman a week ago—"

"Nine fucking torturous days."

"And you're going out with her tonight."

"Affirmative."

"Where?"

"New bistro in Baltimore. I got us the nook seats by the window. My assistant said it's the best table in the house."

"Nice. Wow. This isn't what I expected to hear when I called."

"Yeah, well, it wasn't what I expected when I went to a boring work event either. But, I'm not complaining."

"Dude, you just met her."

Cole pulled into his neighborhood, raking his hand not on the steering wheel through his hair. "I know. And yet—I know it sounds stupid, but as soon as I saw her, I had the sense that I knew her. There was just a...feeling of... 'aaah...here you are.'"

Xander was quiet on the other end for long moments.

"Xan? I lose you?"

"Nah, Colburn. I'm here. Just processing."

"What are you thinking?"

"I'm thinking I've never heard my oldest friend talk about anyone like this."

"I know. It's...it's so strange. But it feels so right."

"Moving kind of fast, aren't you? How do you know she feels the same?"

"I don't." Cole sighed. "That's part of why I'm going nuts waiting. There was so much chemistry between us that night. I keep thinking maybe I imagined it. I had just been thinking how bored I am of the dating scene. How much I want something like my dad and mom had. And then she appears. And it was—Xan, I couldn't take my eyes off her. Couldn't stay away from her. I had to be near her."

"Dude. Just—just be careful, OK?"

Xander's caution was understandable, but it wasn't what Cole wanted. He wanted someone to share his excitement. To join him in the belief that what happened at the Inn wasn't nothing. It was *Something*. Something really big.

He eased into his garage, shaking off his frustration with his best friend. It wasn't Xan's fault. Every time Cole had thought it, and now saying it aloud to Xan, the whole prospect sounded ridiculous. And, yet, every cell in his being screamed that Tiercy was The One.

"You had to be there, Xan. This is, well, it's different. I don't have words. All I know is I've been like a kid on Christmas morning all day, and now I need to take a shower because I smell like a goat."

"You are the GOAT, man. Listen, I'm happy for you. And I want to hear more about her. In particular, does she have any hot friends?" Xan clearly had shaken off his own baggage in an effort to show support. He was a good friend. Rock solid since happenstance made them college roommates at Duke almost twenty years ago.

"Dude. Yes. But I wouldn't subject her to you. Actually, more accurately," he scratched his beard, grinning at the idea, "I don't think you could handle Ross. She's...she's something else."

"Ross," Xander repeated. "She even sounds hot."

"Let it go, bro."

Xander chuckled. "It's good to hear your voice."

"Thanks, brother. Same. You good too?"

"Yeah. Definitely."

"Tell me about these updates." Cole threw his keys in the bowl and then poured himself a cold water from the fridge.

"I think I'm coming home soon."

"Reeeally?" Now it was Cole's turn to drag out the word.

"Yes, fucker. One of my old partners recently had a stroke. He's been teaching some architecture classes at the University of Virginia in Charlottesville since he retired from the firm. He called me from the hospital. He's going to be fine, but his wife is insisting he fully retire. He suggested I take over his classes."

"Damn. Seriously? You gonna do it?"

"I think so. Petey starts kindergarten in September. I need to enroll him in school. It's time to stop roaming around and settle."

"Sucks you can't move here."

"Too far to commute. But close enough to visit regularly."

"Nice. Sounds like an incredible opportunity, and you always said teaching appealed to you." Cole glanced at the clock. Four thirty. "Listen, brother. I gotta hop in the shower and get ready."

"Make sure to trim your old man nose and ear hairs."

"Gross, fucker. I don't have old man hairs anywhere, much less there." Cole laughed. "Hey, thanks for calling. Keep me posted."

"Back at you. I can't wait to hear how your date with the widow goes."

"Tiercy."

"Right, Tiercy. Cool name."

"Cool woman. Gotta dip. Bye, Xan."

"Bye, Romeo." Xan and Cole were both laughing as they hung up.

Cool woman indeed. And spectacular. He was going to make her his.

Chapter Nineteen

TIERCY

Tiercy spent the better part of the afternoon fretting about what to wear. This time, there was no Ross to the rescue. Oh how she wished for an actual fairy godmother or some mice to help her get ready for her date with Cole.

Date with Cole. Just thinking that sent a pulse of anticipation through her. Meeting him at the fundraiser had been...*compelling*...that was for certain. And then there were their funny text exchanges. He seemed like a good guy. And their chemistry had been off the charts—hadn't it?

Tiercy tucked her hair behind her ear. She'd mentally battled herself for nine days, debating if she'd imagined their connection. She hadn't. But that didn't change her dread at this first date.

Ugh. Ross loved the anticipation of a first date. Tiercy had always hated it. When she married Luke, she was thrilled that she'd never have to suffer a pre-first date again.

So much for that.

Tiercy sighed. Some days she missed Luke so much her heart felt like it would shatter with the burden of unfathomable pain. Other times, she was beyond angry at him. Today, she battled with melancholy. Jemma shouldn't be at her grandparents' house. She should be with Tiercy and Luke, and maybe a baby sibling. They would go to the park. Maybe play a game. Cook on the grill. Then they'd put the children to bed. And go to bed themselves—but definitely not to sleep.

Tiercy's daydream was interrupted by the alert of a text from Ross.

ROSS

Hey…getting ready for the Big Date with Thor?

TIERCY

Funny. Yes.

ROSS

How's it going?

TIERCY

About what you'd expect.

ROSS

That bad?

TIERCY

No comment necessary.

ROSS

Wear your new blue dress. It's hawt.

TIERCY

Really? It's not too much?

ROSS

Def wear it. And wear your hair up. It'll show off the wicked back of that dress.

TIERCY

Can't you just go for me?

ROSS

I don't have a wormhole to get from NYC to your house. And, more to the point, Thor has the hots for you, not me, sister. You'll have fun. Trust me. Hell, you might even get laid. He seems like the type who would just rail you into the mattress. Sublime.

Tiercy's eyes focused on two words. *Rail you*. By Cole. Once again, a long-dormant pulse of desire ached in her.

TIERCY

Thanks for the advice.

ROSS

Don't take less than one hundred. Call me when you're through. Take care of you.

TIERCY

Take care of you.

Ross always knew just what to say—even throwing in one of their favorite exchanges from *Pretty Woman*. When they roomed together in college, they'd say it to each other before every date. Ross had dusted off a classic, and in the process, calmed Tiercy's nerves. She was a keeper for sure.

Tiercy walked into her closet and pulled out the dress. She and Ross had bought it at the outlets on the way to the beach. It was pale blue, almost gray. And, Tiercy realized with a startle, eerily similar to the color of Cole's eyes.

With a square neck and thin straps, the garment had caught her eye immediately. But it was the back of the dress that was noteworthy. The straps crisscrossed, and the dress fell into a deep curve to the small of her back. The fabric was simple—a jersey knit with a fitted chiffon overlay, which gave the dress a hint of movement. When she bought it as a splurge purchase (Ross was always a bad influence on that front), Tiercy couldn't fathom when she'd actually wear it. But the stunning design and material had called to her. Feeling low and wanting something pretty with her retail therapy...she bought it.

And now she was wearing it on a date...with a man who was hot AF, as her students would say. And who would—maybe—*rail her*.

She shivered, noticing her nipples were pointed through the thin material.

"Yikes, girl. Tame the nips." Tiercy reached into a drawer, pulling out little adhesive petals designed to camouflage headlights.

Satisfied that her boob boners were under control, she slid on a pair of long silver dangle earrings and a small diamond solitaire necklace her parents gave her on her twenty-first birthday. The diamond nested in the hollow of her neck.

A pair of nude stiletto mules with three-inch heels completed her ensemble. At a little over five ten in bare feet, they'd make her almost six two—but who cared? Cole was at least two inches taller.

Following Ross's advice, she twisted her hair into a simple chignon, allowing a few strands of curls on the side to stay loose to soften the look.

She stood back to survey the results. The flush of anticipation in her cheeks, paired with the flattering dress, made for a becoming result. Tiercy never felt truly gorgeous—not like Ross, or especially Ross's sister, Gaby, who was a total knockout—but she felt attractive. And deep in her belly, which fluttered with nerves, she hoped John Colburn agreed.

Waiting in the kitchen, nervously wiping down counters that were already spotless, Tiercy heard a car pull up and experienced the worst jitters since...well, she couldn't remember. *Walk slowly. No running to the door like a Labrador retriever.* She cracked a smile at the thought of her sniffing Cole's crotch. God, she was turning into Ross.

Sophomoric, but she hid behind the solid wood of the door and peeked through the tinted glass pane. *Dear lord. I wasn't exaggerating my fantasies.* He was as Hottie McHot Pants as she'd remembered. Crisp white button-down, one button opened at the collar. Gray slacks, a shade or two darker than the color of those devastating eyes. Navy sport coat. And a smile that made his eyes crinkle in the corner as he stepped over Jemma's tricycle.

She quickly wiped her sweaty palms on a coat hanging on the rack by the door and reached for the door handle.

Chapter Twenty

*But my body was like a harp and her words and gestures were
like fingers running upon the wires.*
Dubliners, James Joyce

COLE

As Cole pulled into the driveway, he had the strangest sense of having done this before. Everything about this enchanting woman was excitingly new and yet deeply familiar to him—as if his soul had finally navigated to its long-awaited counterpart. Even as he thought it in his head, it sounded idiotic and dramatic. While Cole never considered himself a dramatic man, he had spent a lot of time thinking about her since the fundraiser—too much time.

He was embarrassed at his adolescent behavior that night, constantly placing himself in her path. What was next? Slip a note in her locker? And, yet, he had found himself irresistibly drawn to her. He remembered from chemistry class in college that certain elements just clicked naturally and gravitated to each other. Like hydrogen and oxygen. She was like oxygen to him. When he was near her, he felt he was truly breathing for the first time.

Cole had spent a total of two-and-a-half hours with her, but he had memorized her face. Her bright smile. Wavy reddish-brown hair. An almost regal bearing. She was a tall woman, but didn't slouch as so many did. And she had those blue topaz eyes. Eyes that held so much sadness when talking about her husband.

What kind of a lecher was he, hitting on a woman—pretty aggressively—at an event hosted in part to raise money to honor her deceased husband? Who, according to unnervingly many accounts, was apparently well on his way to sainthood.

Cole took a deep breath. He wasn't accustomed to overthinking dates like this. Perhaps he'd played her up in his mind, and when he saw her, she'd be a mere mortal, not the demi-goddess he'd been painting her in memory.

He parked his Jag and got out, stepping over a tiny purple tricycle on the walkway that must be her daughter's. Jemma. He wondered for a moment how long Tiercy might wait to introduce him.

Slow your roll, Colburn. Let's get through the first date. Besides, she's probably not all that.

Cole knocked on the door, which opened to reveal Tiercy framed in the doorway.

Christ. She is all that. I'm done for.

For at least the third time in their short acquaintance, Cole was caught up in what felt like a forcefield—both of them silently watching each other, both seemingly incapable of speech. Eventually, Cole made a small, incoherent sound and then flushed. He tried again.

"You look stunning. I brought you this." He handed her a single red ginger lily. Cole's fingers grazed hers as he handed it to her, and once again, he experienced a bolt of pure primordial chemistry.

"Thank you. It's gorgeous." Tiercy's smile was shy, and Cole thought he saw her hand tremble.

Realizing they were both still standing in the doorway, he momentarily looked past her shoulder.

Tiercy gave an embarrassed laugh and motioned to her foyer. "You probably don't want to spend the evening hanging out on my front porch. I'm so sorry."

Cole laughed, relieved that she seemed to be as affected as him. He leaned in and brushed his lips on her cheek, observing light freckles on her nose he hadn't noticed in the dim light of the event. Charmed anew, and fighting a desire to kiss those freckles, he entered the house as she stood to the side.

"I-I'll just go and put this in a vase. Please, make yourself comfortable."

As she turned to walk into the kitchen, Cole caught sight of the back of her dress. *Jeezuz...it* was cut practically to her bottom, revealing a pale smooth back of Irish cream. Cole wondered if a dress like that allowed for underwear, indulging himself for a moment in that consideration before rebuking himself. *Down boy.*

Instead of following his baser instinct and going into the kitchen and ravishing her, finding out exactly what she was or wasn't wearing under that dress, Cole settled for standing in her hallway surveying his surroundings. Creamy, light beige walls and large windows with wide-slatted shutters. A soft, chocolate brown couch and a dark green chair in the corner. A dollhouse was in the opposite corner, along with a toybox and a beautiful wooden child's rocking chair. Next to that was a low bookcase filled with children's books. On the far wall were built-ins filled with books, knick-knacks, and pictures. The overall effect was airy and homey. Clearly a home with a child, but not a kiddie disaster area like his brother's living room. Then again, his brother had three young boys. Life was chaos in that house.

But this house felt...like a home. A loving, peaceful home. Tiercy came out of a sunny kitchen with pale yellow walls. In the ice blue dress and high heels, her hair up, the effect was something like a Celtic goddess. *My God, he had a major crush on her.*

Tiercy had a small clutch in one hand and a tremulous smile on her face. *She's as nervous as I am.*

He held out his arm like a medieval gallant. "Shall we go, my lady?" *Corny, dude. Now she knows you're an idiot.*

But Tiercy broke into a huge smile. "I would love to, my Thor—I mean, my lord."

The drive to the restaurant proved an easy compatibility—the Manchester Inn had not been a fluke. Relaxed small talk flowed easily, commenting on basic but not boring topics. She was immensely curious about his car, stroking the seats with admiration and asking questions about the details and finishes so unique to that model. He had debated bringing it, worried it would make him come across like a small-dicked douche hiding insecurities behind a sweet ride. He also had a truck, which he often used when driving to worksites. But the Jag was special, and he wanted to go all out on this date.

Casting occasional glances at his stunning date (although not too many, as he had precious cargo in his passenger seat), Cole explained the significance of the Jag—how it represented achieving his dream of earning his place as CEO and his pride in being able to lead his family's business. Tiercy's eyes softened, scanning his face with understanding, rather than the avarice he was accustomed to seeing in women who clearly were dating him for his wealth portfolio.

For at least the dozenth time since he'd met Tiercy, Cole experienced that tug of familiarity when you connect with someone who is meant to be significant in your life. Certainly, that was the case when he'd met Xan. And with Tiercy...it was that sensation, but on steroids.

When they got to the restaurant, he came around to her side and opened the door, holding her hand as she exited the vehicle. His mother had trained him to be a gentleman. Plus, he suspected those glorious fuck-me heels and her fitted dress didn't lend themselves to graceful disembarking from any kind of car.

Cole had selected a cozy bistro nestled in a city brownstone. Their table was in a windowed alcove, where they could watch the passersby on a beautiful May evening. There was a jazz band playing, and a tiny dance floor. The setting was perfect. He made a mental note to give a big bouquet of flowers to his assistant, Heather, to thank her for the suggestion.

Once settled, they agreed on a bottle of wine. As he studied the menu, Cole secretly studied her as well. She was stunning, but in a down-to-earth way. He noticed several men, including their waiter, checking Tiercy out. Cole allowed himself a moment of uncharacteristic self-satisfaction. *Yes, that's my date. Eat your hearts out, assbaskets!*

As he pretended to debate various main course options (he actually already knew he was getting the filet), Cole entertained his inner monologue—one in which he practiced a series of suave lines he knew were way too corny to actually use. There was a part of him that worried this was too good. She was too beautiful. This chemistry was too strong. Something had to be wrong.

Eventually, he gave up pretending with the menu and just prayed he'd find his groove. They ordered their meals and, in keeping with everything else that seemed to connect with them, their conversation flowed comfortably. The maître d' had placed them caddy-corner to each other, and his long legs periodically brushed hers as they shifted position.

Now all I can think about is our legs properly tangled. Topic change... this napkin won't do much to disguise a boner.

"Tell me about your teaching," Cole asked, his voice cracking just a bit. "High school English, right? How long have you been doing that?"

Tiercy smiled, either not noticing or not caring about his pubescent moment. "I'm in my twelfth year of teaching, which blows my mind. I teach all grades, but the freshmen and seniors are my favorites. The freshmen are so new they haven't become jaded yet. They still have an innocence about them. And the seniors are just...burgeoning. It's amazing to see the difference three years can make in someone's life. They grow up so much in that time. Young adolescence to adulthood, at least by the numbers, is a powerful time of development. And I get a front row seat for that." Tiercy stopped suddenly and took a sip of water. "Sorry, I rambled. I get a little passionate about my students."

Charmed, Cole encouraged her to continue. "You weren't rambling. And even if you were, no apologies needed. I love your passion." Their eyes caught on that loaded word—as if saying 'passion' would trigger acting on it. *Move on, move on.* "Um, so have you always wanted to be a teacher?"

"Yes, even when I was little. Ross and I used to play school, and I'd make her take tests and then I'd mark them up. It would drive her bonkers, but she'd play along. I pretty much knew I'd be an education major in college, and once I did some student teaching, it was clear high school was the place for me. I love the classics, but also newer novels. I wanted to be able to share that. Maybe inculcate that in my students, if I'm lucky."

"Inculcate. I think I need a dictionary for this dinner. Suddenly I feel pretty dense." Cole winked at her, taking a sip of his wine.

"I am so sorry! I don't mean to sound like a word snob. Ross and I have this thing where we like to drop random SAT words into conversation and then call each other on it. It's intentional with her, but sometimes I slip."

"I love it. I feel smarter already." He gently clinked his glass with hers. "What's your favorite novel?"

"Mmmm...good question. I don't have one. I have several. *Pride and Prejudice. My Antonia. The Great Gatsby. Shadow of the Wind. Moby Dick.* Lots of others, including several contemporary romances, but that's a start."

Cole chuckled. "You liked *Moby Dick*? I think you are the only person I know who's actually read the entire thing."

Tiercy laughed. "It's not a beach read, that's for sure. But the writing is...mellifluous. Just gorgeous." She giggled again as Cole mouthed the word *mellifluous*, pretending to write it down. "I love words. And I love how different writers can string the same exact words together, in a different way, in a different context, and create something unique. Words are dynamic and flexible and glorious." She sucked in some air. "Oh my, now you know I'm a dork."

Cole was fascinated. "Quite the opposite. When you talk about your love of words, you practically glow."

They stared at each other for a long moment. Then Cole reached for his glass, shaking his head. "We seem to do that a lot." He cleared his throat, trying not to blurt out just how much she already affected him. "So, *Moby Dick*, huh? Do you have a favorite mellifluous line?"

Tiercy looked out the window, her profile illuminated by the evening light. She began speaking softly. "'Thou touchest my inmost centre. Thou art tied to me by cords woven of my heartstrings.'" She sighed, and then looked back at Cole with a shy smile and an embarrassed shrug of her shoulders.

Cole reached for her hand across the table. "I had no idea. *That's* in *Moby Dick*? Cords woven of heartstrings. Melville was a romantic. Who would've guessed?"

Tiercy smiled. "There are many unexpected gifts in literature. I find treasures in many things I read. I may not love the entire experience of the novel, but so many have these wonderful hidden gems." They shared a smile.

Their waiter approached with a tray, breaking the spell. He placed their meals on the table, refilled their wine and water, and slipped away —but not before his gaze trailed down Tiercy's back.

Cole growled low in his throat—disguising it as clearing his throat —and glared at the waiter, who had the good sense to look chagrined.

Tiercy reached for her fork, thankfully apparently unaware that Cole had just clearly marked his territory. "I feel as if I've monopolized the entire conversation. Now it's your turn. Tell me everything about you...while I stuff my face. I'm ravenous! And—I have to ask...I mean, I've noticed...you are so strong. It's not many who make me feel dainty, but somehow you do. You must work out a lot?" she asked, her face coloring. "Oh, God. I sound like a vapid fool."

He looked at his bicep as in "what, this little thing?" and then flexed. His jacket pulled taut across his arm, and Tiercy's eyes snagged on it and then she laughed.

"Now who's vapid? I just flexed for you." They broke into soft laughter. "I worked construction summers during college. It was my dad's way of showing me the business from the inside out and bottom up. You get pretty strong hauling lumber and cement blocks around day after day. When I was in my twenties, I started working out more. I'm not a gym rat. I have some weights and a bench at home. I've found it's a great way to relieve stress."

"For me it's running," offered Tiercy. "I can put in my earbuds and just get in the zone for a while. I like to run outside, when I can. But it can be hard with Jemma, so I usually just run on my treadmill in the basement. Tell me more about you so I can keep eating." Tiercy grinned and put a large bite of her eggplant parmesan in her mouth, swooning comically at the taste.

The food was definitely out of this world delicious. *Thank you, Heather.* He made a note to order more of her favorite tea from France, which came in posh muslin bags.

Cole laughed appreciatively. "Well, you already know my company does construction. It's a family business, going back to my grandfather. My father continued it. I told you the other night I have four siblings, an older brother, an older sister, and then two younger sisters. My older brother, Brian, wanted nothing to do with the business. He's a suit. A CFO for a technology company. My older sister, Margot, is the CEO of her family. She's amazing. She's a full-time parent, and I don't know how she does it, but she makes managing their kids' education and plethora of activities look like child's play. The sister just behind me, Lara, also works at Colburn. She's freaking brilliant, with an MBA from Wharton.

"And then there's my baby sister, Poppy. Well, Penelope, but Lara couldn't say her name when she was little. It came out Poppy, and it's been her name ever since. Actually, it came out 'PeePee,' and before that one could take hold as a nickname, my parents nudged us toward the name Poppy. Although, sometimes Margot and I still call her PeePee, when we want to piss her off." Cole grinned at her. "Anyhow, she's an artist and a bit of a free spirit. Right now, she's wandering around Europe, probably sleeping with every loser artist she encounters. She drives me batty, but I'd be lying if I said she wasn't my favorite. Margot's a close second, but I still haven't forgiven her for the *Sound of Music* torture."

Tiercy snorted a laugh and hummed a bar from the *Lonely Goatherd*.

"Exactly." He pointed a breadstick at her. "My mom passed away from a heart attack about three years ago. My dad is still fairly active in the business. But he's sixty-six and spending less and less time at work. He travels a lot and recently started dating. Not sure what I think of that."

"Well," Tiercy remarked, pointing her fork at him. "You've done an excellent job of not telling me about *you*. Now I know about your family. Which is awesome—truly. But what about you, John Sims Colburn? Tell me about you."

Cole shifted in his seat. He didn't usually share too much, especially on a first date. But there was something irresistible about Tiercy Somerville. He took a sip of wine and continued.

"I'm thirty-five. My family is from the Washington, D.C., area, so we're locals, which is pretty unusual around those transient parts. I went to Duke for undergrad. My degree is in engineering." He took a deep breath. In for a penny, in for a pound, as his grandma used to say. "I've never been married, but I was almost engaged once."

Tiercy cocked her head and blinked, chin rested on her hand. "And? What happened?"

"I came to the realization that while I might love her on a certain level, I didn't love her the way I think you should love someone when you decide to spend the rest of your life together."

"No one ever...snagged your heart?" Tiercy asked with a shy smile.

Cole was entranced by the pale bloom of embarrassment that touched her cheeks. He reached for his wine and spun the glass to keep from tracing his fingertip along the curve of her face.

"Unsnagged. I know it's unusual to be in your mid-thirties and never married. I'm not opposed to it. I guess in my twenties I had zero interest. But, lately...I've recognized that I've just experienced a very high bar for marriage."

Cole was quiet for a moment, and then continued. "When my mom had her heart attack, she didn't die right away. She lingered for a couple days, although she never woke up. I remember watching my dad by her bedside. He wouldn't leave her. I always knew my parents loved each other, but watching him with her—it was beautiful, heartbreaking, and just beyond powerful. I want something special like that."

He paused, registering the stricken expression on Tiercy's face. *Fuck. Too close to home for her. You are such a clueless ass.*

He wanted to apologize, but got the distinct sense that Tiercy would prefer to just move on. "Now I'm monopolizing the conversation. Have you had enough to eat?" Although his tone was light, he offered her a gentle smile. Tried to transmit his apology with his eyes. Silently ask if she was OK.

Clearly an old-hand at moving through her pain, he watched Tiercy smooth her features. Then she wiped her mouth dramatically with her napkin and winked at him. "Almost finished. I just need to wait a bit and see if I have more room for this...and maybe dessert."

Not fooled, but also not wanting to make her any more uncomfortable, Cole embraced a topic change. Breaking into a grin, he motioned to her. "Excellent. Now it's your turn. Tell me about Jemma while I devour my steak."

His date lit up and gave a light, sweet laugh that sounded like a tinkling bell. She was clearly besotted with her daughter. "Jemma Cathleen. She's four, and a pistol. And before you go calculating, because I can see the wheels in your engineer brain spinning with math, she was conceived shortly Before," Tiercy choked a bit, and then recovered, "—before her dad passed. He never knew I was pregnant. I didn't either, not right away.

"I spent my entire pregnancy sure I was carrying a boy. But they say life is what happens when you're making other plans. Jemma is amazing. She's assertive and funny and sweet. She looks just like her dad. I often wonder if she got any of my genes. She loves ballet, dolls and trucks, and action figures and coloring. I have her in full-day pre-K—it's daycare but with a preschool curriculum woven in. My mom watches her after school, and evenings when I have to work late. Mom is a real estate agent, but really only part-time now. My dad is her business partner. They're the ones who found L-Luke and me our house."

Her face briefly fell, and again she recovered, aided by a timely sip of her Malbec. "Anyhow, when school is out for me in June, Jemma and I will spend the summer together. This fall, we'll go back to our schedule. The following year, she'll be in kindergarten, which I have trouble believing. It goes by really fast.

"Jemma's incredible. Words can't capture this kid, trust me. You'll have to meet her. Oh...oof! I can't believe I just said that." Tiercy pressed her hands to the table, cheeks flamed red, making the endearing freckles on her nose more prominent. "Invite your date to meet your child. Nicely played, Somerville. I'm so sorry. I know we're just getting to know each other."

Cole reached out and gently tapped the back of her hand. "I'd like to meet Jemma. Very much. Three of my siblings are married. I have ten nieces and nephews." At Tiercy's raised eyebrows, he chuckled. "I know! My brother and his wife have three. Margot and her husband have *five*—including two sets of twins. And Lara and her wife have two. Christmas is chaos, as you can imagine. And I'm 'Funcle Cole'—the fun uncle."

"Do you ever want kids?" Tiercy slapped a hand over her mouth, covering an embarrassed laugh. "What is wrong with me? I can just hear Ross screeching, 'Date Foul!'"

Cole grinned at her. "Tell your inner Ross to simmer down. All is good, Tiercy. I like your questions." He topped off her wine and took a sip of his own, giving her a moment to relax.

And providing himself a parallel moment to calm his own racing heart. The fact that she asked such personal questions thrilled him. He hoped it signaled that she was feeling what he was. Taking another sip of the rich red from Argentina, he rested his fork and knife on his plate, no longer interested in the remains of his meal.

"I never thought about it until Petey was born. That's Xan's son. He's my godson. To give Xan a break sometimes—before his current vagabond ways in Europe—I'd take Petey out. It felt really nice to be walking around with a little buddy. I think if I found the right partner, I'd love it. I want to put together a swing set and coach sports. Does that sound trite?"

"Not at all." She smiled at him gently. Her lips were slightly parted, and her hair had come down a bit more, leaving strands curling around her shoulder. She was breathtaking.

The chanteuse performing with the piano player began singing Cole Porter's 'Night and Day' in the background, and Cole mentally thanked his fellow Cole for the romance.

Without thinking, because he didn't want to talk himself out of it, Cole leaned in. "I would like to kiss you. May I?" he whispered.

She pushed a tendril behind her ear. It was definitely her nervous tell, and Cole was charmed. Her eyes dropped to his lips and she nodded.

He touched his lips to hers, which tasted of wine. It was a soft kiss, tender and lingering. Cole pulled back, running the tip of his thumb across the path his lips had traveled, relishing the pillowy softness of her lower lip, before reluctantly dropping his hand and looking over at the small dance floor.

"Tiercy, would—"

"We—"

They broke off, laughing.

"You go first," Tiercy motioned.

"I was just going to ask if you'd like to dance."

Tiercy grinned, a becoming post-kiss blush on her cheeks. "I was just going to say, 'We should dance.'"

Cole rose and took her by the hand, leading her to a small dance floor near the songstress, who exuded an Ella Fitzgerald vibe. Gently, he pulled her toward him, resting his hand on the small of her back. Sparks zipped up his arm as he traced her smooth, bare skin. He was aware of eyes on them and knew the men in the room were wondering how he'd ended up with her.

He trailed his fingers across the soft skin, lingering on the middle of her back, where he toyed gently with those tempting thin strips. How easy it would be to take her home, tear those meager threads, and peel the dress off her.

A thousand jolts of electricity were coursing in his veins. Her right hand curled in his left, and she leaned toward his shoulder. Her fragrance was light and citrusy, and nearly as intoxicating as the wine they'd consumed. Her left hand, bare of rings, rested on his upper arm. He relished the subtle movement of her hand—a soft scratch against his light wool blazer.

He rested his cheek along her head, and they swayed to the music. The words struck him like bolts. About hungry yearning burning inside. About her letting him spend his life making love to her...day and night.

Christ. I want you so much, Tiercy Somerville.

As the song ended, he removed his hand from her back and tipped her chin up, kissing her deeply. The sounds of clapping from the other patrons replaced the resonant tones of the musicians. "I think they're clapping for us," Cole murmured against her lips, smiling.

"I'm pretty sure they're clapping for the singer, Cole," Tiercy whispered back, also smiling but not completely ending the contact of their lips.

Cole sighed. "Enchantress. That's what you are. Next you'll probably tell me you're from a family of Irish fairies."

"I'll wait until the second date for that," she teased.

"Second date? You promise?" Cole's eyes searched hers.

"I promise."

CHAPTER TWENTY-ONE

"It is only with the heart that one can see rightly; what is essential is invisible to the eye."
The Little Prince, Antoine de Saint-Exupery

COLE

They drove home in peaceful silence. Cole was absorbed in the feelings swirling inside him and got the sense Tiercy was experiencing the same. Her head rested against the seat, a soft smile on her face as she watched the passing scenery. The soft strains of Chopin kept their thoughts company. Cole held Tiercy's hand, loving the feel of it in his.

Pulling into her driveway, he battled with himself. He didn't want the night to be over, but he also didn't want to push too hard. She was fragile—clearly still grieving Luke Somerville and possibly, no *very likely*, not in the headspace or heartspace for sex with him.

He turned the music down, unbuckling to face her. "Thank you, Tiercy, for a wonderful evening. It was beyond anything I could have imagined." He coughed. "Uh, not that I was imagining it or anything— Oh, fuck it. I've imagined this date nonstop for nine very long days." He scrubbed his hand down his face and laughed. "I clearly have lost my filter and any 'rizz' I thought I had."

Tiercy burst into her lyrical laugh. "You have plenty of 'rizz,' John Colburn." Her smile faded just a touch, and she reached for her own seatbelt, then shifted closer to him. "You, uh, you aren't alone in your musings over the past nine days."

His heart thudded.

"Will I freak you out if I tell you I've developed a serious crush on you, Tiercy Somerville?"

"No, John Colburn. You won't. But you will make me mad if you don't kiss me again." She broke into a wide smile, leaning further toward him.

Needing no further impetus, Cole pulled her into his arms, crushing his mouth to hers. She sighed against his lips, then opened and took his mouth with matching fervor. Within moments, he had eased her hair free from its confines and ran his fingers through the heavy locks, gently tugging. She gasped and pressed harder into him.

"More, Cole. More."

Cursing the confines of the Jag—his truck would have offered them much more room—he ran his left hand along the decadent length of her lithe leg, lifting her dress along the way.

Tiercy moaned against his mouth, kicking her kiss up another notch and dropping open-mouth kisses along his jaw to the base of his ear, her tongue pressing into an erogenous zone he hadn't known he possessed. His cock was like a steel pipe, straining against his fly. Sensing it, Tiercy reached down and palmed his length through his trousers.

"Good gravy," she whispered, pressing down.

Cole groaned, pressing her back into her seat and removing her hand. When she whimpered her protest, he laughed softly against her mouth. "If we don't slow down, I'll embarrass myself. Your touch feels incredible. Just—just let me touch you for a while."

That spectacular dress was pooled around her thighs. Her hair was mussed and tumbling down her shoulders. Her lips, puffy from his kisses. Cole reached over, watching carefully for any signs of resistance or discomfort, and palmed her breast. He ran his thumb back and forth over her nipple, noting some sort of patch over it. Tiercy's breathing hitched.

"Please, Cole."

"Please what, baby?" He ran his nose along the column of her throat, leaving a trail of chills in his wake. Maybe it was too soon to call her that, but the endearment had fallen from his lips...and he didn't regret it. She didn't seem to mind, as she pushed against him.

"Touch me. More."

Unable to resist, he resumed his explorations along her leg. As his hand moved closer to the vee of her thighs, he could feel the heat she was emanating. Her hips rose subtly, telling him all he needed to know. Gently, he ran the tip of his knuckle across the lace of her panties, right on top of the nub he knew was aching for attention.

"Yes. Please..." Tiercy reached for his hand and pressed it harder against her.

"You want more?"

In response, Tiercy pushed her hips into his hands as she took his mouth in a ferocious, passionate kiss that had him close to spilling in his boxer briefs. He slid a finger under the lacy panel and ran it along her seam.

"Oh, Godddd," she drew out, panting. "Yes, Cole."

He plunged a finger in and then a second. Her back arched off the leather seat, one hand grabbing the handle, the other gripping his shoulder. He worked his fingers, loving the slick of her channel, the tight grab, and wishing it were his aching cock in there instead of his fingers. Soon. Not yet.

Her breathing ratcheted and Cole could feel the beginnings of flutters against his fingers. She was close, thrashing her head against the seat and murmuring nonsense words. When her channel tightened hard against his fingers, he curled them and tapped her clit a few times with his thumb, and then pressed hard.

"Oh...oh, fuck!" she screamed, clearly succumbing to the orgasm. "Fuck, Cole. Harder."

He pumped his hand. My God...it would be amazing when he could really get inside her. She went off like a firecracker, a sexy groan-wail filling his car, the scent and sounds of her arousal surrounding them.

Her hips slowed and she reached down to halt his hand, laughing softly. "Oh...wow. You need to stop. So sensitive. Holy shit, Cole," she let out a huge exhale and then laughed again.

He grinned at her, smoothing her dress partly down her legs.

"Did we...did we just do that in my driveway?" Tiercy looked around, eyes wide, hair sexily mussed. "I hope none of my neighbors were out walking their dogs." She put her head in her hands and laughed again. Then she sat up, eyes fixed on his crotch, where it was clear his hard-on was raging for attention.

"Cole, I'm sorry. I got so caught up in me—it's been s-so long since I felt anything close to that—I forgot about you." She reached for his fly, but he stayed her hand.

"No, beautiful. No. This was all for you. Don't worry about me."

Frowning, Tiercy glanced at her house. "Jemma's not home tonight," Tiercy offered, a slight shake in her voice. "I can't," she gulped and began again. "I can't invite you in. Not for *that*."

She gazed at him with sad but hungry eyes. Her pulse fluttered in her neck. "Take me to your place, Cole. Take me there and let's continue this. Let me make you feel as amazing as you just did for me. I want you to take me to bed, Cole." Her eyes flitted around his face, clearly clocking his reaction.

Cole kissed her again, almost fiercely. For the first time in his sexually active life, he was going to turn down sex with a woman he craved. Touching her. Bringing her to completion—it was amazing. And his cock was definitely on board for part two. But something inside him cautioned against that. Slow down. Make sure she's truly ready—not just her body but also her heart.

Gently breaking their kiss, he put his hands on either side of her face. "Tiercy, there is nothing—and I mean *nothing*—I want more than to take you to my home, carry you inside, and bury myself inside you. I've been imagining peeling that dress off you since the moment you opened your door."

Tiercy smiled shyly, and he could sense the racing of her heart by the flutter of her pulse in that decadent, elegant neck he'd just nuzzled. She scanned his face, a tiny frown emerging between her eyebrows. "But?" she asked, voice shaking.

He kissed the frown and rested his head against hers. "I know I'm going to hate myself for this the second I say it," he said almost to himself. He could feel her brow furrow again.

"I'm not opposed to getting intimate on the first date. But this is—you are—special. Different. Tiercy, this may sound crazy, but, to use an old-fashioned term, I want to court you. I want to get to know everything about you. I want to know it all. I want to go to the movies. I want to take you to the zoo. I want to meet Jemma and go out on a double date with Ross. It would be so easy to fall into bed with you. And right now my body is seriously betraying me." The tell-tale bulge reinforced his words. "But I want to do it right. I want to woo you. I want to fall completely head over heels in love with you. Hell, I'm already halfway there."

He raked his hand through his hair. "Will you let me court you? And then, when it's time, I will take you to bed, where I will touch and kiss every inch of your beautiful soft skin. I want to be inside you, watch your face as—Jesus, I need to stop talking about that." His voice was strangled and his eyes felt hot. "Please, Tiercy. I want to do this right."

Cole was sure that if Tiercy kissed him right now, let the kiss express what they both were feeling, his resolve would crack and he'd take her to bed and make love to her.

"I-I understand. But, Cole," she examined him with eyes that were beseeching, full of yearning...and also troubled. "I want to go home with you. I want you inside me. But I need you to understand this—I can't offer you falling in love. I'm sorry. I feel like maybe that's a dealbreaker for you." She looked away, and started to open the door.

He placed his hand over hers, and pulled her back against his chest. "No, Tierce. Not a dealbreaker. I'm sorry, beautiful. I don't want to push you. I know all of this is very difficult for you. I know it's not something you do."

"You're right. But I don't regret it." She leaned against him, nuzzling his jaw. "I just need you to know there are things you want that I can't give you. You say you're halfway to falling in love with me, but I —I just can't give that. If you want to walk away right now, I totally understand. But if you're OK with that, I would very much like you to court me and then take me to bed."

"Tiercy, I am more than OK with it. What's happening between us —well, it isn't like anything I've ever experienced. And I'm not walking away."

She turned and kissed him softly on the lips, running her hand gently through his hair to smooth what she'd rumpled in ardor. "Good night, John Colburn. I had an amazing evening. Walk me to my door?"

"I wouldn't have it any other way."

They walked hand-in-hand to her door, where she unlocked it.

Cole pressed a kiss to her cheek and then her lips, inhaling her intoxicating fragrance one more time. "Good night, Tiercy."

Then she turned and walked in the door, closing it gently behind her.

Cole stood there for several long moments, only a door separating them, wanting to tear it open and pull her into his arms, but also wanting as intensely the promise of more.

CHAPTER TWENTY-TWO

"The darker the night, the brighter the stars."
Crime and Punishment, Fyodor Dostoevsky

TIERCY

I wish our photos could be like the ones in the Harry Potter films and have movement. What I wouldn't give to watch you laugh again. In every picture I have of you, it looks as if you are about to laugh or just finished laughing. I remember...how you used to rub your hand over your face while you laughed, as if you could rub in the joy to make it last longer. Even better— what if those photos could have little snippets of sound! It's been five years, and I can still hear your laugh. But sometimes, if I try too hard, I can't hear it anymore. It scares me that I will slowly forget the sound of your voice, the timbre of your laughter.

I've watched our wedding video so often. I close my eyes and just listen to your voice. I've got your cadence memorized. But in the quiet of my head, sometimes I can't hear you anymore. I don't know whether to be mad or sad or scared. I can sometimes feel you slipping through my fingers. Please don't leave me that way. You left me physically. I can't bear losing the rest.

That Monday evening, after writing in her journal, Tiercy did schoolwork on her laptop on the deck. It was her favorite part of her home. The house backed up to woods, and the deck was surrounded by mature trees, making her feel as if she were in a treehouse. It was a soothing space, and completely private—except for the occasional deer who wandered into her yard and a fluffle of bunnies that had made a nest by Jemma's outdoor playhouse.

Jemma was in the house with her friend, Marie, practicing their ballet moves for their upcoming recital. Tiercy just needed another thirty minutes of relative peace and quiet to finish grading papers, then she'd take Marie home, put Jemma in bed, and maybe get a few minutes to read for pleasure before she herself headed to bed.

Sometimes Tiercy felt like she was so busy being everything for everyone else, she forgot what it was like to be Tiercy, for Tiercy. She sighed. Not this season of her life.

She didn't want to wish the years away, but the constant treadmill of work and single parenting of a young, precocious child was exhausting.

She overheard Jemma channeling their French ballet teacher with Marie. "First position. Second position. Third position. *Non, non—*cross your foot like *zis*, not like *zat*. Better. Fourth position...*Oui.*"

Tiercy shook her head and laughed. Jemma even had the accent down.

Then, she let out a long exhalation. When she was in labor, the midwife called them 'cleansing breaths.' It didn't really work then, and it sure wasn't working now. She needed to talk to Brinder. She'd been procrastinating for several days. She owed him an apology. And she also wanted a chance to explain in person, this time sober, why he deserved so much more than she could give him.

Just do it, coward.

She tapped on his name on her favorites screen. When the call went to voicemail, she sent a quick text.

TIERCY

I'm so sorry about Friday night. I'd like the chance to explain and apologize.

Fifteen minutes passed, with no return text or call. That was unusual. She was pretty sure he wasn't working, which would normally be the only reason for a delay in response. After close to thirty minutes, she decided to send him an email. Tiercy's hands hovered over her keyboard, unsure what to write. Brevity, she thought. Email rambling would not help.

Brinder, I am so very sorry about Friday night. I owe you an explanation in person. Please call me? I can come to you or you can come by here. I just need to see you and explain. I know I hurt you. I can't stand the idea of us fighting. Please? -Tierce

She reviewed it, took a deep breath, and hit send, turning back to her school document. A moment later an out of office message displayed on her email alert. She clicked on it.

I am out of the country and will return June 18. During this time, I will not have regular access to emails. If you need immediate assistance, please contact Felicity Bowersox, administrative director for the department of radiology. Thank you.

Out of the country? Where? For a month? When did he leave? Was this planned? If so, why didn't he say anything...

Unless it was a reaction to Friday?

No way, Tiercy reasoned. It took much longer to plan a trip abroad.

It must have been scheduled before the fundraiser. Tiercy was confused and hurt that he didn't say anything.

When she finally went to bed that night, there was no communication back from Brinder. Meanwhile, she and Cole had been texting throughout the past two days. Nothing heavy. Just lighthearted text chatter and some discussion about a second date.

Tiercy tossed and turned for a long while, thinking about Brinder, Luke, and Cole—all of whom were causing a tangle of feelings she wasn't sure she could handle.

She turned back to her journal.

It's been five years, two weeks, and three days. But who's counting?

I read an article about an asteroid crater that had been found in Mexico. When it hit 66 million years ago, it killed everything. All signs of life were obliterated. Scientists were going to drill to the core of the crash and research the pattern of life slowly returning to the area. There was a line in the article that resonated, and I read it over and over: "We expect to see a period of no life initially, and then life returning and getting more diverse through time."

I wonder, if scientists drilled to my core, would they see all signs of life as I knew it obliterated, and then a pattern of life slowly returning to the area?

CHAPTER TWENTY-THREE

"You are part of my existence, part of myself. You have been in every line I have ever read... You have been the embodiment of every graceful fancy that my mind has ever become acquainted with."
Great Expectations, Charles Dickens

TIERCY

Over the next few weeks, per Cole's endearing courting request, Tiercy and Cole went out on several more dates. Each time, Cole would bring her a different individual exotic flower. Laceleaf. Orchid. Lobster-claw. Lotus. She was utterly charmed by him. They went to the movies. They visited the aquarium, where Cole arranged a behind-the-scenes tour with an opportunity to feed an injured dolphin. He took her to an opening night fundraiser for a musical at The Kennedy Center, where they had box seats. He wore a tux and looked like a dark-haired Thor in formal attire. Tiercy fought the urge to jump him for most of that evening.

Later, when she'd told Ross about the date, her bestie squealed. "It's like *Pretty Woman*! Did he get some rubies for you to wear?"

Ross was almost as besotted with Cole as Tiercy was herself. As envisioned by Cole in his courtship scenario, they'd gone on a double date. Ross brought a cute but bookish guy named Mike she'd met on the train back from New York. He was a professor of quantum physics at the University of Maryland, but surprisingly hilarious. The four of them spent the evening laughing, the guys enjoying IPA beers and the ladies drinking Kir Royales.

"Slainte!" offered Tiercy.

"Here's to those who wish us well. All the rest can go to hell," added Ross, with her goofy laugh.

After dinner, they went to a bar and happened upon a spirited trivia contest. Forming a spur-of-the-moment team—named The Avengers by a smirking Ross, with a private smile at Tiercy—they ended up coming in second. Mike was their ace-in-the-hole. He came up with the arcane answers, Tiercy nailed the literature questions, Cole had history down (Tiercy learned he was an amateur historian on that date), and Ross, in her black halter top and jeans, had half the guys in the bar in love with her as she answered sports question after sports question.

At the end of the evening, Ross mouthed to Tiercy, *He's amazing.*

I know, Tiercy mouthed back.

Cole appeared at their side. "*Thanks, I think so too,*" he mouthed to them, and winked. They cracked up.

Cole's courtship was...incredible. He sent her sweet and funny texts throughout the day. He planned thoughtful dates. He was engaging and sweet. He flirted. And, to her relief (she was relieved, wasn't she?), he hadn't said anything more about falling in love. Instead, he focused on creating dates that allowed them to get to know each other.

The only issue thus far, for her, had been the intense sexual chemistry incessantly humming between them. Touching him was positively combustive. She was aching to take it to the next level, but he was charmingly, frustratingly insistent about the pace of his "courting." Even when she intentionally wore sexy clothing just to drive him crazy with lust, he always managed to halt things before they went too far. Everything was "above the belt," no matter how much she tried to entice him. His self-control was impressive. And annoying AF. Tiercy had charged her Rose three times in those three weeks.

But their next date was an important one. Tiercy was introducing Cole to Jemma. If that went well, and she had every reason to think it would, the date after that would be The One.

CHAPTER TWENTY-FOUR

TIERCY

The June Saturday morning dawned bright and cheery. Both Somerville women woke with the rising sun, excited for the day's plans. Today, Tiercy would introduce Jemma to Cole. In her heart, which was validated by the butterflies in her stomach, today was almost more important to her than her own first date with Cole.

Worry gnawed at her. *What if they don't like each other? What if Cole isn't good with her? What if Jemma develops an instant dislike of him?*

Jemma was famously mercurial. If she liked you, she loved you. If you got on her bad side, she was shockingly adept at the cold shoulder for a four-year-old little girl.

The environment for the introduction was perfect, though. Cole would pick them up at eight thirty and take them to the National Zoo in Washington, D.C. Jemma hadn't been there yet and had been chattering nonstop about seeing all the animals, especially the monkeys and the pandas.

The second her eyes opened, she bounced into the living room, mop top of blond curls flying behind her. "Mommmeeee! Mommeee! When are we leaving? When is Mr. Cole coming for our playdate?"

Tiercy tore her eyes from her phone, closing the disheartening, short email from Brinder.

Tiercy, thank you for sending the note. I'm in India. Unexpected trip. We can talk when I return. All good. -B.

Tiercy sighed. Worry over losing her friendship with Brinder threatened to overshadow her excitement for the day ahead.

"MOMmmmEEEEE!" Jemma stood at the sliding glass door, hands on her hips. "You are being uhstracted by your phone."

Tiercy smiled apologetically at her daughter and put her phone down. "*Dis*tracted, lovebug. Not *uh*stracted. And I'm sorry. I was reading a note from Uncle Brinder."

"When is he coming over for pizza dinner night? I miss him. I want to show him my ballet dance."

Jemma spun onto the porch and bumped into Tiercy's chair. Tiercy lifted her onto her lap, tickling her tummy. Her daughter's giggles lifted her spirits.

"He will be back around the middle of June. He's in India. I'm sure as soon as he's home, he will come by to see you, lovebuggie."

Tiercy marveled at the ability of the very young to take things at face value and move on. She'd found that preschoolers were great at that, and wished she could do the same—across the board.

Jemma bounced in her lap. "I'm sooooo 'cited for the zoooooo!"

Tiercy laughed and blew a raspberry into Jemma's soft neck. "Meeee toooo!"

Jemma's answering grin was as captivating as her father's. Tiercy pressed her hand against the inevitable sensation in her chest. A tendril of grief—and guilt—curled around her heart, squeezing too tight.

She'd told Jemma she'd been out on "dates" with a nice man named Cole, for which Jemma immediately signaled her approval. She loved playdates, endorsing her mother's with sweet sincerity. "I'm glad you made a new friend, Mommy," she had pronounced. The romance aspect of this was far beyond her ken.

"When's he coming? When's he coming?" Jemma chanted, squirming.

"Soon, sweetness. How about we eat some breakfast, get dressed, and brush our teeth? We don't want Mr. Cole to be grossed out by slimy teeth and icky morning breath."

Unbidden, Tiercy's stomach did a little flip at the thought of waking next to Cole, sharing that moment of, *How bad does my breath stink? I really want to kiss...*, that so many couples face the first time they spend the night together.

"Mommeeee!" Tiercy was snapped out of her little daydream. *Kissdream*, really. "Let's goooo." Jemma's enthusiasm was contagious and they both got ready in record time.

At 8:29 a.m., the doorbell rang. Before Tiercy could even turn the corner from the kitchen, Jemma was at the door, flinging it open. "You're here!!!"

Cole immediately kneeled to her eye level. "I *am* here. I'm Cole. And you must be Jemma."

Jemma nodded and held out her hand to shake his. She had insisted on wearing her pink shimmery leotard from her recital with a pair of white shorts and her light-up unicorn sneakers. Cole's eyebrows went up and his eyes caught Tiercy's, amused and impressed. He put down his packages and solemnly shook her hand.

"Nice to meet you, Mr. Cole," Jemma intoned.

"Nice to meet *you*, Ms. Somerville." Jemma smiled beatifically at him, clearly reveling in being treated like a big girl.

Cole reached next to him, still kneeling, and handed Jemma a brightly but inexpertly wrapped package with the homeliest bow Tiercy had ever seen. He had clearly wrapped it himself and she was touched by that as much as the gesture of a gift for Jemma. In under three seconds, Jemma had destroyed the paper and was peering inside.

Her eyes were big. "Oooo...I like dis big man Barbie," she cooed, examining it closely.

Cole chuckled. "This is G.I. Joe. Your mom told me that you like toys like this. I played with one just like this when I was your age. And maybe even a bit older, too," he winked at Tiercy. "That, plus Legos, were my absolute favorite."

"I love Legos!" exclaimed Jemma. "But Mommy doesn't 'cause she steps on dem and dey hurt her feet and den she says bad words dat we're not 'opposed to say."

Cole laughed out loud, his gorgeous smile crinkling the corners of his eyes. And this time it wasn't Tiercy's heart clenching, it was her lady parts, which were now clamoring for attention.

Good gravy, she'd turned into a raging horndog. If this man didn't get himself between her legs soon, she'd combust.

"Well, maybe when we get back from the zoo, you and I can play Legos. But, we'll be sure to clean them up so your mom doesn't hurt her pretty feet."

Jemma was still admiring the present. "I like Gee Joe."

Cole grinned at the name. "I thought you might like him. And it was fun to hang out in the toy aisle for a bit."

"Coley, dat is very nice of you. Your mommy will be happy dat you bought this and shared." Jemma nodded approvingly. Sharing was a big topic at preschool.

Tiercy's heart melted at the unexpected diminutive "Coley." Cole glanced up, catching Tiercy's gaze, and smiled broadly. He clearly liked it too. Cole tapped Jemma on her button nose and stood up, knees popping. Tiercy was charmed by the sound—even strapping Cole-Thor had joints that popped from too long in one position.

Cole lifted his shoulders sheepishly. "Hmm...pretty sure they didn't used to do that." He smiled and kissed Tiercy on the cheek, resting his lips there for an extra moment and inhaling softly, which was somehow more intimate than the other kissing they'd done.

"And these are for you." He handed her a bouquet of red tulips.

"Thank you, Cole."

Jemma zoomed by, G.I. Joe doll in hand. "Jemma, what do you say to Cole for your gift?" Tiercy nudged verbally.

"Fank you for Gee Joe, Coley!" she called over her shoulder.

"I told you she was precocious. A mini-adult," Tiercy whispered.

"She's awesome." Cole smiled back then called out, "Who's ready for the zoo?"

"Meeee!" Jemma came flying back around the corner, G.I. Joe, He-Man, Skeletor, and Han Solo all grasped against her body. "We're all ready."

"Jemma, how about we leave our friends here when we go to the zoo? We don't want anything to happen to them," Tiercy advised, knowing that she'd end up carrying all of them.

"Or, you could bring them and leave them in the truck," Cole suggested.

Jemma cast a shocked look at Cole. "No! Dat's not safe. It will be *hot* today and you don't leave fings you love in a hot car," she admonished.

Tiercy tucked her head, mortified. Ten minutes and Jemma was already schooling Cole.

Cole slapped his forehead. "Oh my goodness! You are so right, Jemma! How could I not have realized? I am so glad I have such a responsible friend to help me out. Thank you!"

Jemma gave a satisfied smile and set the figures down lovingly on the couch, kissing the tops of their toy heads and warning them in Tiercy-like tones to be good or they wouldn't get dessert later.

Tiercy hid a snicker as she packed the ever-necessary Parent Backpack of All Things Needed. She cast a quick glance at Cole, wanting to gauge his reaction to her daughter's big personality. Tiercy froze, taking in the sheer delight on Cole's face as he watched Jemma tend to her toys. He looked up, eyes snagging on hers and a grin breaking across his swoon-worthy face.

"Looks like we are ready for our zoo date." Cole held out his fist for a bump, which Jemma energetically returned, causing Cole to shake his hand dramatically and wonder aloud about Jemma's superhero strength.

Jemma reached for his hand, dropping a gentle kiss. "Sorry, Coley!" she giggled, smiling up at him from under her long blonde lashes. "Now let's goooo!" She tugged him toward the door.

Tiercy's heart did funny things, skipping beats and dancing in her chest. She rested a hand there, as if to keep it from bursting through.

What sort of magic did this man wield? Both she and her daughter were clearly infatuated.

"I'm coming. I'm coming," Cole laughed, pretending to be dragged to the door. He looked over his shoulder at Tiercy and winked, causing the dancing in her chest to shimmy south and start a party between her legs.

Tiercy shook her head to clear it, then grabbed the backpack, following behind her daughter and her...her what? Boyfriend? Would he be her lover? At the thought, a shiver slid down her spine.

With great effort, she pulled herself out of her confusing feels and locked the front door, automatically heading toward her Accord. But Jemma had spied Cole's truck and was tugging him toward it, insisting on riding in it. Tiercy cast a questioning glance at Cole.

"Fine by me. Do we need to move the car seat?"

Jemma interjected, indignant. "I am a *big girl*. Car seats are for babies, Coley. I use a *booster seat*."

Once again, Cole nodded his head in apology. "I am so sorry, Jemma. I should have known better. Please accept my apology?"

"'pology accepted," Jemma granted grandly, and then squeezed a hug around his waist. Cole's eyes widened in surprise, and then softened, as he bent over and gently returned the hug.

For the second time that morning, Tiercy's heart tugged...hard.

No falling in love, Tierce. Just enjoy him.

CHAPTER TWENTY-FIVE

TIERCY

It was a perfect day for the zoo. Cole surprised them both by arranging yet another private tour. Tiercy's eyes widened, but he just returned her look with a nonchalant gaze. "Remember," he winked, "now I'm courting *two* Somerville ladies. All's fair."

Jemma ran forward with the guide, following the different tracks to animal exhibits. She squealed at the stench of the elephants, was mesmerized by the lions, and went wild when the panda ambled over to just below where they were watching, as he chewed contentedly on a piece of bamboo. "He *sees* us! He wants to be our friend!" she exclaimed.

After visiting most of the exhibits, including the reptile house—which Tiercy adored but Cole did not, citing an aversion to snakes rooted in childhood—they ate lunch at one of the pavilions, which was crowded with parents and children. Jemma swallowed a hot dog in three bites, and then immediately ran to play on one of the animal statues ringing the area.

"Be careful and stay where I can see you," Tiercy called.

She looked over at Cole, who continued watching Jemma, a smile in his eyes. Her heart filled with deep and conflicting emotion for this man. She was obviously in lust with him. She liked him as a person. Over their dates, they had definitely become friends—he was easily one of the most thoughtful people she'd ever known. It was impossible not to feel affection for him.

Then there was the ever-present guilt. And the rumblings of something much deeper. Something she could not—would not—allow to happen. No, whatever this was with Cole, it had to stay at a certain level. *And,* she catalogued his handsome face and defined muscles, *that level better include sex soon.*

She reached over and wiped a bit of pizza sauce that lingered near the corner of his mouth. Cole turned at the touch, and her fingers landed on his lips. He pressed a kiss to them, and when she traced the outline of his mouth, his light blue-gray eyes turned a shade darker.

"Better stop that, young lady, or we're in danger of making this an R-rated zoo exhibit. 'Watch the human mammals in their natural habitat, engaging in love play, leading to long-awaited mating. These two animals have been building up to this encounter for ages...,'" Cole intoned, a la National Geographic voice-over style.

Tiercy laughed, breathless. How was it that a zoo food pavilion could be the scene of an unexpected, but effective, seduction?

The moment was broken by the sound of Jemma running over, small yellow flowers clutched in her hands. "Coley!! Let me see if you like butter!"

"Buttercups! Where did you find them?" Cole tore his gaze from Tiercy and mouthed *Later.*

Tiercy's mind wandered—no, *high-tailed it*—to *later.*

"By the gorilla. I was so kaprised to find dem!" Jemma beamed. "Now, put your chin out."

Cole obeyed, a very serious look on his face and all his attention on Jemma, who promptly put one of the buttercups under his jaw. Tiercy noticed his faint stubble. He hadn't shaved this morning, and it gave him a rakish look. She imagined the scrape of whiskers against her lips... and on her thighs.

"I see yellow! You love butter!" Jemma exclaimed. "Now let's do Mommy."

"May I, Jemma?" Cole asked. "I'd like to *do* your mommy." The double entendre was lost on Jemma, but not on Tiercy, whose cheeks flooded with color at Cole's penetrating stare.

"Here!" Jemma passed him a sweaty handful of wilting buttercups.

Cole carefully selected one. With his other hand, he gently tilted Tiercy's chin up, grazing her neck along the way and sending a current through her body. He peered closely at the underside of her chin, a smile playing on his lips as she fantasized about him kissing her there...and working his way down, with a few scenic stops along the way.

Jemma squeezed in next to him, her arm around his shoulder, and squinted. "Hmmm...Mommy likes butter, but not as much as you," she pronounced. "Now me! Now me! My turn!" She thrust her chin at Cole, and he obligingly put a buttercup under her chin. Jemma closed her eyes in concentration.

Tiercy was completely besotted with her sweet face, eyes scrunched, long pale lashes sticking out.

"You, Miss Jemma, are the winner. You clearly love butter most of all. Why, in my whole life I've never seen such yellow under a chin. From now on, I shall call you Jemma Buttercup," he proclaimed.

Jemma beamed and threw her arms around his neck. "Fank you, Coley!"

I'm in big trouble.

As is the way of things with four-year-olds, after several hours of running around on relatively short legs in the hot summer sun, Jemma started to give in to exhaustion. But she was desperate to see the orangutans. Tiercy thought it was better to begin to head home but Jemma got weepy. Tiercy knew with a mother's practiced instincts that Jemma was on the verge of a meltdown.

She started to stave off an embarrassing tantrum when Cole offered,

"How about if Jemma takes a ride on my shoulders? We'll go to see the orangutans, and then we'll head back. OK?"

"Are you sure?" Tiercy asked. "It's hot, and she's heavier than she looks."

"No problem. I didn't get to work out this morning, so this should count."

Cole looked at Jemma and then whipped her up and began to "curl" her like a free weight, his biceps flexing with the effort. Jemma squealed, her two ponytails bouncing, laughter ringing through the air.

He lifted Jemma onto his shoulders. "Ready for the big monkeys, little monkey?"

"Ready!" Jemma shouted her agreement.

They headed off in the direction of the Great Apes pavilion, Jemma high on Cole's shoulders, her hands grasping the top of his head, and his left hand holding onto Jemma's leg. With his right hand, he reached for Tiercy's.

She turned to him and said, sotto voice, "Way to try to impress me with how you played with Jemma."

He raised a mock-challenging brow back at her. "Did it work?"

"Yes," she admitted with a grin, and he squeezed her hand, answering that with his own broad smile.

When they got to the orangutans, Jemma was beside herself, absolutely tickled with their antics and their human ways. "I love dem, Mommy! Can we get one? Deir hair is sort of your hair color, Mommy," she pronounced earnestly, sending Cole into fits of laughter.

Ignoring Tiercy's disapproving look, he bought Jemma a large stuffed orangutan. "She and mommy have the same hair," Jemma noted lovingly. "I want to name her Niamh."

Tiercy groaned but Cole cocked his head in interest.

"Why Niamh, Jemma Buttercup? That's an unusual name."

"Because, it's Mommy's middle name. She doesn't like when people say 'Nye-amh,'" Jemma explained, offering the common mispronunciation by those unfamiliar with the Gaelic spelling of the name 'Neve.' "She doesn't like her name, but I like it."

Cole turned to Tiercy. "That's your middle name?" Tiercy nodded. "I love it. It's as beautiful as you are." And he kissed her softly.

"Coley! Did you ask Lovie if you can kiss Mommy?" she asked querulously.

"Yes, I did," Cole quickly recovered. "And she said it was OK for me to kiss Mommy."

Jemma trained a discerning eye on him, looking exactly like Tiercy. "Well, OK. Because if you didn't, it would be *direct disdobedience*," she mispronounced, channeling the exact warning often given to her by her mother.

Not for the first time, Tiercy thought to herself that whoever was lucky enough to marry Jemma Somerville one day better be a strong person. And in the ensuing moments, as she watched Cole carrying her four-year-old on his shoulders—who in turn had a stuffed orangutan named Niamh on hers—she wondered if he would be around to see it.

Chapter Twenty-Six

"I know no ways to mince it in love, but directly to say 'I love you.'"
Henry V, William Shakespeare

Tiercy

Jemma chattered nonstop on the ride home. Cole had told Tiercy he was certain she'd fall fast asleep as soon as the truck got going, but he clearly was unpracticed in the ways of preschoolers. Tiercy snickered as Cole responded gamely to Jemma's unrelenting barrage of questions and commentary.

When they got home, as promised, Cole and Jemma played Legos for a while, and then they all had some ice cream. He was helping Tiercy clean up the kitchen and suggested that he work with Jemma to put away the Legos.

Moments later he returned to the kitchen with the sweetest smile of wonder on his face and wordlessly tugged Tiercy toward the family room, where Jemma was sound asleep on the floor, clutching Niamh.

"Let me deploy my hard-earned 'funcle' skills, Tierce," he whispered. With practiced skill, he bent down and gently shifted Jemma into his arms, careful not to disturb her. Jemma smacked her lips in her sleep and mumbled something about a pet orangutan, then snuggled into his chest.

Tiercy's ovaries, already overstimulated, threatened to burst as Cole carried her daughter upstairs to her room. Tiercy stood in the doorway, watching Cole gently ease Jemma into her big girl bed and tuck the soft hair that had fallen out of its ponytail behind her delicate ear. Then he quietly arranged the menagerie of stuffed animals, taking special care to put her elephant and the orangutan on either side of her on the pillow.

She wondered how she could feel so happy and so sad at the same time—the strangest of juxtapositions that happened to those whose hearts have been shattered and then slowly begin to heal. Not fully sad but not fully happy, either. She couldn't shake the feeling that it should be Luke taking them to the zoo, carrying Jemma around on his shoulders, and buying her stuffed animals she clearly didn't need. And, yet, this moment was distinctly Cole's. She was utterly infatuated with him, and he had made the day extraordinary for her and Jemma.

At that moment, Cole turned to her, perhaps sensing her disquiet? Or perhaps he heard the small sigh she emitted. He leaned down and kissed Jemma's forehead, and then quietly closed the door. Taking Tiercy's hand, he led her down the stairs.

They stood in silence at the bottom of the steps.

Unlike previous times, this silence was fraught with tension. Hers for certain, but his as well. Tiercy closed her eyes, struggling to find the right words to convey the torrent of emotions churning within.

"Tiercy," he began eventually, softly, resting his hands on her tense shoulders. "I don't want you to think I'm trying to take Luke's place. That's not what's going on here. And I know you're thinking that Luke should be here, doing what I'm doing."

Tiercy let out a quick exhale, impressed at Cole's perceptiveness.

"And maybe he should. I'll admit to being jealous at the very thought."

Tiercy started to turn away, but Cole kept his hands on her shoulders.

"Look at me, Tierce." He gazed at her with those mesmerizing eyes. "I am falling deeply in love with you. No, not just falling. *Fallen.* I'm there. I know it's only been a few weeks since we've met. This courtship has been a whirlwind. But I also believe that, in our thirties, we know our hearts and we know what we want." He leaned in closer to her, lowering his voice to just above a whisper. "And I know I want you, Tiercy. I want to make it clear that I don't want to replace Luke. I know I never could, and frankly I don't want it. I'd like my own place in your heart, in your life, with Jemma."

Tiercy stood, frozen, a thousand thoughts and feelings hurtling with abandon in her mind and heart. Emotional incoherence tied her tongue.

"Cole—I—it's not that easy," she started, unsuccessfully. Tiercy turned away from him and took a deep breath, one filled with regret, as this would likely signal the end of things with her and Cole. "I loved Luke Somerville more than anything. He was my heart in every way."

She sensed more than saw him shift to examine the handsome, bespectacled man in the picture on the nearby wall. The man who had loved her so deeply, and who she had loved fiercely in return.

"I can never love like that again. That was a really big love, and you only get one of those in a lifetime. He was the love of my life." She took a shuddering breath as he gently turned her to face him again. "You are incredibly special. But you deserve more—so much more—than I can give you. I know what you want. You told me on our first date. And I can't give you that, Cole. I'm sorry." Little fissures tore open in Tiercy's scarred heart, exposing hurt she hadn't experienced in years.

Now it was Cole's turn to exhale a deep breath. He softly traced circles on her bare shoulders, which were pink from the sun. "I'm sorry. I pushed too hard. Too fast. But how about if you let me decide what I do or don't deserve? I'm a big boy. I think I can handle this."

He tipped her chin up and kissed her tenderly. "I'm a patient man, Tiercy. But I want you, in every way a man can have a woman. And I don't think having one really big love excludes you from having another. I've never heard of a love quota system."

His eyes crinkled in the corners with a teasing smile, softened by the kindest eyes she'd ever seen. "How about we just keep having a good time. In the meantime, promise me you'll keep an open mind and think about it?"

Tiercy gave a small laugh. "Trust me, Cole. I've done nothing but think about this for the past several weeks. You...shake me to my core. My feelings are a jumbled mess. They are the emotional equivalent of a junk drawer—I don't think I could sort them if I tried. But in the mess, one thing is clear to me." She heaved a deep sigh and turned smiling, sad eyes on him. "I have fallen for you as well, and I want you in every way a woman wants a man."

"Then *be* with me, Tierce," he breathed, pulling her against him and holding her close.

"Yes," she whispered. "I want that. But...I may not be able to give you more, and I need you to accept that."

"I understand. I'll take my chances." He kissed her forehead and then her lips. "I had an amazing time with you and Jemma today. When she," he halted, swallowing, "when she called me 'Coley' and threw her arms around me, I fell in love with her, too. I need you to know that and believe me."

"I do." Tiercy's voice was barely a whisper.

"Thank you. May I see you again?" he asked, his eyes smiling at her.

"Yes, you may," she replied, channeling Coralee. "Cole...," she hesitated. "Thank you for the lovely courtship."

He softly ran his fingertip along Tiercy's cheek, stopping at her lips, which parted slightly at the gesture, and studied her for a moment with serious eyes. "The pleasure is mine, Tiercy. See you soon."

With that, he turned and walked out.

Through the windows, Tiercy watched his truck leave the driveway. She wasn't experienced like Ross in the ways of dating, but she was pretty sure Cole's old-fashioned courting, along with a generous dose of heady sexual chemistry, was truly special indeed.

She turned and flopped on the couch, eyes landing on her favorite picture of Luke. "Talk to me, babe. What do you think of all this?" But he didn't answer.

Instead all she heard was Cole's voice over and over. *Then be with me, Tierce.*

Chapter Twenty-Seven

TIERCY

Cole's Jag pulling into her driveway set off a case of the schoolgirl butterflies for Tiercy. *"Then be with me, Tierce,"* rang like a refrain in her mind, over and over.

She hadn't seen him since Sunday. It was exams week at County High, and he was swamped with the construction of the medical pavilion, along with a new project that came in. At the thought of the hospital, Tiercy felt a brief pang of sadness. Three Thursdays had passed with no Pizza Dinner Night with Brinder, and other than that brief email, he'd been radio silent. She was sure he would've been in touch by now. She missed him.

But it was Friday at last, and it was her first date with Cole alone at her place. Jemma was with her parents, and Tiercy had spent the better part of the week struggling with the idea of inviting Cole over to her home—one she'd always thought she and Luke would inhabit forever—knowing her intentions centered around getting naked. She'd had a long, teary, agony-filled conversation with Ross on Monday, sharing her conviction that she would be cheating on Luke in his own home.

Eventually, Ross had convinced her she'd feel better if she initiated at her own place—that way, if she "chickened out," she was at least on home turf. Also at Ross's suggestion, Tiercy would take advantage of the guest bedroom, moving any...uh...activities there, instead of her bedroom. She hoped Cole would understand. And with those decisions made, Tiercy had shifted from guilt and sorrow to pure, unmitigated anticipation.

Tonight, Tiercy felt certain, was going to be The Night.

Just like on their first date, she forced herself to slow down and walk calmly to the door. What she really wanted to do was open the door and launch herself into Cole's strong arms, wrap her legs around his waist, and...well...*Probably best not to entertain that line of thought, Tierce, or you'll explode into an orgasm at the sight of him.* She was positively simmering. Just the idea of him was tantalizing.

On the other side of the door, her date rang the bell.

Tiercy took a deep breath and opened the door.

"Hi."

"Hi."

They stood there smiling at each other.

Then both started laughing.

"I guess I should invite you in. Wonder what the learning curve on that is going to be for me?" Tiercy stepped aside and motioned to the hallway.

As he walked past her, he handed her a bird-of-paradise and waved a bottle of Veuve. "I also brought champagne."

"Good man."

In reply, he dropped a gentle kiss on her lips...which went straight to her core. She caught a light whiff of his cologne, an intoxicating spice scent. He had clearly just showered. His hair was damp at the edges and curling. Tiercy wanted to thread her fingers through it and tug. *Down girl*, she thought. *Let the man get in the door.*

"You look gorgeous." He leaned in, softly inhaling, his nose just centimeters from her neck. "And you smell like summer."

She'd tried on about sixteen different outfits before deciding on a short, strapless, white eyelet sundress. She'd slid on a pair of white wedge sandals she knew made her long legs look longer, pulled her hair into a low wavy ponytail, and wore thin gold hoop earrings. In her own homage to his senses, she wore her favorite summer body lotion, which added a bit of shimmer to her skin. The look of approval—and hunger—in Cole's eyes was gratifying.

Tiercy put an extra sway in her walk as she passed by Cole on the way to the kitchen. She could feel his eyes on her and smiled with a blend of satisfaction and anticipation.

"Just relax for a bit. Would you like a beer?" she called over her shoulder. "I don't drink it, but I keep it in the house for all my gentleman callers." At the look on Cole's face, she burst into laughter. "I'm kidding. I keep it stocked for my friend, Brinder." Her voice wavered on his name, a tiny pang of sorrow. "He's into craft beers these days. Grab one and settle in on the deck or the living room, whichever is more comfortable for you. I'm just going to get the last of this dinner prepped for the grill."

"I'll pass on the beer. But," he cocked his head, "Brinder, huh? Should I be jealous?" Cole's tone was teasing, but she could see something deeper in his eyes.

"No," responded Tiercy definitively, and was surprised to find she truly meant it.

"I'm happy to help prep dinner. I'm a great sous chef. I'm also excellent at pouring drinks."

"No, I'm good. Please, just get comfortable. I'll only be a few minutes. I thought I'd be ready before you got here, but Miss Jemma had to find her Skeletor before she left for her grandparents, so it was an all-hands-on-deck search party. I got a bit waylaid. Thankfully, we found him, nestled in her sock drawer...where he belongs, apparently." Tiercy smiled and shook her head at the funny, randomly willful ways of preschoolers.

"I'm not sure what to comment on first there—Skeletor or his hiding place."

Tiercy laughed again, her heart light.

"Skeletor belonged to her dad. I mentioned to you that my mother-in-law saved all his childhood toys and sent them to Jemma. Ever since then, Jemma's been inseparable from him and Han Solo. As for the sock drawer, apparently Skeletor likes it there because it's 'cozy,' according to Jem. But she forgot that was his 'cozy place.' After thirty minutes of frantic and somewhat tearful searching, she remembered where she put him. By then I was behind in getting ready. I just have to 'shish' the kabobs and then throw everything on the grill. Make yourself at home."

"You know, little filly," Cole drawled in an amusing attempt at a cowboy accent, "the grill is the man's domain. Why don't you rest your purty little feet and I'll do that heavy liftin'."

Tiercy laughed. "I'm very proprietary about my grill."

"Hmmm...well, if I'm a good cowpoke, maybe I could earn a chance to touch your...*grill*?"

Cole smiled wickedly at her and a blooming blush heated Tiercy's cheeks...and parts lower.

"OK, but be careful. It's hot," she all but purred, proud of herself for the matching flush that crept up Cole's neck.

"You sure I can't help?"

"Nope," she popped the P. "You're my guest. I'm not putting you to work." She waggled her brows suggestively. "Yet..."

"Eat dinner fast, Cole," he whispered loudly, and then winked at her. "If you're sure, I'll just chill out in your family room and play with Han Solo." He waved the action figure, which had been sitting on the hall table. "It's not who I really want to be playing with, but..." he added under his breath, clearly meaning to be heard, and cocked a playful eyebrow at her.

Before Tiercy could attempt another witty retort, her eyes caught on the toy and she registered what he was saying.

"Oh no. Jemma is going to be distraught that she left Han. She was so busy looking for Skeletor, she forgot him. I'm surprised I haven't gotten a text from my parents. Ah, well. My mom will distract her with sugary treats, I'm sure. Plus, she has *Niamh*," Tiercy noted playfully. "She hasn't let go of it since the zoo."

Casting another quick glance at Han, she lifted her eyes back to Cole's. "Perhaps later, if you're a good boy, you can play."

Cole's eyes flared, the black of his pupils overtaking the gray-blue. He turned and subtly, but without embarrassment, adjusted himself, and then wandered into the family room on a dramatic, throat-clearing cough.

Tiercy grinned, relishing her ability to, well, get a *rise* out of him. *Lord, I really am turning into Ross.* Unable to stop herself, Tiercy followed him, and then halted, the smile sliding from her face.

The juxtaposition of the newness of Cole with the everydayness of her life stole her breath. As he scanned the room, a neutral expression on his face, Tiercy detected well-hidden curiosity in his eyes, and couldn't help but examine the space through his perspective.

Images of her life were thoughtfully scattered throughout the cozy space. Pictures of Jemma at various ages; her parents at a recent anniversary celebration, arms wrapped around each other and laughing; Tiercy and Jemma; Ross and Jemma; Tiercy and Ross; and a wedding picture of Luke and Tiercy graced various surfaces.

A photo collage in rustic wood frames hung in a place of honor over the fireplace. In the middle of the frame was an up-close picture of two pairs of entwined legs hanging from a dock. "Kal and Luke... It's A Really Big Love" was inscribed in calligraphy across the bottom. Luke gave it to her when they'd moved in, after she'd lamented not having a beautiful piece of art for the spot. Nearby on the built-in bookshelf filled with classics she'd collected over the years, sat a custom piece of artwork featuring a fancy treatment of the names Kal and Luke—a gift from Ross on the anniversary of Luke's...his *death*, she forced her mind to say.

As she watched Cole's eyes roam the photos, wondering what he was thinking, Tiercy herself studied them with fresh eyes. She looked so...light. So happy. In every picture of Tiercy and Luke, they were touching—cheeks, foreheads, hands, legs. The love they had felt for each other emanated from the photographs.

Tiercy rolled her lips, worry gnawing at her. She should never have offered to hold their date here. Too much "Tiercy and Luke," when it should be about her and Cole.

Her and Cole. Was there a 'her and Cole'? Is that what she wanted? And if it was, would she ever truly be able to reconcile her new life with the one that was stolen? Luke still owned her heart. He always would. She couldn't lose that, couldn't let that change, because it would be like losing him all over again.

And, yet...with every interaction, Cole had anchored himself more firmly in that scarred, aching place, slowly filling the emptiness with something wonderful...and scary.

Chapter Twenty-Eight

"It's no use going back to yesterday, because I was a different person then."
Alice's Adventures in Wonderland, Lewis Carroll.

Cole

Cole studied Luke's photo closely. He'd heard so much about him, both from Tiercy and at the hospital, where he'd discreetly inquired. But this was his first time really examining photos and being confronted by the image of Luke as Tiercy's husband. From the way people talked about him at Fellowship-Unity, he half expected to see a halo floating above his tousled blond crew cut. A broad smile with a hint of a dimple in one cheek. Hazel eyes in a tanned face. Wire-frame glasses that gave him a bookish air. In most pictures, he looked as if the photos were snapped mid-laugh. Cole knew guys like this in school—the ones all the girls had crushes on, and the guys couldn't help but like despite it.

Cole turned away, feeling a bit like a voyeur, and frankly—he was mature enough to admit—vibrantly jealous of the laughing handsome doctor and his gorgeous wife, so crazy in love with each other.

What are you doing here? She is still hung up on him. She told you herself. You can't compete with a beloved dead husband. Walk away, Colburn. Walk away.

He had just about convinced himself that he would eat a quick dinner, stay long enough to be polite, and then end the evening. End it all. He would never measure up to Saint Luke. Damn the chemistry. Damn the wooing. Damn his heart.

And then Tiercy walked toward him, an expression of both sorrow and understanding on her face. She was backlit by the evening sun and her smile was soft and warm. Just like the first time he saw her, it was like being punched in the solar plexus. She positively *radiated* beauty and warmth, and like a magnet to metal, he found himself irresistibly drawn to her side.

"It's too much, isn't it?" Tiercy asked in a low, sad voice. "I'm sorry. We shouldn't have done this here. We can leave if you want. Go to your place..." she trailed off uncertainly.

A beam of sun touched the floor by his feet, dust motes dancing, and Cole had the distinct sense of standing on a precipice. He knew if he followed through on a plan to leave, with or without her, this would end tonight. If he left alone, well, that would be the death knell in and of itself. And if he took her to his place, he was equally certain they would end up in bed...and then she'd walk away. Likely for good.

No. Cole had to show her he could co-exist in her life, in her heart, with Luke.

"No, beautiful. It's not too much. *You* are never too much." He reached for her free hand, the other still holding the champagne. Her blue eyes fastened to his hand and he watched the elegant column of her neck as she swallowed. "You promised me your grill, and I'm not leaving until I taste your...offerings."

"Ok." Her voice was shy, uncertain, but also held an unmistakable smoky undercurrent of desire. She squeezed his hand and then broke into a wide smile that made him feel like a pubescent teen with a first crush. "Ready?"

"Readier than I've ever been. Let's do this."

Replete with a simple but delicious al fresco meal, and relaxed by the bottle of crisp champagne, they stretched out like lazy, basking cats in side-by-side chaise lounges, enjoying the warm summer evening. They held pinkies and talked aimlessly about this and that, but Cole was distracted by the building tug of sexual anticipation. Perhaps it was foolish, but in the glow of the setting sun, he asked the question that had been on his mind since looking at her pictures.

"May I ask you something personal?"

Tiercy nodded, but a small furrow creased her lovely forehead.

"I noticed something in your family room. Why did Luke call you Kal?"

The frown disappeared, replaced with a wistful smile different from anything he'd seen from her. *The many faces of Tiercy. I want to learn them all.*

Her eyes gazed into the distance of memory, and she was quiet for a moment.

"I'm sorry. I shouldn't have asked. It's none of my business—"

"No, please don't apologize. It's fine. Really. It's a long story so I'll try to give you the Spark Notes version, even though as a literature teacher I'm firmly opposed to those, by the way."

"Duly noted." Cole winked. "I promise I did all my assigned reading in school."

"Good boy. There will be a quiz at the end of the evening." Tiercy laughed, a melodic waterfall, and Cole was entranced. He was tempted to wrack his brain for a funny joke just so he could hear it again. It was more intoxicating than the champagne.

"Remember the SAT word competition that Ross and I have? When Luke and I started dating my senior year of college, there was a night when we did a group bar hop with a bunch of friends. Ross and I were on a roll with the big words. Luke, being the competitive sort, keyed in on it. The next time we went out, he had his word all ready.

"He was in his first year of medical school, and I was student teaching plus taking classes, so we didn't have a lot of time to spend together. He'd finished his first block exams and wanted to take me out to celebrate. He planned an evening picnic, overlooking a reservoir. It was fall and the air was crisp. He had blankets, and wine and cheese, a crusty loaf of bread. As it got darker, the stars came out and we just sat there watching them appear, first one at a time, and then hundreds popping out, until the sky was full of them."

Cole watched her, lost in her memories, and recognized a hard truth. He was in love with her, but he actually wasn't sure he could co-exist in her heart with Luke. There might not be enough room.

Tiercy continued with the story, her voice far away.

Chapter Twenty-Nine

"Sometimes you will never know the value of a moment, until it becomes a memory."
Dr. Seuss

TIERCY

"Kalon," *Luke whispered.*

"Hmmm?" Tiercy asked, only half listening, as she lay on the soft blanket with Luke's legs as her pillow, marveling at the heavenly display.

"'Kalon,'" he said again. "It means the ideal of beauty."

"Mmm-hmm," Tiercy hummed her agreement, almost too relaxed to speak. "It's gorgeous tonight."

"I wasn't talking about the sky." At his tone, tender and low, Tiercy turned to look up at Luke. He was gazing at her intently. "Kalon. Per the Greeks, the ideal of physical and moral beauty. Synonym: Tiercy Niamh Flynn."

He bent down, gracing her with the kiss of true love—one that starts in the heart, the lips its messenger.

"Good SAT word," Tiercy whispered against his lips.

Tiercy surfaced from the memory. "And that's how it started. For a while, he'd call me Kalon, but after a while, it just became 'Kal.' He called me that more often than he called me Tiercy. It was just his thing. And I loved it."

"If you don't mind me asking...How did he die?"

Tiercy scanned Cole's handsome face, looking for signs of pity. Instead, she was relieved to see a patient understanding expressed in those stunning blue-gray eyes. If there was any chance of them being intimate, and getting past her...well, *her* past, she owed him the gist of the story.

Tiercy sighed deeply, her heart suffused with a familiar sadness. "It was a thoracic aneurysm. He was dead almost immediately. Apparently, the warning signs are difficult to detect, particularly in an active young person."

"That's awful. I'm sorry. And I've made you sad. That wasn't my intention. I'm an inconsiderate dolt, forcing you to dredge up memories." He shifted on his side to face her, rubbing his thumb across her knuckles.

"Not at all. I feel like I've broken Widow Dating Cardinal Rule Number One: Don't wax melodramatic about your dead husband when on a date with a special guy you really care about." She tucked her chin, feeling wobbly and shy.

"Later I want to hear more about these widow dating rules. But, first," Cole broke into a wide grin, "a special guy you really care about, huh?"

Tiercy swatted him playfully. "Don't be cocky."

"Oh, I'll be *cocky* with you, Tierce. Just you wait." He laughed at his own double entendre, and Tiercy couldn't help but join in.

After a moment, she composed herself and inhaled a shaky breath. "That's just it, Cole. I don't want to wait anymore."

Cole's smile faded, his eyes turning a shade darker, his piercing gaze penetrating her until the building warmth of desire soaked her panties.

He stood, holding out a hand, telegraphing his intention. She rose, taking his hand and meeting his gaze head on. *Go for it, Cole. Don't make me wait any longer.*

Cole pulled her into him. "Are you sure, Tierce?" He stroked the line of her jaw, eliciting chills up and down her spine.

"Very," she whispered.

Cole nodded. And then he crashed his lips to hers.

Stunned at the ferocity of his kiss, Tiercy grasped his shoulders....and let him take her on the ride. Their tongues tangled, soft moans escaping. Tiercy wasn't sure if they came from her or him.

Under the pale light of the half moon, Cole proceeded to worship her mouth. Small bites at her lips, which he then salved with the tip of his tongue. He sucked her lower lip into his mouth, and Tiercy knew the moans were hers. He shifted to place light nibbles along her neck—nip, a light touch of his tongue, another nip, all the way to her shoulders.

He traced her clavicles. "How much champagne do we have left," he murmured against her skin.

Confused at the non sequitur, Tiercy looked to the small table between the abandoned chaise lounges.

"About a third," she managed, struggling to make her voice work amidst Cole's sensuous assault.

Cole nipped at her collarbone and Tiercy gasped in pleasure, her senses converging in the pleasure zone between her legs with increasing pressure.

"Plenty." He growled again, licking along the bone and laving into the hollow. "Christ, I love these."

Tiercy's chills had chills at this point, and her arousal was potent. She tapped one of Cole's hands, which had wandered to skim her ass, causing another wave of desire.

"Cole," she whispered, arching away.

He leaned toward her, kissing his way up the other side of her neck.

"*Cole,*" she laughed, managing a louder voice.

"Mmmm," he mumbled against her skin.

"Let's go inside. The neighbors can't see us from here, but I'm pretty sure they'd be able to hear."

Cole shifted back. His hair was rumpled. His eyes hot with desire. Tiercy's eyes traveled down his body, and widened. His pants were so tented they looked like they might burst. Sort of how she felt right now.

"Come." She tugged him toward the sliding glass door.

"Oh, I plan to." He followed closely behind her, enough that she could feel the heat emanating from his body. "But not before you do, at least twice."

Tiercy halted, and then took a deep breath, dropping his hand. "Tierce?"

Ignoring the momentary confusion from Cole, Tiercy turned and faced him. Then she winked and ran for the stairs, laughing.

Cole barked out a laugh as she sprinted for the guest bedroom, him hot on her heels.

There wasn't even time to admire her preparatory handiwork. The fresh sheets. The throw pillows already off the bed and stacked in the rocking chair that had been her grandmother's. The candles waiting to be lit. Within moments, Cole had whipped her into a gentle turn, pressing her against the wall.

Tiercy ground against his hard length, eliciting a groan from him. She knew from getting handsy with him a few times—which he always halted before she got to see the goods—that he was packing down there. Now, she was on fire to get him naked and feel that gorgeous hardness inside her.

Reaching behind her, Cole slid her zipper down. Not breaking eye contact with her, he eased the dress from her body, revealing a barely there lacy strapless bra and matching thong. With one hand, and a sexy half smile, he flicked the bra open so it dropped to the floor.

Tiercy's nipples were tight buds, begging for his touch.

Cole said nothing, taking her in. But his faster breathing told her everything. That he was as close to exploding as she was.

Still in silence, punctuated by their panting breaths, he pushed her dress further down and off her hips, leaving her standing in only a tiny lace thong.

"Turn around, baby," Cole rasped.

Tiercy faced the wall, placing two shaking hands on it to steady herself.

"Gorgeous." Cole eased behind her, pressing into her. "Take off your panties, beautiful."

Again, Tiercy was powerless to do anything but obey. She slid her panties down, reveling in the decadent sensation of being naked while Cole was still fully dressed. As she bent to remove her panties, she brushed against Cole's arousal. His sharp inhale sent waves of desire to her clit, which tightened in anticipation. She was positively throbbing for his touch.

And yet, it wasn't his touch she felt then, but a gentle kiss of cooler air as he stepped away.

"What—?" Tiercy started to turn, confused.

"No, baby," he commanded. "Stay facing the wall. I just want to look at you for a minute."

Tiercy turned back to the wall, her legs shaking with desire, and yet utterly unembarrassed. She could feel Cole's hot perusal, almost as tangible as his touch.

"Fuck, Tierce." Cole stepped in closer again. "You are beyond beautiful."

He dropped a kiss where her shoulder met her neck, and she melted at the brief flicker of his tongue. Who knew that was an erogenous zone?

"I want to kiss you, Tierce. Everywhere you'll let me. I want to make you feel good, baby. I've been wanting to do this for so long."

Tiercy leaned further into the wall, arching her back and pushing her ass into him, then grinding.

Cole groaned. "So fucking sexy," he muttered pressing back into her. "May I?"

"Take off your clothes, too."

"All in good time, beautiful." Cole's voice had gone down an octave, and every word was like a well-placed flick to her clit.

"What are you waiting for?" Tiercy all but purred, wriggling against him and then gasping as he grabbed her hips. He pressed kisses down the length of her spine, stoking her flames, until he knelt behind her.

"What—"

"Trust me, Tierce?" He paused, his lips hovering at the base of her spine, his breath gliding across her ass.

She looked at him over her shoulder, her hands still anchored against the wall. His eyes, dilated with his arousal, sought hers and held. She knew he'd stop at one word from her. Even one nonverbal cue that might indicate hesitation.

She closed her eyes, turning back to the wall, savoring the sensation of his large hands bracketing her hips, the tips of his fingers so close to where she desperately needed them.

Again, she pressed her hips back into his hands, a wordless assent.

Another gasp as he kissed each globe of her ass, tenderly. Then he bit her right cheek and she emitted a shocked squeak. He smoothed his tongue over the area, then did the same to her other cheek. This time, it was a moan that rolled out—hungry, aching, needy.

He nudged her legs. "Wider, baby. Let me see you."

Tiercy widened her stance, too aroused to feel even a slight embarrassment at what she knew he saw: her wet arousal, dampening even the tops of her thighs.

"Now lean forward a bit."

Again, Tiercy complied.

"Good girl. Let me see that gorgeous pussy."

Holy gravy. Cole was a dirty talker? Yes, please. She was here for it.

He held onto her cheeks, pulling them apart. A zing of need pulsed through her and she could feel his eyes on her tight pucker. Tiercy was also very glad Ross had talked her into a full Brazilian. She was smooth and ready for his mouth.

"I don't need to know if anyone's ever been here. But I do need you to know that one day, I will slide my fingers deep in your ass. And you will love it. You'll come so hard for me. Not today. Not this time. But it will happen." He ran his thumb along her crack, pressing gently where he stated his intentions to go. "And after that, after I get you used to it, I'll bury my hard cock in there."

"Fuck," Tiercy breathed as her legs started shaking harder.

"Easy, baby. I'm just going to taste you."

Cole's tongue trailed to her opening, and then further forward. He pressed the flat of his tongue against her clit and Tiercy's hips bucked. "Oh...God, Cole."

In a lightning fast move, Cole turned her by her hips so her back rested against the wall. Then he lifted one of her legs, hooking it over his shoulders. She was wide open, wet, panting, and she knew her pussy was visibly pulsing as it sought to be filled.

"Pretty pussy." He leaned in for a long lick. "Tastes amazing too."

Before Tiercy could even formulate thoughts, much less words, Cole dove in, French kissing her pussy and lighting her up. She was already on the verge, and he knew it. He worked her clit with his tongue, circling it and building her higher and higher.

He paused and inhaled deeply. "Fuck, Tierce. You smell so incredible." And then he dove back in, owning her with his mouth.

"Yes, Cole. Oh my—there. There. Please don't stop. There," she chanted mindlessly, every atom in her body focusing on that hub of pleasure where all her senses had coalesced into one aching need.

Then Cole slid two fingers inside her. "Fuck," she yelled, her body clamping down on the welcome intrusion.

Cole kept at it, teasing her clit and fucking her with his fingers.

"Soclose. Soclose. Soclose."

All coherence evaporated as Cole curled his fingers, finding and hitting that sweet spot again and again. The sound of her own arousal wound her tighter as he worked his fingers in and out. Then he sucked on her clit, hard, and she exploded.

"Cole!" she screamed, as waves of sheer pleasure coursed within her.

He kept working his fingers, lightly flicking her bud, as her orgasm kept crashing through her.

Tiercy's clit was beyond sensitive and she started to push him away so she could finally get him naked. But Cole wasn't having it. "More, beautiful. Give me more."

"I can't," she laughed, breathless.

"You can," Cole growled. Then, not waiting, he wiggled his fingers, somehow magically activating that internal zone that so many men never could find. He definitely didn't have that problem.

He brought his mouth back to her and patiently licked through the painful sensitivity until Tiercy's hips were thrusting against his face. He pulled back, and Tiercy whimpered as he dragged his finger through the combined glorious dampness of her own juices and his saliva. Then he reached up and rubbed her arousal over one of her distended nipples.

"Holy fuck." With that one move, he catapulted her into a frenzy of desire.

She tilted her hips and he read the movement accurately, filling her with his fingers, covering her clit with his magnificently talented tongue, and rubbing her nipple until she was sure she would die of pleasure.

She grabbed his head on both sides, pulling him closer. "More. More. More."

He lightly blew on her clit and then began a series of rapid flicks that had Tiercy panting in unison. Her legs shook. Her pussy was impossibly tight, contracting in that glorious way that signaled imminent release. Cole issued one last swipe around her clit and flicked it hard as he pinched her nipple in perfect tandem.

Tiercy detonated, screaming his name again.

CHAPTER THIRTY

"License my roving hands, and let them go/Before, behind,
between, above, below."
To His Mistress Going to Bed, John Donne

TIERCY

Before she could even recover, Cole swung her into his arms and carried her to the bed, seating her gently on the edge. Grinning, he jogged back to the door and grabbed the champagne bottle where he'd left it, just next to where he'd brought her to orgasm. Twice. And she still hadn't seen his cock.

She started to lean back on her elbows, exhausted, body still humming from back-to-backers.

"Uh-uh. Sit up, baby." Cole fastened his gaze on her, taking her in.

Chills rose again under his tender but ravenous surveillance, and her nipples tightened, ready to party again. Tiercy was riveted as he stalked toward her, exuding the grace of a panther in the jungle. God, he was gorgeous.

Cole stopped inches from her, placing the bottle on the nightstand.

Without breaking eye contact, he pulled his shirt over his head—using that one hand behind the head maneuver that was so patently sexy.

He removed his slacks, but not before retrieving a condom from his pocket and placing it on the nightstand next to the champagne, leveling her with one of the sexiest looks she'd ever received.

Tiercy wasn't sure how it was possible, but as he stood there in only his boxer briefs, Cole's impressive bulge was even...bulgier. Her heart skipped in anticipation and she clenched her legs. That was going to either hurt like hell or feel amazing inside her.

Cole reached for the champagne bottle. "Humor me?" He tipped the bottle, aiming it at her collarbones. With a sexy smile, he poured a small bit into the hollow of her clavicles.

Tiercy gasped at the cool, fizzy wetness against her skin.

Cole leaned down and licked up the liquid, a satisfied hum vibrating his lips against her and adding to the sensual assault.

"Holy gravy, Cole," she whispered, reaching for him.

But he shifted away, practically melting her with the same ministrations on her other collarbone.

She looked down and was treated to the perfect view. Cole's self-control appeared to be waning, the tip of his cock emerging from the briefs, a touch of precum at the tip that Tiercy longed to flick with her own tongue. Instead, she ran her thumb gently across the tip.

Cole jerked and hissed his own pleasure, blindly reaching back to put the champagne on the table and missing. The bottle plopped the short distance onto the carpet, unbroken, the little liquid remaining leaking out.

"Oops," Cole breathed, turning to pick it up.

Tiercy placed a staying hand on him. "Leave it."

Like lightning, Cole shifted back and pressed her into the mattress, lifting her arms above her head and holding her at the wrists with one large, strong, but gentle hand.

He pressed his erection into her and she instinctively arched into it, wrapping her legs around his waist.

"I can't wait any longer, Tierce. I need to be inside you." His voice was strained, but Cole's eyes were soft. "I need you, beautiful."

"Yes." Tiercy could barely hear her own voice over the thumping of her heart.

Cole released her, standing quickly and shoving down his boxers.

"Oh holy fu—" Tiercy sat transfixed as Cole's cock sprung up, thick, long, hard...and pointing right at her like a divining rod. The head was angry and red. Tiercy licked her lips, involuntarily telegraphing her intention to take him into her mouth.

"Not right now, Tierce. I need to feel your beautiful mouth around my cock more than I need oxygen. But not this time. I can't wait any longer. I have to know what it feels like to be inside you."

"Then stop talking, Cole, and fuck me." Tiercy leaned back and spread her legs.

"Jesus, fuck." Cole wiped his hand down his face and then grabbed for the condom, quickly sheathing himself.

He reached down and tested her entrance. "So wet for me," he murmured.

Then Cole eased back over her, holding his weight above her, bracketing her face with his arms. A tattoo wrapped around his upper biceps—an intricate Celtic ring.

Tiercy turned and licked it.

"Tiercy," Cole growled. "Kiss me."

She turned back and he sunk into a sexy, claiming kiss. His hard length prodded against her opening as he ravaged her mouth, alternating between tender and rougher kisses. Plundering.

Tiercy's hips rose. "Now, Cole."

He shifted up, pinning her with a fierce gaze, and then slammed into her, burying himself to the root.

"Fuck," they both breathed in unison, and then smiled at each other.

He felt immense inside her. Hard. Hot. Throbbing. Tiercy's body, long out of practice, both strained to take him and welcomed him. She wiggled beneath him, needing more. Needing him to move.

"You OK, baby?" Cole's face was etched with tender concern.

"Better than. I feel so...incredibly...*full*."

He scanned her face quickly and, assured she was indeed better than OK, the worry cleared from his eyes, replaced by a look of pained restraint. "Good, beautiful." He touched his lips to hers, so very softly, still holding back.

"Cole," she began again, restless and needy, "I need you to move. I need you to fuck me. Hard."

Cole's eyes flared. He pulled his hips back, waited a beat, and then thrust in, hard, just like she wanted. Again and again, he pistoned into her. Skin slapped. Hands groped. Lips met and kissed and bit.

"Harder. Harder. Harder," Tiercy cried out, arching against the sheer pleasure of being absolutely nailed to the bed.

Cole complied, taking up a faster, harder cadence, grinding his hips periodically against her and lighting up her clit. He leaned down and sucked on her nipple, and Tiercy clenched. She was close.

Attuned to her, Cole shifted up onto his knees, lifting up her hips.

Unbelievable. How does this feel so amazing?

He slid even deeper, hitting a spot that sent her flying. Then Cole started up again, filling her over and over.

Tiercy's ears were buzzing. Every piece of her was centered on the building, aching, pulsing tension between her legs. Cole pulled back once more, pressed his thumb to her clit, and slammed in. She exploded, clamping around him, her body's lubrication easing the way for the deep, erratic thrusts that were pounding her pussy.

"Yes!" she screamed, thrashing her head.

Cole dropped onto one elbow, pulling up her hips. Sweat trickled down his brow and chest, and the veins popped on his arms. He pulled almost all the way out and pumped into her hard. Then did it again, faster, harder. Again. Cole panted, threw his head back, and slammed in one last time, shouting his release as Tiercy clenched him as tightly as she could.

"Fuck," he groaned, his thrusts slowing down. "Fuck, Tierce. You strangled my cock." He bracketed her again between his arms. "And I loved it."

She tilted her hips slightly and clenched again.

"Woman," he chuckled. "You're killing me. In the best way."

Cole's voice was soft, satiated. He exhaled, and the motion caused little wisps of her hair to tickle her face.

She giggled, pressing her face against his shoulder. "Right back at you. Cole," she flared her eyes comically, "I don't even want to *think* about how you got so good at that. But," she laughed, "I'm grateful."

He laughed and rolled onto his back, pulling her into his side. "Grateful isn't the word I'd use, although I am, don't get me wrong."

"What word would you use?"

"Words. One isn't enough. Delirious. Destroyed. Rebuilt. Astonished. Inspired. Breath-taking. Celestial. Ethereal"

"Oooh, nice SAT word, Colburn." Tiercy threw a leg over his body. His cock, softening, but still half hard, was a thing of beauty.

"Just trying to keep up with my lady." He pressed a kiss into her hair, stroking it lazily with one hand while the other trailed across the shoulder closest to him. "I mean it, Tierce," he said, suddenly serious. "That was...like nothing I've ever experienced before."

When Tiercy opened her mouth to reply, he pressed a gentle finger to her lips. "It's OK. I know I was incredible."

Tiercy, certain he was quieting her to relieve her of the awkwardness or pain of comparing their encounter with her intimacies with Luke, burst out laughing against his fingers. She guessed he did spare her that. Not the serious way she expected, but with humor. As she nipped his sexy, thick fingers, he started to ease them away from her lips.

But then Tiercy sucked his forefinger into her mouth, swirling her tongue around it the way she fantasized doing to his cock. Tiercy tasted herself on him and was turned on all over again.

"Baby," Cole laughed. "Are you asking to get railed again?"

"Mmmhmmm," Tiercy hummed, still tasting his fingers.

"Hey," he whispered. "I'm not saying no, but," he looked at the nightstand clock. "It's almost ten. We left our phones downstairs. Do you want me to grab them so you can check for a message from your parents?"

Tiercy sat up, touched by his thoughtfulness. Anytime her parents watched Jemma overnight, they'd leave her a message letting her know when Jemma was asleep, and it always eased her heart. Tiercy couldn't believe, in the throes of off-the-charts passion, she'd forgotten about her daughter. Guilt and worry stabbed.

"Tierce, it's OK. I'm sure she's fine. Your ringer is way up, so I'm pretty sure with your mother hearing," he winked, "that you would have heard it, no matter how loud you were screaming my name."

"Hey!" Tiercy laughed, swatting him. "I didn't scream."

"Who knew that my beautiful lady was a screamer," Cole mused, as though to himself.

Tiercy fake punched him again. "You wish."

Cole just grinned at her. Tiercy tentatively swallowed. Ok. Her throat was a *little* tiny bit sore.

Watching her, he laughed softly and whispered, "My screamer," propping himself against the headboard and pulling her gently to his side. "I'll go downstairs in a minute and get our phones, and some water for us. I don't know about you, but I worked up quite a thirst."

Tiercy relaxed against him, nuzzling against his muscular chest as she trailed her fingers across its planes, enjoying the smattering of dark hair that moved down his torso in a sexy trail that led to...the promised land. She rubbed her face into his chest, stifling a giggle. "You were pretty loud too, you know?"

"Oh, I know. You were choking the life out of my cock and the spirit moved me." He waggled his brows and patted her bottom. "I was calling out to God, 'Thank you for this woman and her magic pussy!'"

Tiercy snorted. "See if I let you in my magic pussy again."

"Oh, you will." He trailed his fingers across her body, setting off a chain reaction of contentment and desire. "We are just getting started, beautiful."

Tiercy shifted up on an elbow, tracing the pattern of his tattoo.

"I didn't know you had this. I like it."

"It's high enough on my arm that you wouldn't see it, even in a T-shirt. When I started making noises during college about getting one, that was the only ask my mom had...no visible tattoos. She wasn't opposed to them, but she was worried that visible ones might be off-putting to the various corporate types we need to work with to secure contracts." Cole chuckled. "Little did she know many of those corporate types also had tattoos. Things you find out in a locker room after a round of golf." He shook his head fondly.

"When did you get it?"

"Study abroad in Dublin my junior year. Xan and I went together when he came to visit over spring break."

She traced the pattern again. "What did he get?"

"Oh, Baby Xan didn't get one. He chickened out. There was a big dude getting a back tattoo in the other room, and his yelps freaked Xan out. But by that point, I was already in a chair, a design picked out. And," he grinned, "the tattoo artist was hot. She did the work."

"And then you did her," Tiercy surmised, rolling her eyes.

"Yep." He cocked a brow. "You still like my tattoo?"

"If you are asking if I'm jealous of some Dublin tattoo artist from more than a decade ago...no. I'm not. And I do still like it." Tiercy leaned in and kissed him. "A lot."

Cole frowned.

"What is it?" Tiercy asked, feeling the shift in energy.

"Speaking of jealousy, I'm debating saying something."

Tiercy sat up, wrapping the sheet around her. Cole tugged it back down, grinning wolfishly.

"Don't spoil my view."

Tiercy laughed. "Out with it, Colburn."

He sighed and blew out a breath. "I just...I noticed where you brought me." He motioned around them. "To the guest room."

"Cole, I—"

"It's OK, Tierce. I just wanted to say that I'm glad we're here. You know I don't ever want to make you uncomfortable or in any way feel that I'm trying to step into Luke's place. I told you the last time I was here that what you had with him was special and I honor that. Honestly, I don't ever need to step into your bedroom. I just need you."

"I need you, too," Tiercy whispered, tears of relief filling her eyes.

"Don't cry, beautiful."

"I'm not crying."

"Ok. Then I'll just kiss this random moisture leaking out of your gorgeous eyes." His lips were gentle against her eyelids as she laughed softly.

Between them, his cock had hardened again.

Just as he shifted her on top of him, the sound of her cell phone ringing came from the kitchen.

"Ignore it," Tiercy commanded, ignoring a pang of guilt that it was probably her parents. She straddled him, pressing into his length. He trailed kisses along her neck. The phone stopped ringing and their kisses continued unabated.

Then Tiercy's cell phone started chiming again. She lifted her head away from Cole with great reluctance. They were both breathing heavily. "I better get that." She eased herself off Cole, wrapping the sheet around her. Padding downstairs, she spied her phone. Two missed calls from her parents.

"Shit," Tiercy exhaled, as she called her parents back.

Her mother picked up immediately. As Tiercy listened intently, it was clear their evening was over. Assuring her mother that she hadn't interrupted anything—ha!—she acknowledged their ETA and then hung up.

Cole eased behind her, wrapping an arm around her waist and tugging her to his front. "Jemma Buttercup?"

She looked back at him with remorse. Her lips felt puffy from kissing, and she knew she had his whisker burns on her neck and shoulder...and elsewhere.

"Yes. She started throwing up an hour ago and she has a fever. Mom and Dad would have kept her, but she's in tears and she wants me...and Han. I think maybe Han a little bit more. They're bringing her home. Listen, I'm sorr—"

"Don't you dare say you're sorry. I understand, Tierce. Jemma doesn't feel well and she wants mommy...and Han." He turned her and gave her a tight squeeze. "I'll get out of your way."

Tiercy felt the loss of him immediately...physically, but also more.

Cole was already pulling himself together, tugging on the pants and shirt he'd brought with him into the kitchen. The impact of their passion on him, albeit interrupted, was embarrassingly apparent.

Tiercy's eyes flicked to his pants, and then quickly back up as her cheeks reddened. She hesitated. "Cole, this obviously isn't how we both wanted the evening to end. I-I hope we can have a do-over."

"You take care of Jemma Buttercup. We'll do this again. I promise." And based on the look in his eyes, Tiercy knew that to be more than just lip service. A shiver of anticipation, along with regret, ran along her spine.

"Tiercy, would you like some help with Jemma?"

She smiled gently, but decided to forego his presence and support, tempting as it was. Jemma adored her 'Coley,' but when she was sick, she might see him as competition for her mother's attention and resent his presence.

"You're thoughtful to offer. But I've got this. She's probably almost finished throwing up by now, so the rest of the evening will be about getting her settled, some Mommy-Jemma snuggles, and then checking on her overnight. I think I can fly solo on this one. But...thank you for asking."

"You sure? Sometimes it's nice to have help."

Tiercy nodded, suddenly on the verge of tears again at his thoughtfulness.

Cole tipped her chin up and kissed her softly. "Thank you for tonight. You are so beautiful, Tiercy. Inside and out. I loved being with you. And I can't wait to do it again. Not just the sex. Just being with you." He kissed her nose and smacked her softly on the behind. "Now get some clothes on, beautiful."

"I had an amazing time too," Tiercy whispered, torn between worry for Jemma and regret that their evening was over just as it was getting started. "Goodnight, Cole."

"Goodnight, Tiercy."

CHAPTER THIRTY-ONE

"It is difficult to know at what moment love begins; it is less difficult to know that is has begun."
Henry Wadsworth Longfellow

TIERCY

The next day she received a text from Cole.

COLE-THOR

How's Jemma Buttercup?

TIERCY

Better. She didn't throw up again, and her fever is mostly gone. We're just relaxing in our jammies, drinking ginger ale and eating toast.

COLE-THOR

Sounds cozy. Do you need anything?

TIERCY

Nope, we're good. I hope it's psychosomatic, but my stomach is upset too. I hope I'm not getting sick. Oh no! And you've been around Jemma and me.

COLE-THOR

Don't worry about me. I'm impervious to kid germs <puke emoji>. Call me if you need anything. I'm heading to Northern Virginia later for a concert at my niece's school. And maybe we can talk about our next date…

TIERCY

Definitely.

Unfortunately, as is the way with these things, within hours Tiercy hurried into the bathroom, emptying the contents of her stomach. After a couple hours of the same thing, her abdominal muscles were so sore it was like she'd done a thousand sit-ups.

Sweet Jemma, who was much better and had been enjoying a Disney movie marathon, brought her a ginger ale. As she handed it to her mother, an unexpected ray of sunshine, Tiercy's heart filled with both deepest love and deepest sorrow. Jemma resembled Luke so much, and clearly, also like her father, had a caregiver's heart. Once again, as had happened a myriad of times before, Tiercy had the sense that Luke was with her, keeping an eye on things.

Later that afternoon, she reached for her phone to text Ross and saw a message from Cole, which must have come in earlier when she was napping.

COLE-THOR

Checking in. How's Jemma B? How are you?

She immediately tapped a response.

TIERCY

Sorry it took me a while to reply. Was napping and missed your message. The good news is Jemma is better. Just one of those short viruses that's out of your system once you puke everything up. The bad news? I got Jemma's bug. Haven't been sick in a few hours but now I'm just exhausted.

COLE-THOR

I'd bring you some chicken soup, but… guess what? I never made it to the school concert. On the DC beltway, I had to pull over and decorate the shoulder with my breakfast and lunch.

TIERCY

Oh no!!!! Cole, I am so sorry. And mortified.

COLE-THOR

Don't be. It makes me happy.

TIERCY

I think you must be delirious with fever.

COLE-THOR

It's just that it makes me feel closer to you. Our first shared sickness. That is a major relationship milestone. In some cultures, we'd essentially be engaged. 😌

TIERCY

You are crazy.

COLE-THOR

Crazy for you.

Tiercy chuckled. How was it that she could feel sick and gross and wonderful at the same time? Cole was special medicine indeed.

Chapter Thirty-Two

"But one man loved the pilgrim soul in you, And loved the sorrows of your changing face."
When You Are Old, William Butler Yeats

Cole

That evening, Cole sat in his home office, reviewing emails and fine-tuning details on a job bid. He was exhausted from the stomach bug, but strangely content.

As he worked, a scene played out in his mind. In a cute bungalow ten miles away, the woman who owned his heart sat ensconced in an oversized chair with her beautiful little girl. Cole imagined her reading to the girl, the soft light of the lamp a nimbus around her auburn hair. He envisioned himself in the scene, walking into the cozy room, about to drop a kiss on the two precious heads. His attention turned toward movement in the picture behind them. The laughing, handsome face with the wire-rimmed glasses changed into an angry scowl, glaring directly at Cole. Cole saw himself dissipating from the scene, unable to get back to her and deeply saddened by that.

The sound of his cell phone ringing startled him awake. He must have drifted off. The memory of Luke's angry face shook him—even though it was a dream—but not as much as the awful feeling of being kept from Tiercy and Jemma. He swallowed some water from the glass he'd placed on his desk to rehydrate after the sickness, glanced at his iPhone, and the caller ID picture brought an immediate smile to his face.

A close-up of the middle finger of his best friend, Xander Grace.

"Xan...what's up, brother?" Cole's voice was craggy.

"Dude, you sound like shit." Xan put on his best Spicoli voice from *Fast Times at Ridgemont High*. "Are you sick, drunk, or hungover?"

Cole laughed. "The first. Getting over a bug. And I just woke up from the craziest dream."

"Cole, it's seven at night eastern time and you've been asleep? When did you turn into such an old man?" Xan razzed. It was always this way with them. They could go weeks without talking and then immediately fall back into easy banter.

"Since I started hanging out with a four-year-old who shared her stomach virus with me," Cole responded archly.

"Which niece or nephew is that?"

"Not one of them. Jemma. The daughter of—" Cole hesitated, and then blurted, "The daughter of the woman I'm going to marry. That is, if her husband lets me."

"Wait—what?? Her hus—*Are* you drunk? Cole, you got engaged?? What the hell? I go away for a few months to nurse a broken heart, and you freaking lose your mind? And what happened to that widow you met at the Manchester?" Xan, who was as urbane and unflappable as anyone Cole had met, was definitely flapping.

Amused by this uncharacteristic response, Cole began to laugh. And as much as he was sorely tempted to drag this on a bit just to tease his friend, decided to better explain himself.

"First of all, *five* months, bro. You've been in Europe nearly half a year. Life goes on without you, you know."

"Not as much fun, though," Xan mumbled.

"XanFun is definitely its own breed of fun," Cole admitted.

"Apparently not as much fun as dating a married woman with a puking kid," Xan responded in mock sarcasm, but affection tinged his voice. "C'mon man, what's going on? What happened to that Tiercy woman?"

"Tiercy's who I'm talking about. Xan, Tiercy is—she's incredible. She's everything...gorgeous, smart, funny, tender, and an amazing mom. I-I've fallen in love with her."

Xander let out a long, low whistle. "Moving kinda fast, huh, chief?"

"Yes, and yet, no. I could use your advice."

"I'm so confused. I thought you said she was widowed the last time we talked. But now you're talking about her husband like he's still in the picture."

"Tiercy is a widow. Her husband has been gone for five years. Aneurysm. And, apparently, he was a saint. Saint Luke. Everyone at the hospital—he worked there—liked him. They're naming a damn training room after the guy. And Tiercy...well, she adored him. She was head over heels in love with him. His death shattered her heart. And the thing is? He seemed like a cool guy. We'd probably have hung out with him. He played basketball. Drank beer with his friends at a sports bar. He had everything. Awesome wife. Great job. And then he died. I met her at this event and, *bam*, it's like suddenly everything has shifted in place in my life."

Cole paused as he let everything he'd just said play back in his mind. "I sound like an idiot. I'm an idiot, right? I've fallen in love with a woman who is still in love with her dead husband. And I'm talking about him like he's still in the picture because he very much is still in the picture. I'm trying to be cool about it, but I'm so fucking jealous of Luke Somerville." Cole rested his head on his hand. "I'm the asshole. You know that Reddit thread about 'who's the asshole?' Yep. It's me—"

"Dude, breathe. I think you said all that in one breath." Xan cleared his throat. "Man. This really is serious. Let me get this straight. You meet a hot, young widow with a kid at a work event at my Inn?"

"Yep."

"And you've fallen for her—hard, it sounds like. Does she feel the same way about you?"

"Yes. I mean, I'm pretty sure. The thing is, she won't let herself completely love me. But I know she wants to. I can feel it when we're together. But there's the Luke Factor. I'm not sure how to handle it.

Apparently, it's even seeping into my subconscious. When you called, I was having the craziest dream. I was in her family room, with her and her daughter, who's awesome by the way. I was about to kiss them on their heads, when the photo of her husband started glaring at me. Like he was going to reach through the frame and jack me up. It was nuts."

Xan was quiet, clearly absorbing this unexpected topic of conversation. "You said you were going to marry her. Have you proposed?"

"Not yet. I don't think she's ready, although I know I am. I guess I'm OK with the fact that she still loves her husband, but I hate his guts for it sometimes. I'm crazy jealous of a dead guy. Dude...I want to punch a dead guy."

"Yeah...that pretty much confirms it. You're the asshole."

They both laughed.

"I love her, Gracie." Cole stopped and breathed deeply. "But I don't know how to navigate this Luke thing. I'm stuck. And I don't want to blow it."

"Can't you call Margot or Lara for some wise counsel? I feel like I suck at this stuff. I fucked up my own marriage. Are you sure you want advice from me?"

"You didn't fuck up your marriage. That bitch ran out on you. And Petey. That's not you, man. Now help me so I don't end up a miserable, lonely bastard like you."

Xan ignored the jab. "It's weird, Cole. I've known you a long time and I've never heard you like this. Your voice sounds different when you talk about her." He was quiet for a moment, and Cole could almost picture his friend dragging his hand down his face, Xan's tell for deep thinking. Eventually, Xan cleared his throat. "You know what I say? Go for it. Be patient with her. But go for it. She'll come around. I've never seen a woman able to resist the charms of John Colburn for too long."

Cole released a breath he hadn't realized he'd been holding, the endorsement of his oldest friend carrying more weight than he realized.

"Ha...I wish. I'm a patient man. I'll wait until she's ready. But I need to know that she will even let herself be ready. I feel like she could really break my heart."

"I'm no expert, man. But my thought is that if you love her that much, it's worth taking the chance. The deeper the love, the more potential for heartbreak. Love like that makes you vulnerable. But, when it works, the more potential there is for something amazing. And this Tiercy sounds like someone who would take very good care of your pathetic, vulnerable, loving heart." Xan paused. "Man, that was fucking profound. I am a freaking love philosopher. I should get my own show."

"That would just be an excuse for you to bang groupies."

"This is sounding better and better. I know my next investment."

As the guffaws died down, Cole closed his eyes, intentionally reimagining that scene from his dream—only this time with the ending he wanted, where he kisses her and stays. And perhaps another small child—or two—in the tableau. "Thanks, brother. For an asshole, you're a pretty good guy. I want you to meet her."

"One: You're welcome. Two: You suck too. Three: You bet I'm going to meet this chick. She has a ball of fire best friend, right? One who I will happily let eat me up and spit me out. Isn't that what you said?" Xan snickered at his adolescent joke. "Wait. Strike that. I'm boycotting the female species."

Cole scoffed. "As John Wayne would say, 'That'll be the day.'"

"Now that we're finished with your little love drama, can I tell you why I called? I'd like to make this about me now."

"Go for it, brother."

"I'm coming home."

"Finally! When?"

"One week. Petey starts kindergarten after Labor Day, and I need to get him settled in. We're officially finished with our bachelor gallivanting around Europe. And I have officially landed the professor gig at University of Virginia. I'm moving to Charlottesville."

"Xan! Brother—that is amazing news! Congratulations! When did all this go down?"

"While you were busy falling head over heels, I was busy trying to build a new Aubrey-less life for Petey and me. The university needed someone to run my former colleague's syllabi and fill a void. And I had my own void that needed to be filled. Fucking profound *again*. Damn I'm good. So there you have it."

"Been a busy summer for us."

"True."

"I'm happy for you, *Professor Grace.*"

"That actually sounds pretty cool. Listen, I'll be in touch with details, including when I'll be in your neck of the woods. I want to check on the Inn. But first I need to get Petey and me settled. I'm renting a place while I see if I'm suited to a life in academia. In the meantime, about your lady? Just love her. Oh...and be kind to the dead guy. He may still have a part of her heart. But I'm thinking there's room for you. Now, enough relationship talk. We're going to have to turn in our Man Cards at this rate. I'll email you my new work contact info. G'night, Cole-Feel-the-Burn."

"Goodnight, Gracie."

Cole hung up and checked the time on his iPhone. Seven thirty. Hand shaking, but filled with a feeling of rightness in his heart, he tapped Tiercy's name on his favorites list. She picked up on the second ring.

"Hey, beautiful. Checking in. How are you and Buttercup doing?"

"It's run its course for both of us, thank God. She's sleeping on my lap right now," Tiercy whispered. "She fell asleep about a half hour ago, but I haven't felt like moving. Jemma's just so sweet like this. I feel like she's always in motion, and I love this opportunity to watch her at rest. It's magical. How are you?"

"Also much better. And even better now that we're talking." He noticed he was whispering too, unnecessarily, but had no intent to change it, enjoying the intimacy of the shared hushed tones.

Cole took a deep breath. He could feel his heart thudding in his chest.

"I love you, Tiercy."

There was silence on the other end of the phone for several painfully long beats.

Cole, sick that he'd once again pushed too hard too soon and scared her, immediately started talking to fill the awkward pause. "I'm sorry. I shouldn't have told you like that. You're sick, and I'm probably going too fast for you—"

"Cole—" Tiercy interrupted, laughing softly. "Can you let a person respond? I—you—well, you just took me by surprise, is all. I wasn't expecting that. Not today, with sore abdominal muscles and greasy hair and a sweaty child's head on my lap. You picked an interesting moment in your courtship, Cole, to say some really huge words." Tiercy breathed a nervous laugh. "Say them again."

He let out a quick sigh, and realized he'd been holding his breath. "I love you. I love you, Tiercy."

"I love you too, Cole." Cole heard a small sniffle, wondering if Tiercy was fighting the same battle to compose herself as he was. "I love you," she whispered again. "God help me," she added even softer.

They were quiet then, the only sound the hum of the cell phones.

Cole broke the silence with a low laugh. "Interesting twenty-four hours. Getting laid by the hottest woman I've ever met after weeks of the world's worst case of blue balls. Barfing on the side of 495. And now finally telling you how I feel...and hearing it from you. This is the best stomach virus I've ever had. If we get strep, maybe I'll even finally get in your ass."

This time Tiercy laughed loudly. He loved how he could make her laugh, even when the emotions got really big.

"Mama—" Cole heard Jemma's sleepy voice in the background. The laughter must have awakened her. And then there was Tiercy's muffled response.

"Hey, baby. Mama's going to take you up to bed. Let me just say goodnight to Cole."

"I wanna say g'night to Coley," Cole heard the sweet, sleepy little voice say. There was a rustle of the phone being passed.

"G'night, Coley," Jemma whispered loudly into the phone. "Don't let the bed bugs bite."

"Good night, Buttercup. Sweet dreams."

"Love you, Coley."

Cole felt his heart catch in his throat. "I love you, too, Jemma Buttercup."

A rustle of the phone again, and Tiercy's voice. "Good night, Cole," she breathed quietly into the phone.

"Good night, my love."

Two declarations of love from two Somerville women in one night. It really was the best stomach virus ever.

CHAPTER THIRTY-THREE

"It is not time or opportunity that is to determine intimacy; it is disposition alone.
Seven years would be insufficient to make some people acquainted with each other,
and seven days are more than enough for others."
Sense and Sensibility, Jane Austen

TIERCY

Ask any teacher, and they will tell you the end of the school year has a kind of magic. It goes beyond the simple relief of summer vacation in grasping distance—and just about everyone at County High was grasping for summer vacation. There's also a tremendous sense of accomplishment—milestones achieved, lessons taught and learned, students growing academically, physically, and emotionally.

At the high school level, Tiercy always felt it was even more powerful. Watching seniors getting ready to fly out of an environment grown too small for their new wings brought a bittersweet sense of pride. Juniors were ready to rise to the top, rule the school, and build their own launchpad for the following year. Sophomores, whose metamorphosis from underclass students to upperclass students, with an emerging maturity, was fascinating to observe. And freshmen looked forward to taking the leap from newbies to seasoned high schoolers. The energy to the end of the year created a current all its own—the hallways were louder, the smiles brighter, and the achievements more satisfying.

One of Tiercy's favorite days was the annual Awards Assembly. Every year, the entire student body would gather to recognize and honor academic, athletic, community, and other achievements. The principal at County went out of her way to make it fun, inclusive, and validating. There were surprise awards and ones that warmed everyone's hearts. Tiercy looked forward to it the way many of her students counted down the days for prom or homecoming or big games.

As the teachers processed in, the students would stand and clap and cheer, calling out the names of teachers and high-fiving. Tiercy sat with her colleagues in the English department, reflecting on just how fortunate she was to be part of such a great team. She'd been at the school seven years and couldn't imagine working anywhere else. They had something special at County.

The principal ran a smooth assembly, moving it along at just the right pace, building to the top awards. Toward the end, they did funny teacher awards. "Most Likely to be Running Late for Class," "Most Stylish Teacher," "Teacher with the Cheesiest Jokes," and "Caffeine-addict Teacher" were perennial favorites. The capstone awards were the County Character awards, given to five students in each class year who represented role model behaviors. Tiercy clapped heartily along with the full auditorium, even wiping tears away as some favorite students were recognized.

Then came the final award of the assembly: Educator of the Year. This award, along with the County Character awards, required nominations from both students and fellow faculty. The selection was made by a committee of County students and parents from the PTA, with input from teachers from a nearby district high school.

The principal, Dr. Teisha Shields, walked to the front of the auditorium. With a flair for performance that came from a community theater background, she signaled for silence. The room darkened, and the AV team adjusted the lighting, shining a spotlight on the empty stage. The Black-Eyed Peas' 'Gotta Feeling' played in the background as Dr. Shields began reading from the nominations for the winner, pulling her reading glasses from their perch on the top of her closely cropped hair.

"This faculty member received more nominations than any other member of the team this year." The audience clapped appreciatively. "This person was recognized by students for always believing in them, for making learning—and I quote—'actually fun.'" A wave of laughter spread through the room. "The students also noted this teacher's flexibility, focus on fostering love of learning of the subject, and for making quote 'words beautiful.'" Dr. Shields was beaming. "Her colleagues—yes, it's a woman," excited murmuring began to build as the students and parents in attendance speculated, "noted her contagious excitement, her team leadership, her positive attitude in putting her students first, even when she's exhausted, and her creative lesson planning, where she's always pushing to find new ways to teach the classics. A single mom, this educator has been a role model of balance between family and work, infusing passion into her teaching and fostering deep feelings of loyalty, respect, and appreciation among both students and colleagues alike."

Tiercy's cheeks began to burn. Her colleagues were turning to her and smiling, nodding.

"The County High School Educator of the Year is...Ms. Tiercy Somerville!"

The auditorium burst into cheers, with students stomping their feet and hooting approval. The music amped up. Fergie and the Peas were singing about how the night was going to be a good, good night. Tiercy's team lead came over and helped her to stand, throwing her arms around her. "We knew you would win! Hop up there and get your award."

In a haze of shock, and fighting tears of disbelief and joy, Tiercy climbed the stairs to the stage on shaking legs. Dr. Shields greeted her with a massive hug, handed her a gorgeous lead crystal vase on a wooden base, and then left her standing in the spotlight. Between the klieg lights shining in her eyes, and the tears spilling over, Tiercy could barely see.

But she could tell that she was the recipient of a humbling standing ovation. The cheering went on and on, and the senior class president handed her a bouquet of flowers and guided her to the podium.

Tiercy stood for a moment, truly at a loss and beyond overwhelmed. The students began yelling 'Speech!' Tiercy laughed, put down the vase, and wiped her eyes. When she caught her breath, she leaned toward the microphone, set lower for the diminutive principal.

"Oh my gosh, you guys…" she began, and the cheering, which had begun to subside, started again. "Wow…OK. Wow. After all my lessons about the beauty of words, I find that they fail me now." The audience laughed appreciatively. Tiercy fought to collect herself and come up with something intelligent and heartfelt—on the fly. "Samuel Clemens once said, 'I have tried simply to write the best I can. Sometimes I have good luck and write better than I can.' That is how I feel. I have tried simply to be a good teacher and a good teammate, and teach the best I can. I guess I've had some good luck and teach better than I can, especially being here, at the greatest high school, with the most amazing colleagues, and rocking students!" The cheers erupted again. As the room quieted, Tiercy tried to calm her racing heart, taking a deep breath and then continuing. "I will never have the right words to express how much this moment means to me. Instead, I will shamelessly steal from the Bard—hey, you knew I'd get my pal Bill S. in here somewhere—and say, 'I can no other answer make but thanks, and thanks, and ever thanks.'" The audience rose again.

Tiercy picked up the award and flowers, posed for a photo, and walked down the steps of the stage, immediately engulfed in embraces from students and teachers alike. Someone took her vase and flowers, placing them on a nearby table to free her hands. She smiled gratefully, and saw that it was Ross, who was standing there just beaming at her. They hugged tightly. Next to Ross were her mom and dad, who were both crying like the good Irish they were. They embraced Tiercy in a three-way hug. Around her legs, Tiercy felt a fierce squeeze and looked down to see Jemma.

She dropped to her knees and gathered her daughter into her arms. "How did you all know?" She was crying anew, burying her face in her daughter's soft blond curls, which smelled of Johnson's Baby Shampoo and Play-Doh. She was delicious.

"Dr. Shields called us last week when the committee selected you," her mom shared, her dad nodding vigorously, his leonine white hair flopping with the intensity. "We're on your emergency contact card, so she reached out to us, and then swore us to secrecy."

"She's fierce!" her dad added with mock terror.

Tiercy laughed her assent.

"Then we called Ross, because we knew you would want her here," her mom continued.

"I thought you had to go to New York?" Tiercy asked Ross, who winked in reply.

"That's next week. I just fudged the date as a cover story. We didn't want you to suspect. And then we pulled Jemma out of preschool. No way could she miss this!" Ross reached down to tousle Jemma's hair. "I also called Brinder's secretary, but he's not back yet." Ross watched Tiercy's face as she mentioned Brinder, and Tiercy was careful to keep as much of a poker face as possible. "I know he would want to be here."

Tiercy gave her a small, honest smile in return, signaling she was moving toward a place of peace about Brinder. "I'll tell him about it next time I see him."

Jemma chimed in, "Good job, Mommy. But dat present isn't fun," she announced, looking askance at the vase. "Dey should have given you a toy, like Gee Joe!"

Tiercy laughed and stood up, still holding Jemma, whose legs were now wrapped around her waist. "Dat was a lot of clapping. Dey made me hide in the room with the lights so you wouldn't see us. Teddy let me touch the button for the music!" Teddy was the head of student AV services and ran the control booth for the various school productions.

"He did? Well, that was special. I bet you did great!"

"I did. Teddy said I can help him again." Tiercy and Jemma high-fived.

Still reeling from the shock of the honor, and then seeing her parents, Jemma, and Ross, Tiercy shook her head to clear it. "I still can't believe this. And that you're all here to see it happen. I just don't know what to say."

Her mom beamed with pride, tucking her wavy ginger hair behind her ears. "We are so proud of you. I'm sure you have a lot of people to greet. We can wait by the refreshments in the cafeteria, and then we're all going out to dinner tonight to celebrate."

"Chuck E. Cheese!!" Jemma called out, clapping wildly. The adults laughed.

"Not this time, sweet girl," her dad smiled, reaching for Jemma, who clambered into her Gramps's waiting arms. "Somewhere for Mommy this time."

Tiercy rubbed her aching biceps. Between the heavy crystal vase and then carrying Jemma, who was getting to be an armful, her arms felt like she'd just done fifty reps with a twenty-pound weight.

"Oh, there's one more special guest who wanted to be here," Ross announced, standing there looking like the cat that ate the canary.

Without hesitation, Tiercy just *knew*. She could practically feel his presence, the signature of his own unique energy. Her gaze shifted to the back of the auditorium. Standing there, holding the largest bouquet of mixed tropical flowers she'd ever seen, was Cole. He was grinning from ear to ear. For the second time in twenty minutes, Tiercy found herself breathless, as a feeling of warm happiness spread through her. She knew she had a big, goofy smile on her face, but she couldn't help it.

Cole strode down the aisle toward her, never once breaking eye contact. Tiercy wasn't sure if it was his natural authority or curiosity from students and teachers who were watching this unfold, but people shifted out of his way, clearing a path from him to her. In one smooth motion, Cole passed the bouquet to Ross and gathered Tiercy in a crushing embrace, lifting her and spinning her. Perhaps it was the thrill of the award, or the thrill of seeing Cole, or some potent combination of both, but Tiercy buried her face momentarily in his neck, breathing in the gorgeous scent of him.

He whispered in her ear, "That was amazing, Tierce. *You* are amazing." Then he let her down slowly, framed her face with his hands and kissed her, sweetly and then deeper. From the back of the auditorium came friendly catcalls and cheers. Tiercy and Cole broke away, laughing and maybe a little embarrassed, but certainly a lot happy to see each other.

Jemma launched herself at Cole. "Coley!! You came to see me!"

He lifted her expertly, perching her on his arm. "I sure did, Buttercup. And your mom, too. It's a big day for her. Your mommy is awesome!" Keeping Jemma in his arm, Cole wrapped his other arm around Tiercy, and her parents exchanged meaningful looks, one of those conversations that long-married couples can have without talking.

Cole turned to her parents, smiling warmly. He lifted his arm from its perch around Tiercy and held it out, first to Cate and then Neal. "I'm John Colburn, Tiercy's friend. Cole for short. I've heard so much about you both. It's a pleasure."

At the word 'friend,' Ross offered a small snort, causing Tiercy to shoot her a warning glance. Ross just smiled innocently.

Neal returned the introduction first. "Neal Flynn, my wife Cate. Cole, it's very nice to meet you as well. We've heard about you too from Tiercy, and Ross, and a lot from Jemma, so it's nice to meet you in person."

"Nice to meet you, Cole," Cate added. "Tell me, why do they call you 'Cole'? I mean, I know it's short for your last name, but John is a lovely, strong name."

Tiercy fought the urge to roll her eyes at her mother's nosiness. Some things never changed. During Tiercy's teen years, Cate was an inveterate, unapologetic griller when it came to her boyfriends. Her dad, meanwhile, would just stare menacingly if he didn't like the looks of the guy. Thankfully, that didn't seem to be the case here. Her dad was smiling at Cole as he explained the origins of his nickname.

"I have a pretty big family, and there are seven Johns among us. My parents began calling me Cole out of clarity and I maintained it out of self-preservation. It can get confusing."

Her father nodded, white hair flopping across his forehead. "Ah, makes good sense. Jemma tells us you're a master Lego builder."

Cole flashed a smile at the little girl and tickled her under the chin. "Occupational hazard. I'm in construction management by trade, and by genetics. Plus, I spent my childhood...and far longer into adolescence than I'd like to admit...building with Legos," he offered self-deprecatingly. "But Jemma Buttercup here is a champion builder herself. She imprisoned me in a Lego dungeon on Saturday afternoon. I had to bribe my way out."

"And how did you manage that?" asked her dad as he unabashedly sized Cole up.

Tiercy guessed she couldn't blame her father. After all, Cole had literally just swept his daughter off her feet.

"Ice cream," responded Cole sagely and Jemma broke into a grin.

"Tutti-frutti!" she cheered. "Let's get some after Chuck E. Cheese!"

"Jemma-lemma," Ross cut in, "We are not doing Chuck E. Cheese today. In fact, we are going someplace very special—the new restaurant on the water, Starboard."

Her dad let out a low whistle. "How did you manage that? It's one of the hardest reservations in town."

"Turns out that 'Coley'"—Ross gave him a teasing smile—"and his firm built it, so he's kind of a VIP. And we are shamelessly exploiting it to celebrate our Educator of the Year."

Tiercy had been silent, still processing the shock of the afternoon. Once Cole had shaken her parents' hands, he put his arm back around her, gently pulling her against his side, the sheer solidness of him a comfort. She was also watching her parents assessing Cole—and being quite obvious about it at that. She'd told them about him in a cursory way, but kept the details to a minimum. There was a part of her that was afraid her parents would see right through her casual façade and recognize how deep her feelings were for Cole. But Jemma apparently had been her little motormouth self.

While part of her wanted to be annoyed at the scrutiny of Cole, she really couldn't blame her parents. She'd probably do the same in their position. Besides, it was hard to feel anything but glorious as she basked in her unexpected recognition and in the presence of her parents, Jemma, Ross, and Cole. She found that she could not wipe the smile from her face. It had been a long time since she'd felt this happy. Since Before.

In his typically unassuming way, Cole added, "I hope it's OK with you, Mr. Flynn. When Ross called me and told me about Tiercy receiving this award, I was very excited. I made the reservation first, and then checked with Ross second. I'm sorry if I overstepped. We can certainly go somewhere else. And I don't need to be there if you'd prefer just family—"

"Nonsense, and please call us Cate and Neal," her mom interrupted, resting her hand on his forearm. Her eyes flew briefly to Tiercy. Well, it *was* a nicely muscled arm. "The more the merrier to celebrate my talented daughter. Besides, I've been wanting to go there ever since I read the reviews. What time are the reservations?"

"Six p.m. I thought earlier would be better, so Jemma Buttercup isn't up too late." He smiled at Jemma, still perched in his careful hold, her arm hooked around his neck.

Tiercy watched her mother telegraph something to her dad and rolled her eyes.

"Come over here, young man," her dad boomed. "Let's you, Jemma, and me take a closer look at this fancy-dancy award and let my wife catch up with my baby girl a minute."

"Smooth," Ross snickered, sotto voice, as her dad led them away.

Once they were out of earshot, her mom turned to face her, eyes alight.

"Well," she drew out. "Well, well, well."

"Spit it out, Mother." Tiercy rolled her eyes again, catching Ross's eye. She was clearly enjoying herself.

"Oooo, you 'Mother'ed me. Now I'm in for it," her mom teased.

"I know you have something to say, and I suspect it's about Cole, so hurry it up because I have a few people to chat with."

"I just wanted to say that it's been a long time since I've seen you look so...happy. Cole arrived a bit late and was standing in the back of the auditorium to the side. When Ross pointed him out to us, while we hid in the control booth that smelled a lot like weed, I might add—"

Tiercy snorted. Her parents had never hidden from her that they partook on occasion.

"—I had a perfect vantage point to observe him closely."

"And so you did," Tiercy added dryly.

"Of course I did." Her mom winked. "You barely talk about him, but Jemma is an excellent spy for us."

"I'll keep that in mind."

Her mom continued, ignoring Tiercy's fond snark. "And based on the look on his face as you went up to receive your award, I'd say this John Colburn Cole has strong feelings for my precious daughter. Lord, I felt like I was in a tennis match during the announcement—torn between watching you and watching Cole watch you. The look on Cole's face could only be described as... besotted." Her mother cleared her throat from the obvious tears that were clogging it.

Tiercy was saved from responding by the loud reemergence of her dad, Cole, and Jemma into the small circle she'd made with her mom and Ross.

"Well, that's quite an award. Quite an award."

Third eye roll. Tiercy's dad would not be receiving any acting awards any time soon.

"Indeed," her mother replied. "So, six o'clock, you say, Cole?"

Her mother wouldn't win any either.

And Ross...she was clearly eating it all up, looking on with unfettered glee.

"Yes, ma'am," Cole replied, taking her hand again.

"Well, that's perfect. It gives Tiercy time to greet her adoring multitudes, who have been waiting not-so-patiently to talk to her." Her mom motioned to the group of faculty and students gathered nearby. "And then we have about an hour to get home and freshen up, and then get downtown."

Her dad added, "Why don't Cate and I drive together, and you four can work out your plans."

Clearly not wanting to be a third wheel, Ross offered an obvious white lie. "I'll meet you all there. I have a couple errands I need to run, and I don't want to hold anyone up. But I promise I'll be there by six."

Cole turned to Tiercy and smiled. "That leaves you, Jemma, and me. I'm happy to drive. How about if I follow you home? Then we can move Jemma's booster seat into the back row of the truck. Sound good?" Jemma clapped with glee at the idea of riding in Coley's truck again.

Tiercy felt as though someone had turned on an electric blanket inside her body, as heat spread through her. Fergie was right. Tonight was going to be a good night.

"Sounds perfect."

CHAPTER THIRTY-FOUR

*"I cannot fix on the hour, or the spot, or the look or the words,
which laid the foundation. It is too long ago. I was in the middle
before I knew that I had begun."*
Pride and Prejudice, Jane Austen

TIERCY

Squinting shouldn't be hot, right? Of the many sexy faces a man could produce, intentionally or not, squinting would not be tops on Tiercy's swoony list. And, yet, as Cole squinted behind his Aviators against the glare of the sun off the car in front of them on the DC beltway, Tiercy nibbled her lower lip, her ovaries trilling in harmony as she shamelessly checked him out.

Tiercy shifted a bit more toward him in the passenger seat of his truck, enjoying the look of his profile and the play of muscles on his forearm, which rested on the steering wheel. Tiercy marveled, astonished by the jolts of desire Cole could elicit in her with actions as ordinary as driving, squinting...and, let's face it, breathing.

The fact was, she had it bad for John Sims Colburn. But beyond the intense physical attraction, a deep connection had emerged, stunning her even more than her own physical wanting of him. Emerged was the right word. Not developed. Because, honestly, it felt as if it had always been there, only waiting to be known. As she'd done a billion times in the last week, she relived their incredible night together—even if it had been interrupted by a poorly timed stomach bug—and the ensuing revelations about the depth of their feelings. He was in love with her. And, despite her deep worries about her inability to give him what he clearly wanted, she was in love with him.

Live in the moment, she kept telling herself. *You don't have to figure it all out at once.* But love and guilt and worry commingled inside her, coiling confusing tentacles around her heart to such an extent that she had done the only thing possible—she compartmentalized, as she'd done with Luke's passing, and focused on Cole and only Cole when she was with him.

Well, as much as she could. Because Luke was always with her. Even if it felt like his presence within her was fading as much as an early morning fog gives way to sunshine.

"Nickel for your thoughts." Cole's deep voice rose gently over the hum of the road and Jack Johnson on the radio.

"Hmmm...inflation," smiled Tiercy.

Cole grinned back at her, but his eyes telegraphed worry. "You were far away, Tierce. Where were you?"

"Just...thinking."

"Hopefully not about how much you don't want to do this." Cole smiled again, but there was apprehension behind it. And sadness?

Tiercy was tempted to unhook her seat belt, lean over, and kiss the crinkle she could reach at the corner of his right eye. *Seriously, how could a squint crinkle be so freaking sexy?* Thoughts of the winding curves and kamikaze drivers of the DC beltway convinced her to stay buckled. Instead, she reached over and smoothed the back of his hair, which was still damp from his pre-date ablutions.

"Hardly. I've been looking forward to this all week. I finally get to meet the Colburn Clan. Although I'll admit the idea of it is slightly terrifying." Tiercy gave a mock shiver that she hoped didn't give away her true case of nerves.

She'd also compartmentalized those jitters, which made themselves known about zero-point-six-eight seconds after Cole's midweek invitation to a cookout at his dad's home. But now they were bubbling up in force.

"I'll protect you. Especially from Margot." Cole snickered. "No *Sound of Music*, I promise."

He glanced over quickly, and they shared a grin. *More eye crinkles. Gah.* She could not go into this Colburn family gathering all kinds of turned on and emanating fuck-me vibes, which she knew was happening based on the follow-up heated glance Cole zapped her way.

No sexy thoughts, Tiercy Niamh. Compartmentalize! Subject change!

"Jemma has been talking nonstop about it." Yep, Jemma was always a most excellent distraction, even thoroughly in the land of Nod, as she was at this moment.

Cole glanced at the sleeping preschooler in his rearview mirror. She had belted Niamh in next to her, opened a book, and then proceeded to fall asleep within the first ten minutes of the drive.

Tiercy looked over her shoulder to where her daughter was emitting endearing, soft child snores. "Soporous."

Cole flashed her another glance, this one with a half smile. "Outstanding SAT word. Ross would be proud. Context clues tell me this would be a highfalutin way to say 'asleep.'"

"Correct." Tiercy nodded her approval, enjoying his banter.

"Impressive," he intoned. "Suffice it to say, she's zonked. I'm honestly surprised she's sleeping. I thought the sugar rush from cake and ice cream would keep her awake for a week."

"She ran her little legs off at that birthday party this morning. I hope she's not a monster for your family."

Tiercy cringed internally at the thought. It was nerve-wracking enough to meet your boyfriend's huge family. *Hey there. Here's Cole's girlfriend who's a widow. And here's her cranky, growly four-year-old newly awakened from a sugar-crash sleep coma. Such a catch.* What a first impression. Tiercy sighed.

"*What* are you thinking?" Cole asked, quirking an eyebrow curiously. "That's the second time you disappeared into deep thought."

Tiercy started to lie, but then gave up and admitted her thoughts. "I'm not exactly a marquis girlfriend. I mean, your family is clearly close, and I know they think you hang the moon—don't deny it!" She pointed a finger at him. "And now you're bringing home some widow with a cranky kid, when you could have anyone you want." Tiercy's eyes filled with tears and she quickly turned to the window, dashing at them with the heel of her hand.

Cole turned off the cello concerto that had been playing quietly in the background, and reached toward her, resting his hand on her left leg. He stroked her softly with his thumb, just above the knee.

"Tierce. Beautiful. You are being very unfair to yourself. And to Jemma. I'm captivated by you—everything about you. You are so much more than just 'some widow.' We all have baggage. I'm just 'some thirtysomething dude who's always been a bit of a commitment-phobe' if you want to be plain about it. But I know better. And so do you. And as for my Jemma Buttercup, please don't worry about her. She is amazing. And if she happens to be cranky, she'll likely be in good company with my ten nieces and nephews. Trust me. The Colburn family is quite familiar with cranky kids. Any gathering of all the cousins is a special breed of Colburn Chaos."

Cole gave her knee an affectionate squeeze, and then subtly stroked a bit higher on the inside of her thigh, reigniting her compartmentalized lust for this incredible man.

"Marquis girlfriend?" He laughed. "Tiercy, you are mucho marquis. As for me being able to have anyone I want, I don't know about that. What I do know is that I want you...very much."

"You're giving me goosebumps doing that *thing* with your thumb on my leg."

"What thing? This thing?" Cole asked innocently, a wicked smile gleaming, and intensifying his efforts.

"Cole—" Tiercy laughed, stilling his hand with her own. "Down boy. This is hardly the time or the place for foreplay."

"I'm trying hard to get in your pants again."

"Clearly." The look on his face, and (she couldn't help but glance down) the growing bulge in his shorts, left no confusion that Cole definitely wished it were the time and the place. "Let's see if I make it through this family shindig and then we'll see about my pants. Deal?"

"Deal." He slid his thumb meaningfully along her knee one more time, and then dramatically placed his hand firmly on the wheel. Tiercy didn't miss the way he subtly stroked the leather with his thumb. *Brat.*

As Cole's truck pulled into the driveway of the large Victorian house, Tiercy's eyes widened. Milling around the generous wraparound porch and the front yard were what had to be at least twenty people. And they were all looking in the direction of the driveway.

Cole's family.

They were clearly waiting for them to arrive. It reminded Tiercy of the way the servants lined up outside of Downton Abbey. A small, nervous giggle escaped her lips as Cole quirked an eyebrow at her.

"What?" he asked, smiling.

Before she could respond, Jemma—her body sensing the stilling of the vehicle—startled awake. "Are we here?" she exclaimed, grabbing to undo her seatbelt from the booster seat.

As Cole came around to open the door for Tiercy, she marveled at her daughter's ability to go from sound asleep to wired in a nanosecond. When he reached to open Jemma's door, the little girl catapulted out of the truck.

"Helloooo! Hello, Coley's family!" Jemma sang, practically hopping up and down.

Tiercy could hear a wave of appreciative laughter, and instantly relaxed. She smoothed her white denim shorts and her navy halter top. Everyone was dressed casually for the backyard barbecue. At first, Tiercy was worried she'd underdressed. But Cole, dressed in athletic shorts and a black Under Armour tee, assured her it was going to be a very low-key gathering.

He reached for her hand, guiding her toward the wide front porch stairs. A distinguished older man was walking toward them, greeting them at the top. He had the look of Cole. His father, no doubt.

"Hello. I'm Jake Colburn. You must be Tiercy. Welcome."

Cole had told her that Jake was in his late sixties, but Tiercy thought he looked a decade younger. His hair was mostly silver, but his face was youthful and smiling. Tiercy noted that his eyes crinkled in the corner, like Cole's did, and she found herself immediately comfortable with him, his warm hand encircling hers.

"Very nice to meet you, Mr. Colburn. Thank you for inviting us to your beautiful home."

"Call me Jake, please."

"Hello, Mr. Colburn. I'm Jemma," came her daughter's young but personable voice. "Nice to meet you. I can't call you Jake or I'll get in trouble, OK?" Jemma had reached the top of the stairs right after Tiercy, and placed her hand confidently in the older man's.

"Oh, I'm so sorry—" Tiercy felt her cheeks burn and started to correct her precocious daughter's manners.

But Jake merely threw his head back and laughed, an echo of a gesture she'd also seen in Cole. "Yes, it's very nice to meet you too, Jemma. How about you call me Mr. Jake?" Jemma grinned at him in assent. "Everybody," he called, "This is Jemma. Kids, introduce yourselves and show her where the swing set and treehouse are." Then he turned to Jemma and whispered, "We have some buttercups by the field. Maybe you can show the cousins how you earned your nickname?"

Tiercy allowed a relieved sigh to escape. The apple hadn't fallen far from the tree. Jake was as charming and down to earth as his son.

Jemma cast a questioning look at her mother, and, receiving the nod of approval, took off for a group of children, ponytails bouncing.

Jake turned to his son, folding him into an embrace. Tiercy's heart warmed even more. It was a good sign to see a father and son hug. Still smiling, Jake asked Tiercy, "Are you ready to run the Colburn gauntlet?"

Tiercy laughed. "I hope so!"

She and Cole made their way through the siblings, their spouses, and a gaggle of nieces and nephews. There was Brian, Cole's older brother. He was shorter than both Cole and Jake, although still about six feet. With his salt-and-pepper hair, wire-rim glasses, and Congressional

Country Club golf shirt, he had a manner that conveyed a man of means and comfort. Tiercy remembered he wasn't a part of the family business, instead working as the CFO of a large technology company. She tried to remember what his company did exactly but came up frustratingly blank. Brian shook her hand firmly, but without the warmth of his father.

His wife, Sharon, appeared to be the classic country club wife, with blonde bobbed hair and tennis-toned arms and legs. Tiercy's first impression was quickly revised when Sharon grabbed her into a quick but kind embrace, whispering in her ear, "We have been so eager to meet you. Cole never brings *anyone* home."

Sharon blushed at her overshare of Cole's dating habits, and pushed her hair behind her ear, revealing very large diamond studs. "Don't let us overwhelm you. We're harmless. Even Mr. Distracted here," she motioned affectionately to her husband, who had already turned to his iPhone. "I'm sorry. He has a big work deal going on, so he is unusually preoccupied." Brian, as if by way of apology, looked up from his phone and offered a small but genuine smile.

"And those are our children. Johnny is twelve, Martin is ten, and Gussie is seven," she added, motioning to three nearby boys, the oldest of whom was climbing on an elaborate side porch railing. "Get off there! You're going to break your necks, or worse, Granddad's railing," she called and then shook her head. "Boys."

Tiercy laughed and smiled sympathetically, warily noting that Jemma herself was eyeing those railings covetously.

"I thought Granddad told you to go find the treehouse. Vamoose," Sharon shooed, laughing.

Next was Margot, who was in a rocker, nursing a baby. Once again, Tiercy consulted the mental dossier she'd quickly compiled and memorized, haranguing Cole for details so she'd at least have a fighting chance at keeping her head above water. Luke had been from a large family, too. Tiercy had to apply all her hard-earned tricks to survive in that kind of whirlwind. The youngest was a "bonus baby" who surprised Margot and her husband, Max, after two sets of in vitro twins. The oldest twins were ten, and the next set was seven. Tiercy's mind blanked. She couldn't remember any of the names. Fuck. She'd have to run into the bathroom at some point and consult her Notes app on her phone.

"I'm Margot," the woman smiled kindly. "I'd get up, but…" she motioned to the baby nursing contentedly.

"I completely understand. Congratulations, by the way."

"I just hope she's way more chill than her siblings. And cousins." Sounds of laughter and good-natured yelling from the backyard traveled. "Sorry for the corruption of your daughter that's about to happen."

Cole leaned down and kissed his sister's cheek, softly rubbing the baby's head. Tiercy melted a bit more. Then he turned and bear-hugged a man so huge—he had to be six-foot-seven—he made Cole look small. "This is Max, Margot's husband."

Tiercy's eyes goggled. He was like a giant bear. He had the biggest hands she'd ever seen. He wasn't overweight, but the sheer size of him made her think of an NFL linebacker.

Max embraced Tiercy in a hug as big as the one he'd given Cole. "Tiercy, we finally get to meet you!" he exclaimed, with just the slightest hint of a Russian accent. "You are far too beautiful to be with this ugly lug. Is it a mercy date?"

"Da, comrade." Cole jokingly punched at Max's massive arm. "Max and my sister met at Harvard in grad school. Max is a big-time sports agent."

"Big maybe." He held out paw-like hands. "But not big time."

"Would I know any of your clients?"

"Depends on how much you like sports." He winked.

"A good amount. Not as much as my bestie, but enough."

"I have the good fortune of representing several hockey players and a good number of baseball. I specialize in retired athletes, but I have an active roster as well."

"Ross, that's my bestie, is good friends with a retired third-baseman. Gideon O'Grady?"

Max let out a bellowing laugh, which startled the baby and earned him a good-natured glare from Margot, who smoothly resettled the little girl.

Could a laugh have an accent? Tiercy was fascinated by the big man.

"Gid! Yes, he's a client. What a small world. I'll have to send him a message."

Tiercy grinned and caught Cole's eye. He winked, beaming at her. So far so good.

"Max and Margot have two sets of twins, in addition to this little beauty. The older ones are Eli and Trish, and then they have Alex and Irina."

"That's right," Tiercy smiled, picturing her notes. "You named one set of twins so he named your younger ones."

"And Cole helped with this nugget, since we were all out of names we could agree on at this point. Or we were just too tired to think of anything." Margot shrugged with a smile and Max bellowed out another —this time softer—laugh.

Tiercy turned to Cole, cocking her head and glaring in mock accusation. "You didn't tell me that!"

He held up his hands good-naturedly. "I have so many nieces and nephews, I just forgot," he laughed.

"Liar." Max shoved into Cole. If Cole were any smaller or less muscular, he probably would've been propelled off the porch by the innocent force of his brother-in-law.

"Sorry, beautiful. I dropped the ball on your dossier."

Tiercy, thankfully, was saved from the embarrassment of explaining.

"I'm LaTonya, but you can call me Lattie," came a voice from behind her. Tiercy turned to face a stunning Black woman, long braids cascading down her slim shoulders. She was easily six feet tall. Tiercy was accustomed to often being one of the tallest in the room, but this was a family of giants. So far only Sharon was under five-feet-five. "I'm Lara's wife and Cole's favorite sister-in-law."

"Hey!" Sharon shouted from the edge of the porch, where she was clearly headed to put eyeballs on the rambunctious brood in the backyard. "It's a tie!"

"Yes, completely," LaTonya called back over her shoulder, and then turned and whispered, "Not really" with a wink.

"I heard that. I have mother hearing," Sharon laughed, turning the corner.

Tiercy knew she should have felt overwhelmed and overstimulated, but she was loving every minute of this loud, large family.

Lattie enveloped Cole in a big hug, not as impressively consuming as Max's, but just as genuinely affectionate.

Was there not a family pariah? Didn't every big family have one? Good God. Please don't let me be the pariah.

Tiercy was saved from her catastrophizing by Lattie pulling her into a hug. It wasn't as big as the one she gave Cole, but still affectionate. "Lara is in the house. One of the girls managed to lock herself in the first-floor bathroom. Clearly the Colburn genetic material." Lattie added the last part sotto voice to Tiercy. "Go find her. She's dying to see you, *Coley*"—Lattie nudged Cole at the nickname—"and meet *you*," she added, winking at Tiercy.

Her head slightly spinning with that lightning round of introductions, Tiercy allowed Cole to navigate her into the house toward an expansive, sunny, great room. "This is gorgeous, Cole," Tiercy breathed. "It's both cozy and open at the same time. What a fabulous space." She examined the room with an appreciation that came from years of trailing her real estate agent parents to various homes. She motioned to a mirror made from a rustic wooden window frame. "Lovely. All of it."

"Thanks," Cole smiled softly. "It was my mom's handiwork. She loved it here. When they stumbled on this house in the late seventies, it was a mess. They bought it 'as is' and it became a labor of love for her. I can't walk in here and not feel her. It's been three years since she passed, and yet every time I come here, it's like I expect her to walk around the corner." Cole's eyes were wet as he scanned the room.

"I know," Tiercy whispered, her own throat tight with tears. "I know how that feels."

CHAPTER THIRTY-FIVE

TIERCY

Cole instantly turned toward her. "Of course you do. I'm sorry. That was insensitive of me. Sometimes I forget that you haven't always been mine. That you had an entire life before me."

He held out his arms and pulled her close, resting his lips on the top of her head. "My mom would have adored you. And if you want to know what she looked like and acted like, just wait until you meet Lara. She is my mom's clone, in every great way...and some of the annoying ones, too."

Tiercy tipped her chin up. "I know I would have adored her too...because she made you."

As she kissed him, Cole reached around and played with her hair. Feeling the brush of her ponytail on her bare back sent a spark of longing through her, and she nudged closer to Cole, reveling in the solidness of him and deepening the kiss.

"Ahem. A-HEM."

Cole and Tiercy startled apart like teens caught making out on the couch. Then Cole laughed. "Caught in the act."

Tiercy's cheeks were flaming red as the woman crossed the room to them. No doubt—this was Lara. While she physically looked nothing like Cole, she had the same pale blue-gray eyes, the same self-assured walk, and the same knowing cock to her head. But where he was dark, she was blonde. Where he was tall, she was positively petite—maybe five feet-three inches, and if she were one hundred-twenty pounds soaking wet, Tiercy would be shocked.

For a moment, her mind marveled at the idea of Lattie and Lara together. They were physical opposites, and yet each exuded such similar warmth. Tiercy found herself instantly liking Lara, as she had Lattie.

Cole wrapped an arm around Lara in a brotherly hug-slash-headlock. "Hey there, Sis. How long have you been standing there?"

She wriggled away, pinching the inside of his arm and making him yelp. "Long enough to tell you it might be a good idea to take it down a notch or it will be just like you and Jenny Douglass in the tenth grade."

Lara grinned impishly at her older brother. They seemed to slide into easy, practiced banter. Tiercy imagined that's what working side by side in the family business for years, and with only thirteen months separating them, would do.

"We wouldn't have been busted if *someone* hadn't ratted me out to Mom and gotten me grounded for a month."

"And *you* weren't supposed to have your girlfriends in the house. Besides, she was a skanky ho. That needed to end."

Lara smiled in the same blindingly stunning way Cole did. The wattage was enough to light the room. Tiercy imagined Lattie was as gobsmacked at first sight of Lara as she was with Cole.

Cole's younger sister turned her warm gray eyes to Tiercy. "Hello, Tiercy Somerville. Welcome to Crazy Town." Tiercy found herself being drawn into yet another hug. "Get ready for six thousand questions by the family. We are insanely curious about you, and merciless."

"Be nice, Lara," Cole said warningly, and pulled Tiercy to his side. "Don't worry, Tierce. Remember. I promised to protect you from them."

"Where is your daughter? Jemma, right?"

Tiercy looked through the large floor-to-ceiling window to the backyard. "Yes, Jemma. That's her, hanging upside down on the monkey bars with...oh shoot. I don't remember his name."

"Eli. One of Margot's twins," Cole supplied the elusive name.

"We should wear name badges for Tiercy," added Lara.

"No, no. I'll be fine. I'm a teacher. We need to learn a lot of names very quickly each September. I'm a pro at this. And where are your daughters? Lizzie and Sasha, right? Your oldest is named after your mom, right?"

"Good job." Lara smiled approvingly. "Sometimes I can't even remember everyone's names, and I have the misfortune of being related to these people."

She glanced toward the other room. "I freed Sasha from the bathroom. She ran in there to escape one of her cousins, who was chasing her with a frog. The lock is wonky and it got stuck. I expect she's back outside to inflict revenge. Lizzie is probably with Margot and the baby, Juliana. She is absolutely obsessed with her baby cousin."

Cole's sister cast a furtive glance around the room and lowered her voice. "Listen, I need to tell you something. Tiercy and Jemma aren't the only special guests here today. Dad brought Caro. She's in the kitchen right now, prepping the appetizers."

Tiercy saw something flicker across Cole's face—sorrow? hurt?— and then disappear just as fast. He sighed. "I figured she would be here. I mean, they are getting ready to take a cruise together. I guess the jig's up. He's serious about her."

"Cole, you know it's a good thing for him. He needs to have fun."

"I know. I'm happy for Dad. And I like Caroline a lot. She's lovely. It just feels wrong seeing Dad here with another woman."

Tiercy gently squeezed Cole's hand, a gentle press of unspoken support, and he returned the squeeze, offering a small but genuine smile.

Lara, clearly not one for mincing words, seized the moment. "And is the jig up here, too? Are you two serious? Is this the real deal? Will we be seeing something sparkly soon on Tiercy's left hand?" Lara's tone was joking, but Tiercy saw in Lara's eyes the same scanning consideration she often saw in Cole's when he was sizing up a situation and preparing to cast judgment.

"Yes. Yes, we are serious and yes, it is the real deal."

The brevity and surety of Cole's response to Lara stunned Tiercy into silence. Their private 'I love yous' made her stomach flip-flop with joy. She was absolutely in love with him. He filled her waking thoughts, and the sleeping ones too. But hearing Cole say it aloud to his sister like that was shocking to her, and forced her to consider something she hadn't been prepared to face. At the thought of an engagement ring, she unconsciously ran her thumb across the base of her left ring finger, almost expecting to feel Luke's ring.

Suddenly Luke's face flashed before her and it felt like a dagger in her heart. Tiercy closed her eyes for a moment and tried to conjure Luke's face again, to assure herself that she was still his, and he hers, forever.

When she couldn't see his face—couldn't make it reappear—Tiercy was stricken with the dangerous pull of grief and guilt.

Cole looked at her with concern. "Are you OK, Tiercy?"

"Yes," she quickly replied, putting on what she hoped was a bright smile. "I'm fine."

"You sure?" Tiercy could hear the concern under the question.

"Really. I'm fine. But I'd love a glass of whatever Sharon was having."

Tiercy was sure she saw Lara frown ever so quickly, before replacing it with a hearty smile. "Rum punch," Lara supplied. "Summertime Colburn house special."

Just then, two children came flying into the room—nephew Gussie (Tiercy remembered his name!) and who had to be Lizzie or Sasha. "Mom! Uncle Cole! Tell Gus to *stop*!! He is trying to put a *frog* down *my shirt*. Make him *stop.*" A miniature version of Lara stood before them, emphasizing her speech with the drama of a nine-year-old girl. "He is a *disgusting brat.*"

Cole reached out and put a warning hand on the back of Gussie's neck. His voice was hard but held an undertone of warmth. "Augustus Colburn, you leave your cousin alone now or I will personally ensure you eat that frog, alive, for your dinner, instead of a hamburger. You hear me?"

Gussie's neck turned pink with embarrassment. "Yes."

"Yes what?" Cole responded.

"Yes, sir."

"Good. Now apologize to Lizzie."

"Mmmmssorrry..." Gussie mumbled.

"Excuse me?" Cole probed. "I didn't hear you."

"I'msorryandIwon'tdoitagain," Gussie rushed, and then hurried out of the room.

"I *accept* your *apology*," Lizzie called out after him with the superiority of an older cousin. "Thank you, Uncle Cole." She tiptoed to kiss her uncle's cheek and then turned to Tiercy. "Hi there. Nice to meet you. OK, bye," she said quickly, with the barest touch of politeness, and then stalked off.

Lara shook her head. "And she's barely a preteen. She may not make it. Sorry about that. Sasha is seven. She is a much easier child than her older sister. Mostly."

"No worries. Unfortunately, Jemma can act in a similar way, and she's only four—going on fourteen." The women exchanged the knowing smiles of mothers of spirited daughters.

"OK. Now I'm off to the kitchen to help Caro, our dad's *girlfriend*." She emphasized the last word and shot Cole a warning look. "You can help too, brother."

"Please, let me help," Tiercy offered. "Have to earn my meal today."

"You don't have to earn anything, but company is always welcome. I am way more comfortable in the boardroom," Lara nodded toward the kitchen. "We'll drink while we prep. It's the only thing that makes setting up—and let's face it, cleaning up—palatable."

Tiercy returned Lara's smile as she took Cole's proffered arm and headed toward the kitchen, trying to ignore the small frown she'd seen flicker across Lara's face reflected in the windowpane mirror as they walked by.

CHAPTER THIRTY-SIX

"One half of me is yours, the other half yours—Mine own, I
would say. But if mine, then yours, And so all yours."
The Merchant of Venice, William Shakespeare

TIERCY

The afternoon passed in the blur of copious food, jesting, and general din that is often the signature of large family gatherings. Tiercy met Caroline, whom everyone but Cole seemed to call Caro, and struggled with mixed emotions. Caro was lovely, but clearly Cole struggled to see his father with another woman. Loyalty to Cole and compassion for Caro, who had privately confided to her that she longed to break the ice with Cole, warred within Tiercy.

Eventually, Tiercy nestled in an Adirondack chair on the back lawn with a rum punch, recognizing in herself that wonderful feeling of fitting in. The adults were engaged in various activities and Cole, who had been next to her watching and occasionally refereeing the kids, had left in a hurry to help his father fix something in the house. Enjoying the moment of solitude, she watched Jemma play with the Colburn grandchildren and realized that her daughter was experiencing the joy of cousins—even if just vicariously. Two of Luke's three siblings had children, but they were much older and lived far away. For the millionth time, Tiercy reflected on the belief that she didn't want Jemma to grow up an only, lonely child.

"May I join you?" Lara's question broke her reverie.

"Of course." Tiercy smiled up at Lara, flashing briefly to the frown she'd seen earlier. She'd hoped it wasn't about her. Maybe Lara had been preoccupied with something else. But Tiercy couldn't quite shake the gnawing in the pit of her stomach that she'd done something wrong.

The women chatted quietly about this and that in the way of playground parents passing time and enjoying that their children are entertained and—thank God—expending some energy.

"So, Jemma calls Cole 'Coley'?" Lara commented with an amused smile.

"Yes. I have to admit I cringed when it first came out. I mean, here I am on what is still one of our first few dates, and my daughter calls your macho man brother Coley." Tiercy rolled her eyes in embarrassed recollection.

"How did he react?" Lara raised one eyebrow in curiosity.

"He took it in stride. He's never actually said anything to me about it, but I think he kind of likes it. It's their 'thing,' you know? Something special between them. She calls him that and he calls her 'Buttercup.'"

"He's really taken with her. And with you, Tiercy." Tiercy fought to remain still and maintain eye contact as Lara studied her, not unkindly. "I've truly never seen him like this. He's different. I've never seen him so —*effortless* with someone."

"Really?" Tiercy knew she was blushing and smiled shyly at Lara. "I don't have that kind of context, or point of comparison with him. I just know he's fabulous."

"Yeah. He is—even if he is my annoying older brother," Lara agreed. "And I can see that you are fabulous too, or you wouldn't be here."

The women exchanged smiles and resumed watching the children.

After some time, Lara turned to Tiercy with a frank gaze.

"May I ask you something personal?"

Cole had told her Lara was a straight shooter, but facing it so early in their acquaintance was momentarily shocking. She nodded, then waited. Maybe it was the tone of Lara's voice, but Tiercy found herself bracing.

"What was that earlier? When I first met you and asked if you and Cole were the 'real deal,' you got a strange look on your face."

Tiercy knew it was pointless to be evasive or lie. There was something about Lara's gray gaze that was too close to her brother's. Tiercy had a feeling she'd see right through her, just as Cole had the ability to do.

"It was…just a little…shocking to hear Cole say that to you. You know, about us and our relationship." Tiercy fumbled for words and cursed herself internally for sounding like an idiot.

"You mean he's never said that before?" Lara raised her eyebrows. "Kinda dorky to profess your feelings for your girlfriend for the first time in front of your kid sister. He hasn't been that much of a loser since high school."

Lara clearly joked to ease her discomfort, and yet Tiercy remained unsettled. She knew meeting Cole's family might bring some probing questions, and she'd thought she was prepared. But…nope.

"He—we, well, we *are* serious. And we love each other. A lot. I'm crazy for him, and I know he feels the same. He's amazing with Jemma, and she is so attached to him."

"But…" Lara led.

Tiercy inhaled quickly and let it out, almost a sigh. "Earlier, when he said that to you, it was the first time he and I have publicly acknowledged the nature of our relationship. I mean, I talk about him to my best friend. And he told his friend Xander about us. But the way he said it to you, with me next to him and in your family home, just makes it so much more real."

"You still aren't telling me everything."

Tiercy gave a shaky laugh. "Cole said you are whip smart and perceptive. He said no one is better at reading a room than you."

"Then what did I read? Tiercy, do you not love Cole the way he loves you? When he said that, you were holding back. He was elated and beaming. And you looked like you'd seen a ghost."

"A ghost," Tiercy whispered, gazing off into the distance. "Maybe. Yes." Lara was watching her intently. Tiercy shook her head to clear it. "I do love Cole very much. More than—more than I can even comprehend." She added the last part in a whisper.

She looked toward the yard, watching Jemma so instantly comfortable with the horde of cousins. Just like Luke—neither ever met a stranger. Tiercy herself was an "extroverted introvert," who could turn on peopling skills (required as a teacher), but then usually dealt with a drained 'fun tank' after.

"Cole told you I'm a widow?"

"He did. So did my dad. And Sharon. And Margot. You've been the talk of the family. Even our little sister Poppy called from Italy to gossip about you."

Tiercy cringed at the idea of being discussed, but surely her parents had endlessly discussed Cole after their celebratory dinner.

"She's just like her dad." Tiercy motioned to Jemma. "I look at her and I see him." Tiercy felt her eyes fill with unwelcome tears and dug her fingernails into her palms to stifle them. "Earlier, when Cole was talking, it was like Luke flashed before me. Except I couldn't see him. Couldn't conjure his face. I worry that Cole will overshadow him in my heart, and I can't lose Luke again. I can't. It would break me." She turned away, watching Jemma taking one of the cousins to task for some infraction.

"I've been watching you—" Lara interrupted herself, laughing softly. "Not in a creepy way. Just in the way of a nosy sibling who cares. I can see why Cole loves you. And I know you love him too. That much was clear while I was intentionally eavesdropping on you in the family room." Lara shrugged self-deprecatingly. "Bratty little sister habits die hard."

Tiercy started to respond, but Lara held up her hand. She scanned Tiercy's face with warm eyes. But there was steel behind them. "All kidding aside, I need to say something. I really like you, and I don't want this to come off as bitchy. But I need to say it."

"I really like you too. And I don't think you have bitch in your nature. So go on. Say it."

Lara muttered under her breath, "He's probably gonna kill me...and if he doesn't, Lattie will." She took a deep breath. "I will not have Cole hurt by you. He looks so big and strong, but he has the gentlest heart of all of us. When our mother died, he was devastated. You have never met such a devoted mama's boy, in the best possible way. In addition to being mother and son, they were friends. All of us kids would have been stupid jealous, except my mom was amazing at making each of us feel like her favorite. Anyway, I'm the one who heard him crying in his office late at night when he thought no one was around. He still doesn't know that, by the way."

Tiercy could hear Cole talking with his father on the screened-in back porch, coming closer.

Lara lowered her voice to a whisper. "All I'm saying is this: please do not hurt him. He loves you so much. If you can't love him fully, if you are still hung up on your late husband, you need to let him go. Anything else is cruel."

Cole came up behind them and must have keyed in on the disquiet. "Everything OK, ladies?"

For the second time on her brief visit to Cole's family home, Tiercy put on a bright smile. She could feel Lara's intense eyes still trained on her. "Everything is great. What was wrong in the house?"

Cole grimaced. "Toilet. Turns out a couple of inquisitive grands decided it would be fun to do an experiment—what flushes best: burgers, pie, or cupcakes? They clogged it all up, and we had to snake the plumbing. That was delightful coming back up." Cole made a gagging face, shaking his head.

"Who did it?" Lara asked.

Cole scanned the lawn. "Innocent until proven guilty, but I notice that Eli and his twin Trish have conveniently disappeared. Max is going to hunt them down, and then shake them down." He and Lara grinned at each other, cracking up.

Tiercy couldn't help but join in their laughter, despite fighting against the ache in her heart.

The rest of the evening passed in a blur. Periodically, Lara would offer her a conciliatory smile, which Tiercy would return. From time to time, Tiercy even managed to forget the despair in her heart at Lara's ultimatum and the thought of not having Cole in her life. She was, after all, the queen of compartmentalizing pain—it was how she'd survived the past five years. Her well-honed skill helped, and Tiercy eventually was able to relax and enjoy the fun—despite an undercurrent of sadness she couldn't completely squelch.

After the farewells had been said, Tiercy helped a sleepy Jemma into her booster seat, and then climbed into the truck. As Cole was closing the door, he leaned in and kissed Tiercy gently on the cheek. "I don't know what my sister said to you. But whatever it was, it made you sad. And I *will* find out what she said. You did a good job of not letting it show, but I know your heart, Tiercy Somerville. And your face is glass to me."

Tiercy blinked back tears as he settled in and started the engine, easing the truck into drive. They drove in silence for a bit, Jemma falling asleep in a happily exhausted bookend to their earlier drive.

"I know you were thinking of Luke earlier, Tierce. I just want you to know, it's going to be OK."

Tiercy could hear Lara's voice echoing in her head. Resolutely, she pushed it away, ever the expert at compartmentalizing. "All I'm thinking right now is that I love you, Cole. And I want you to make love to me. We are going to tuck Jemma into bed, and then you are going to—"she checked over her shoulder to be sure her daughter was sound asleep"—fuck me into orgasmic oblivion. But, you know"—she motioned to Jemma—"quietly."

Cole looked over at her, a slow smile spreading across his handsome face.

This time, when she smiled back at him, it was from her heart.

CHAPTER THIRTY-SEVEN

COLE

Leaning back in the overstuffed chair in the corner, Cole stretched out, enjoying the peaceful night and the heartwarming sounds of Tiercy moving around in Jemma's room as she settled her into bed. He reached for his whiskey and took a sip. Based on how the ride here ended, he was pretty sure they were going to end up in bed. And he cared less and less that she hadn't invited him into her bedroom yet. He understood it represented a private place where she'd shared the deepest of intimacies with Luke. It was a frontier he wouldn't cross. Maybe ever.

If he was lucky, perhaps, with time, he could convince her to move them in with him, where he—and she—wouldn't constantly be surrounded by memories of Luke.

He tipped his glass at the picture of Luke on the mantle. For as intensely jealous as he was, he couldn't help but admire the guy. And, yet, he also resented him. Resented the place he held in Tiercy's heart as her professed love of her life. He wanted to have that kind of love from her. Wasn't it possible to have two soulmates? Surely God, with all His everlasting love and all that (which Cole mostly remembered from his all boys Jesuit school) could create capacity in the human heart for two beautiful loves?

He heard the gently creaking stairs first. Then the gorgeous woman who had stolen his heart appeared, a happy, satisfied smile on her face.

Cole knew exactly how that felt. The day had been...everything he'd hoped. Tiercy fit in seamlessly with his family. Watching her with his dad, his siblings, their spouses, and his horde of hooligan nieces and nephews...even Caroline...was like something from a dream. It was like the universe had collected all its special and unique matter and then fused it into the woman who would fill the empty place in his heart.

Later, when she'd held little Juliana, rocking her gently in the early evening breeze, Cole had been seized by a desire he'd never had. He wanted to fill her with his seed, watch her belly grow round with his child, and one day she'd be swaying with their baby.

He knew he was romanticizing. But, hell, he was in love. And Tiercy...she was beyond special. She was his.

His cock had also called dibs. All day, as she'd pranced around in those white shorts, and that sexy halter top he was pretty sure she was wearing without a bra, he'd struggled against the urge to grab her and tug her into one of the upstairs bedrooms. They could be quick. He could bring her to an orgasm, then slide into her and find his own pent-up release. He'd thought about it a few times, wondering if she'd be comfortable leaving Jemma, even for a short bit. Every time he started to make a move, Lara would catch his eye and grin and then pull Tiercy into an Important Conversation.

That fucker. Lara knew him too well. She was an unrepentant cockblocker when they were teenagers, and she still apparently took great joy in instigating his blue balls.

But now they were back at Tiercy's, with no Lara, no loud family, and a tired little girl who was sound asleep when he carried her in. At Tiercy's request, he'd transferred sleeping Jemma Buttercup into her mother's arms. Tiercy had been a little off since he caught her deep in conversation with Lara—this one clearly legit—after he and his father fixed the toilet. He'd asked her a couple times after that if she was OK, if she wanted to talk. Each time, she'd smiled, her beautiful head cocked, and told him she was just fine. And when she grinned at him and told him her intentions involving fucking and orgasmic oblivion...well, perhaps he was just connecting dots to make the wrong picture.

She padded toward him, her bare feet sinking into the beige and white area rug covering most of the hardwoods in this room. He looked down at her pink toes and then traveled up, up those long, toned runner's legs. He wanted to unzip her white shorts with his teeth and devour her.

"What in the heck are you thinking?" Tiercy laughed, sinking into his lap.

Christ, she felt amazing in his arms.

Before he could reply, she wiggled into him and laughed hard. "Ah, I know what you were thinking. The iron pole in your shorts gave you away." She wiggled harder, pressing her delectable ass into him.

"Minx," he chuckled, pressing a kiss behind her ear—a place that never failed to elicit chills on her ivory skin.

She turned her face and captured his lips in a sensual kiss.

"I've been thinking the same thing. I don't have an iron pole, but there is definitely other evidence of my...impure thoughts."

He reached for the button on her shorts. "Let me investigate."

"Not yet." She put her hand on his, halting his progress. Easing off his lap, she stood in front of him, her pupils dilated so much there was just a thin ring of topaz visible around them. "There's something I've been needing to do." Her eyes strayed to his cock, which was tenting the front of his shorts. "Stand up." She licked her lips, telegraphing her intentions.

Fuck. He had been dreaming of her mouth on his cock since the first time he kissed those lush lips.

He stood. "Tierce. My beautiful girl," he rasped, "Are you sure?"

She licked her lips, he thought unconsciously, once again. "Very."

"Then take off your shorts while you do it. And that halter top."

Tiercy's eyes flared with desire. Wordlessly, she eased down her shorts, revealing a tiny, nude lace thong.

Fuckety fuck. He should have jacked off this morning. He was going to blow in twenty seconds.

"Now," he gritted out, "your top." Christ, he was setting himself up to be a two-pump chump.

With a sexy half smile, Tiercy crossed her arms over her body and lifted her top, pulling it off and tossing it on the chair behind him.

Yep. No bra. "Holy fuck, beautiful." He reached for her.

"Uh-uh," she chided, and then drifted down to her knees.

Cole knew even if he lived to be a decrepit old man, he would never forget how Tiercy looked in this moment. Moonlight passed through the shutters, vertical lines playing across her soft, firm breasts, nipples budded in anticipation. Her glorious hair, now released from its ponytail, cascading halfway down her back. Her legs slightly separated. And, fuck, he could smell the intoxicating tang of her arousal.

Without breaking eye contact, a charged gaze linking them in a way that was so resonant of the first night they met, she shifted forward and took his length in her hands. He hissed in appreciation, his cock jumping at the attention. And then...finally...the tip of her tongue, dancing on the head of his cock. Licking. Tasting. Flicking. She trailed her tongue from the base of him to the very tip, stopping at the top to swirl it around his engorged head.

Cole groaned in agony. "Please, beautiful."

Tiercy gave a sexy smile and then...took him into her mouth.

"Fuck," he called out, probably too loud, his eyes rolling back into his head as he repeated the cry on a hoarse whisper. "*Fuck.*"

She began working him, taking him deep and then pulling back with suction so intense he had to recite high school Latin in his head or he'd explode. At the same time, she worked him with her right hand, twisting and pulling with just the right pressure. *Holy fuck. Holy fuck.*

"Tierce," he tried to pull back, but she followed him and redoubled her efforts. "Baby, if you don't stop, I'm going to come in your mouth."

He could see the start of a smile grace her lips, despite the fact that they were gorgeously stretched around his shaft. Then she took a deep breath and brought him to the back of her throat.

It was heaven. He'd died and gone to heaven. Her mouth...her throat. She kept working him. Mouth. Tongue. Hands. Throat. All his senses blurred and he wasn't even sure he could stay upright much longer. He wove his fingers into her hair and she bobbed harder, gripped him tightly, and...God help him, when he thrust further into her throat, they both groaned.

"Baby," he managed. But that was all he could get out because while she was doing something amazing with one hand, she reached between his legs with her other hand and cupped his balls, which were tight against his body. She pressed her finger behind them, brought him back even further into her throat, and swallowed.

It was too much. He tried to pull away, but she swallowed again and tugged...and he exploded. He worked his hips as gently as he could as his release spurted down her throat. How she wasn't gagging was a miracle. He was fully in her throat and still pumping.

Shaking with the intensity, he eased her off his cock, aroused all over again at the sight of it emerging from her puffy lips, a line of spittle mixed with his cum connecting his dick to her lower lip. Tiercy licked it and then swirled her tongue once more around his head. His cock, although as spent and satiated as he was, pulsed. Laughing, he leaned over and pulled her up.

"That was nice," she murmured, laughing against his still-heaving chest.

"I'm not sure there is an adjective created that can describe what I just experienced. But I can tell you 'nice' doesn't do it justice."

He cradled her face in his hands and kissed her deeply. She tasted of rum punch...and him. It was unbearably sexy and he had to taste her where he'd been longing to all day.

"Your turn, beautiful."

"Cole, no. I need you inside me. Now." In the moonlight, Cole could make out the damp spot on her panties. She pressed against him.

"I have to taste you. Hold on." He dropped to his knees and draped one of her legs over his shoulder. She wobbled and then grasped the top of his head for balance. "What part of hold on didn't you understand, beautiful?" He winked.

She swatted him. "You took me by surprise."

"No surprises here. I've been plotting this all day."

"Then get to it," Tiercy murmured and then gasped as he pulled her panties to the side and slid two fingers into her.

He fastened his lips to her clit, which was begging for attention, and sucked. "Ah...fuck!" she cried, rocking her hips.

"Ssssh," he laughed against her. The vibration of it must have done something because she shifted her hips into him. He pumped his fingers, adding a third, and made a shushing sound against her clit.

"Why...why does that feel so good?' she moaned. She rocked her hips again, this time more frenetically. She was drenched.

He eased his hand out and she made a noise of protest. "Hang on, baby." He took his very lubricated index finger and trailed it from her opening to her back entrance.

"Cole," she rasped, working her hips. "Yes..."

With that greenlight, he slid two fingers from his other hand into her warm channel, curling and pressing along that sensitive front wall. As she clenched, choking his fingers, he eased his index finger, which had been patiently waiting for action, into her tight pucker.

"Of...fuck...fuck."

Past one knuckle. Past two. And all the way in. Her hips were flying, rocking back and forth. He worked her, pussy and ass, until she was panting and wildly thrusting. He flicked his tongue rapidly on her clit. She had grabbed onto his head with both hands now, burying his face in her pussy. He could barely breathe, and he loved it. His chin and lips were covered in her juices, and it was decadent.

"Cole. Jesus, fuck. Cole, more." The sounds of her arousal had turned his cock back to iron, the tip weeping and begging for entrance. He needed to finish this and get inside of her. Now.

He slid a third finger into her, pumped in and out of her ass, twisting on the way out, and sucked on her clit. Hard.

"Cole!" she screamed, collapsing forward, breathing hard as she steadied herself with shaking hands on his shoulders.

He looked up and winked. "My little screamer." Cole eased his fingers from her body.

"I didn't," she started to protest.

"Mommy?" A tiny voice called out in the distance.

"Oh shit," Tiercy shot up, eyes darting to the stairs. "I think I woke her."

"You think?" Cole teased. "Does your throat hurt?"

"Actually it do—"

"Do you need to go to her?"

"If we're quiet, she may settle back down"

"Mommy?" Jemma called again, this time louder.

"Or not." With a wry grin and a shrug of her elegant shoulders, Tiercy scurried for her shorts and the top that she'd flung on the chair as Cole reached for his own shorts and slid them up his legs.

"Mommy?" This time more of a plaintive whisper.

"Coming, lovebuggie!"

"Yes, yes we did," Cole chuckled.

"Ass," Tiercy laughed, hustling to the stairs.

"Yes, your ass is quite nice. And if you liked my finger in there, just wait until I bury my—"

"MOMmmmeeeeee!" Jemma hollered, cutting him off.

Tiercy blushed a becoming rose color and sprinted for the stairs. "On my way, Jemma!"

He followed her, watching her ascend the staircase. He thought about going in with her, but didn't want to create any confusion for Jemma.

At the top of the steps, Tiercy stopped and wiggled her bottom. "I can't wait," she whispered, her little taunt sending a fresh surge of blood to his cock.

"I'll just be here," he whispered as she sashayed to her daughter's room, "trying not to come in my pants at that visual."

CHAPTER THIRTY-EIGHT

"I loved her against reason, against promise, against peace, against hope, against happiness, against all discouragement that could be."
Great Expectations, Charles Dickens

COLE

As it was, the evening did not end—ha, no pun intended—as both he, and Tiercy, had wanted...with him inside of her, any way she'd have him.

Once awake, Jemma had fussed, her body overstimulated from too much excitement in one day. Tiercy had tried to calm Jemma to no avail, eventually returning briefly (and apologetically) to the family room to send Cole on his way. Jemma had begged to sleep in the "big bed" with her mommy and wouldn't settle until Tiercy joined her. Cole and Tiercy had kissed goodnight, tenderly, wistfully, and he'd shooed her along back to Jemma Buttercup.

It had been one of the best days of his life, and he was still thinking of it the next day in the office. Colburn Construction held space in a building in Bethesda, about three miles northwest of DC. His grandfather, the eponymous John, for whom many in both his immediate and extended family were named, had established his business in DC, moving it out to the suburbs when they began securing more contracts in Baltimore and needed more space. Today, Cole held one corner office and Lara held another. His semi-retired father, who only came in about once a month, preferring to visit their various construction sites, used an interior office that had been designed for hoteling.

Cole spun his chair to gaze out the window. The sun was blazing in the sky, with temperatures in the high nineties. At some point, the humidity had to give out. In this region, that was usually precipitated by a thunderstorm. They definitely needed the rain.

Sighing, Cole reread his texts from Tiercy this morning. At around midnight last night, his Buttercup had finally settled and slept in until nine, which, according to Tiercy, is the latest she'd ever slept when she wasn't sick. Tiercy told him she'd slept in as well.

Getting home after ten thirty, Cole had sunk into a deep, dreamless sleep. When his iPhone alarm chimed at five a.m., he'd rolled out of bed, a spring in his step. His morning workout had a little extra, adding some more to his "pull" day and hitting his treadmill. By seven thirty he was at his desk, eager to start the day. He had back-to-back meetings, starting at nine and running until at least six, and then he was hoping to swing by and pick up his girls for dinner at a new burger place that had opened near Tiercy.

His girls.

Cole grinned, picturing Tiercy and Jemma snuggled in bed, sleeping in, and then splashing around in Cate and Neal's pool, which Tiercy had texted was how they'd planned to spend their day.

Whistling, he turned back to his computer, determined to put a dent in the emails that had accumulated over the prior week. Heather did a great job sifting through most, but there were still dozens that required his personal attention.

"Someone's in a good mood." Lara stood, propped against the doorway to his office, a shit-eating grin on her face.

"Well, I was...until you came in," Cole teased.

"Har-dee-har-har, funny guy. You know you're happy to see your favorite sister."

"Oh, is Poppy here?"

"Stop!" Lara laughed, closing the door and plopping down in one of the chairs across from his desk. "I swear, Sasha had Lattie and me up at the crack of dawn. She and Lizzie leave for camp on Saturday, and she's been after us nonstop to get her packed. I know it's her first time, but the girl has got to get some chill."

"Hmmm...like her mothers?"

"Shut up," Lara laughed.

Cole waggled his brows. "Empty house for the first time. Or, should I call it a loooove shack?" Christ, it was so easy to slide into his annoying big brother role.

Lara cracked up. "You can call it that. I think first we'll sleep for two straight days. Then maybe I can ravage my wife the way I can't when those mini-cockblockers are around."

"Things I don't need to hear about, Lara," Cole chastised, only half joking. "You still planning to take next week off?"

"Damn skippy."

"Nice." Cole rocked back in his chair. "Now, why don't you tell me why you really came in here."

"What?" Lara replied, eyes wide with innocence. "I can't just come in here and shoot the shit with my brother?"

"Nope." Cole popped the P. "Out with it. Let me guess. This has something to do with my guests at yesterday's barbecue."

"I think guests is downplaying it significantly, no?" Lara arched a brow.

God, in that moment, she looked so much like their mother, Cole's heart stuttered. As Lara got older, she looked more and more like their mother had when they were growing up. It was uncanny. The rest of them favored his dad. But she was all Mom. It both hurt and soothed.

"I love her very much, Lara. I think I made that clear yesterday. And Jemma."

"I know." Lara frowned, the small vertical line between her brows an exact replica of the one their mother used to get when she was worried.

"Spit it out, Mrs. Colburn-Barnes."

Lara sighed "I just—I have reservations."

"Reservations?" Cole's ire rose. "Pray tell, sister." He knew he wasn't going to like this.

"She's wonderful, Cole. Kind. Smart. An amazing mom—"

"I know."

"—and still very hung up on her late husband."

Cole sighed and closed his laptop. Those emails would wait a little longer.

"Lara, you are very perceptive. It's what makes you a formidable business leader. But Tiercy's feelings for Luke aren't exactly breaking news."

"I—"

"Tiercy loved Luke very much. He was, by all accounts, a really good guy who died way too young. But," he held up a finger as Lara started to interrupt again, "she loves me too. It's still relatively early days for us—"

"And you'd slap a ring on her finger so fast Usain Bolt would look like a turtle in comparison." Lara raised her brows.

"Does Lattie mind all your interruptions?"

"She adores me, and all my wonderful imperfections," Lara replied primly.

"There's no accounting for some people's taste, I guess." Cole snickered, and then narrowed his eyes at his sister. "That said, I have no doubt I'm going to spend the rest of my life with Tiercy."

"And that's what I'm worried about." Lara pointed her finger at him.

"Put your finger away, Lara, before I snap it off." Cole rolled his eyes. Outwardly, he might appear calm, but inside? Every ounce of blood was simmering to a boil.

Lara sighed and dropped her head, the offending digit lowered. "Cole, you never jump in. You're never rash. You think everything through. Measure twice, cut once, blah blah. It's what makes *you* a formidable business leader," his sister continued, echoing his earlier comments to her. "But you're moving really fast on this one. And, based on what I observed yesterday, I don't think she's capable of loving you the way you deserve, Cole."

"Dammit," Cole rolled his chair sideways, unable to look at his sister. "That's an unfair assessment of someone you've only met once, and for just a few hours."

"And that was enough. I saw her face, Cole. I saw it. Just the idea of loving you the way she knows you should be loved breaks her heart. I talked with her and she admitted as much."

Cole stood and rounded his desk, yanking over the other chair so he sat close to his sister. He took a calming breath, leveling an accusing glare. "I knew it. I knew you fucked with her mind. She was fine...and then she wasn't. She's a pro at putting on a happy face, but when I came out, I could *feel* her sadness. Fuck, Lara!" He stood again and began pacing the room. "Why would you do that?"

"Because I'm your sister and I love you. Yes, I probably stuck my nose where it didn't belong—"

"Probably?" Cole huffed, incredulous at the balls on his sister. He'd seen her in action at work as she smoothly guided a situation to her desired outcome, and she had absolutely been an annoying, cockblocking tattletale as a teenager, but this was the first time she'd truly inserted herself in his life in a damaging way. "Jesus Christ, Lara. You *hurt* her!"

"No, she just showed me her hurt. I didn't make her feel anything she wasn't already struggling with." Now Lara stood, facing off with him. "Cole, I told her not to hurt you. If she couldn't love you fully, as much as Luke, or more, then she needed to walk away."

"And that wasn't your place!" Cole almost never yelled, and now this was three times in the last five minutes. Heather was probably debating the merits of storming the office to break up the sibling battle.

He calmed his voice as he leaned against his desk to support his shaking legs. Losing his temper would not help. "This is my relationship, not yours. And I will decide—*Tiercy and I* will decide—how that plays out."

"She's going to hurt you, Cole," Lara whispered, eyes penitent. "The kind of love you have for her? It's the kind that makes you feel like you have wings. And that's awesome. But it's also the kind that can shred you. And I'm worried that is exactly what will happen if she decides she can't emotionally handle your love. Or if you decide you don't want a life of fighting for a place in her conflicted heart."

"That'll never happen. I won't walk away from her."

"She still loves Luke, Cole. Deeply." Lara moved next to him, and settled back against his desk, crossing her ankles. Like this, even in her heels, she barely came up to his shoulders. "She may never be able to get past that. Are you OK being number two for the rest of your life?"

Cole opened his mouth, but no words came out.

Lara squeezed him in a side hug, and when he didn't move, she sighed and headed for the door. Turning, with sad eyes that reminded him so much of his mom, she whispered, "Think about it. Mom would want you to have what she and Dad had. You deserve that."

CHAPTER THIRTY-NINE

"What wound did ever heal but by degrees?"
Othello, William Shakespeare

TIERCY

The early day started benignly, as do many days that deliver soul-crushing pain. The gentle morning held no warning sign of what was to come, as Tiercy rose sleepily from bed and stretched. She felt her muscles pop a little. She'd love to get an outside run in, no matter how hot it was.

The forecast was a classic mid-Atlantic summer day—hazy, hot, and humid, with the possibility of a thunderstorm in the afternoon. Jemma had a birthday party that day, a pool party, to be followed by a sleepover, her first one, so Tiercy was a bit apprehensive. But this one was at Marie's, and Jemma was very comfortable at her best friend's house. Just as Tiercy had been at Ross's at almost the same age.

Tiercy looked out the French doors—bright sun already shining. A perfect day for a pool party. Jemma would be thrilled. She'd been practicing so hard at her lessons, and could now swim the length of the pool without stopping.

She walked down the hall and headed downstairs, the floors creaking 'good morning' in response. Tiercy loved the early morning, when the house was quiet and then would slowly come alive. First Tiercy rising, then the coffee maker going, the rustle of breakfast preparations. All of this would be followed by the sweetest of wake-up rituals...and then the tornado of an energetic four-year-old.

Coffee on and the homemade cinnamon rolls Ross had dropped off before leaving for Manhattan warming in the oven, Tiercy went back up to wake Jemma.

Walking in the room, her heart filled with love for her baby. The room remained in the blue and green color scheme she had selected for the unborn child she'd nicknamed 'Perseus,' but now the room featured a Jemma-like mix of dolls, action figures, a soccer ball, ballet slippers, and a children's microscope that she had insisted on getting for her birthday. She liked to pick up things in the house and outside and look at them under the magnifying lens. She truly was Luke's daughter; he'd been a science nut.

Jemma was nested in a pile of pillows, her tiny body barely visible in all the mess of stuffed animals. Clutched in her hand was the stuffed orangutan "Niamh" (Tiercy shook her head and smiled fondly at the use of her middle name) that was now essentially an appendage. Jemma went everywhere with it. Tiercy thought Jemma's crush on Cole was almost as big as her own.

Quietly, Tiercy moved to the edge of the bed and gently sat down. Jemma's soft breathing filled the room. Tiercy always knew she wanted to be a mom, and she'd understood on an intellectual level the type of love a parent can have for a child. She'd certainly experienced it herself as a daughter. But nothing prepared her for the encompassing, almost ferocious love for her daughter. It was as if every cell in her body were full of love for Jemma. Sometimes the love was so big, it almost hurt. She just wanted to cherish every moment—even the crazy moments, and there were plenty with Jemma Cathleen.

"Rise and shine, Sweetness." Tiercy stroked the velvet soft cheek, and Jemma's long, pale lashes fluttered. "Time to wake up."

Jemma stirred, slowly blinking. Her eyes fixed on her mother and she smiled sweetly. Then she popped up, throwing her arms around her neck like long-separated friends. "Mommy!" Tiercy squeezed her back, the now fully awakened Jemma vibrating with a new day's energy.

It was impressive. And also just like her father. Luke had shot out of bed like a cannon. He would go from sound asleep to instantly awake. Conversely, he could drop to sleep in a snap. Tiercy would alternate between jealous admiration and frustration at this skill Luke claimed came to him naturally, but had been perfected during his residency.

Tiercy pulled Jemma onto her lap and rocked her. Nothing is cuddlier than a small child in the morning, still warm with sleep. "Did you have sweet dreams?"

"Yes, Mommy. Lola Elephant was in it. And Niamh. And Coley." Tiercy's heart tugged.

"How nice! Well, we can't lollygag. You have a party to go to today, and we still need to pick up a present. I have Aunt Ross's cinnamon rolls warming up for us. And then we'll run to Target for a present. I already have your bathing suit and towel packed up."

"'K, Mommy. I'll get dressed." Jemma hopped off the bed, a surge of excitement for the party giving her an additional boost of morning adrenaline.

Aaaand she's off. Jemma would be wound up now for the rest of the morning until it was time for the party.

Jemma rummaged through her drawers, muttering to herself, selecting things and then discarding them. Within minutes, it looked like a college girl's dorm room on date night. She turned to her mother. "'Scuse me, please. I need my privacy."

Tiercy's jaw hit the floor. Who was this child and where did she come from? She left the room feeling quite certain, for about the billionth time, that she was in big trouble in another ten years.

She headed downstairs, plated the rolls, and poured a cup of coffee. Luke had always programmed their coffee the night before. No matter what, he always had it set so the next morning, her coffee—her lifeline to sanity and reason—was ready for her. She didn't miss it right away... After. First, she was in such a deep funk, she was barely functioning. Then when she found out she was pregnant, there was no coffee for her. Even decaf was out as the scent of coffee became one of her pregnancy aversions.

It was later, when Jemma was a newborn, that Tiercy began drinking coffee again. One morning, after getting up several times for Jemma to nurse, Tiercy stumbled into the kitchen. Some deeply ingrained habit awakened from its latent state, and she automatically reached for the coffee pot.

Cold and empty. Just like she felt.

Months passed before Tiercy felt normal making her own coffee. Sometimes just the sight of the pot would be enough to trigger a crying jag. Eventually it got better, but Tiercy still felt a pang at times when she reached for her morning brew.

Sipping her coffee, she heard the sound of a Clydesdale on the hardwood steps. Jemma appeared, clomping in the kitchen in a pair of pale pink cowboy boots Ross had given her. She'd chosen to round out the ensemble with hot pink shorts and a white top with ruffled short sleeves and a glittery butterfly on the front.

"You look stinking cute," Tiercy announced.

"I don't stink, Mommy. Dat's not nice," Jemma frowned.

"No, lovebuggie. I didn't mean that. I just meant you look really cute in that outfit." Jemma had climbed on the bar stool next to Tiercy and had already shoved part of a roll in her mouth.

"Mfpmh mhu," Jemma replied.

Tiercy dropped a kiss on her head. "We don't talk with our mouths full, and you forgot to say grace. But, I think you said, 'thank you' so I will say 'you're welcome.' Now, let's say grace—better late than never."

"Dear God, fank you for dese yummy foods dat we's eating. Watch over Eli, and Trish, and Alex, and Irina, and baby Juliana, and Lizzie and Sasha, 'specially Sasha because she's my friend, and Johnny even though he's not as much fun, and Martin 'cause he can burp his name, and even Gussie even though he's mean to Sasha."

Tiercy's eyes goggled at Jemma's recitation of the litany of Cole's nieces and nephews, and swallowed a smile at her editorializing. Then Jemma tore her heart open.

"And give Daddy a hug from us. Tell him I'm being good, 'cept for when I pinched Gussie because he chased Sasha with a frog. Amen."

Tiercy fought the urge to correct her grammar, and also fought to hold back a rise of tears. The reference to Luke tugged at her heart.

Sometimes she could just feel him in the room. She knew, without a doubt, that she'd get some kind of a sign from him today. It hadn't happened in a while. Months. And if it didn't happen today. Well, how many times could a heart break and then heal? She'd clearly tested the outer limits of that, and she suspected she wasn't finished.

After a restorative gulp of java, Tiercy reached over and smoothed Jemma's hair.

"OK, sweetness, let's finish up. We've got a present to buy."

Having purchased a pink kids' camera that Jemma insisted Marie *had to have*, and then a Star Wars gift bag, which Jemma also insisted on because it featured Han Solo, Tiercy dropped Jemma off at Dom and Giorgia's house. Sure enough, Giorgia had a little belly popping out. Tiercy congratulated them and handed them a baby gift that she'd picked up when they were at Target.

Kneeling down, she looked Jemma in the eye. "Listen, Jem. I know you are going to have a super fun time playing at the party. It's very important that you are a kind guest and a good listener. Do not go near the pool unless there is an adult watching. And be a good friend. Don't be bossy, OK?"

Jemma nodded, positively vibrating with barely concealed excitement for the "big girl party." Seven girls were coming to the party, but only Jemma, as Marie's best friend, was spending the night.

"If you want to call me tonight before bed, Ms. Giorgia has the number. You are going to have fun at your first sleepover! Go to bed when you're told and be good." She squeezed her daughter, who hugged her back, but then quickly squirmed to get away.

Tiercy stood and gave a surreptitious swipe to a wayward tear that had appeared. Jemma had certainly spent the night away before, but never with a friend. It was a rite of passage, and Tiercy marveled at how fast time flew when you had children.

"Are you sure you're game for this? I'm happy to stay and help. Seven four- and five-year old girls is a heck of a lot of mini-estrogen!"

Giorgia laughed. "Dom and I have it covered. We bribed Ana and her friend to come help. We told them we'd pay them like babysitters, and then they'd have money for movies or makeup or clothes. I'm worried they may be worse than the little girls!" The women giggled companionably.

"Ok. If you're good, I'm out of here. Jemma keeps glaring at me. She very much wants to do this party 'without mommy.' You've got my number if you need me."

Tiercy hopped in her car, driving off in the summer sunshine. Ross was meeting with an author in New York and her mom and dad were on vacation on the Gulf Coast of Florida. Cole was working on the building site. Things were moving along but it was a critical phase of construction. He'd been spending a lot of time there over the past several weeks. They'd had several more dates, relying on her thirteen-year-old neighbor to watch Jemma for a few hours at a time. But with both Ross and her parents away, there'd been no opportunity to spend the night together—something she'd been craving.

While they'd spent plenty of time in the guest room after Jemma was asleep, she hadn't been ready for him to spend the night with Jemma in the house. Tonight, she and Cole were going to meet up for dinner and drinks at his place, which she'd yet to see, and she had a feeling it would be an important night for them.

In the meantime, she had an entire day to herself. It was glorious.

She went for a manicure and pedicure, getting a bikini wax while she was at it. Her thoughts turned again to Cole. Tonight he would get to see the aesthetician's handiwork for himself, with a whole, glorious, uninterrupted night to enjoy and not worry about waking up her daughter. Just the thought of Cole's ability to make her scream in senseless abandon sent a shiver of anticipation through Tiercy. Desire tugged between her legs.

Later, stretched out by her parents' pool, she read the new Samantha Christy romance novel she'd just purchased. There was a place for Shakespeare and there was a place for this. It was summer—time to indulge a different genre of books.

She moved the chair under an umbrella and put a gauzy cover-up over her legs. If she wasn't very careful, her Irish skin would burn...and burst into frecklepalooza, neither of which was acceptable. Warmed by the sun and made lazy by the relaxing day, she dozed a bit, awakened later by a text alert.

She had sent several messages to Brinder, asking for a chance to talk, with no response. She knew he was finally back from his trip. Maybe this was finally him? Stretching languorously, she peeked at her phone. Not Brinder. But it was hard to be disappointed, since the message was from Cole.

COLE-THOR

Will be a bit later. Need to sort through an issue with our subs and I may have to drive to the office. Should be at your place to pick you up by 7. That OK? Eat in or go out?

Tiercy checked the time on the phone. 3:45 p.m. Good. She'd have time to shower and throw something portable together for dinner. She didn't want to go out. Staying in was definitely on her mind.

TIERCY

Eat in. I'll make something to bring to your place and heat up.

COLE-THOR

You sure?

TIERCY

Yes. In fact, why don't I drive to you? Save you the trip.

COLE-THOR

Nope. Your place is between the job site and my house. So what are we heating up? I mean...besides us...[flame emoji] [eggplant emoji] [water drops emoji]

Tiercy burst out laughing.

TIERCY

Did you really just type that?[cracking up emoji]

COLE-THOR

I mean…yes?

TIERCY

I can't wait to see you. Now I want to eat eggplant.

COLE-THOR

Eat eggplant…or "eggplant"?

Tiercy giggled again.

TIERCY

You'll find out. [kiss emoji]

COLE-THOR

[gif of excited dancing] [kiss emoji]

Tiercy practically skipped into the house.

CHAPTER FORTY

*"The world breaks everyone and afterward many are strong at
the broken places."*
A Farewell to Arms, Ernest Hemingway

TIERCY

J ust before five p.m., Tiercy was sitting at a stoplight, a bag of
groceries and a bottle of wine for tonight's dinner in her front
seat. Her windows were down, the music turned up. It was a
flashback weekend, and Tiercy was singing to Nirvana as her mind
wandered to her and Cole...and *eggplant*. Tiercy giggled, basking in the
glorious sensation of being truly content.

As the song wrapped, the announcer cut in, "How about this one
for a way-back flashback?" The opening beats of "Doctor Doctor" by
The Thompson Twins filled the car. It had been her ringtone for him.

There it was. Tiercy had known Luke would send her a sign today.
She'd been feeling him all around her since the morning. Tiercy laughed
out loud. "I love you too, Luke."

The light turned green and Tiercy pulled forward. Movement in the corner of her right peripheral vision caught her attention. A sudden flash, and then the sound of metal squealing.

Tiercy ricocheted off the driver's door and then was propelled forward, her head thrust against the exploding airbag. Pain radiated in her left shoulder. *Accident. Something's wrong.*

Then everything went black.

CHAPTER FORTY-ONE

TIERCY

She came to with the sound of sirens. There were a lot of people talking. A voice cut through the din. "Ma'am, my name is Officer Warner. You've been in an accident. You're OK." Tiercy kept her eyes closed and focused on the voice, warm and authoritative. "The ambulance will be here any second. I can hear it coming."

Tiercy nodded, pain jolting down her arm. She fought to open her eyes, to focus, but her vision was hazy and she had trouble focusing her eyes.

Breathe, Tiercy. Inhale. Exhale. You are OK. You are OK.

Her radio was still playing. What had been on? Oh yeah. Luke's song.

Tiercy focused her eyes. In front of her was a police officer. He had a kind face. "The EMS crew is here now," he assured her.

Her head was beginning to clear. The initial shock of the accident had worn off, and she slowly assessed her surroundings.

Officer Warner filled her in. "You were T-boned, on the passenger side. I was in the gas station and saw it happen. It wasn't as bad a hit as it could have been—the driver braked at the last minute—but it deployed your airbag. I think your left shoulder must've hit the window frame. You were holding it when you came around. I'm going to step aside and let the EMT care for you, but I'm right here."

Tiercy nodded. Her head and shoulder hurt and her legs were sore. She felt a little woozy, but was gaining clarity with every passing second.

The EMT came to stand in front of her. "Ma'am, my name's Ian. I'm going to take care of you. Did you hit your head? Does anything hurt?"

Tiercy considered. "Yes, I think I blacked out." Gingerly she shifted sideways, pain stabbing down her arm. "My arm hurts. And I'm woozy."

The EMT carefully examined her.

"You've definitely hurt your arm. You aren't bleeding anywhere, but we need to take you in and get that arm checked out. Looks like you have a concussion too. Those airbags are lifesavers, but you've hit your head pretty hard on the airbag and on the headrest. I'm going to pull up a stretcher and we'll help you on it."

As he eased her onto the gurney, his words sunk in. Tiercy grabbed at him with her good arm. "Taking me in? In where?"

"To Fellowship-Unity hospital, ma'am. Memorial is on bypass so Fell-U is the next closest. You need to get checked out and they'll take good care of you."

"No. Not there. Please no." Tiercy was frantic and tried to get up from the stretcher.

Suddenly Officer Warner was there, holding her hand with his large, comforting hand. "Ma'am. It's OK. Fellowship-Unity is a great hospital. I promise. Who can I call for you?"

"Please not there. Can't you take me to University? It's not much further."

"I'm sorry, ma'am," the EMT shook his head. "We have to take you to the closest available hospital. You have a concussion and you've injured your arm pretty badly."

Terror filled her body and she began to shake. She didn't want to go back to that hospital, and definitely not to the ER. Luke's ER. She couldn't go there.

"Ma'am, your blood pressure is sky high. You've been in a serious accident. Please, let us take you there." The EMT looked earnestly at her.

Officer Warner came back with her purse. Pain was searing through her arm and she felt dizzy. Suddenly Jemma's sweet face appeared before her. What if something bad had happened in the accident and something was really wrong with her? Jemma couldn't lose another parent.

"O-OK," Tiercy reluctantly agreed. "If you're sure we can't go to University."

"I'll come with you," Officer Warner offered. "May I call someone for you? Or you can call."

"Let's get her in the ambo and then she can call," the EMT offered, watching her carefully. Years with a physician husband confirmed that he was likely worried she was beginning to show signs of shock. She was worried about that too.

Once in the back of the ambulance, Tiercy hit the "recents" list on her cell with a shaking hand, dialing Cole. It went straight to voicemail. She debated sending him a text, but instead called Ross, instinctively hitting the second number on her favorite's list. The first was still Luke's number. She'd never deleted it. That call also went to voicemail. She was probably still meeting with her client in New York.

This time Tiercy left a shaky message. "Hey, Ross. I'm OK, but I've been in an accident. They are taking me to F-Fellowship. I don't want to g-go but we can't go to U-University. Can you call my parents and let them know, but tell them I'm OK?"

She thought about trying Cole again, or even Brinder, but the EMT motioned for her to hold her arm still. He wanted to take her blood pressure again, and was talking about starting an IV line.

"Please, I'm fine."

He'd put an ice pack on her arm, on which an impressive bruise had bloomed already. The ambulance bumped over the road, and Tiercy must have closed her eyes.

They flew open at the feel of the ambulance coming to a halt, double doors opening. They were wheeling her into the ER.

Tiercy concentrated on not throwing up. The pain in her arm, and the shock at being back *here*, was nauseating. She kept flashing... flashing...to That Day.

"Tiercy!" Chris King, the lead physician assistant, who had worked closely with Luke, hustled out from behind the clinical hub. "What've you got?" he asked the EMT.

"MVA. Shoulder injury. Possible concussion. No visible lacerations. Possible shock, but she refused an IV."

"Thank you. Alright, Tiercy. We've got you." He turned to a nearby tech. "Put her in room three."

As they wheeled her to one of the front bays, Tiercy said a silent prayer of gratitude that it wasn't the back of the ER. She kept her eyes forward and refused to look in that direction. This was Luke's ER. And where Luke was pronounced dead.

Tiercy closed her eyes. And just like that, it was five years ago. The smells were exactly the same. The sounds were the same. She began trembling, and slowly leaned back against the stretcher.

Within minutes, the doctor came in to perform a gentle but thorough exam. She didn't recognize him. It made sense that there would be new faces. After all, it had been five years. Somehow, seeing a stranger made her feel better. It was hard enough seeing Chris and some of the staff. A nurse came in and gave her oral pain meds—just a strong ibuprofen. Tiercy didn't want any narcotics.

She was in the bay, waiting on the CT scan and ultrasound, when there was a knock on the sliding door. "Come in."

The door opened, followed by the curtain that had been pulled across it to offer her privacy.

Brinder. He was in scrubs and a lab coat, with a five o'clock shadow. His hair was mussed, like he'd been running his hand through it, and his face was etched with concern. The sight of him opened a floodgate of tears that she'd been fighting to contain.

He hurried toward her, leaning into her good side with a gentle hug. "Tierce—my god. Chris buzzed me and told me you were here. And then I got a frantic message from Ross. You were in an accident?"

Tiercy nodded, wiping her eyes with her good hand. "T-boned, leaving the grocery store." She inhaled a shaky breath, already calmer just looking at his dear face. "Brinder, I am so sorry. So sorry about that night. Why didn't you return my messages? I owe you—"

"Sshh, Tiercy. We don't need to talk about that right now. It's not important. The main thing is that you are OK." His eyes scanned her body, as if they could do the work of the CT scan.

"B-but, you disappeared. You left the country? Why? You didn't say anything. Just disappeared. You never answered my texts."

"Tiercy, love, you've been injured, and we need to get you to the imaging suite. Let's not talk about this now. There will be time enough. Let's just get you checked out. That arm looks painful."

"They just gave me something."

"Mmm," he nodded, looking in the computer at her chart. "You want something stronger?"

"No. I don't like how I feel on that stuff. And being loopy on meds in here reminds me of—reminds me of—" Tiercy cleared her throat with effort. "I'll be OK. It's just..." she started.

"Just what?"

Tiercy choked on a sob. "I just hate being here. I hate it. It h-hurts so much to be h-here." Brinder sat on the edge of the bed, still on her uninjured side, and held her, kissing the top of her head. "I know. I'm sorry, love. I will get you out of here as fast as I can."

There was a knock and the door opened again. It was patient transport, ready to wheel her to imaging. Brinder helped him unlock the stretcher and walked with her to the elevator. He waited while they did the CT scan and X-ray, and promised her he'd personally read them.

Brinder clearly greased the skids for a streamlined patient experience. She was in and out of imaging fast, and then back in the room. He said he needed to look at the results, and possibly consult with ortho and neuro, but then he'd be in.

Tiercy's phone rang. It was her parents. They had her on speaker. Her mother sounded frantic with worry, while her dad was clearly working hard to stay calm. She told them she was OK and that Brinder was personally overseeing her care. They talked for a bit, then Brinder came back and spoke to her parents, assuring them he'd look after her.

His British accent was warm but authoritative. He was in his element, and Tiercy felt better just listening to him. Her parents offered to find a way home immediately, but Tiercy insisted that they stay.

Just as she ended the call, she heard a commotion at the entrance to the ER from the waiting room. There was a deep male voice, insistent—almost angry. Brinder stepped out to check on things. "I'll be right back."

CHAPTER FORTY-TWO

"Into each life some rain must fall, some days must be dark and
sad and dreary."
Little Women, Louisa May Alcott

COLE

From across the ER, Cole saw the authoritative man in a lab coat stare in his direction, and he hurried toward him. "Doctor, I'm looking for Tiercy Somerville. Can you help me?"

The doctor frowned at him. "Sir, I can't confirm any patients. Who let you back here? Have you checked in with security?"

A vein in Cole's forehead pulsed. He grabbed a hospital vendor badge in his pocket and waved it. "I have this. I'm John Colburn. I'm a contractor here, working on the new building. A friend of Tiercy Somerville's called me and told me she's here. I need to see her." Brinder's eyes flicked to the bay, telegraphing her location. Cole followed his glance. "Excuse me," he said, and swiftly strode past the man.

"You can't—Wait—"

Before he could say anything else, Cole was in the room. He saw

Tiercy on the stretcher and relief flooded his body. He almost dropped into the chair.

"Cole—" she began, holding out her right arm to him.

He moved toward her, heart racing from the frantic dash to the ER. He hadn't told Tiercy he'd be here today. He just referred vaguely to a job site, of which there were several active. Cole knew mentions of Fel-U stirred up painful memories, so unless she asked, he avoided any talk of the project.

He'd had all sorts of horrible scenarios playing in his mind as he rushed from one end of the hospital campus to the other, leaving his truck parked haphazardly by the ER portico. He'd move it later. For now, he just needed to touch her, assure himself that she was OK.

"Jesus, Tierce. My God. What happened? Are you OK? Ross tracked down my assistant and called me from New York, worried sick. She said you called her. That you'd been in an accident. Then I saw I missed a call from you." Cole was at her side, gently skimming his hands along her and kissing her face. "I was at the new building in a meeting and I'd DND'd my phone. I rushed over as soon as I heard."

"I'm OK. Brinder's taking care of me. I'm alright." She motioned to the door.

Cole swung around to face the same doctor who had not been very helpful moments earlier. The guy was standing stiffly, arms crossed and an unreadable expression on his face.

Cole frowned. On instinct, he was wary, and he didn't like how he was looking at Tiercy. He appeared professional, but there was something under it that he recognized from how he himself looked at Tierce.

The doctor stepped forward and held out his hand. "Brinder Desai. I'm a radiologist here and a good friend of Tiercy's."

The guy emphasized *good* and moved, almost protectively, to Tiercy's other side.

"John Colburn. Tiercy's *boyfriend*." Cole put similar emphasis on the word, standing up and reaching his hand out across Tiercy.

They silently shook hands, sizing each other up. Cole realized they were like lions fighting over a pride, and she was the fierce lioness. Only there was no fight. Brinder was her friend. Cole was her boyfriend. Loved her.

Aaaand...from the look of it, so did this guy.

At the word 'boyfriend,' Brinder's gaze jerked toward Tiercy. A look of shock crossed his face and then was quickly gone as he arranged his features into neutrality. He turned back to Cole, his tone calm and polite.

"Well, Mr. Colburn, nice to meet you. I've been away. I didn't realize Tiercy had a—had a...well, anyway, I was just coming in to share the imaging results with Tiercy. If you'll excuse us, I can review them." He motioned to the door to the bay.

"No, Brinder, it's OK. Cole can stay."

Cole tried, and failed, not to be jealous at the warmth and familiarity in Tiercy's voice. *I wonder if she knows he's in love with her?*

Cole's eyes pinged between the two, settling on Brinder, whose brow furrowed.

Cole sat on the edge of the stretcher again, arm protectively around Tiercy as he gently rubbed his thumb across her hand. The doctor's gaze fastened there. It was a moment before he began again.

"Yes, well. Your CT scan on your head came back fine. I had Dr. Spelman in neurology look at it. She agrees that you sustained a mild concussion in the accident. Nothing too bad. But you're going to have quite a headache, and you'll need to take it easy. I'll have the medical assistant print out some instructions on that.

"As for your shoulder," he turned to the computer and brought up some images. "You likely have a small tear in your rotator cuff, from the trauma of the accident. I don't think you're going to need surgery. I did a quick ortho consult with our new chief of orthopedics. We recruited him from Hopkins and he's incredible. He agrees that with rest, ice, and time, you should heal on your own. You may need a cortisone injection, so I'm going to give you a referral to him. He said he'd see you in a couple days. He wants to give it a little time to calm down on its own."

Brinder Desai looked up from the screen, now clearly avoiding eye contact with Cole.

But Cole was regarding him intently. *Yep. I'd bet my left nut Dr. Brinder Desai is in love with Tiercy.*

"I will be back with the instructions and the discharge papers. Why don't you get dressed and I'll put in an order for patient transport? It's mandatory with our concussion protocol. You're a falls risk, love. We're slammed this evening, but it shouldn't take too long. I told them we have a VIP. Then, once you are dressed, I'll bring you a sling. You'll need that for a while to keep your left arm stable while it heals. I will send in one of the nurses to help you."

"No, that won't be necessary. I'll help her." Cole's voice was firm. He was a man accustomed to being in charge and heeded, and he knew his tone evidenced that.

Brinder, to his credit, looked at Tiercy for confirmation. She nodded her assent and then darted her gaze to Cole—her eyes and facial expression conveying a mixture of relief and sadness.

Cole tucked her closer against him. Christ. He'd come close to losing her today, and his heart still hadn't settled into a healthy cadence since Heather had come running into his meeting with the news.

Brinder inhaled and closed his eyes for a half second. "Right then. Let me see to that paperwork." He smiled at Tiercy, nodded curtly at Cole, and stepped out.

Cole watched Brinder leave and then turned to face Tiercy. "So, how long has the good Dr. Desai been in love with you?"

Tiercy's eyes widened. "How did you—?"

"It's written all over his face."

Cole let out the deep sigh of relief and exhaustion that comes from the letdown after an adrenaline surge. He ran his hands through his hair. "Tiercy. My God. When I got Ross's message, I almost lost my mind. I literally dropped everything and ran. I'm so glad you're OK." He pressed his lips to hers, sinking into a deep kiss. Eventually, with a shaky sigh from Tiercy, they broke apart.

He touched her cheek, running a fingertip down the smoothness. "Thank God," he whispered and then reached for her clothes, almost whimpering as he got a good look at her arm. It was a mess. And she had a red mark on her forehead, probably from the airbag. "Come on, beautiful, let's get you dressed."

Tenderly, he dressed her, helping her into the shorts and T-shirt she'd been wearing. He noted her thong underwear and firm backside.

Despite the shock of the ER and the circumstance, he felt a jolt of desire. Tiercy turned at that moment, her eyes colliding with his. She knew exactly what he was thinking.

He quirked a guilty smile at her. "Not exactly a great place for foreplay, I guess?"

Tiercy breathed a small laugh. "Not really." Her voice dropped to a shaky whisper. "Actually, it's a terrible place. I hate it here. I asked them to take me somewhere else, but they couldn't." Her chin wobbled and tears filled her eyes, made even bluer in the harsh light of the ER.

Cole startled, suddenly putting it all together. "Oh, Tierce, baby. My God. I hadn't even thought—you haven't been back here since—"

Just then the door opened. It was a different nurse with the paperwork. She gave Tiercy a quick hug and then reviewed the papers, getting Tiercy's signature. Another guy came in just as she was signing. Thankfully, her right arm, which was her dominant one, wasn't injured. This guy shot him a glance too, but not anything like the way Brinder had scrutinized him. Nope. This one wasn't a threat.

"Hey, Chris. This is my boyfriend, John Colburn."

Engaging in a triumphant internal high-five as he noted Tiercy's lack of hesitation when she introduced him as her boyfriend, Cole gently squeezed her hand.

"Nice to meet you." Cole held out his hand and the other man shook it affably.

"Boyfriend, huh? I can't wait to tell Ramon."

Tiercy laughed lightly and shook her head. "I forgot what a gossip you are," she teased and then turned to Cole. "Chris and Ramon are two PAs here. They met, fell in love, and even married in the hospital chapel."

"And Tiercy was my 'flower girl.'"

Tiercy laughed.

Cole's heart expanded in his chest at the sound. She was OK. She was fine. But she was shaken up. And he knew, despite her laughter, she needed to get the hell out of this ER. Stat...as they say. And he was going to bring her home and take care of her.

"One of my favorite memories. Anyway, I came in to tell you that Dr. Desai got called back down to radiology to look at a stat image. He said he'd be back up as soon as he could, and asked me to get you situated with this sling."

As Chris began maneuvering the sling into place, Tiercy winced in pain. Once her arm was stable, Chris leaned in for a hug.

"I'm glad we could take care of you today, Tiercy. It's personal for us. We take great care of everyone, but you are one of our own. We all felt Luke watching us today with the eyes of the chief, making sure we gave exceptional care to his wife." Chris choked a bit at the end. "Call us if you need anything. Make sure you follow those instructions and get some rest." He cast a quizzical look at Cole, smiled at Tiercy, and left the room.

Cole exhaled. He hadn't realized he'd been holding his breath. Chris's words, while offered with the best of intentions, had to be like a dagger to Tiercy's heart. Cole squeezed her hand.

"Tierce? Let's get you out of here. This isn't good for you."

He rose and covered the distance to the door in two strides, spying the nurse. "Excuse me. Sadie, right? Can we get Tiercy Somerville out now? Where is transport?"

"I'm sorry for the delay, sir. We've called them." The nurse's voice was calm as she explained, "It's a busy night, and both our transporters had to take patients to other areas for testing. They will be here as soon as possible."

Cole turned back to Tiercy, whose face was white. She looked on the verge of collapse.

"How much longer, do you think? I need to get her out of here." He lowered his voice. "This is really hard for her."

Sadie shook her head. "I'm not sure. Not long, but I can't say for certain." She looked past him to Tiercy, registering his meaning. "I'm sorry, sir. I understand. We'll be as fast as we can."

Cole's face hardened. "Not good enough. She has all her paperwork right, and she's signed out?"

"Yes, sir. She just needs transport to escort her out."

"No. She doesn't." Cole turned on his heel and strode back into the bay, a powerful protective instinct swelling from deep within.

"Come on, beautiful. Let's get you home." He gently slid one arm under her knees, the other around her back, keeping her good side against him. Tiercy was a tall woman, but Cole lifted her as easily as he had Jemma.

Tiercy opened her mouth to argue but clearly saw the look of determination on his face. He wasn't going to brook any argument.

He carried her out of the bay, passing patients on stretchers, careful not to jostle his precious cargo. Nurse Sadie stepped aside, mouth agape, as Chris hustled around the hub.

"Sir. Sir! You cannot do that. She needs a transport escort. Sir!" But Cole just kept walking.

Making his way to the exit, Cole watched Chris reach to call security, conflict etched on the PA's face. He clearly didn't know whether to listen to Cole or follow protocol.

A voice cut across the ER din. "It's OK, Chris. Let him take her. It's for the best."

Cole nodded at Brinder and then offered conciliatory smiles at Sadie and Chris.

As the double doors closed behind them, Tiercy sighed and then choked out a laugh.

"Well, one thing's for certain. The hospital grapevine will be humming for days over this one."

CHAPTER FORTY-THREE

TIERCY

Cole insisted on carrying Tiercy into her house. She rested her head against his strong chest, breathing in his woodsy spice scent. Tiercy had to admit—it was definitely better than a wheelchair. It was also better than walking. The little she'd done had jostled her shoulder, and ibuprofen was barely touching the pain.

He nodded toward the living room. "Do you want to be here or in your bedroom?"

"Here, please. For now," she answered, motioning toward the living room, dusky in the evening light. He kissed her brow tenderly and laid her on the couch.

"I'm going to get some ice for you, and a pillow. I'll be right back." Cole left the room just as a flash of lightning lit the sky. A low rumble of thunder answered the lightning—the storm they'd forecast was imminent.

Tiercy lay back on the couch, grappling with delayed shock at the accident, grief from being in the ER, pain from her arm and several other places on her body, and utter exhaustion. She heard Cole moving around in the kitchen and then heading upstairs.

Her phone indicated three missed calls and two voicemails. It must have rung while she was in imaging. She listened to the messages. The first was her insurance company. Officer Warner had found her insurance card in her glove box and called on her behalf. Her car had been towed to a nearby body shop, and they'd do a review in the morning to see if it could be repaired or if it was totaled. Tiercy sighed. She hadn't even thought about the damage to her car.

The next message was Ross, sounding deeply worried. "Tierce, I got your message. I've called Cole. And Brinder. One of them will be there as soon as they can. Call me so I know you're OK."

Tiercy tapped Ross's name on the phone. It was 8 p.m. Ross was supposed to have dinner in Manhattan with Honor Wheatley, a child star descended from acting royalty who'd successfully transitioned into adult roles. She'd won a best supporting actress Oscar last year for her portrayal of a fighter pilot who gets picked up by enemies and manages to save herself and a captive orphan. Phenomenal movie. And now Ross was trying to convince Honor to write a memoir.

But, dinner with a star or not, Ross picked up immediately. "I need you to assure me you are OK."

Tiercy could hear the anxiety in her friend's voice. "I'm OK," she responded quickly.

Tiercy heard Ross blow out a sigh. "Thankfully Dr. De-sighhhhh called right after you left the ER. He told me everything. He said he wasn't supposed to, but I threatened him with disembowelment. But hearing it from him and hearing your voice are two different things. Crikey. I can breathe now. I was going bonkers staring at my phone and waiting to hear from you. I cannot believe it took you so long to call. I've been worried sick. Jesus, Hooker Hips. You took ten years off my life." Ross's laugh was shaky.

"I'm sorry, Ross. I did call you and leave a message."

"I know. From an *ambulance*. Where you sounded like shit. And then you didn't pick up when I called you back. Twice. And I needed to *talk* to my bestie." Ross sighed theatrically, but Tiercy knew there was real distress behind it.

"I really am sorry, bestie. I called my parents on the way home, and we just got in the door. I promise I'm OK. Shoulder injury that should heal on its own. Mild concussion. Some bumps and bruises. I'll be alright."

"Thank God." Ross paused. "Dr. Hottie McHot Pants also told me Cole was there. How did *that* go?"

Tiercy looked toward the stairs, where she could hear the creak of Cole's steps on the hardwood floors in her bedroom. Lowering her voice, she offered just the barest details. There'd be time to rehash it all later over a bottle of Prosecco. "Cole is here with me now. Let's just say it was awkward and Cole definitely showed his alpha side—"

"Hawt."

"Tell me about it," Tiercy whispered, suddenly feeling very tired.

"I'm glad Cole is there." Tiercy heard someone talking to Ross in the background. "Listen, I have to run. Now I'm that obnoxious person on the phone in a restaurant. You sure you're OK? I will rent a car and drive home immediately."

"Really, Ross. I'm fine. I'm going to just rest a bit. Thank you."

"OK. I'll be home tomorrow. I'll come by. Love you."

"Love you too."

Cole was standing at the bottom of the steps, two pillows under his arm, an ice pack in one hand, and a cup of ice water in the other. "She's an amazing friend, isn't she?"

Tiercy smiled. "The best."

"When she called me earlier, I could hardly understand her. I've never heard Ross like that. It scared me as much as what she was saying."

Tears pricked Tiercy's eyes. "Ross has seen her fair share of bad things. She's generally pretty stoic, but accidents bring up bad things for her. Her parents were killed in a horrible car accident. It's been almost twenty years. She doesn't talk about it really, but accidents freak her out."

The storm outside was picking up. Although it was only a little after

8 p.m., the room was getting dark from the green sky. Cole put down the pillow and water, and turned on a lamp, the amber light casting shadows across the planes of his handsome face.

"Wow, I had no idea. That's awful." He let out a huge sigh. "When I was in the kitchen, I realized that neither one of us has eaten. You hungry?"

"A little."

He handed her the water, carefully arranged one pillow behind her and the other under her arm, gently placed the ice on her shoulder, and went back into the kitchen. Tiercy heard the doors to her refrigerator and pantry opening and closing, along with cabinets and drawers. A few minutes later, Cole came back in with some cheese and crackers, and a sliced apple. "This is the best I could do on the fly."

"It actually looks really good. Maybe I'm more than a little hungry."

"And I brought us this." He handed her a snifter with a finger of whiskey in it, and then poured himself a similar amount. "Not enough to get you drunk. Just enough to calm both our nerves. It's been quite an afternoon." He sat down in the chair across from her, intense blue-gray eyes searching her face, as if to reassure himself again that she was safe and OK.

They ate in easy quiet, the silence broken only by the sounds of their eating and the rumble of the storm picking up in intensity.

"I hope the storm doesn't get too bad. I'm worried about Jemma getting scared at the sleepover."

"I can get her, if you want," he offered.

"No, I guess it's best that she stays there. I need some rest, and I don't want to upset her with how I look. I'm sure I'm a wreck."

"You are gorgeous, Tiercy," Cole whispered.

He joined her on the couch, carefully picking up her legs before settling down and resting them on his lap. When he began giving her a gentle foot rub, Tiercy moaned in ecstasy. After the physical and emotional trauma of the day, the massage was bliss. He'd rolled up his sleeves in the kitchen, and she was mesmerized watching the play of muscles of his tanned forearms.

Once again, they sat in peaceful silence, listening to the sounds of the summer storm. After a while, Cole cleared his throat. "I'm sorry for the dramatic escape earlier," he offered sheepishly. "I just needed to get you...out of there. Your face—It was like nothing I'd ever seen. I just needed to get you out."

Tiercy nodded, her breath catching. "Don't apologize. I appreciated it, unconventional as it was. It was hard enough being there, and the shock of the accident and whatnot. And then when Chris said what he did, I—" Tiercy broke off.

"You don't need to explain. I understand," Cole answered softly.

"You can't understand. Not really. I barely understand, and I was there. It's just that—have you ever returned to a place you once knew really well? It's the strangest feeling of déjà vu. Like no time has passed at all. The sights and smells are the same. And you're just...back...where you were. It's surreal. For me, this afternoon, it was five years ago. I was there again. And I could feel myself slipping into the past."

"Tiercy, we don't need to talk about this now. You need to rest."

Tiercy continued, ignoring his gentle shushing. "I call it 'That Day.' That's what I call the day Luke—the day Luke died. *That Day*. I never talk about it. I never let anyone talk to me about it. Even in the grief support group they dragged me to. I could talk about other things. Before. Right After. But not That Day. I never really wanted to." She took a shuddering breath, and in a small voice added, "Until now."

Cole watched her intently.

"Tell me about That Day, Tiercy."

Tiercy listened to the summer storm brewing. There was low thunder in the distance. The sky was a heavy gray, tinged with green. She could almost feel the electricity in the air from the repeated lightning. She looked over at him and her eyes rested on his hands, softly stroking her legs. Even seated, she could feel the muscle of his thighs on the backs of her legs. He had a band-aid on his left index finger, peeling at the edges. There was dried blood visible underneath. He must have cut it at work. She could not stop looking at it. Another rumble of thunder. The trees began swaying harder.

Tiercy didn't remember deciding to talk. She heard speaking, softly, and realized with surprise that it was her own voice. Small. Far away. Remembering. *That Day*

CHAPTER FORTY-FOUR

"We need never be ashamed of our tears."
Great Expectations, Charles Dickens

TIERCY

It was a Sunday.

Luke and Brinder, with a bunch of doctor friends, had played on a hospital basketball team they'd coined The Hemoglobin Trotters. It was part of a basketball league of doctors from hospitals in the region. He was going to hang with the Trotters. It wasn't a game. Just some of the guys shooting around. The early May weather was absolutely perfect. You know, it's always beautiful weather on that day, since then. I don't know about...Before.

Luke's back had been hurting pretty bad off and on, and I suggested he stay home and rest it. He said he wanted to get outside, take advantage of the gorgeous spring day. He thought I should go for a run, but I was getting over a cold, courtesy of my students, and feeling run down.

I know I was cranky with him. He made me some soup and ginger ale, and he kissed me. He told me he loved me. 'Take a nap, Kal. You'll feel better. I love you.' I still remember those ten words. Those ten simple words. They were the last he'd say to me.

He left, and I took a little nap.

After I woke, I puttered around the house a bit. He'd been gone a while and I texted him to ask approximately when he'd be back. It was unusual for him not to respond. I waited, and then sent a few more texts. Later, I'd read and reread those texts obsessively—as if I could will him to respond.

TIERCY

Luke, what's your ETA home? Thinking about dinner…and dessert XXOO

TIERCY

Did you decide to go out for a drink with the guys? Sorry I was a whiny baby earlier. I love you.

TIERCY

Kal to Luke. Come in, Luke. Basketball practice that much fun? I can think of another fun activity…

TIERCY

Making tacos for dinner. Also have cornbread. Feeling much better. Can't wait to see you. Wanna get it on tonight?

Luke had been stressed at the hospital. Everything was about looking for savings, faster patient throughput, and all sorts of administrative things. Luke loved being chief, but he also missed just being able to focus on patients. He was the youngest chief of service, but so respected. With all that, we hadn't made love in close to a week. That was unusual for us. But I was feeling better that afternoon…and frankly a bit horny.

You know what's crazy? What I can't get rid of? I remember that feeling of anticipation…the thrum of my body. I just wanted to jump him. I could picture him walking in the door. He'd sense it right away and give me that knowing little smile that quirked up in the corner. The tacos would have to wait.

I sent him one more text.

TIERCY

I love you. I bet you forgot your phone in the car. I love you. I want you. Did I mention I love you?

I knew he'd see it as soon as he got back in the car, which would be any minute now. I held my phone and waited. As soon as he called me, I'd slip upstairs and get ready. I was somewhat impatiently holding my phone when it rang.

It was a ringtone Luke and I had set the week before. I'd gotten a new phone that day, and he was flirting with me like crazy in the store. I flirted back. The clerk was not amused. We came home so turned on and had the most amazing sex. Later, we sat in bed, drinking Malbec and setting up the phone. We got silly. He downloaded a ringtone for himself— "Doctor Doctor" by the Thompson Twins.

Anyway, finally my phone rang...it was The Thompson Twins singing about burning with love.

Luke!

I didn't know whether to be annoyed or happy.

A long bolt of lightning snapped across the evening sky. One. Two. Three. A massive clap of thunder. The storm was getting closer. Tiercy could feel Cole's warmth and breathed in his unmistakable scent—like woods, and spice, and something else distinctly Cole. She closed her eyes and inhaled again.

Cole said nothing but she felt him shift toward her. She wanted to stop, but now that she'd started, she needed to just be in it. She was powerless to halt the flow of words. It was like she was outside of her body, watching herself, narrating That Day five years ago.

I picked up without listening. "Hey, you sexy mutha. Get your cute basketball playing butt back home. I made spicy tacos, and if you're lucky, I may let you have some other good old-fashioned spice...

"Hello?"

There was a voice I could barely hear. "Chris?"

I could hear him say my name. "Tiercy. Tiercy, are you at home? Is Brinder there yet?" And then, "Luke...Luke..."

He just said his name. Twice.

"Chris, why do you have Luke's phone? Why is Brinder coming over? What's going on?"

His voice sounded so weird. I could barely hear him. I pressed the phone tighter to my ear.

"Chris...what is it? Yes, I'm home. What about Luke?"

I could feel a dull ache somewhere near my heart and a rising feeling of panic. Why was Brinder coming over? Why was Chris using Luke's phone? Why wasn't Luke on the phone?

"Chris?"

"Brinder should be there any second."

Then the doorbell.

I put the phone down without even hanging up or saying anything. Like I was in a trance, I walked to the door.

Brinder was standing there, and a police officer. I'd never seen Brinder look like that. He was pale, almost gray. He looked bad.

"Tierce, I...Luke...something's happened. Luke collapsed on the court today. They were taking him by ambo to Fellowship. We have to get there. Tiercy. It's bad."

I just stood there, in a stupor. Mute. I didn't move. I didn't react. I'm not even sure I was registering what he was saying.

The officer stepped in the house and put her hand on mine. "Mrs. Somerville. Your husband collapsed playing basketball. He's at the hospital. I'm here to give you and Dr. Desai a ride. Mrs. Somerville, I need you to come with me."

Something in her tone cut through my torpor. I kept blinking my eyes, trying to process. My ears felt fuzzy and I was nauseated. I thought I might pass out. And then Brinder, pleading almost, "Tiercy, please, he needs you."

I don't think I grabbed my purse or closed the door. Brinder must have done that. I just walked out of my house and got in the police car. The sirens sounded like they were a hundred miles away. It's amazing how many cars don't pull over for emergency vehicles. Brinder kept yelling at them to move. I just needed us to get there. I'd done that drive gazillions of times. It was the longest drive of my life.

In the back of the squad car, Brinder was trying to talk to me...to explain. Luke had seemed off. He told the guys he was probably just getting sick. Caught what I'd had. No big deal. He went up for a rebound.

As Brinder said that, I remember thinking how awesome Luke's tapered doctor hands were under the boards.

And then he went down. Collapsed.

The guys started CPR. They called 9-1-1.

When we got to the hospital, it was eerily quiet. I knew that ER like the back of my hands. The doctors, the nurses, the techs. They looked at me, and I knew. I could feel my heart thudding. No-no. No-no. No-no. With every beat of my heart, I kept praying No.

And then I saw Dr. Walker. He led me to a treatment room with a few chairs and sat me down. "Where's Luke? Is he up in surgery or something?"

You know, they train them how to do this? In residency, they actually train them on how to break bad news. It's terrible. I can't imagine having to practice that. Luke told me that no amount of training ever prepares you for having to tell someone the worst.

"Tiercy, Luke is dead."

I looked at his lips, trying to read them because I was sure I didn't hear it right. "I'm sorry?"

"We did everything medically possible. We worked on him for more than forty-five minutes. But he was gone almost right away."

You would think at that point I'd have started screaming or crying. I'd heard what he said, but it just didn't sink in.

"Where is he? Can I—I have to see him."

It was so strange. I'd heard people talk about out-of-body experiences. And now I totally get it. I was there but not there. I was moving with Dr. Walker toward a trauma room in the back, but I don't know how I actually made my legs work. The whole time, Dr. Walker was talking softly to me.

Brinder was calling my mom, and Ross, and Luke's parents. He'd grabbed my phone on the way out apparently. And Chris still had Luke's. They must have been going through the contacts.

And then I saw him. He was on the gurney, and it looked like he was sleeping. Just resting. My God, he was so handsome.

Dr. Walker had his hand on my shoulder. "He's gone, Tiercy. I am so sorry."

It was unreal. I walked over and hovered my hand over his hand. I loved his hands. Elegant hands that healed. That saved lives. I was afraid to touch him. And then I was afraid not to touch him. So, I did...

They told me later that I just howled. Apparently, I threw myself across him and I wouldn't let go. I've seen footage of women doing that in funeral processions. And now I understand. The need to just be with them is so strong. It's as if you could just infuse your life into them. Maybe if he felt me near him, he'd wake up.

'Please wake up, Luke.' They told me later I begged him over and over again. I wouldn't let go. I honestly don't remember it.

They gave me a strong sedative, guided me onto a gurney, and put me in another room. By then, Ross and my parents had arrived. They sat with me while I slept. Ross said she'd never heard an ER so quiet. Even the sickest patients knew something bad had just happened. His colleagues were in various pockets sobbing. And poor, sweet Brinder had to watch his best friend be taken to the morgue. Had to call the family and tell them their son and brother was gone. And I just slept.

Eventually, they must have roused me enough to get me home. I wish I could fully remember, but I can't. Only disjointed moments. Brinder says it was the sedative. That it gives you a kind of amnesia until it wears off. But, eventually it does wear off. And you have to face it. Face that he's gone.

I didn't do too well. There were always people around. Touching me. Talking to me. Holding me. And yet, I was alone. It's so odd how you can be in a crowd of people, and still totally alone.

Tiercy sobbed on the couch, whispering Luke's name over and over, lost in fresh grief. She rocked, oblivious to the pain in her arm. Only slightly aware of Cole kneeling on the floor by her side, holding her good hand.

By now, the rain was coming down hard. Pockets of thunder boomed, following on the heels of lightning snaking across the sky. Another flash, and the lights flickered. A hard boom of thunder, and the lights went out.

Cole waited a moment to see if the lights would come back. Rising, he went into the kitchen and grabbed the grill lighter, followed by the taper candles in the dining room. All while Tiercy sat, soaked with her own tears, lost in another world. Lost in That Day.

CHAPTER FORTY-FIVE

"I have not broken your heart—you have broken it; and in
breaking it, you have broken mine."
Wuthering Heights, Emily Brontë

TIERCY

Tiercy must have fallen asleep. She woke to find herself curled on the sofa, sore arm propped up, a blanket tucked around her, head resting on Jemma's (once Luke's) nubby Batman pillow. It was dark outside, with just the soft light from a reading lamp illuminating the room. The clock on her DVD player, which she only kept to watch her wedding video, was blinking. The house must have lost power for a while in the storm. Cole was in the chair with his feet up, *Moby Dick* splayed across his chest, sound asleep.

Tiercy smiled. "Kind, good man." She had the strangest feeling of relief juxtaposed with a lightness she hadn't experienced in a long time. It was never her intention to share That Day from her perspective with anyone, much less Cole. She'd never even told Ross some of what she'd shared with Cole. What was it about him that made her face the core of her grief after all these years?

The intensity of her feelings for him scared her more than a little bit.

Cole shifted in the chair, and Tiercy rose to reciprocate his TLC, leaning over him to gently place the blanket across his tall sleeping form, wincing when pain shot through her shoulder. He was a beautiful man. Awake, he exuded such power and grace. His dark looks and chiseled features, along with his muscular build, didn't connote much in the way of softness. But asleep, ah...here was something different.

She'd not had an opportunity to observe him like this. It is tenderly intimate to watch someone you care for sleep, when they are at their least guarded and most vulnerable.

Cole's long, dark eyelashes rested upon his cheeks. *Any woman would kill for those.* His jaw, strong even in sleep, was covered in a day's stubble. He had a noble nose, as her mother would have said jealously. Both she and her mom hated what they called their 'snub' noses of their Irish ancestors. Cole's lips were full but not too heavy. Just right.

Tiercy closed her eyes and imagined, just for a moment, those lips on all her forbidden places. The thought gave her chills. *My God, I want him. Badly.* His dark hair fell across his forehead, and when he frowned briefly in his sleep, Tiercy reached out a tentative hand and smoothed his hair away. Even asleep, it was like touching an electric wire, and she began to throb with need. Once more and then she'd walk away and let him rest. She lifted her hand to touch him again.

Sensing the movement, Cole's eyes flew open. Light gray steel fixed on her in the pale light. Wordless energy sizzled between them—a current connecting them so powerfully she couldn't have torn her eyes away, couldn't have moved her hand, even if she wanted to.

He watched her penetratingly, something intense playing behind his eyes. Desire. Longing. Passion. And more. It scared her, the depth of this feeling that pulsed in her.

Cole slowly raised his own hand and, without taking his eyes off her, tenderly brushed her hair behind her ear. He slowly leaned forward, and Tiercy's breath caught in her throat. He kissed her softly on the forehead, resting his warm lips there for a long moment. Then he pressed his forehead gently into hers. They stayed that way for a beat, and then another. And another. They didn't touch at all except where their foreheads lightly connected. Tiercy could feel his breath on her and wondered if he could hear her heart beating in the whisper quiet of the room.

Eventually Cole lifted his head away and placed his large hand on the side of her cheek, slowly brushing the velvet skin with the side of his thumb. "It's like alabaster. So lovely." He continued to stroke her cheek.

Her body was aching for him. She wanted him, and she could see the same desire reflected in his eyes. Tiercy watched him struggling to say something and then finally he found words. "I was so scared when I heard you were at the hospital. I didn't know what I'd do if you were badly hurt. I can't ever lose you, Tiercy."

Tiercy swallowed, and then mirrored him, placing her hand on the side of his face. "Make love to me, Cole."

Tiercy watched a dozen emotions play across his handsome face. She could see the pulse beating in his neck.

"Tiercy, you know there is nothing I'd love more than to bury myself inside your body," he said, his voice thick and husky with desire. She raised her face, moved her lips toward him. But Cole shifted back, keeping his hand in place on the side of her cheek. "It's late, Tiercy," he whispered. "Today has been a hard day for you, physically and emotionally. You need to rest." She watched him swallow, and then clear his throat. "I'll stay in case you need me. I can sleep on the couch."

Rest? Tiercy was confused. His words were out of tune with what was passing between them. All she knew was that she hadn't felt this way in a long time. Maybe ever. No—she quickly silenced her heart, feeling traitorous. *Focus on the right now. Not the what if.*

"Stay." Tiercy's own voice was strong. "I don't need you to stay, but I want you to stay. And not on the couch or in the guest bedroom. I'm finished with wooing. I want you, Cole, in my bedroom."

The room sizzled with the voltage of a thousand unspoken words and the primal surges of chemistry. The clock in the kitchen ticked softly in the background, a metronome accompanying her desire.

"Tiercy," he began haltingly, removing his hands and raking them through his hair. "I'm in uncharted territory here, and I'm trying hard not to really screw this up. You shared something with me earlier tonight that I don't believe you've ever shared before. You're raw. Vulnerable. You just relived the worst day of your life. After that, you just closed your eyes and went to sleep. I've never seen anything like it. You were utterly exhausted, emotionally and physically. I watched you sleep for a long time. Do you know you cried in your sleep?"

Tiercy's hands went reflexively to her eyes, where she could feel the salt of dried tears in her lashes.

"I want you, Tiercy. I want you so badly I could take you, right here and right now. It's all I've wanted from the first moment I saw you. And I know you want it too, as badly as I do." His voice dropped. "I can smell the desire on you. My God. I want to stay here with you. In your bedroom, and not on your damn couch or in your guest room. But there's something else. As much as I want to touch you everywhere, kiss your soft, tender skin, and make you cry out, explode with you, I want you even more in a different way. I want you, and I want all of you. Not just some small part you feel you can give me. I want all of you, Tiercy. And I don't want to be second place. I want our own really big love."

"Cole—"

"Right now, I cannot believe myself. I'm here, crazy turned on with an equally turned on woman I have longed for, hungered for, dreamed of. I don't know what you've done to me, but I can't do it. You've made me want more. I want you to be fully mine. I want to build a life with you. I need you to make room in your heart for me. I want it all."

"Cole," she began again, "I-I can't give you all that. I can't. That belongs to Luke. But why won't you take what I *can* give you?"

"No!" Cole pounded his hand on the arm of the chair, the sudden action shocking them both. "I'm sorry," he whispered. Then he stood, and turned his back.

Tiercy watched him take several calming breaths. Eventually, he shifted to face her, his tone calmer but strained. "No. Maybe in the very beginning I might have been satisfied with that, but we've known from the start that this was special. Different. Big. I know how I feel, and *dammit* I know you feel the same way. My love for you is bigger than anything I've ever felt. Let me love you. Let go and let yourself love me the way you know you want to."

"I can't give you what you're asking for!" Tiercy cried out, standing and reaching for him. He turned, eyes full of anguish and conflict traveling her face. Tenderly, oh so tenderly, he leaned into her, easing her against his chest and gently wrapping his arms around her.

Home. It felt like home.

Tiercy's heart was shredding, and it hurt way more than her arm right now. "Why do you ask me for something I can't give? Why can't you just let us be...us. As we are now. We love each other. Why do you need more? You ask too much. It's not mine to give anymore. I had a big love once, and I can't do it again."

Cole leaned back and searched her face again. "Why not?" The fire in Cole's eyes burning a hole in her resolve, Tiercy closed her eyes.

"Because I can't," she whispered, defeated. "I just can't."

"Then I can't either," Cole answered, anger and sadness echoing in his voice.

He dragged his hands through his hair again, the cowlicks making it stand up. Tiercy's fingers ached to smooth it. But the spell was broken, leaving something cold in its place, seeping around her fragile heart. She could feel it breaking all over again.

"What are you saying, Cole?"

"Lara fessed up about what she said to you at the barbecue. She told me she gave you an ultimatum—to love me fully...or let me go." Cole's voice was jagged as shattered glass. "I think she was right."

Tiercy swayed a bit on her feet. She tried to speak and found her vocal cords failed her. Her heart thudded in her ears. Tiercy swallowed and tried again. "What does that mean?" she croaked out.

"That I don't want to be second best. I don't want to battle a dead man for your love and watch you feel guilty for loving me."

They stared at each other in a silence so unlike the ones that punctuated their first meeting.

Tiercy eventually found her voice. "So what does that mean for us?"

"It means...I leave. I go home. You go upstairs and sleep. Tomorrow, or later today, technically," he added, looking at his watch, "we start fresh. We do our own things. Alone. We move on."

"We move on," she repeated woodenly. "Because you're stubborn. Because you want something I can't give."

"Because you would rather have the memory of a love than the chance at a new one. Because I want it all. Because, Tiercy Somerville...I love you. I *love* you, and only a part of you will never be enough for me."

"Please, Cole—"

He kissed her on the forehead. Gentle. Oh so gentle. Then he picked up his keys from the table and opened the door.

Tiercy's senses were assaulted by the tangy post-storm air.

"Get some rest. Goodbye, Tiercy." And then softer, "Petrichor."

Tiercy looked at him quizzically.

"It's the smell that frequently accompanies the first rain after a long period of dry weather."

And then he walked into the night.

Tiercy watched him get in his truck and willed him to walk back. She watched him reverse down the driveway and willed herself to walk out the door and chase after him and tell him what he needed to hear. And then she watched as he drove down the street, away from her.

She closed the door softly, rested her body against the wood, ignoring the pain screaming in her arm, and slowly slid down until her head was on her knees. "Good SAT word," she said, sobs shaking her body.

CHAPTER FORTY-SIX

*"The loneliest moment in someone's life is when they are
watching their whole world fall apart, and all they can do is
stare blankly."*
The Great Gatsby, F. Scott Fitzgerald

COLE

The Jag's tires crunched on his father's driveway. Cole sat for long minutes, staring at the house where he and his siblings had been raised. Where his parents modeled for their children the kind of marriage that became a beacon, a life goal for him. It had been a few years, but Cole still expected to see his petite, blonde mother skip down the steps, delight on her face like she hadn't seen him in years, even if it had been only days.

Christ. He missed her. Missed her voice. Her advice. Her laughter.

Cole wiped his hand down his face, feeling bleary. He glanced in the rearview mirror, where a haggard version of his face stared back with bloodshot eyes. He hadn't slept much in the week since he and Tiercy—he could barely even think the words. *Broke up.*

Motion on the front porch caught his eye. He looked over to see Caroline standing there, indecision and unease written all over her face. Sighing, he exited the car and headed toward the house. He halted at the bottom of the steps, where only a couple weeks before, with so much hope and excitement for their future, he had introduced Tiercy to his family.

Cole blew out his breath and reached for the railing.

Caroline moved forward, initially hesitant but then with purpose.

"You look like shit." Her words, delivered not unkindly, were tempered with a sad smile. "Jake popped out for a bit. Costco run before the cruise. You look like you could use a drink. Maybe a sympathetic ear too."

Cole sighed again and moved up the steps, following Caroline into the house.

"It's nine a.m., Caroline."

She kept going toward the kitchen. "And? Never heard of a breakfast cocktail? Bloody Mary or a mimosa? Screwdriver?"

Cole huffed a remorseful laugh. "Since I've beyond screwed up, a screwdriver would seem to fit the bill."

"Coming up." She reached for orange juice in the fridge, then paused, motioning to the high-back counter stools. "I'd tell you to take a seat, but this is your house and that feels presumptuous."

Suddenly, awareness hit. How had he missed it at the barbecue? He looked around the kitchen and beyond it to the great room. Little signs of feminine habitation, like he hadn't noticed in years.

"It's your house now too, isn't it, Caroline?" he asked, too weary for any rancor.

She smiled sadly as she passed him a drink, and then took a healthy sip from her own glass. "I wish you'd call me Caro. I-I understand that you don't much care for me. But Caroline was my great aunt. My mother named me after her. Why, I'll never understand. That woman was a nasty hag."

Cole almost did a spit-take, wiping his 'breakfast cocktail' from his mouth.

Caroline grinned at him. "Sorry about that. I can be very blunt."

"No, it's fine. Just surprised me."

"So, listen, I know I'm not your favorite person. I'm probably one of your least favorite—"

"That's not true—"

"Don't bullshit a bullshitter, John Colburn." She smiled and shook her head. "You are so much like your dad. You both think you have this impressive poker face. But your tells are actually pretty powerful. Anyway, when did you break up with Tiercy?"

This time Cole choked on his drink.

"Left arm up. Opens up the airway," Caroline commanded, one eyebrow raised and a kind smile on her face.

When he recovered his faculties, Cole raised his eyebrows. "Remind me never to play poker with you."

"I can't promise I won't take your money in a poker game—I love a good game of Texas Hold 'Em—but I can promise you I'm a good listener."

Cole examined his drink as he considered her offer, swirling the pale orange liquid around. Nodding, he took a deep breath and blew it out so his lips trilled. "Why not?" He ran his hand through his hair and took a bracing gulp. "Last week. We broke up last week." There. He said it.

"I'm sorry. You or her?"

"Me. Because I'm an idiot."

Caroline cocked her head. "I don't think you're an idiot, Cole. But perhaps you did something idiotic?"

"Oh, there's no perhaps about it."

"What happened?"

"Do you mind if we move into the family room? I've slept maybe two hours and I feel like I might tip off this chair. Also, someone included a healthy pour of Tito's in my screwdriver."

Caroline broke into another smile, dimples he'd never noticed before emerging. Objectively, he could understand why his dad liked her. She was average height—not as petite as his mom, but not nearly as tall as—his heart skipped a painful beat—Tiercy. Caroline looked to be in her early sixties. Her hair was the yellow-silver of a true redhead in senior years. It had a nice shine to it, and she wore it long, almost to her shoulders. Brown expressive eyes. Nice smile. In good shape, but with expected age-softening of her body. Cole knew, just from overhearing—not direct conversation—

that she'd swum competitively in high school and college. She and his dad both now swam most mornings at their local fitness center.

As he catalogued her, Cole realized with a start that, beyond the most basic of observances, he'd never actually looked at her. And he felt like an ass for it.

"You done scrutinizing me? I'm starting to think I've got a bat in the cave or something in my teeth."

Cole barked out a laugh. "No, that's not it. You're—you're fine. Actually, better than. I was just thinking I can see why my dad likes you. And realizing that I've never really...well, I've never really looked at you."

Caroline's eyes were sad. "I know, Cole. But I also understand. You loved your mother very much. And I'm not Elizabeth. Can never be her. It can't be easy to see someone else with your dad. Loving him."

Cole tipped his head in assent, then stood and moved into the living room, Caroline following him. He dropped onto the couch and she settled in on the nearby overstuffed chair, facing him. They drank their breakfast cocktails, accompanied by the sounds of the washer humming, the ticking of their old grandfather clock in the dining room, and a neighbor's dog woofing deeply but happily. How could he tell it was a happy bark? Cole didn't know, but it was.

His mind wandered, inevitably, to the woman who'd stolen his heart, and he wondered if Tiercy had ever thought about getting a dog for her and Jemma. The visual emerged of him and Buttercup playing with a large dog in his yard, as Tiercy watched and laughed. He shook his head to clear it.

It hurt too much to think about that.

Cole swallowed, returning to his conversation with Caroline, who was waiting patiently for him to emerge from the Land of Lost in Thought. He'd spent a lot of time there over the last week. "So you love him, huh?"

"I do." Caroline smiled. "Very much."

"He's a lovable guy."

"Most of the time." Caroline winked and they shared a smile.

"I'm not trying to take Elizabeth's place, Cole."

"I-I know that. I do."

"It's not an easy thing, stepping into a fully formed family and trying to fit in. Trying to find your place. It's a delicate dance, honoring the one who is gone, who was so deeply loved, while still establishing your own place and identity with your partner and the family, not to mention friends. But," she motioned toward him, "I think you know something about that."

Cole closed his eyes and leaned back onto the couch. He was so fucking exhausted. Not just physically. Emotionally. Mentally. Bone-fucking-tired.

"You want to tell me what happened? Might help."

"Tiercy was in an accident."

"Oh my God. Is she OK?" Caro held a hand to her chest, immediate worry written all over her face.

"She was T-boned, on her way home to make dinner for our date. Mild concussion. Her left shoulder is banged up, but it should heal in time."

"My God," Caro breathed. "Was Jemma in the car?"

"No, thank God. She was at a birthday party."

"Double thank God." Caro puffed out a breath. "She's lucky it wasn't worse."

"Well, it was worse, because they took her to the ER where her late husband used to be the chief. And where he was pronounced dead. It was the last place she ever saw him."

"Oh my fucking God." Caro shook her head, as if to clear it.

"My sentiments exactly."

"How is she doing? Have you talked to her?"

Cole hung his head. "I haven't," he sighed, battling the ever-present guilt. "I've started about six billion texts. Hovered my hand over her contact so many times a day. And night. And I keep thinking I'm probably the last person she wants to talk to at this point." He sighed again.

"But I did talk to Ross, who chewed me a new asshole...after she updated me on Tiercy. Physically she's doing better. Ortho confirmed she wouldn't need surgery on her shoulder. But Ross wouldn't give me any more than that, other than to call me a colorful name. I think her exact words were 'asshat gobshite chickenshit.'"

Caro hummed, clearly amused by the nickname, despite her apparent sympathy for Cole. "I'd like to meet this Ross. She sounds like a piece of work."

"She is." Cole smiled fondly, although he knew it wasn't powerful enough to overcome his sad eyes. Or his sad heart.

"So I'm trying not to push here, Cole, but how did that terrible car accident and whatnot end up with you breaking up with her?"

Cole scratched an eye. It felt like there was sandpaper under his eyelids. "I hear a bit of a twang, Caro."

"I was born in Dallas and spent my first eighteen years there, until I met my late husband. He was military, so we moved a lot. Until we divorced."

"But you didn't have any kids?"

"Wanted to. Couldn't. It all worked out. Now I have bonus grandchildren out the wazoo." She winked at him.

"That you do."

"Now stop avoiding the subject. What happened?"

"The accident, as you'd imagine, stirred up all kinds of horrible memories for her. She—she sort of went into this...trance...and relived the whole thing. Caro...it was...fuck...it was excruciating to listen to. I watched her heart break all over again, and with it, my own broke. I realized...I realized that she wasn't even close to being over the loss of Luke. And that Lara was right. I will probably always be second best to a dead man."

"Oh, lordy," Caro shook her head. "What the tarnation did your sister say to you?"

"She just pointed out how obvious it was that Tiercy was still deeply in love with Luke and that I was setting myself up for a lifetime of hurt."

Caro plonked her glass onto the table. "Oh, bullshit."

Cole's eyes flared. "What?"

"I said 'bullshit.' And I meant it. Lara was out of line *and* she was way off base. For a smart woman, she missed the mark."

Caro leveled a means-business gaze at him. "Listen to me, Cole. You might not have really looked at me until today, but I've looked at you plenty." She rolled her eyes at him and smirked. "Not in *that* way. I know you observe your siblings and the love they have for their spouses —especially Ms. Busybody Lara and her Lattie. I know you had the best example of a strong marriage in Jake and Elizabeth. Who wouldn't want to strive to achieve that in their own lives? And I watched you at the barbecue. With Tiercy. With that precious, and precocious, nugget Jemma. And," she waved a hand at him, "I watched Tiercy with *you*. Cole, you daft man, she is beyond head over heels for you. Her issue isn't that she doesn't love you enough. It's that she's worried she loves you too much."

Cole stared at her in stunned silence.

Caro stood, taking their empty glasses into the kitchen. Eventually Cole rose, like a zombie from a crypt, and joined her, leaning on the island for physical support.

Caro loaded the dishwasher. "Your girl is scared, Cole. She's gone and fallen in crazy, deep love with you. As has that little girl. And then she literally got shaken the hell up in an accident—"

"And taken to the worst possible place for her."

"Or," Caro drew out, "maybe it was the *best* place for her, because it forced her to face some things she needed to." Caro closed the dishwasher with a bump of her hip. "And then you went and issued an ultimatum, didn't you?"

Cole dropped his chin to his chest, fresh remorse flooding him. "Yes," he sighed.

"This one's actually pretty dang easy, Cole. You need to give her space and time—"

"That's what I—"

"I'm not finished," she chided gently. "And if you were just gonna say 'that's what you did,' I call bullshit again. You didn't just give her time and space. You broke up with her."

"Thanks for making me feel worse."

"No, Cole. Not my intention. There's nothing that can't be fixed when two people truly love each other. It might be a lift. It might take time and patience. But a love like that? It's worth cultivating. It's definitely worth the effort. We all break things in our relationships— sometimes intentionally, but more often unintentionally with some notion of positive intent behind it. What separates a relationship that can go the distance is that both parties want to do better. And they recognize it and work at it."

Caro moved to the side of the island across from him, mirroring his stance with elbows on the island counter. "Cole, this isn't the end of you and Tiercy. It's just a pivot point."

He dropped his head into both hands. "So now what do I do?"

"You love her, Cole. You find her and you tell her you love her and you just...be by her side, no matter what. She'll figure it out eventually. She's a special woman."

"When we started dating, I courted her."

Caro's eyes lit up. "That sounds special."

"I think I need to restart Operation Court Tiercy, which is a part of Operation Prove to Her that She's My Everything and I'm not Going Anywhere."

"I think a part of that is also Operation Grovel Sincerely." Caro chuckled.

"Indeed ..." Cole blew out a long breath. "Well...this isn't how I expected my morning to go." He quirked a smile at her.

"No. Me either. But I'm glad it did."

"Me too, Caroli—Caro." He emphasized her preferred name and thought he saw a sheen of tears in her eyes, accompanying the smile that had bloomed on her face. "Me too."

He shifted and then rounded the island closer to her. "And I want to apologize. For being less welcoming. For making it...harder than it should have been."

"You don't owe me an apology, Cole. But I do accept it. We're all on our own journeys. Doesn't matter how long it takes. Just matters that we allow ourselves to move forward."

"My dad's a lucky guy."

"I think so." Her smile lit up her face. "I'm lucky, too. I never expected to find someone like Jake. Kind. Funny. Sexy. Great in be—"

"La la la!"

They burst into laughter.

"Now that's a sound I like to hear." Cole's dad walked into the kitchen, a broad smile on his face, each arm loaded with the ubiquitous Costco boxes used to carry purchases.

"Let me grab one of those, Dad." Cole hurried over and grabbed what looked like the heavier of the two boxes, both of which were loaded with the necessary and random unnecessary things people (including him) seemed to pick up at the warehouse store. He put it on the far kitchen counter.

"Thank you, Son." Jake set his box next to the one Cole had deposited, then turned and enveloped Caro in a hug, pressing a kiss to her cheek. "Caro, I hit the jackpot at Costco today."

"Did you now? Shocking. And at your favorite place in the world. Who'da thunk it?" Caro's dimples were deep and her eyes shone.

How had he missed this? His dad and Caro were deeply in love. And they both deserved to enjoy it, without a surly son making everyone uncomfortable. In that moment, Cole decided he'd put the full force of his support behind them. His dad deserved happiness, as did Caro.

"Well," his dad boomed, arm wrapped around Caro. "What brings you here this morning, Son?" Cole observed his dad scan him, clearly noting the strain on Cole's face with a concerned frown. "Everything OK?"

"Everything is much better. I came by to talk with you, but... instead, I had a really good chat with Caro."

His dad's eyes flared in happy surprise at the use of her preferred name and the warmth in which he conveyed it. "Well...well, that's..." His dad seemed at a loss for words. "That's great, Cole. Caro is an amazing listener."

"So I've found out." He aimed a warm smile at Caro, who returned it.

"Where's our incredible Tiercy?"

"I'm going to see her tonight. I've got to wrap something at the job site, and then I have a few stops to make as I plan a really special night." Cole smiled at both of them, the picture of contentment in the homey kitchen. "I'm going to get out of your hair. I know you have prep to do for the cruise."

His dad and Caro walked him to the door, and he hugged each

goodbye, putting a little extra into his for Caro—making up for lost opportunities.

He bounced down the porch stairs, the weight of the last week lifted, giving him a spring in his step...and purpose.

Just before he slid into the Jag, he called out to his dad and Caro. "Oh, by the way, congrats on shacking up!" Grinning at his dad's shocked expression, Cole waved, his heart light and anticipation humming through his bones.

CHAPTER FORTY-SEVEN

"If it's true that there are as many minds as there are heads, then
there are as many kinds of love as there are hearts."
Anna Karenina, Leo Tolstoy

TIERCY

Seven days had crept by since she'd communicated with Cole. They were marked by an agony Tiercy had only experienced one other time in her life. As her body healed, it became clear the most grievous injury had been to her heart.

She'd grabbed her phone dozens of times a day, looking for—hoping for—a message from him. An equal number of times she began a message to him, only to delete it. Eventually, Ross grew short-tempered with her and colorfully told her to shit or get off the pot.

She agonized over her feelings, acknowledging the ironic parallel. She had, dramatically, dumped Brinder because she couldn't doom him to a life where he'd only ever be second place to Luke. Why would she subject Cole to that?

Because.

Because he was different.

Because, if she was being honest with herself, she could live without Brinder's romantic love. But the same was not true of Cole's.

Screw Lara and her admonishments to leave Cole. Tiercy's clenched jaw popped in defiance. She and Cole had something special. They needed to just enjoy it. And somehow she had to get Cole to be OK with Luke's place of prominence in her heart. Anything else was...well, it was unimaginable.

On the seventh day after her accident, and their subsequent breakup, Tiercy rose early, dropped Jemma off with her neighbor, and called Cole's assistant to find out where he was working that day. She was a woman on a mission. Why throw something amazing away just because you can't have it exactly as you might want it?

With a well-rehearsed, cogent argument prepared, she set off for his field office, located in a trailer on the far side of the hospital.

Tiercy cringed as she pulled onto the hospital campus, even though it was the opposite side of the ER. She studiously avoided looking in that direction, focusing instead on the trailer. A security officer stopped her, and she rolled down her window.

"Tiercy Somerville here to see John Colburn."

He said something into a walkie-talkie, waited for a response, and then motioned her through, pointing to a few coned-off spaces by the trailer.

Tiercy's legs were shaking as she climbed the metal steps. Before she could put a hand on the door, it opened. Cole was standing there, cell phone to his ear. His eyes lit up, and his sculpted lips formed a tentative smile. He motioned to the phone, indicating that he was wrapping up, then sat down at his desk to finish the conversation her arrival had interrupted.

She smiled uncertainly at him, having driven there fully expecting him to be angry with her. She'd played out various scenarios in her head, and all involved him greeting her coldly...or hurt...or even slamming the door in her face. She wouldn't blame him. She knew it was on her to hold out an olive branch, even if he snapped it in half.

Instead...he looked almost relieved. Happy. As he listened to the person on the other end of his call, he scanned her face and smiled gently at her, frown lines fading from his forehead.

She couldn't help but notice he looked worn down. Like he'd been through the wringer. Her stomach tangled around itself in guilt.

"Yes, I completely understand what you're saying. But I need you to understand me. This delay is a result of your lack of accountability in this, not ours. You agreed to deliver by yesterday, and it's still not here. It's putting us at an unacceptable risk of even further delay, and I won't have that." He consulted something on his laptop. "My expectation is that you solve this. Period. I will look forward to your return call with the solution. Today. Thank you." He hung up the phone and sighed, running his hands through his hair.

"Wa-was that for real?" she rasped, struggling to find her voice and grabbing into the superfluous. "You sounded so...badass."

He sighed as she ate him up with her eyes. "Yes, unfortunately that was for real. I was talked into going with a supplier I don't normally use, but there's a relationship with a hospital board member. You can fill in the rest based on what you just overheard." He scanned her intently. "No sling?"

"No sling. I got the cortisone injection and it's beginning to feel better."

Cole hesitated and then reached a hand out to her. "Tiercy. Please. Come over here. I'm not sure why you're here, but I need—"

Not letting him finish, she rushed toward him. He pulled her into his lap, and kissed her long and deeply enough to leave them both a bit breathless.

"Why are you here, Tiercy? After last week, I wasn't sure if you would ever want to talk to me again." He nuzzled into her neck, trailing his fingers across her collarbone. "I was just about to...to head out and try to see you. I had this whole scenario worked out. I was going to come sweep you off your feet. Court you and..." He looked at her hopefully. "And now you show up in my office on *this* campus of all places, and I think maybe you deserve the floor first."

Tiercy shifted off him and took a seat on the edge of his desk, needing to look him in the eyes for this. She inhaled deeply and launched into her opening statement. "Cole, did you ever hear the phrase 'don't throw out the baby with the bathwater'? Well, that's what we have going on here. You and I love each other. And we clearly have amazing chemistry. I mean, we're about to combust right now. I know you've already thought about locking the trailer door and taking me on this desk." She situated herself so his leg was between hers, and as she'd anticipated, Cole's eyes darkened.

"I love you Cole. I want us to be together, the way we both know feels so right. The best way we can. You can't deny the chemistry. It doesn't lie." She reached for him, hopeful, pleading.

Cole leaned forward with an intensity that startled her. He took her outstretched hand and threaded his fingers through hers. "Don't you get it, Tierce? It *is* chemistry, pure and simple. You put a couple elements together, and you get a powerful reaction. Massive. Gorgeous. Awe-inspiring. But that doesn't mean it's the only possible combination of elements. Every other combination isn't ruled out—or doesn't even get attempted—because the first one was so amazing. You mix some other elements and you get a new and different reaction. Still powerful. Still massive and gorgeous and awe-inspiring. But different. They aren't mutually exclusive, and one doesn't negate the other."

Tiercy gave a shaky laugh. "I was an English major. I took 'Biology for Non-Majors' in college. No chemistry for me." But she heard his meaning.

Cole's eyes lit up with inspiration. "How many books have you read in your life?"

Now Tiercy really laughed. "Is this a trick question? Thousands. Easily."

"OK. And how many have you really loved? How many books have really touched you to the core?"

Quietly, she responded, her heart beginning to pound. "Three. Maybe four. That I really love."

"And when you read the first one, did you swear off all books forever more? Take a vow of literary chastity, if you will?"

"Cole, you are a wordsmith under all that brawn," Tiercy teased, trying to deflect and break the spell he was weaving. She could see what he was doing. He was breaking down her carefully constructed barriers using her love of books as a wrecking ball.

"Tiercy," he pressed, "did you stop reading altogether after that first amazing, life-changing novel?"

Her response was lower than a whisper, just her trembling lips forming the word. "No."

"No. You didn't. You were open to the possibility of another magical novel, weren't you?" Cole implored.

Tiercy was chewing on her lip, fighting something raw inside her. She needed him to stop. She needed to think. She was overwhelmed by the emotions churning and the thoughts spinning around in her mind.

But Cole was relentless.

"And when you found a new novel that consumed you, that touched your 'inmost center'"—Tiercy jolted at Cole's use of her favorite line from Moby Dick—"did it take away from your love of the first novel that filled your heart?"

Again, the pull of the truth. "No."

"Then why not let me all the way in? Why not let us try?"

"Because." Tiercy was shaking now. The feelings and the fears she'd been tamping down since the moment she met Cole were pressing up dangerously against the fragile, protective surface that was barely staying intact. If it shattered, she might shatter too. "Because I can't do that."

"Why can't you?" Cole pushed.

Her heart was pounding in her ears.

He kissed each of her hands, holding both between his, gripping them tightly and pulling her toward him. "Why, dammit? Talk to me. Say it. Why can't you?" And then harsher, "Why?!"

"Because I'm afraid I'm going to love you more!"

Tiercy dropped her face into her hands, unable to hold back the gut wrenching sobs unleashed by her confession.

Cole froze in stunned silence.

"Don't you get it? Luke was the love of my life. He's gone, but I feel like I'm betraying him. Us. What we had. Kal and Luke. If I let myself love you, the way you want me to—the way *I* want me to—what does that mean for my feelings for Luke?" Tears coursed down her cheeks.

"What if I love you more?" she whispered past the thickness in her throat.

She wanted to stop, but couldn't. Cole had splintered, and then decimated, her protective shell, and she was powerless to stop the deluge of words that poured from her. "What about Jemma? Would you b-be her dad? And where does that l-leave Luke? Do you usurp him in her heart? She never even got a chance to know h-him. That's not fair. And w-what about Luke's parents? They'll h-hate me for loving you and they'll think I've f-forgotten their s-son. And when I die, who am I buried next to? You or him? And in heaven, where he's waiting for me, then what? Is it both of you? Do I have to choose? Or will I be a—an *eternity bigamist*?"

Tiercy punctuated each question with a wave of her good arm, practically wailing the last sentiment.

"I only had eight years with Luke. I'm thirty-four. You and I could feasibly have *fifty* years together. Our love would eclipse my love for Luke, and I'm not sure I can let that happen. Because I'm pretty sure that what I feel for you, I've never felt before. It's-It's...you...you are...all I want. All I can think about. I just want to be yours, completely. And I want to give you all of me so much it aches. I feel like I'm going to explode with wanting you, with loving you." Tiercy halted suddenly, took a great shuddering breath and looked at him, blurred through her tears.

"And what if I love you more?" she whispered again

Cole pulled Tiercy back into his lap, and she allowed it, boneless with weary grief and beyond comforted in his strong arms. He held her in his arms and stroked her hair. "Sssh, Beautiful. It's OK. It's going to be OK. I promise."

"How? I just don't see how," Tiercy sniffled into her sleeve, and then gave him a shaky smile as he passed her a tissue from the box on his desk.

"Tiercy, do you ever think about having another child?"

She gave a half-hearted pummel to his chest. "How can you ask me that right now?"

"Hear me out. You love Jemma with a massive, powerful love. One that consumes your heart. Right?"

"Of course. You know that."

Cole smiled, eyes crinkling in the corner. "Indeed I do. And if you were blessed with another child, or several children, would you love Jemma any less?"

"Of course not!" Her wobbly voice strengthened with the conviction of her boundless love for her daughter.

"Of course not." He stroked her cheek. "Because when presented with the opportunity, the heart expands to bring in and hold more love. Letting yourself love me fully in *no way* diminishes your love for Luke. And the joys and sorrows we will share in no way diminish or negate what you shared with Luke. You will always have it, and you will always love him in a special way. Just as you love me in a special but different way."

A slow tear trickled down Tiercy's cheek. Cole gently kissed the tear, and then Tiercy's lips. She briefly tasted her own salt, and then the warmth of his mouth, and felt that familiar stirring he could arouse at a touch, or even a look.

"Let's take the rest of this piece by piece, which is exactly how I handle a complicated construction project. For your eventual burial, I move that we worry about it in sixty years. But, I can see by your face that you want to settle it now. So, you be next to Luke...and I'll be on your other side. And people will say, 'That lucky bitch. She had two hot men lusting after her.'"

"Stahp!" Tiercy laughed. "Don't make fun of me." But the image soothed her as much as his humor eased her pain. "Would you really do that?"

"My love, if it would ease your heart, I'd do whatever you wanted."

He continued, like a lawyer making final arguments. "Luke's parents? They love you as a daughter, and like any parents, they just want their child to be happy. I promise you they will celebrate this for you. It may hurt a bit—I can't imagine that it wouldn't. But that doesn't mean they want you to live the rest of your life pining for their son."

Cole's eyes softened, his voice thickening with emotion. "And as for Jemma Buttercup, I can never and *would never* take Luke's place. He is her father. I promise to always honor that, and help you keep him alive in her heart. But I'd be lying if I said I didn't want to be a father to Jemma. I love her so much, Tierce. She's already a child of my heart. I can't love her the way Luke would have—simply because that would have been his unique love for her. And we can never know what that would have looked like or replace it. It's a part of the grief and loss that you and Jemma will always have. But I pledge to you that I will love and care for Jemma Cathleen, my Buttercup, for the rest of my life with my own unique, fierce, powerful love as a bonus father. I would be honored."

Tiercy's eyes filled with fresh tears and she started to respond, but Cole held up a hand, clearly fighting to contain his emotions. "Hold on. I'm on a roll now." He continued professorially, "As for the afterlife, I figure Luke, you, and I have an eternity to figure it out. Maybe I'll arm wrestle him when I get to the Pearly Gates. St. Peter officiates, and winner gets you for eternity?" She swatted him fondly, unable to form words beyond the massive love for him that was bubbling over. "No? OK. Maybe I get you on even eternity years and he gets you on odd eternity years? Or we switch days? Hey...we could be heavenly brother-husbands."

"*Cole...how* do you come up with this stuff!" Tiercy threw her head back and laughed.

"I love that lyrical laugh. Truly, it's music to my heart." Cole's blue-gray eyes, light and merry, turned serious. "Tiercy, I'm not a theologian or a religious expert. But I believe that *our* love is a gift from God, just as your love with Luke was. If He sent both of us to you, I'm sure He'll have the rest figured out as well. Who are we to second guess God? Best not to argue with Him. That's how you end up," he pointed his finger dramatically toward the floor, "down *there*."

"You are bonkers."

"Not at all. I'm in love. It's pretty close—they sometimes feel a lot alike." He smiled softly at her, stroking her shoulder as she rested against him, content in the succor of his embrace. "But I've never been of sounder mind. I love you, Tiercy, and I trust in what we have." He shifted back, and cradled her face in his hand. "Tiercy, 'Thou touchest my inmost center. Thou art tied to me by cords woven of my heartstrings.'"

He'd memorized her favorite line from *Moby Dick*. From any novel.

"Tiercy, I love you. And I know you love me. But I also know you've been living with one way of thinking for more than five years now. It's not fair of me to expect you to just do a one-eighty."

He squeezed her hand, caressing her face with his soft gray eyes. "Here's what we're going to do. I want you to take some time. Think about it. Talk to your mom. Talk to Ross. Talk to *Luke*. But just promise me you'll be honest and give this a fair shake. And I will be here waiting, maybe not so patiently. And probably taking a lot of cold showers. But you're worth it. And so is Jemma. I want us to be a family. I want to knit together our own really big love, with cords woven of our heartstrings. So, when you're ready, come to me. I'll be ready. Deal?"

He held out his hand, palm up. Tiercy reached to place her own in his, and hesitated.

"What if the answer isn't something you want to hear?"

Cole looked at her with sadness and love. "Then I will spend the rest of my life grieving the loss of you."

Tiercy took a deep breath, placed her hand in his, and squeezed gently. "I don't know if I can do this. I just don't know. What you say makes sense. It *does*. But I can't help worrying that if I give myself to you, I lose Luke all over again. And I can't do that." Tiercy squeezed his hand harder, echoing the brutal squeeze on her heart. "Cole, I think Lara may be right. If I can't love you fully, I have to let you go." Tiercy hiccupped a sob.

Cole's desk phone rang, shattering the moment.

Tiercy stood, wiping the drying tears on her cheeks and smoothing her shorts. "I have to go. You need to get that. I shouldn't have come to you at work."

He waved an impatient hand at the phone. "They'll leave a message with Heather. And there aren't words to describe how happy and relieved I am that you came to me here."

Cole stood, and gently ran a knuckle along her tear-stained cheek. "Tiercy, I love you, and there is nothing I want more than to spend the rest of my life loving you." He rested his forehead against hers. "Please, Tiercy..." he whispered.

With effort, Tiercy lifted her eyes to meet his. "I don't know, Cole. I

—I have to go. We'll talk, OK? I just...I need to think." In a whirl, Tiercy spun away, yanked open the door, and scurried down the stairs as he called out her name after her.

As she flung herself into her car, Tiercy was hit with a wave of grief and longing she hadn't felt in years—five to be exact. The idea of hurting Cole was worse than the reality of her own pain, and the thought of losing Cole was devastating. It took her to a place she had firmly refused to visit. *Oh Luke. Talk to me. Tell me what to do.*

CHAPTER FORTY-EIGHT

TIERCY

Tiercy robotically ascended the stairs leading to her bedroom. The sky had turned gray in parts, not unlike the color of Cole's eyes, she noticed with a slice of pain in her heart. But there were bits of sunlight and swaths of blue sky peeking through. Tiny splashes of rain began to drop, gentle intermittent patters that splashed on the window panes and rolled down, softly smearing the view of her front yard. It reminded her of the "fingers" on a good glass of red wine.

Instinctively, Tiercy walked over to her nightstand, reaching for her most recent journal. She paused a beat. And another. Then she reached into the back of the drawer. Feeling around, she pulled out her first journal from five years before. She knew it by touch. It had a green, velvety cover. Ross had bought it for her after the grief counselor recommended journaling.

Curling into her favorite armchair, covered in whimsical toile, she opened to the first page and read the passage from July 2—the summer *Right After.*

> They tell me I should journal. In the bereavement support group that mom and Ross dragged me to this week, they went on and on about how journaling helps you to process the things you're feeling. I don't know if that's true. But I'm so miserable and tired I guess I could try. I'm not even sure what to write or how to begin. I'm such a jumble of emotions, it's hard to actually write how I am feeling.
>
> Only one thing comes to mind. At the support group, they kept talking about "bereavement." That is definitely me. I am bereft. I try to nurture the love of words in my students. Words in a novel or in a poem aren't just words. You have to look deeper to uncover their full meaning. Take the word "bereft." It comes from the Old English "reafian," which means to rob. Those who are bereft are robbed. I've been robbed of Luke. Cruelly robbed. And I want him back.

Tiercy closed the book and took a deep breath. This was going to be excruciating. Yet she knew this was something that she needed to do if she was going to give her love with Cole a fair chance. Tiercy opened the journal and continued reading.

> July 4
>
> Independence Day. I was supposed to go to her aunt's beach house with Ross. But I just can't go. Too many things associated with Luke. Every beach tradition I have now as an adult is connected to Luke. The way

he'd call out Latin names for body parts while we played flag football—his medical student play-by-play. 'Somerville extends his brachium to capture the flying pigskin...' It was ridiculous. And it always made me laugh. Or the way he'd insist on turning his steamed crab the opposite way so the 'poor dead crabbie won't look at me while I consume him.' And the way he'd tip his head back drinking his Stella. He'd look at me and wink. I'd watch the convulsion of his neck as he swallowed and think 'I cannot wait to kiss him exactly there.' We'd watch fireworks on the beach. He'd say "ain't that purty" to all his favorites. No. I can't go to the beach. It's not my independence day. I'm imprisoned in memories. And I don't want to escape.

July 5

I cannot stop this painful, incessant wrangling with my guilt. For at least two weeks prior to 'That Day,' Luke complained of back pain. He is (was...will not be getting used to that change of tense) an ER doctor, for Pete's sake. I figured if it was serious, he'd be the first to know. He is a doc, works with docs. Don't they talk? At school, I can tell you when one of my teammates has an ingrown toenail. I guess we share more than he and his colleagues did. But I can't help but think...why didn't he say something to them? Even more: Why didn't I pursue it? Why didn't I make him get checked out? Whywhywhy? I failed him. I broke our wedding vows. I didn't look after him in sickness.

And now he's gone.

Brinder says a thoracic aneurysm is commonly missed and misdiagnosed in young, healthy people. So, even if he had it checked out, no guarantees they'd have caught it. I think he feels guilty too. We're all mired in guilt. It sucks.

July 6

Today I drank an entire bottle of wine. It felt good. Until it didn't. I've been vomiting nonstop. I'd like to say it's the first time I've done this. But it's not.

July 7

It's exactly nine steps from my side of the bed to the bathroom. Does this count as a grief journal entry?

July 9

My boobs are killing me and I'm bloated. I must be getting my period. Which explains why I'm cranky and ravenous. It's no fun PMSing without Luke nearby to offer to rub my back and feed me chocolate. He had a way of making PMS fun. Seriously. Leave it to a doctor to take shark week and turn it into an event. Just realized I haven't gotten one since...Well. Since. I will say since "Before."

July 10

Today is our anniversary. 5 years ago today, we said 'I will.' I keep watching our wedding video over and over. I just pause it on his face. At one point he smiled at our videographer. I kept it on pause and walked over and kissed the TV screen. Traced my fingers on the outline of his face.

July 11

I heard something today at the support group. It was from a really wonderful Episcopal priest, Mother Rebecca, who comes to pray with us sometimes. She said, "The pain of grief is an expression of depth of love." Well, Luke, based on the pain I am feeling, there is no doubt I love you deeply.

July 13

I am writing this at 1 a.m., so I guess it's technically July 14. I cannot even begin to process what happened today. It's surreal. And, for the first time since May, I'm not alone. I guess I wasn't alone before. I just didn't know it. I can't even write fast enough to put this all down.

OK. Back up. This week we hit the three-month mark. Luke's been gone three months. In some ways it feels like three minutes. In other ways, three years. Time is so elastic right now, and I can't figure it out. My plan was to do something original and stay in bed all day. Ha...

Instead, Mom and Ross did this intervention thing. They basically stormed my little grief fortress. They bullied me out of bed and told me if I didn't get in the shower, they'd put me in fully clothed. I gave them my meanest teacher look, but honestly, Mom saw worse from me as a teenager and she is totally impervious now.

I stood in the shower for a long time. I was grateful for Luke's ginormous water heater. I let the water just run all over me until my fingers were pruned and the water was getting cold. Ross started hollering that she was sending in the SEALs to come rescue me, unless she jumped the hottest one first and had her way with him on my bed. Which made me laugh in the shower.

I was so mad at her for making me laugh when I just wanted to wallow. My boobs were killing me. I needed chocolate. When I finally stepped out of the shower I caught a glimpse of myself in the mirror. It was pretty steamed up, but I could see enough. I look emaciated. I ran my hands along my torso. Ribs and bones. My hip bones jut out. I smeared the mirror with my forearm to get a better look. It was terrible. I look positively gaunt. Somehow my boobs were spared and seem to have retained their fat. Score one for the genetics, I thought at the time. More than that, I thought about Luke - how he'd call them his "fun bags."

Freaked out by how I looked, I got dressed. Nothing really fit, so I just threw on a maxi dress. You know those scared straight films they show teens? I was basically scared straight. I resolved to immediately eat the biggest burger I could find. All I could think was, Luke would be horrified. He'd probably slap an IV in me or something.

When I left the room, Mom and Ross were waiting in the living room. Mom had her keys. I asked where we were going. She said, "The doctor." I asked why. But I knew. The mirror didn't lie. If they were seeing what I saw, I'm sure they were freaked too. They were surprised when I didn't fight them. And also when I grabbed a couple cookies from the tin Ross must have brought.

When we got in the exam room, the doctor took all my vitals. Asked me a ton of questions. Told me I needed to gain 20 pounds. (I'd lost more than that in the three months since That Day, which is how I will evermore think of it.) The phlebotomist took some blood and I peed in a cup. Good times. The doc tried to talk me into an antidepressant. And, honestly, if she'd asked me the day before, I probably would have said Why Not. But for some reason, it was like a curtain had been lifted. My mind was feeling clearer. I can't explain it. I think seeing myself in the mirror triggered something primeval in myself...some survival instinct going back to our caveman days. She sent in the prescription anyway, telling me that even though I was feeling better it was normal to have ups and downs. That I didn't need to take it but I'd have it if I changed my mind.

Then we went out to lunch. I ate a huge burger. And fries. And a milkshake. I could see Mom and Ross trying to look at each other surreptitiously. Except they were so totally obvious. Then my cellphone rang. It was the doctor.

This is where it gets mind-blowingly, completely crazy. And yet I knew what she was going to say. Because the realization had been building since I saw myself after the shower. I'm not alone.

I'm pregnant.

July 16

I haven't written in a couple days. It's been a blur. I'm pregnant. Almost 15 weeks, according to the doctor. And I know exactly what day I got pregnant. The day I bought the phone. The day we flirted at the store. Retail foreplay. It had to be that day. I can't quite believe it. Luke left me a gift. A part of him. I immediately freaked out. I haven't had prenatal vitamins. I've consumed way too much alcohol. I've barely been eating. This poor little baby. I've inebriated it and starved it. The doctor told me not to worry. She said this happens sometimes (well, maybe not the extreme circumstances and probably not the drunken, grief-stricken wallowing), and that these fetuses are hardier than we can imagine.

I didn't like that word "fetus." I'm suddenly very attached (emotionally in addition to literally) to this little person. She said to just start taking my folic acid right away and prenatal vitamins. And to gain weight—which should not be a problem. I'm hungrier than the teenage boys I see with two trays of lunch in the cafeteria and then they go back for dessert. It's impressive. I should challenge them to an eating contest when I get back to school. I'm technically in the second trimester. Given this start to his life, he'll probably need therapy. Oh, that's the other thing. I'm sure, very very sure, that this is a little boy. Luke's son.

I talk to Luke every day. I mean, out loud. And now I'm talking to the baby too. I guess I don't feel quite as lonely.

July 17

I am happy and sad and mad and thrilled and overwhelmed. Today I heard Perseus' heartbeat. Yes, I'm calling him Perseus. After the great Greek hero who slays monsters. This baby slayed my grief, at least in its prior debilitating form. Maybe I won't really call him that, but he needs a nickname. This baby is epic already and deserves an epic nickname. Ross calls him Percy for short. But I like Perseus.

It was my first appt with my new midwife at the birthing center. I've been researching online, and I know that's what I want. I'll chew glass before I step back in Fellowship-Unity. I can't go back into that hospital. I won't ever again—not willingly.

First, she dropped a piece of news I wasn't prepared to hear—and yet it didn't surprise me at all. Based on my last period, she told me that Perseus was probably conceived on...That Day. I mean, the sex happened sooner. But the actual implantation? That Day.

Then I heard his heartbeat. So fast!!! Whoosh whoosh whoosh whoosh. Ross was holding my hand.

And then I just started sobbing. Luke should be here. He should be hearing this. He'd go nuts. The doctor in him would be all over this. He'd be measuring me, and analyzing things, talking to the midwife, and reading up. I know it. He's missing out. And I'm missing out. He should be here with me and it's not fair.

Crying in solidarity with her past self, Tiercy skimmed ahead to the end of August.

August 27

School starts in a couple days. And today I got my first ultrasound. I'm 20 weeks. Halfway there. Mom, Dad, Ross, and Brinder came. They all crowded in. It was ridiculous in the room. The poor tech. She didn't know what to think. I was on the table, cold jelly on my cute little belly. The tech moved the wand around. At first, it looked like nothing. And then I could see it. See him. My baby!

Brinder was watching intently. The tech took a bunch of pictures. Nodded and smiled. Everything looks good. She printed a few pictures and we oohed and aahed. Then the midwife came in and nodded at me. She goggled at Brinder. Pretty sure she has the hots for him. Brinder just gave his awkward smile. She asked us if we want to know the sex of Perseus. But I said No. I already know. Luke sent me a little boy. Brinder smiled. I think he saw. He's a radiologist for God's sake. He better have seen. I purposely didn't look too closely. All I needed to see was Perseus swimming in there. And everything appearing OK (despite his early starvation and inebriation via his mother).

His mother. I think this is the first time I've written it. I'm a mother. Good God.

She flipped ahead more pages. The rain was coming down steadily, but she could see the sky beginning to brighten. The sun even shone in places, despite the rain. Classic summer storm.

Sept. 29
Tonight I stood in the shower and cried for a very long time...

Oct. 31
I look like I have a pumpkin on my abdomen. Hard to believe next Halloween I'll have a 10-month old. Perseus kicks so much. I'll be in class, and he just kicks away... He prefers the Brits—very active in Brit Lit, but less so in American Lit.

Nov. 3
I am incredibly sad. Tonight, I was alone in the house. Completely alone. And Perseus was doing acrobatics in my belly. I just watched him, mesmerized. But I was alone in bed. No Luke. I'll say it again for the thousandth time. He should BE here. I want to talk with him about this. Confide my fears (childbirth???). I want Luke. I want Luke. I want Luke. I just want Luke.

Thanksgiving

Last year, Luke worked in the morning, but he had off the rest of the day. I did a Turkey Run. It was biting cold, but the air on my face was exhilarating. I crested a hill, and as I caught speed on the descent, I wondered why everyone doesn't do this. I got home, freezing cold and basking with the happy exhaustion of filling my lungs over and over again with fresh, crisp air and pushing my muscles to their limit. All of Luke's siblings were in town last year, and my mom and dad hosted a big dinner. Ross came (refusing again to go to the farmhouse in Virginia, despite her grandmother's pleas).

It was my favorite holiday dinner ever. Luke and I had decided to "pull the goalie" in the next year, and we both sat there wondering if next year I'd be pregnant, or we'd even have a little newborn. We kept smiling secret smiles.

This year, he's gone. I still can't believe it. Sometimes I just randomly burst into tears. I'm not sure if it's grief or baby hormones or both. I feel like I can't be totally happy about Perseus because it would somehow undermine my grief. And Luke deserves to be grieved. So, I can't be totally happy about the baby and I can't be totally sad about Luke. So, Happy Thanksgiving. Or whatever.

Dec. 31

I would seriously kill for a glass—hell, a bottle—of

champagne. Ross and Brinder are over, and he made this amazing Indian meal. Then we had English crackers, where you pull them apart and you get a crown and a toy and a joke. Mine: Why do melons have weddings? They cantelope. Ross, working on a nice buzz, laughed so hard she snorted champagne out her nose. Brinder gave me the most amazing foot rub. It was positively orgasmic. I also asked them tonight if they'd be Perseus' godparents. We did this spontaneous little group hug. It was special. But I'm feeling overwhelmed, so I sneaked into my room to write a little while they clean up. They are trying hard to keep the mood light and I am too. It's exhausting not saying Luke's name. So I'll just say it here: I love you, Luke. Happy New Year.

Jan. 17

It's 3 a.m. and I woke about an hour ago from the most intense dream. It was about Luke, and he was going down on me and touching me. Rubbing me. His fingers were inside me and his mouth was on me. The tension built and built. I woke in the midst of a mind-blowing orgasm. My heart was racing, and I was sweating and so damp between my legs. For a second, I thought my water broke.

I read in my pregnancy book that this type of sleep orgasm is not uncommon—a side effect of raging hormones. It made me realize that I haven't had an orgasm since early May, and I don't know when I

ever will again. The idea of making love to anyone but
Luke is unimaginable. So now I'm tossing and turning,
and incredibly horny. Luke's side of the bed is
untouched. And that is how I will remain, I guess.
Untouched.

Jan. 31

I went to the midwife. A fingertip dilated. 5%
effaced. She said I could stay this way for a while.
Brinder took me out for very spicy Indian food to try
to get things going. Now I'm sitting in the bathroom
with the worst heartburn ever. Perseus is also not happy
with me. But no labor.

Feb. 2

Today is my due date. No action. I'd kill to go for
a run. But I'm hugely pregnant. Oh...and it's 25
degrees out. But other than that...

Feb. 5 - 5 a.m.

I am officially in labor. I just got out of the
shower. The midwife told me to take a long hot shower to
see if the contractions space back apart, but they are
coming on strong and long.

Feb. 6

I am a mother. Of a girl!!! Perseus is a girl! We
got to the birthing center at 5:30. I was already 7 cm.
and mostly effaced. I thought I would curse a lot or
cry a lot. It hurt like crazy. But honestly, I welcomed

the pain. With every contraction, Luke's baby was closer to joining me in the world. I was so calm. My midwife, Theresa, told me to feel free to yell or scream or cry. But I didn't. I was laser focused. And almost out-of-body calm. I swear I could FEEL Luke's presence. I know he was in the room. Ross was on one side and my mom on the other as I urged my little baby into the world. But I could just...see...Luke at my feet. He was there.

I had made a music mix to play during labor. Just as the baby was crowning, Luke's favorite song came on, "Are You Ready for This," from Jock Jams. 'Y'all ready for this?' It's not exactly soothing, but it was his "get pumped up" music and he would always play it when he needed to psych himself up for something. When the song came on, just at the peak of a contraction, I let out a laugh. The force of the laugh pushed my baby into this world. She was born in laughter. Then we all started laughing. I know it was Luke, letting me know he was here with me.

Then I cried. Mom cried. Ross didn't. (She never cries. It's a thing with her that goes back to when her own parents died. But she did get a little misty. I saw it before she turned away to compose herself.) Brinder came into the room. He is totally besotted with the baby. Everyone was waiting for me to name her. I Facetimed with Luke's parents. His mom said the baby looks just like her mother, Jemima, whom everyone called Jemma. Luke adored his Grandma Jemma. So there it is:

Jemma Cathleen Somerville.

Feb. 7

Welcome home, Jemma! I can't journal because this baby is attached to my breast incessantly. Here I thought she was a parasite inside me. I was worried she'd suck me dry, but my milk just came in and apparently I could be a wet nurse.

April 10

I dreamed of you last night.

Thank you for coming to me in my dream, Luke. I loved seeing your beautiful hazel eyes and your crooked smile. In my dream, I heard your voice. I woke, and for a moment, I forgot you were gone. And when I remembered, it was devastating. I fed Jemma and sobbed, my tears falling on her as she nursed contentedly. The side of her head was wet from it. I am so sad. And yet, if it's the only way I can have you, I would love for you to come visit me in my dreams again. Even if temporarily forgetting and then remembering was so shattering.

May 12

One year. I can't write. I can't anything.

Tiercy flipped through more pages. The entries were sporadic, and with the distance of time, she could see a clear pattern. Entries about Jemma and her milestones. Entries about Luke and her grief. Grief that morphed from the raw to the steady hum of sadness that would periodically crest in a stealth wave, sending her tumbling. Anger and regret when there would be something special with Jemma that she wanted Luke to be a part of. Frustration that she could never totally immerse herself in her joy because of the guilt she'd feel. Guilt for the times she allowed the bliss to seep in and she just reveled in her beautiful daughter.

Her journaling became more and more infrequent, triggered by deep joy or deep sadness...and sometimes a juxtaposition of both that would leave her emotionally disoriented and physically drained.

She looked ahead, scanning for a specific set of entries. The summer shower had stopped, leaving the grass a bright green, the rich hue activated by the rain.

There it was. Two years ago.

May 12

Today, I took my wedding rings off. It's been three years since Luke died. I am still every inch his wife, and I always will be. But something has been happening inside me lately. I feel like my rings are a symbol of the past, and I need to move forward. I will never stop loving Luke, but I'd been having thoughts about taking off my rings. I was thinking of putting them in the safety deposit box, and then when Jemma turns 16, melting the gold of his ring and mine into a new setting for Jemma, with my diamond solitaire. But then I felt so guilty. I asked Luke for a sign to let me know it's OK. He sends me signs all the time.

I waited for it. He never lets me down. Here's the thing. Jemma, at age two, looks just like Luke. She has his coloring—hair and eyes. She even has his mannerisms. It's freaky sometimes. Dad was reading to her, a funny little story about Grover called The Monster at the End of this Book. Jemma burst into laughter...and she rubbed her hand on her face, just like Luke used to.

But there's more. Forever, Mom has been trying to get Jemma to call her Gigi. Luke would always call my mom "Lovie" ever since a funny conversation we had one night when we all were talking about what character on Gilligan's Island we'd be. Dad insisted that he was Thurston Howell III, so that would make Mom Lovie. But no one has called her that since Luke died. My dad will occasionally call my mom 'my love' and I'm sure Jemma has heard that. But just after Jemma finished the book with Dad, and she made him re-read it to her, she turned to my mom and said, "Fank you, Lovie." We were all floored.

As I write this, my rings are in my safe in the basement, and in fourteen years, I'll make Jemma a very special setting. For the first time in eight years, I'm not wearing my rings.

Sept 18

I'm tired of being lonely. And maybe I wanted to test myself. To see if I could still be a "normal" woman after almost three-and-a-half years of this bizarre existence without Luke. So, I did something. Last night, I went out on a date with an English teacher from another school in the district. We met at a teacher professional conference for the county, and he asked me out. It was so nice to just be Tiercy. Not

Tiercy, Jemma's mom. Or Tiercy the tragic widow. He knew that I have a daughter, but I think he just assumed I'm divorced.

Ross has Jemma with her. She took her for pedicures (at age 3??, but Ross insisted there's always little girls at the salon and she'd love it) and a movie. Then they were having a "sleepover." And I went on a date.

He's a nice guy. Masters in Shakespearean studies, and we had a fascinating conversation about the Bard. I picked up some good info for when I teach the section on Romeo and Juliet to my freshmen in October. We had cocktails before dinner. Then a bottle of wine. He's handsome in sort of a brainy way. Just a little bit taller than me. Maybe 5'11." But he has a cute smile. Outside the restaurant, he leaned in to kiss me. I let him. I kissed him back. It was nice. Then he asked if I wanted to go back to his place to look at his Shakespeare collection—which struck me as the funniest line I'd ever heard. I just started laughing and told him that I didn't want to see his Shakespeare. That I wanted to see his 'spear.'

He laughed at my pun, and I laughed. And then we both realized I wasn't kidding. We caught an Uber to his place and made out in the back. When we got to his townhouse, I had the strangest feeling of not really being there. I just went through the motions. When he slid on a condom and slipped inside me, I just closed my eyes. It wasn't bad and it wasn't good. It just...

was. And then it was over. We made an attempt at pillow talk, but it was useless. He got up to get us some water, and while he did that, I got dressed.

When he came back in the room, wearing just his boxer shorts, he saw me fully dressed and ready to go. He just set down the water and nodded. He helped me with my jacket. Called an Uber for me. We kissed goodnight, but it was pretty chaste, considering he'd been inside me not 45 minutes prior. I got in the car. I made it all the way to my kitchen before I just lost it.

I screamed myself hoarse. I broke a vase. I stripped off my clothes and scrubbed myself until I was practically raw in the shower. The crazy thing is, I was so horny. But not for that guy. For Luke. It was like something ignited in me. I touched myself until I came, calling out Luke's name. And then I dried off, got into bed naked and fell asleep.

Oct. 16

I am so angry tonight. Just pissed off. Everything went wrong at work. And when I dug down and summoned some reserves that I didn't even realize I have, I picked Jemma up from preschool and she proceeded to barf all over the car…and then the hallway. She even puked in my hair as I carried her up the stairs. 102 fever. She's been sick at least five times. I had dried barf on the ends of my hair, which I could smell every time I moved my head. There is vomit in the seams of the hardwoods in the hallway, which I'll need to clean with a brush. I finally got her settled, and then I had to go clean out my car, which I'm sure will smell like vomit for who knows how long no matter what I do.

And all I can think is: Luke would have helped me clean the car. You probably would have run out and gotten me one of those deodorizer trees that smell like pine or vanilla. And you would have helped me clean the floor. You would have sung to Jemma while I washed my hair, and teased me about it later. You would have been here. And maybe I would have gotten a little break today. Maybe you would have listened to me sympathetically while I complained about work.

And we would have worked together to soothe our little girl. She's still so tiny. We would have partnered to get through it. And when we finally settled her down, maybe we would have collapsed in bed together, praying that we didn't catch this crud. We would have read or talked. Just chilled out together. Listened for Jemma together, in case she cried in the night. I am so fucking out of gas. I'm on empty.

All I can think of right now is the line from Wicked about going to a land of what might have been.

That's how I feel. Tonight, I lived an entire parallel universe, where you were with me. Where you, Jemma, and I were a family. Where we cared for our sick little girl, and while we did that, quietly planned for a brother or sister for her. Where you listened to me gripe about my day. Where we talked about the hospital. Where we were us, as we should have been. As it was supposed to be.

That's what I did tonight, Luke, when I was running on empty. I went to the land of what might have been. And I loved it there.

Tiercy flipped through more pages to another entry from this past January—one that made her stomach roil as she recalled the evening in excruciating detail.

Jan. 1

I rang in the new year in an unexpected way. Ross and I went out to this cool bar. She's hooking up with the owner, and he set us up with free hooch all night. The bartender was about 25 and oozing with hotness. He was, quite literally, the most gorgeous thing I've ever laid eyes on. And for whatever reason, he seemed into me. I was pretty buzzed. At midnight, he kissed me. Ross hugged me, waggled her eyebrows, and then she and the owner disappeared. A bit later, he leaned into me and told me he was going on break. As he walked into a back room, he turned and motioned with his head to follow. I followed. 30 seconds later, he was sheathed in a condom, and taking me up against the wall. It was wham-bam…and hot.

And soulless.

This morning I made a pact with myself that I will never let another man touch me like that again. I've tried twice to feel like a woman again. And twice I've *failed, and felt so cheap and guilty after. I don't want to sully what Luke and I had. So that's it. Ross says never say never, and that I might feel different if I actually loved the other person. But I can't imagine ever loving again. Not like that.*

There it was. The words she had been seeking all afternoon. "I can't ever imagine loving again. Not like that."

Not like that. But...what if loving Cole was completely different? What if the only thing her love with Cole had in common with her love with Luke was...her?

Chapter Forty-Nine

"He's more myself than I am. Whatever our souls are made of,
his and mine are the same."
Wuthering Heights, Emily Brontë

TIERCY

In the three days since her emotional conversation with Cole, Tiercy'd had three fitful nights' sleep, myriad vacillatory conversations with Ross, and daily anguished conversations with Luke, begging him for a sign to indicate his approval...or not.

Jemma spent day four in Cate and Neal's backyard pool, practicing what she called her "bread stroke," recently learned at her swim lessons at the Y. Cate had urged Tiercy to come and enjoy the summer day, but Tiercy needed time to think in peace and quiet.

During typical summer days, her focus was on Jemma, along with enjoying the seasonal break from the demands of teaching teenagers. She loved the extra time with her daughter, but sometimes felt that her cadre of one hundred thirty students across five classes was infinitely easier than one mule-headed four-year-old.

After the constant barrage on her heart—grappling with Cole's logic and love versus her own inner turmoil—being Jemma's only parent was exhausting. Tiercy was the main recipient of all her questions, her drama, her attitude—and also her sugary sweet kisses, her sticky hugs, and her love. Jemma had many who adored her fiercely, including her grandparents and her godparents. But Tiercy was Jemma's axis, and sometimes the demands of that solo status were crushing. When Cate asked if Jemma wanted to play in the pool, Tiercy almost cried tears of relief —commingled with guilt—when Jemma squealed her agreement.

The afternoon sun was slanting through the French doors when Tiercy heard her mother's car door slam shut, followed by the slapping of Jemma's tiny flip-flops on the floor. She couldn't make out a single word, but she could hear a steady stream of chatter coming from her daughter, and an occasional murmured reply from her mother.

The hall bathroom door opened and closed. Tiercy listened to the sound of running water through the pipes in the shared wall. A soft tapping at her door was followed by a flash of ginger hair, and then her mother's concerned face, peering around the frame. She had clearly been in the pool. Her chin-length hair—faded a bit from her younger days, but still maintaining a golden luster—had dried into chlorine-supported waves.

Tears pricked behind Tiercy's eyes, and she held her arms out to her mother. Sometimes you just needed your mommy. This was one of those times.

"Oh, my baby girl. Is this about Cole?"

Tiercy nodded, wiping her eyes.

Her mom listened to ensure Jemma was well-occupied with her dad and then closed the bedroom door. "Gramps is overseeing bath time. Which means that there will be more water on the floor than in the tub when it's over." They shared knowing smiles.

Going around to the side of the bed where Tiercy was stretched, wadded tissues scattered around, her mom sat down and gathered Tiercy into her arms. As Tiercy quietly wept, her mom stroked her hair and rocked her as she had so very long ago.

Rays of sunlight filtered through the sheer curtains, dappling the bed in their diffused glow. Slowly, Tiercy began to pour out her heart, in the special way a daughter can with her mother.

"Mom, you know that ever since Right After, I've always had signs from Luke. Whenever I really need something, really need *him*, I talk to him and ask him for a sign. And he always sends something. Always. Some people are skeptical, but I *know* it. I know he's reaching out to me."

Tiercy spoke haltingly, struggling to say aloud what had been in her heart since the moment she realized her feelings for Cole had blossomed to something far greater than she could have ever imagined. "I need Luke to tell me—to let me know...it's OK—that *he's* OK...better than OK...with me and Cole..."

"You want a sign from Luke indicating his approval for you to give your heart fully to Cole," her mom finished for her. Then she paused, looking out into the distance, brow furrowed in the way that signaled she was gathering her thoughts. "You want a sign from Luke, and I understand why, my sweet. But many times in life we don't have signposts guiding the way. Instead, we have to rely on our hearts. The sign that matters most of all is what is in here." She gently tapped Tiercy's heart. "Luke loved you beyond words, but he would never want you to miss following your heart while you waited for some definitive sign from him that may or may not come."

"In my brain, I know you're right. But in my heart...I can't let go of that."

Her mom smiled gently. "Tiercy, when Luke proposed, did you make him wait until you received some kind of sign?"

"No..."

"Then why are you holding Cole to a different standard? He loves you, Tiercy. And Jemma. He's devoted to you. You'd have to be blind not to see what happens between the two of you when you're together. Makes me want to tell you to get a room!"

"Mom!" Tiercy gave a shocked yelp, and then laughed.

She waved a dismissive hand. "You all think you invented sex. Let me tell you, I'm pretty sure your dad and I invented it. We're really good at it."

"Mom! Over-share alert!" Tiercy slapped her hands over her ears dramatically as her mom broke into her husky laugh.

Sounds of splashing, high-pitched laughs, and her dad's deeper one drew their attention.

"I better check on the kids—the little one and the big one." Her mom rose and walked to the bedroom door. "You follow your heart. Luke will let you know." Her mom blew her a kiss. "Now," she added briskly, "get yourself together. We have a date with a bossy four-year-old for a mac and cheese dinner, and then to act out Star Wars for her bedtime story. I call dibs on being Princess Leia. I'm going to win Han back from Skeletor."

That night, after kissing Luke's picture, Jemma wrapped her arms around her mother's neck. "Mommy," she asked, her voice sleepy, "is Coley going to be my daddy?"

Tiercy opened her mouth and realized she had no idea how to answer.

"I miss Coley. I hope he's finished with his big project soon." That was the lie she'd told her daughter to explain his absence. "Because I like him. Do you like him, Mommy?" she asked.

Tiercy's heart compressed and stuttered. "Yes, sweetness. I like him very much."

"Does Daddy like him?"

Tiercy was taken aback by her daughter's prescient question, which in many ways echoed what she herself had been wondering. She waited a moment, collecting her thoughts.

"Well, lovebuggie, there is no way of knowing for sure..." Tiercy could barely finish, her throat tightening in sorrow.

"I think Daddy likes Coley very much," Jemma pronounced, in her 'that settles it' tone that was so reminiscent of Luke. Satisfied with her own answer, she rolled onto her side, snuggling into her pillow, Niamh tucked under her arm. "G'night, Mommy." She puckered up for a kiss.

"Good night, Jemma. I love you."

Tiercy left the room, and instead of feeling relieved with the important endorsement from Jemma, struggled with the fact that— even if it seemed absurd—she still needed a sign from Luke.

CHAPTER FIFTY

TIERCY

Tiercy had never experienced such mental anguish. She had loved deeply and buried a husband just as their lives should have been beginning. But this was different. It was a high stakes game where her heart, and Cole's, were the wager. Now it was her bet. Choose wrong, either way, and hearts would be broken. And this time, Tiercy feared, hers would not heal again.

Tiercy needed to run. It was seven a.m. and already eighty degrees, but she craved the slap of her running shoes on blacktop, the sensation of burning lungs as she forced oxygen through them. She required the mindless oblivion that often came to her when she pushed her body to its physical limits.

Quickly dressing in her running gear, she called her mother and asked her to watch Jemma, who was still sound asleep. It was early, but her dad was going to be showing a house to a prospective buyer, so they both were up-and-at-it.

Tiercy was already stretching in the living room when her mom pulled in twenty minutes later. They exchanged a wordless hug, and Tiercy walked out the door she had left open, ready to run it out.

At about the ten-mile mark, Tiercy realized she was running in a direction that surprised her. It was as if her feet were moving of their own volition and she was instinctively following. Up a hill. Around a bend. Down a tree-lined driveway into a parking lot that abutted a large park with tennis courts, a baseball field, and three basketball courts. Tiercy headed in that direction.

There was a lone figure shooting hoops on the far court. Lay-up after lay-up. Shot after shot. The sound of rubber bouncing on the asphalt was a familiar sound, and one she'd avoided for years. Tiercy ran closer, and then stopped short, recognizing the form.

Brinder.

Beyond the disastrous encounter at her house, and then the hospital after her accident, they had barely communicated. Nothing more than a few quick texts.

Breathing heavily from her exertions in the heat, she sat on a bench by the side of the court. A plaque on the top wooden slat had heated up in the sun, and she pressed her back against it, welcoming the burn. She knew what the brass plaque said without looking.

In Memory of Luke Somerville, MD
The Ultimate Hemoglobin Trotter
Shooting Threes in Heaven

His friends had cleared it with her first, and of course she'd agreed. They'd invited her to see the bench and plaque when it was installed, but she couldn't go. Wasn't ready to face the court—the place where Luke had breathed his last. Even now, she couldn't quite believe she was there.

Brinder had stopped shooting. He was facing the net, ball tucked under his arm.

No longer winded, Tiercy's heart rate slowly settled. "You've been avoiding me."

He kept his back to her. "I know. I'm sorry." Brinder continued quietly, "It was right here. He was standing here when it happened. I could see he wasn't right. His game was off. He was missing his threes from the perimeter. Missing easy lay-ups. Something was wrong. At first, I thought he was in a fight with you. But it was different. Why didn't I stop the game? Why didn't I just *ask* him?"

Tiercy rose on surprisingly steady legs and walked over, putting her arms around him and resting her cheek against his back. Brinder sobbed.

"I am so sorry, Tiercy. I should have seen it. Should have known. I was his best friend, and a doctor, for God's sake. If I had just—"

"Brinder. Stop." Tiercy released her hug and moved around to face him. Sweat was pouring down his face, mixed with tears. Heart aching, she stroked his cheek as she would Jemma's. "Luke was a doctor, too. Heck, every single one of you playing was a doctor. He worked every day with doctors. You were his best friend. *I was his wife.* Why didn't he say anything to any of us?" .

"I had a professor of philosophy in college who used to say there is the unknown and the unknowable. This falls into the category of the unknowable. We will never know why, Brinder. We have to stop berating ourselves for something we can't undo or understand."

Brinder looked at her and tilted his head. "How did you know I was here?"

"I didn't," Tiercy shrugged. "I woke up this morning in emotional knots and I just had to go for a run. Without thinking, I ended up at the court. And here you are. Why are you here?"

"I have a shift later, but I was feeling restless. Luke's been on my mind a lot lately. I feel like—like I betrayed him with my schoolboy infatuation with you... I feel like such a wanker. That's why I haven't been by to see you...and Jemma."

Brinder took a couple steps and grabbed his water bottle from next to the basketball pole. He swallowed a large gulp, and then offered it to Tiercy. "You look to be in need of some hydration as well," he gestured to the front of her running shirt, which was soaked with perspiration. "If you don't mind sharing some germs." He held the bottle out to her.

"We've shared germs before. I think it's OK." Tiercy offered a rueful smile and gratefully accepted the water.

"Tiercy, I am so sorry about that night. I was wrong to take advantage."

"I'm the one who should be apologizing. I made the first move. Then you bared your heart, and I stomped on it. Which seems to be my M.O. these days," she added dolefully. "What I don't understand is, why did you leave the country without saying anything? And then you didn't respond to any of my messages."

Brinder sighed. "I needed to get away. I'd actually been thinking of the trip for a while. I had a ton of vacation and was in a use-it-or-lose-it place. My cousin and I have been in touch on Facebook, communicating for some time. I thought perhaps it would be good to meet my father's family. I have an entire family in India I don't know. My grandparents are dead. There is no reason to continue this exile just because my parents had the gall to buck not one but two very ingrained cultures. I've been curious for ages, and when Sanjay invited me, I just went. He'd sent the message the day before the fundraiser. Then the—interlude— with us happened. I talked to Ben Lopez the next morning, arranged for coverage with the radiology team, and I just...went."

"But you didn't say anything."

"Tiercy, I was incredibly hurt—both my heart and my stupid pride. And I was upset. But mostly at myself. Look, I think it's pretty obvious I've fancied you for quite some time. I had even convinced myself Luke would have wanted it this way, for us to be together."

"Brinder, I—" Tiercy began.

"No, I'd like to finish, please." Brinder's voice was gentle but insistent. "Let's sit." He took her by the hand and they sat on Luke's bench.

"I thought I could do right by him—love you and be a father to Jemma. But when we were kissing, in Luke's bed, I knew it was wrong. It felt wrong emotionally, even if physically it felt good at the moment." He gave an embarrassed smile. "So, I ran. But not from you. I just needed to clear my head.

"I'm thirty-five years old, Tiercy. And I've spent the past four years believing I was in love with my best friend's widow, deluding myself that it was the right thing. And when I suddenly realized it was the wrong thing, the only way I could straighten my brain and my feelings was to go somewhere far away, where everything would be new. I went to Sanjay's and stayed for almost a month."

"I never thanked you for taking care of me that day in the ER," Tiercy whispered. "I was just in a state of shock, and then I hadn't seen you since that night...and it was awkward."

"Mmm, and then your massive bloke came barreling in and literally swept you away." Brinder watched her face carefully. "He is your bloke, right? He called himself your boyfriend. I don't know what that was between you two, but it was pretty intense. Sadie was wagging her tongue within seconds of your rather dramatic departure, and the hospital buzzed about it for ages."

Tiercy sighed. "Yes, well, my 'massive bloke' is why I've been doing some running myself." She pointed to her running shoes.

"Do you want to talk about it?"

"Brinder, don't you find it odd that I've never come here before and when I do, you just happen to be here?"

"What are you saying, Tierce?"

"I'm saying that I think Luke brought us here together today. He knew I needed some medicine from Dr. Desai."

Brinder gave his yummy posh laugh. It was so good to hear that sound again.

"First of all, I do come here a lot, so perhaps it's not as coincidental as you think. But, assuming you are correct, and Luke wanted me to assist you, please continue. Let's see what I am able to diagnose. I'm good at that."

"Imaging studies and affairs of the heart. You are a multi-talented diagnostician."

"I'm here to serve." He rolled the basketball toward her with his foot. "Now, shoot."

Tiercy took a deep breath, holding it for several seconds and then exhaling. "Cole is in love with me."

"Can't say as I blame the guy. And I'm assuming you return his feelings?"

"Yes, but that's the problem. We've fallen in pretty deep pretty quickly. He's amazing. Jemma adores him. And I...well, I have some really big feelings for him. And that's the problem."

"Doesn't sound like much of a problem to me."

"But don't you see? It is. I'm not sure I can let myself love him the way I desperately want to. I'm scared."

Brinder was quiet for a moment. He looked up at the sky, as if searching for the right thing to say. "Radiology isn't the sexiest field in medicine. We sit in dark rooms and look at disembodied images. But in those images, there are moments of crystal clarity. That's the art of what we do. Behind those images, there are real people. People who are in some kind of health crisis, whether large or small. And it's our job to get as close to the truth as possible so we can give them hope. Tragedies happen, Tierce. I see it every day. But I see miracles happen as well. The tumor that appears malignant and diabolical, ends up being benign.

"What I'm endeavoring to say, and quite badly I might add, is that Luke saw those miracles too. We doctors are people of science and medicine, but things happen that are beyond science and medicine. There is something bigger than us out there, Tiercy. Different cultures and faiths call it different things. But it's there and it's real. And I know, beyond a doubt, Luke is still with us. And that he would want you to be happy. If this Cole fellow fills your heart with joy, then just *love him*. That kind of love is too rare to discard."

"But don't you see, Brinder," Tiercy cried, "I'm a swan. Swans mate for life. I had my mate, and he died here, not five feet from where we're sitting. I can't love again. Not like that."

Brinder cocked his head and smiled, as Tiercy swiped at her tears. "Why are you smiling?"

"Oh, my sweet Tiercy, who was an English major and not a zoology major. Do you want to know something about swans? They do mate for life, that's true. But you only have it partly right. When one swan dies, the remaining swan finds another mate, and they in turn mate for life. You *are* a swan, love. And now you have an opportunity to mate again for life."

"Are you making that up?" Tiercy looked at him skeptically. "You weren't a zoology major either, Brinder Desai."

"I am telling the truth, and I also watch a lot of animal documentaries on Nat Geo. Google it. You'll see I'm right. Tiercy, Luke would want you and Jemma to be loved. If he couldn't do it, he'd send someone who could."

He gathered Tiercy in his arms and held her, rocking her like a small child while she wept, tears of sorrow and tears of relief.

And in the place where Luke breathed his last, Tiercy found new life.

Brinder and Tiercy sat quietly for a long time. Eventually she asked the question that had been bothering her since May. "So, what about us? Where does that leave us?"

He quirked an eyebrow. "What do you mean what about us? I don't want to lose your friendship, and Jemma needs her godfather. I've already lost one friend, and I don't mean to lose another." He tapped her on her freckled nose. "Right then. Go get your swan."

Chapter Fifty-One

"She couldn't make him look like just any other man to her. He looked like the love thoughts of women. He was a glance from God."
Their Eyes Were Watching God, Zora Neale Hurston

TIERCY

There are moments in life when you just *know* something. When every cell in your body, every neuron in your brain, and every beat of your heart are in complete alignment.

Tiercy awoke with the warmth of the morning sun on her face. She squinted against the light, realizing she'd forgotten to close the shutters on her windows the night before. Her room faced east, and even with them closed, the room would brighten delightfully on sunny mornings —a beautiful wake-up from Mother Nature.

She sat up and stretched, feeling tight muscles pop. Her legs were sore from the long run the day before. She kicked them out from under the covers, stretched them out in front of her and reached forward, enjoying the delicious pull. Turning her head to the side, she looked at Luke's side of the bed, still smooth. An untouched homage to a man who had left her too soon, breaking her heart, and almost completely breaking her.

She lifted her head. But she *wasn't* broken. She had survived. And now it was time for her to live completely again, instead of enduring this painful, bizarre half-life she'd been ensnared in for more than five years —never fully sad or fully happy, even since Jemma was born.

A feeling of surety settled in her body. It reminded her of moments she felt as a student in school when something previously difficult to understand just clicked and it all made sense. Something that once bewildered and frustrated, a foreign concept, became fully known and understood.

"I love you, Luke. You are the love of my life. And now I'm going to go get the other love of my life," she whispered. "Please understand."

Resolution firm within her, she reached over and messed up Luke's side of the bed. She nodded at her handiwork and jumbled the sheets a bit more. It was intoxicating. Tiercy stood on the bed, and began jumping around, hopping all over the mattress and laughing like a loon.

Her daughter poked a sleepy, confused head around the doorframe. Spying her mother bounding all over the bed, Jemma called out, arms akimbo. "Just what are you doing, young lady?"

Tiercy burst into laughter and held her arms open for Luke's beautiful daughter. Jemma leapt on the bed at the invitation, grabbing her mother's hands. Together, they jumped on the bed, hitting each other with pillows and filling the early morning with sounds of glee.

Flopping breathless on the comforter, she pulled Jemma in her lap, cuddling her baby. "Jemma Buttercup, would it be OK with you if I go see Coley today? I think I want to kiss him."

Jemma offered a toothless smile, so like the gummy smile of her infancy, her second bottom tooth having fallen out the night before. "Yay, Mommy!" She threw her arms around her mother and squeezed.

"I'll take you to Lovie and Gramps. And then maybe Coley and you and I can get something to eat later."

"Chuck E. Cheese!" Jemma cheered.

Tiercy laughed. "Maybe." And then laughed even more, her heart soaring. "Now, I need to take a shower."

"OK, Mommy. I'm going to look at my ottopus book from the

'quarium. Did you know an ottopus has eight testicles? Dat's what Uncle Brinder says."

"Tentacles, Jemma. *Tentacles*."

"Oh, whatsa difference?"

"I'll explain later," Tiercy evaded with a quiet laugh, heading into the bathroom, shortening the nine steps into seven. She had a life-changing conversation to have.

CHAPTER FIFTY-TWO

COLE

Cole picked up on the first ring. "Tiercy." He'd been anticipating and dreading her call for days. It was the worst agony of his life—this rollercoaster of emotion. He'd played out the best scenarios in his head and been filled with joy. Just as plausible was the ending where she chose Luke, stubbornly holding fast to her notion of one love of her life versus a life of love with him. He thought his heart would shatter at the possibility.

"Where are you?"

"I'm at the construction site, in the trailer."

"Can you get away? Could you meet me at the park by the water, about a mile from the hospital?"

Cole's heart skipped a beat. "I know the place, and yes, I can get away." At the sound of her voice, hope and despair waged an epic battle in his heart.

"Fifteen minutes?"

Cole checked his watch. It was nine thirty a.m. He'd already been at work since six thirty, unable to sleep and figuring he'd at least make the best of his Tiercy-induced insomnia by getting more work done. Since their last parting, he'd worried incessantly that he'd pushed too hard and, as a result, he'd lost her completely.

The thought of that filled him with the deepest despair. He was in uncharted waters, inexplicably paralyzed. Aching to be with her but too scared to go to her, fearing she'd decided she couldn't commit to what he wanted.

"I'll see you then." Cole disconnected the call and strode to the little mirror his assistant Heather had affixed to the trailer wall. He hadn't shaved in days and his beard was growing. His eyes were haggard from sleepless nights, and he needed a haircut. Giving in to the reality that he'd have to face her looking like a frat boy recovering from a week-long bender, he did the best he could to smooth his hair and splashed water on his face in the tiny bathroom sink. He sniffed his underarms and added a bit of the deodorant he kept in the bottom desk drawer; he knew Tiercy liked the scent of it.

When Cole arrived at the park, he saw her immediately, as if his heart guided his eyes. That same heart began thudding in his chest. Was she there to shatter him...or would she grant him his greatest desire?

He made his way on the paved path toward the gazebo where she was standing, facing the water.

Without turning, she began to speak. "Something I always love about novels is the unexpected way a story can unfold. First it's the thrill of the unknown, and then it's the satisfaction of watching the pieces and parts come together. There's a magical moment, when the story knits together fully, revealing itself. And you think, 'Aha...there it is.'"

She faced him, her eyes brimming with unshed tears but a smile on her face. Cole loved her blue topaz eyes, and the glints of sun on her auburn hair, which had grown well past her shoulders. He reached over and rubbed the silky strands softly between his fingers.

Tiercy continued, "I had one of those moments this morning, Cole.

I woke alone in my bed, as I've done almost two thousand times since Luke died, and I felt my story knitting together, revealing itself. I don't know how my story ends, Cole. I just know I want you in it. The plot took an unexpected twist for me again this past May, and I love it." She put her hands on his face. "I love *you*."

Cole's own eyes filled with tears, and he grasped her in a fierce kiss, his fingers tight on her shoulders. Suddenly, he pulled away. "I want a big love, Tierce. With you. Can you love me like that? I can't be second best."

Tiercy took his trembling hand and squeezed it, her eyes full of hope and love.

"The last time we talked, you reminded me that the heart expands to bring in and hold more love. This morning, as I lay in my bed, basking in the sun on my face, I felt *different* inside. Everything clicked. And I just had to see you...to tell you this. I don't want you to take Luke's place. And you couldn't, even if you wanted to, even if I wanted you to. I want you to take *your* place, which my heart grew...just for you. Will you do that, Cole? Will you take your own special place in my heart?"

Cole had to ask it. "Can you have two loves of your life?"

Tiercy smiled. "I ran into Brinder the other day."

Cole's eyebrows raised.

"We had a good talk. We've both struggled with why Luke never said anything to either one of us when he had to be having some kind of symptoms. Maybe we could have done something. Saved him. But then I reminded Brinder, and myself, that some things are unknown and some are unknowable. But I know this: I will love Luke Somerville until the day I die, and beyond. But I love you too. And I know I don't want to live my life without you. I've already lost one love of my life. I don't intend to lose the other."

A tear escaped down Cole's stubbled cheek, and he collapsed to his knees in relief, softly crying. He leaned his head into her, and she stroked his hair. After a moment, he looked up at her. "Thou touchest my inmost center, Tiercy."

"Thou are tied to me by cords woven of my heartstrings," she whispered in response.

He rose and wrapped his arms around her waist, lifting her off the ground and kissing her deeply, relief and the stirrings of passion coursing through him in equal parts.

They stayed that way for a while, holding and kissing in the hot July mid-morning. Eventually, Tiercy ran her hand over his unshaven face. "I like this." Just like when they first met at the Manchester Inn, he felt powerful sparks of electricity as she ran her fingertips lightly over his face and neck. She tilted her head up, a mischievous look in her eyes. "My mom says we need to get a room."

Cole barked an incredulous, embarrassed laugh. "She actually said that?"

Tiercy nodded, grinning.

"Well, as long as I have Lovie's permission..."

Any thoughts of work disappeared, he'd called Heather and told her to clear his schedule for the next three days. He wanted to be with his girls.

Tiercy followed him to his house in her car, not wanting to leave it in the city or risk seeing Jemma if she dropped it off at her place, teasing that once Buttercup saw her Coley, any thoughts of Tiercy and Cole being intimate (at least until after Jemma's bedtime) would be scuttled. The whole way there, a solid forty-five minutes, Cole knew he was beaming. He couldn't wipe the smile from his face. His heart had settled into a not-quite-calm cadence—Cole was too hyped to finally have her in his home...and in his bed in his home. This ride from the city to his place that he'd done thousands of times was filled with a distinct, powerful, pulsing anticipation.

He'd been half-hard since they'd kissed in the park.

Embarking on a lightning-fast tour of his house, Tiercy laughed in delight as he pulled her from room to room, with the bedroom his focal destination. There'd be time for a leisurely tour later...after he ravaged her body and made her scream at least twice.

Once at his bedroom, he moved to reach down and sweep her into his arms just as Tiercy reached down to remove her shoes. The timing was such that Tiercy's chin collided into Cole's nose with a resounding thunk.

"Oh my God—" Tiercy's hand flew to her mouth.

Cole staggered back, holding his nose.

"Is it broken?" she whispered. "Let me see it."

She stared at him, utterly horrified. And then with confusion when she realized he was laughing...hard.

His shoulders shaking, Cole wiped his eyes and tried to compose himself. "I'm fine, Tiercy. Really." He fought to contain his laughter. "It's just that, I finally get you to my place and we're about to make love, and *this*"—he gestured to his nose—"happens. You could sever my arm and I'd still be aching to get in your pants."

Tiercy began to laugh as well. "I promise no appendages will be severed. I can't promise I won't have my way with my favorite one, though."

Her pupils dilated, and Cole's already rock hard 'appendage' turned to steel.

She placed his face gently between her hands and kissed his nose, her husky voice further signifying her arousal. "Are you sure you're OK?"

"I'm great." Cole's own voice was an octave deeper. "And I'm about to be even better. Come with me." He held out his hand and looked at her with a crooked grin. "Let's both walk, shall we?"

She giggled and followed him to the foot of the massive platform bed—a custom build that ensured he had plenty of room to stretch out —decorated in shades of gray and blue, care of his sister-in-law Sharon.

She halted and tugged him closer. Cole's heart thrummed.

"I missed you so much, Cole." Her eyes searched his face. "I am so sorry I put both of us through the past couple weeks."

He pressed a gentle kiss to the side of one of her eyes, inhaling her unique scent. "Never apologize, beautiful, for following your heart. It's been difficult for me, and I've missed you beyond words. But I also know how important it was for you to examine your feelings. You've been on an excruciating journey, Tierce. And now it's my honor to continue that journey with you, by your side."

"Cole," she whispered, her eyes twinkling. "I'm tired of examining my feelings. I'm tired of talking. And I'm tired of waiting for you to touch me the way I've been aching for."

In response, Cole moved a step closer, fighting his own sense of urgency to have her *now*. He traced his fingers along her cheek and neck, swirling them along the tops of her breasts. Her breath hitched.

"The first night I met you, I couldn't take my eyes off you." His voice was low and husky with the memory of that nascent desire. "I imagined myself kissing you over and over again. And everyone would know you were *mine*." He leaned in and kissed her, then gently took her lower lip in his mouth, sucking and running his tongue softly. His pulse was beating a ferocious tattoo.

Pulling away, he turned her around and lifted her shirt over her head, exposing the long, lithe line of her back. "And then," he continued, dropping kisses down her spine, "there was our first date. You answered the door, and I almost dropped to my knees on the spot to beg for mercy. When you turned, and you had on that amazing dress cut down to your waist, it was all I could do not to reach out and touch your beautiful ivory back." He trailed his fingertips along her spine. "Like this."

"Cole—" she rasped.

His heart was accelerating in a cadence of intense desire, his nerves so electrified, every touch of her soft skin brought excruciating pain and ecstasy at the same time.

"I have to know. Were you wearing underwear the night I met you?"

"Barely," Tiercy replied, turning her head to see his response, a sultry smile playing on her lips.

Cole growled, nipped at her shoulder, and kissed along her neck to just below her ear. She writhed against him, pressing herself into the front of him.

"Please," she moaned, working her succulent ass against his cock.

"Not yet. I'm going to take my time, touching all the parts of you I've missed so much." He traced the delicate nobs of her spine, stopping at the uninterrupted band of fabric. "A front clasp. Tricky. Good thing I'm an engineer."

He reached around and undid the front clasp of her bra. Standing behind her, his mouth again on the side of her neck, he ran his hands over her breasts. Tiercy's nipples stiffened and she gasped as he ran his hands over them, sending jolts of desire between his legs. His cock was weeping in his boxer briefs, screaming for release from the confines of his dress pants.

"Cole—" she tried again, gasping as he rolled and lightly pinched her nipples. "Please. I need you inside me."

Cole slid her bra from her shoulders and turned her to face him. Now it was his turn to gasp. "I always thought you were a Celtic goddess. Now I know it. Show me more, beautiful." He fumbled as he unhooked the front of her shorts, his own racing adrenaline making him clumsy. Tiercy placed her hands on his shaking grip. Together, they pushed her shorts down. As they pooled around her ankles, Tiercy stepped out.

"Those," Cole scraped out, motioning to her thong underwear, her eyes boring into his with an intensity that stoked his own fires. His voice was strangled. "Take them off."

Without breaking eye contact—another echo of their first meetings —Tiercy slid the lacy silk off.

Cole's eyes roamed her body. "My God." Dropping to his knees, he pressed his head into her stomach. "My God," he repeated, wrapping his arms around her waist. "You are so breathtaking. With my body, I thee worship. I never understood those words until now." He looked up at her, his eyes filling with tears. "I love you."

She bent down and kissed him, softly and then with more intensity. "My turn," she murmured against his lips.

She stepped back as he rose. Tiercy reached out for his shirt and unbuttoned it, her own hands nimble in her urgency. Removing his shirt, she pressed her breasts against his bare chest. Cole groaned, pulling her tight against him, his resolve to go slowly all but disappearing. Tiercy reached down and undid his slacks, and, in one smooth motion, pushed everything off.

"You are a beautiful man, John Sims Colburn—inside and out," her eyes devoured him and she smiled. "And one part of you is considerably...out." Tiercy took him in her hand and pumped, working her hand twice along the length of him, rubbing his pre-cum across the head of his cock.

They'd had the protection and birth control conversation weeks prior, and Tiercy had shared she'd restarted the Pill after their first date, but he had a condom, just in case. He reached for his pants, and Tiercy halted him. "You won't need that, Cole. I want to feel you."

He sucked air between his teeth. "Enough."

Cole couldn't wait any longer. He lifted her into his arms and gently placed her on his bed. Tiercy lay back and closed her eyes, her expression one of pure bliss. He nudged her legs open wide, settling in against the vee of her body, her arousal glistening on her bare pussy. Moaning, he pressed kisses along her upper thighs, as she squirmed and used her hands to try to guide him closer to where she clearly wanted him.

He chuckled against her sex.

"Stop playing around, Colburn," she groaned, tilting her hips.

"Who's playing, beautiful?" he murmured against her, rubbing his lips across the smooth petals that hid nirvana. "I'm just having a little appetizer before I feast on the most delicious pussy ever created."

Languorously, decadently he kissed her, his mouth and tongue teasing and igniting. Tiercy was quivering, her hips writhing.

He slid three fingers into her, prepping her for the way he'd fill her soon.

"Cole," she moaned. "Mmmm..."

His fingers were already soaked with her arousal, and he could feel the start of her pulsing. With his other hand, he pulled open her lips, exposing her nub that had hardened in desire, echoing exactly what was happening in his own body on a much larger scale.

"Please..." She worked her hips more against him, grabbing the sides of his head and pulling him against her. Hard.

He could barely breathe...and it was heaven.

Small flicks of his tongue against her clit. Then slow circling. He curled his fingers, pumping hard, and worked his tongue against her.

She detonated, screaming his name.

Even as she laughed breathlessly and tried to push him away from her sensitive nub, he kept at it, building her back up quickly.

"Cole, oh God. Cole, please."

"Please what, beautiful? Please keep loving this pussy? My pussy? It belongs to me now." He thrust his fingers, sucking on her.

"Yes. Yes. It's yours. Yes. Oh, please. Please make your pussy come."

"Whatever my beautiful woman wishes, that's my command."

He rapidly flicked his tongue, with some pressure, against her nub, then curled his fingers and pumped.

"Yes!" Tiercy screamed, clenching against his hand. "Yes!" And then a gush of fluid ran down his hand. She squirted. And Cole nearly lost all control, about to spurt his own release.

"Cole, need your cock. My pussy needs your cock. Fill me up."

Cole looked up at Tiercy, naked and yearning for him, and moved on top of her. Tiercy's hips raised and pushed against him.

"Tierce, baby," he murmured, nudging her legs further apart with his own, "as much as I love being tied to you by my heartstrings, right now, I really need to be connected with you in another way."

With that, he thrust inside of her, again and again. When she screamed his name a third time, Cole exploded into a thousand tiny pieces, amazed that he had never felt more whole in his life.

They lay wrapped in each other's arms, their legs entwined. Cole reveled in the glorious feel of her naked skin against his, the soft cotton of his sheets drenched in the scent of their ardor. He lifted up on his elbow and trailed his hand across her chest, delighting at her satiny soft skin and watching her goosebumps rise. That wasn't the only thing rising.

"Again?" she teased. "I thought you'd need more time to recover after..." she raised her eyebrows, her skin flushing a becoming shade of pale rose.

"Tiercy. Beautiful. Now that my cock has 'touched your innermost center,'" he quoted her Moby Dick line with a wink, "it's insatiable. Now...sit on my face so I can eat my pussy."

She rose wordlessly and straddled him. Just like the first night they met, and again at their first date, their eyes caught and held. Hers glistened with unshed tears.

"This is definitely a thing with us. I just...I can't stop looking at you."

"Never stop, Tiercy. And never stop loving me."

"Always," she whispered.

"Always."

Epilogue

"He who has felt the deepest grief is best able to experience supreme happiness."
The Count of Monte Cristo, Alexandre Dumas

TIERCY

One Month Later

It was a special day, and Tiercy wanted it to be a golden moment in Jemma's memories. Despite a morning that had started with a ground-dampening August rain, Tiercy and Jemma were going to play at the tire park. The sun had burst out from behind the clouds, and the forecast called for sunny skies for the rest of the day. They'd play for an hour or so, and then they were meeting Ross and her mom to pick up Tiercy's wedding gown, Ross's maid of honor dress, and Jemma's flower girl dress. Cole and Tiercy told her she could pick out whatever she wanted to wear for "their" wedding.

Jemma had been debating between a He-Man costume and something more traditional, as she was newly in a princess phase. But when she saw an "Elsa blue" dress, Jemma was enchanted...and that was it.

Butterflies danced in Tiercy's stomach. They were getting married at the Manchester Inn the next day. Xander was back from Europe to be Cole's best man. If Xan's son, Petey, wasn't headed to his grandparents' place in Kiaweh for an annual trip with them, he would have been the ring bearer. Instead, Jemma announced she would be the "ring and flower bearer girl." *Perfection*.

Following the wedding, she and Cole were squeezing in a week at a private villa in Barbados before she had to report to County High School with the rest of the teachers.

The sun glinted off the cushion cut diamond on her ring finger. It had been four weeks, but Tiercy caught herself looking at it all the time. Ross had teased her for gesturing excessively with her left hand.

The sound of laughter across the park caught her attention. Jemma had found a new friend, a little boy who looked to be about the same age. Naturally, she was bossing him around, and naturally, he was letting her, following her around like an adoring puppy dog.

Tiercy sighed. She definitely was going to have her hands full in ten years.

"Are you thinking what I'm thinking?" A friendly voice called over to Tiercy from the bench next to hers. Tiercy looked up and then followed the woman's gaze to Jemma and the boy. "I'm thinking I'm going to be in big trouble in a decade or so. My son is already girl crazy." She shook her head ruefully and laughed.

Tiercy joined in. "I was just thinking the same thing." She walked over and sat next to her. "I'm Tiercy Somerville."

Tomorrow she'd be Tiercy *Colburn*. Le sigh. And as much as Cole had initially worried about her grieving the loss of Luke's last name, letting her know it was more than fine with him if she kept Somerville, only excitement flooded her body when she thought about her new name.

"Deborah. Nice to meet you."

"I thought Jemma and I would be the only people here today. The ground is pretty wet."

"Oh, we come here a lot, even in some gross conditions. We've been here in rain, snow, mud. My son loves it."

"We do too. I'm surprised we haven't run into each other before." Tiercy added, "We'll probably see each other all the time now."

The women smiled companionably, watching their children run and play. Deborah called out a warning to her son. "Take it easy, Cal. You don't need to play so rough."

Chills rose across Tiercy's body and her heart started pounding. Deborah looked over at her, concerned. "Is everything OK?"

Tiercy struggled to find her voice. "D-did you say your son's name is Cal?"

"Yes. I don't like traditional names, but Calvin is a family name on my husband's side, and it meant a lot to him. I agreed to it, but on the condition we use an alternate spelling—so, it's Kal...with a K."

"Beautiful," whispered Tiercy, smiling into the sun.

The End

*Next up is Ross's story, **Arches**. Here's a sneak peek.*

Arches

ARC Editon

CATHRYN LYONS

Prologue

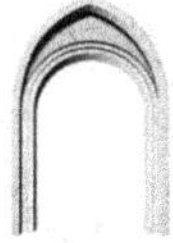

Ross

10 months ago

A soft tap signaled his arrival. Ross smoothed the neckline of her silk robe, the atypical flutter of her nerves pairing a symphony with the thrum of arousal that had been building since they'd shared a charged look across the room earlier that evening.

She opened the door and, with its reveal, sucked in her breath, her pulse racing, heart pounding in anticipation. *Damnation*, he was a Hottie McHot Pants.

Ross tugged him into her room, grinning over her shoulder as she guided them in further toward the bed. "Best man and maid of honor hookup after the rehearsal dinner? We are such a cliché, but...shall we?"

He laughed, a deep sexy sound that amped her desire higher. "I've never been one to appreciate a cliché before, but I believe I need to revise my opinion. A beautiful woman brings me to her bed and has her naughty way with me for hours on end? What's not to like?" He cocked a grin at Ross, endearing dimples appearing in his cheeks.

"'Hours on end,' you say?" Ross raised her eyebrows. As her heart kicked up another notch, she wondered if the heat she saw in his maple-syrup brown eyes mirrored her own.

"*Hours*, Maid of Honor," he whispered against her ear, causing a bloom of chills to cascade down her arms.

Somehow, she found her voice, raspy with anticipation. "In that case, Best Man," she murmured, touching her lips to his, "in for a cliché penny in for a cliché pound."

Preorder now! Available June 10, 2025.
https://books2read.com/Arches-CathrynLyons

Looking for your next read?
Heartstrings by Cathryn Lyons is out now.

BLURB

What happens when you bury your heart with the love of your life—but someone gives its strings an unexpected tug?
Tiercy Somerville is quite sure you only get one love of your life. But just as she was building a life with hers, he was torn from her forever. Five years later, the popular high school English teacher and single mom has healed to a place of grief-tinged acceptance and peace, but her love of a lifetime still very much fills her heart, leaving no room for any other really big love. Or so she believes.
John Sims "Cole" Colburn is tired of playing the field. The construction firm CEO longs for the harmony, partnership, and deep abiding love his parents had. The problem is...his standards are probably impossibly high.
When their paths cross, the chemistry is instant, but neither is prepared for the intensity and passion of the journey ahead of them.

As their love deepens, Tiercy finds herself emotionally torn, questioning what she's always known. How can one person have two soulmates? And having found the love of his life, Cole must decide if he can bear not being the love of hers.

CHAPTER ONE

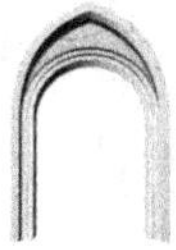

Traffic crawled along I-81. The winding four-lane highway through the Shenandoah Valley was a popular pass-through for eighteen-wheelers, which struggled up and down its hills. Right now, one semi was trying to pass another—sort of like the faster turtle passing the slower one—bogging down the rest of traffic.

Ross unleashed her impatience on her steering wheel with a resounding whack. "Move, you douche-nugget! Get over." She was in a bad mood and the traffic wasn't helping. She'd been dreading this drive since her grandmother talked her into it. Not the traffic so much. Rather, the destination. And what it held in store.

Although she'd been on this road as a passenger many times in her youth, Ross had only driven it once before. The summer she'd turned sixteen and was learning to drive, her intrepid dad had deemed her ready to try an interstate. And the scenic route to her grandmother's was his selection.

She tilted her head back and sighed. It was to be expected—these unbidden, unwanted, visceral forays down memory lane. She was almost thirty-five years old and returning to a place she hadn't visited in more than half her life. Ross had resolved never to go back to her grandparents' home...a place she, her older sister, and her parents had visited regularly until her sixteenth year.

Ross forced herself to stare down the memory of the drive that presaged the start of the most awful summer of her life. She didn't often allow herself to dwell on the specifics of that time, but the ache was always there—a faint pain her mind would seek out and linger on, just like a tongue repeatedly finds a rough spot to worry on a tooth.

Her phone buzzed and Ross turned down the alternative rock/new wave playlist she'd been listening to on the drive. A man she'd been seeing (a term she used loosely), had turned her on to the genre. Ross's favorite photo of her best friend, Tiercy, popped up on her iPhone. Ross grinned at the image of Tiercy wearing an elegant Carolyn Bessette Kennedy-style wedding dress, with her eyes crossed and an exaggerated pout...Ross photobombing in the background, holding two thumbs up.

She tapped the hands-free. "What's up, Hooker Hips?"

Tiercy's laughter filled the car, magically easing Ross's crotchety mood. "I'm just checking in. How's the drive?"

"I'm on eighty-one, behind a string of obnoxious tractor-trailers that won't move into the slow lane. I wish my car had a missile launcher on it. Or that I had an Inspector Gadget car with tires that extend out and up, and I could just go over these asshats. Also, I need to pee, and I really should get some gas, but I don't feel like stopping. And, of course, with every mile, I get closer to the inevitable."

"That good, huh?" Ross heard the smile in Tiercy's voice. Her best friend waited a beat, hesitated, and then jumped in, deploying her bestie mind-reading skills. She knew the emotional tightrope Ross began navigating when she stepped in her car and headed south. "I know this sucks, Ross. Want to talk about it?"

"No, I don't really want to talk about it." Ross didn't believe for a second her bestie would let her get away with that. She drove in silence for a few moments, accompanied only by the hum of her car's tires on the interstate and her friend's patient breathing through the Bluetooth speakers. Eventually she cleared her throat and voiced the thought that had been beating an incessant tattoo. "I'm dreading this, Tierce." *Seriously, fiercely dreading this.*

"I know, sweetie. I'm sorry."

"It feels so surreal to be doing this drive. I look back on that teenager driving my parents' car, and I know it was technically me, yet she and I have nothing in common. It's me but it's not me. Time is bizarrely elastic."

"Trust me, I remember that drive. I was praying with your mom in the backseat."

"Ha!" Despite herself, Ross chuckled at the memory. "Remember when I threatened to drive up the runaway truck ramp?"

"Your dad was so ticked off when you pretended to turn the wheel toward it," Tiercy reminisced.

"'Now, Adam. She's just kidding. Ross is a very responsible girl.'" Ross giggled as she parroted that long-ago conversation, ignoring the pang of loss that shot through her heart. She forced humor into her voice, wondering if Tiercy would see through it. "If she only knew how wild we were that summer!"

Tiercy laughed. "I remember your sister driving your mom nuts complaining about *everything*. She was so mad to be stuck in the back of the minivan with your mom and me."

"Gaby—whatever." Ice coated her response. "Didn't she want to bring her own car so she'd have it there for the summer, but Dad wouldn't let her? She was always wound up about something." Ross turned on her blinker to pass another slow truck.

"Sorry. I shouldn't have gone there." Tiercy quickly changed the subject. "What's your ETA?"

"If I don't stop to empty one receptacle and fill another, I guess about thirty minutes." Ross gnawed on her cuticle, a bad habit she'd broken in young adulthood. She looked down in horror. God...she *was* going back in time. She rubbed her hand over the dull ache in her chest and groaned. "Tiercy...I don't know if I can handle six weeks at Hon's."

Ross's grandmother had been born and raised in Baltimore. Her husband used to tease her with the popular local idiom, which was short for Honey. When Gaby, ten months Ross's elder, began talking, she called her grandmother "Hon" one day, having heard it thousands of times. From then on, Hon's plans to be called something glamorous and Continental, like Grand'Mere, were scuttled.

"I know, bestie. But you can call me whenever you need me."

"You know I will," Ross replied, brightening her voice even as she battled the soul-drenching darkness the drive evoked. "I'll FaceTime you and text you nonstop."

"You better," Tiercy warned. "I can't believe you're leaving me. My hubby told me to stop with the pity-party. He knows what you said about us being in touch nonstop isn't hyperbole—"

"Oooh! Good SAT word." Ross smiled as she thought about the ongoing competition the two friends had, dating all the way back to high school SAT prep, to drop big words into their everyday conversation.

"I know, right?" Tiercy laughed and then added on a whine, "But what will I do without you right here with me?"

"Have more fun than I will?" Ross complained.

"It'll be fine, Ross. The days will fly by. You'll help Hon pack the farmhouse and get settled in her condo, and then you can head home, finish packing your own place...and then head to your new gig in New York as the world's most amazing memoir editor."

"I can't believe I'm spending my time off between jobs doing this. I should be topless on a beach in Tahiti, drinking a cocktail from a coconut, a hot man by my side nibbling my toes *and* my ladybits. Instead, I'm about to spend six weeks in the Shenandoah Valley, that hotbed of glamor and sophistication. *And* I'll be living under Hon's roof. I probably won't get laid for almost two months. I'll be practically re-virginized when I get to Manhattan." She sighed, her mini-diatribe finished. "I hope Gideon's in town when I get there."

"Aw, poor you. You'll figure something out. Hey," she announced, "you can always sneak out of your bedroom window like the old days." Tiercy snickered at her own suggestion.

"Ha! Tempting. *Not.*"

"You just need to suck it up, buttercup," Tiercy cajoled. "Enjoy the downtime. Catch some rays by Hon's pool. Read for pleasure instead of work. Find a new cocktail to enjoy. I'll be down soon for your birthday and we'll relive the glory days."

"God help us!"

Much-needed laughter filled the car. As it faded, Tiercy asked the next hard question. They'd danced around it for weeks. Ever since Hon announced a condo had become available in an "active seniors" community and she was moving. And then requested Ross's help at the Virginia farmhouse her grandparents had bought and renovated in a labor of love over the years. "How do you feel about her selling it?"

"It's the right thing to do, Tierce." Ross knew Hon couldn't keep the big house up. Gaby had her own place. And God knew Ross herself would never want the farmhouse. She swallowed past unexpected dryness in her throat, taking a swig of water from her Yeti despite the protestations of her full bladder. "I'll do what needs to be done, get her moved into the new place, and that's that."

"So many good memories," Tiercy mused. "Best summers of my life."

"Yep," Ross agreed, equally wistful. "A lot. But some really crap memories too. I'm not thrilled at the idea of Gaby wallowing in all that and losing her shit again—especially so close to the anniversary of Mom and Dad's deaths. I can't deal with her theatrics. Maybe she and I can help at separate times."

"Come on, Ross. She's not that bad," Tiercy admonished. "She's a completely different person now."

"You think?" Ross heard the snark creep into her voice, a common occurrence when discussing her sister.

"I *know*," Tiercy rejoined. "People change, Ross. You just said you looked back at the teenager doing that drive all those years ago, and you know it's the same person, and yet you feel so different. Why can't it be that way for Gaby?"

"Bitch. I hate it when you're reasonable," Ross grumbled. "You're a good man, Charlie Brown. I don't know what I'd do without you." She heaved a sigh. "Almost there. I'm finally moving faster than a herd of turtles stampeding through peanut butter."

"See? Things are looking up."

"Oh yeah. Everything is hunky-damn-dory."

"Seriously, Ross Ellen Beaufort. You've got this. I know it's hard, but Hon needs you. And *you* need to do this. Ross...you have unfinished business there."

Ross was quiet, absorbing her friend's gentle reproach. Tiercy was right. And that was one important element of a true friend—to say the things that needed to be said.

"I guess sometimes you've just gotta chuck it in the 'Fuck-it Bucket,'" she muttered in resignation. "You're right. I know you are."

"Of course I am," Tiercy soothed, and Ross smiled at her friend's teasing lilt. "I'll see you soon in person and talk to you even sooner." Tiercy paused. "When I see you, I have something I want to talk to you about."

Ross's Spidey-senses alerted. "About...?"

"Never mind. It'll keep."

"You sure? I have a rock-star bladder. I can easily hold it at least another seven minutes before I need to pull over into a field and pee."

Tiercy laughed. "Classy. We'll talk when I see you in person. This will keep. Now, drive carefully, Speed Racer," she admonished. "And... hey, Ross? Take care of you."

"*Take care of you.*" The line from *Pretty Woman* was their standard closer before any big undertaking. Ross herself had said it to Tiercy just before she went out on her first date with Cole—the handsome, thoughtful man who'd healed her widowed friend's heart.

Ross disconnected the call, turned her music back on, and raised the volume as she lowered her windows, enjoying the rush of air.

"Let's do this, Beaufort."

The sooner Ross got there, the sooner this tour of duty in hell could begin. And then she could go home. Or, rather, go to New York and her new job. She was both nervous and excited about it. Tiercy had her new beginning. Now it was Ross's turn.

Over the car's speakers The Cure sang about how boys don't cry.

Neither do I, Ross thought as she sang along. *Neither do I.*

ACKNOWLEDGMENTS

It's a bit surreal, and magical, to arrive at this place. Having fantasized for years about publicly thanking and celebrating the countless individuals who have supported me on my writing (and life!) journey, I find my fingers stalling on the keyboard. As Maria says in *The Sound of Music*, let's start at the very beginning (oh, and this is gonna be loooong). [To anyone I leave out, please forgive me. It is unintentional and the product of an overwhelmed, overjoyed brain! I'll fix it. I promise.]

To Mom and Dad (in heaven), you already earned the dedication of my first novel, simply by loving me...and putting up with me. I know I put you through your paces. I love you so much and am grateful to be your daughter for eternity.

Special thank you to the late, amazing John DeSimone, MD, for the medical insights. If I got something wrong, it's my honest error. To my many beta readers over the years, thank you for your input, your enthusiasm, and your amazing edits. Big thanks to the world's best seester Cyndi, to Joyce (rest in everlasting light), Marlena, Michael, Alexis, Emily, Rose Ellen, Kim, Lexi, and Heather. To Lara and Trish, who formed two-thirds of my "standing committee" all those years ago, thank you for reading so many chapters/versions/snippets and for helping me shape my story. And to the other third of that committee, my Chief Reader and the best bestie who ever bestied, Rebecca. Honestly...it is so difficult to find the right words but...you really are the best. Love you, Bestie. This book never would have happened without your steadfast and insightful support. You're definitely the smarter bestie.

To the team who brought the rough manuscript to fruition: I get emotional thinking about the way connections happen. Michelle Fewer, world's most insightful and incisive editor, I celebrate the day I first saw your name in the back of a novel written by an author I adore. Then I kept seeing your name in other amazing books, and I thought...take note. Take note! And then we discovered a mutual friend, which created a connection I will always treasure. You've made my work so much stronger. You've guided me, calmed me, made me laugh...and become a lifelong friend. You truly are the ultimate book doula. And you led me to Rhon House. Oh, Birthday Twin...wow...so much to say here. You do the Authory Stuff so very well. You are a rock of support, a shining light, and now a dear friend. Without you, this would not be happening. Thank you also to Julie Collier for sharing your expertise. Nancy McLaughlin, thank you for your amazing graphic design talent for so many things. Cookie, it's been 25 years (holy moly!) and I'm so grateful to you and to John ("let me get it up") for the years of friendship. You are a kick-ass designer. And a piece of your love with John is woven into this story. Thank you to Maria at Steamy Designs for a gorgeous cover and to Wander Aguiar for a stunning cover photo of Valerio.

Decades ago, my Aunt Agnes pronounced that one day I'd be a published author. She made me promise I'd dedicate a book to her. It's coming...I promise. I'm sorry I couldn't manage this while you were with us, but I know you are smiling down as you crochet in heaven and laugh with Grandmom, Great Aunt Agnes, and Aunt Joanie. You called it!

To Sutter, the world's best dog who is so much more than a dog... thank you for supervising me in my office and for the emotional support via furry nose smooches and belly scratches (yours not mine).

To my three sons: When I was a little girl, a friend of the family had her third son. I gasped, horrified, unable to imagine this. No girls??? Well...twenty-one years into this Boy Mom thing and I have to say: It's fabulous! I wouldn't change a thing. Thank you for being such outstanding gentlemen. Words cannot convey my love for you. Thank you for your patience as I disappear into the writing cave for entire weekends and evenings. Thank you for loving me (and for the great hugs, which you definitely inherited from your dad/papa).

Speaking of...Robert...my heart. You do All the Things. You check All the Boxes. You fill my heart. You lift me up. You make me laugh. Best father. Best husband. The love of my life. You are tied to me by cords woven of my heartstrings. I love you, Spice. XO Always—Sugar.

ALSO BY CATHRYN LYONS

SECOND CHANCE AT LOVE SERIES

Heartstrings

What happens when you bury your heart with the love of your life—but someone gives its strings an unexpected tug?

Tiercy Somerville is quite sure you only get one love of your life. But just as she was building a life with hers, he was torn from her forever. Five years later, the popular high school English teacher and single mom has healed to a place of grief-tinged acceptance and peace, but her love of a lifetime still very much fills her heart, leaving no room for any other really big love. Or so she believes.

John Sims "Cole" Colburn is tired of playing the field. The construction firm CEO longs for the harmony, partnership, and deep abiding love his parents had. The problem is...his standards are probably impossibly high.

When their paths cross, the chemistry is instant, but neither is prepared for the intensity and passion of the journey ahead of them.

As their love deepens, Tiercy finds herself emotionally torn, questioning what she's always known. How can one person have two soulmates? And having found the love of his life, Cole must decide if he can bear not being the love of hers.

Arches

A sexy summer fling. A tangled past. A second chance at love.

Ross has a plan: pack up her grandmother's farmhouse, avoid old wounds, enjoy a little no-strings bedsport, and move on in Manhattan. She doesn't expect to rekindle the scorching chemistry with a hot, opera-singing single dad—or confront the shocking family secrets buried long ago.

Single dad Xander Grace has sworn off serious relationships—until Ross Beaufort, the unforgettable one-night stand who's haunted him for months, shows up at her grandmother's farmhouse...next to the property he's renting. She's only there for six weeks. A perfect summer fling.

As desire turns into something deeper, Ross must decide if she can let go of the past and fight for the future she never saw coming.

Stardust

A beloved silver screen star

A playboy doctor

Two scandals

One solution—fake date your long-lost first love

When two scandals unexpectedly reunite long-estranged first loves almost two decades after their painful breakup, can they put hurtful bygones aside to help each other? Will their surprising alliance lead to lost love found?

Honor Wheatley's world has just imploded. A decorated film actor, the beloved "nepo baby" and darling of the silver screen flees to the Shenandoah Valley to escape the fallout from a devastating scandal. When Honor's arranged lodging floods, she finds sanctuary in an unexpected place—the home of her first love and the man who shattered her surgically repaired heart years ago. And when Brinder agrees to be her personal guide on a sexual exploration journey as preparation for a film role—what could go wrong with that?

Dr. Brinder Desai has a well-earned reputation as a player, earning him the nickname Dr. Desiiigh. A fabricated scandal jeopardizes his dream job. Brinder needs to show stability or risk losing the position he loves. Having Honor Wheatley—the woman who broke Brinder's heart a lifetime ago and ruined him for relationships—in his home is a prescription for chaos he doesn't need. Except—fake dating the woman he lost could be the very thing he needs to keep his job.

Stardust is a steamy, humorous, emotional contemporary romance about lost love found, healing, redemption, and second chances.

About the Author

Cathryn Lyons loves novels. Seriously loves them. Especially romance. Reading (often devouring) them...and writing contemporary romance novels of her own. She has been writing since before she could even properly hold a pen.

She is happily married to her real-life MMC and they share three sons and the world's best and derpiest rescue Golden Retriever (from Turkey!). She is a lifelong Marylander, but wonders if her short stint in London counts as being cosmopolitan (the attribute, not the drink; although those are quite delicious).

Cathryn fills her creative bucket by writing stories she hopes bring as much joy, laughter, escapism...and sexy feelings...that she herself has experienced through the gift of others' words. She hopes you love her stories, and welcomes hearing from you. Visit her Website, you can Email her, or follow her on Facebook and Instagram.

Want to have a bit more unfiltered fun? (Sorry, Mom.) Join her Facebook reader group, Cathryn Lyons' Romance Den to connect with other lionesses and lions who roar for joy at romance.